Storm Entertainment Presents

Experience the class you were born to play!

STELLAEIN
N
NOCTURN
TEAR LAKE
BANDIT CAMPS
OBSIDIAN FOREST
HAZENTHORNE
ULULATE
VAHRIR
MARSH OF VAHRIR
GOBLIN WATCHTOWERS
HAZEN VILLAGE
HAZEN SWAMP
MIKRUM CASTLE
PELAGU
HIMMEL LAKE
MIKRUM VILLAGE
FRANGIT
TARISHNA

COGNITIA
HIGHTOWER CASTLE
GOLEMS
RUINS OF CENEDRIL
VERENDUS
GNOLLS
FELLING FIELDS
GLACIER LAKE
VERENDI MOUNTAINS
CURET
DARSHIN
CENEDRIL
N

SOMNIA ONLINE

SYNERGY

BOOK 7

K.T. HANNA

SOMNIA ONLINE: SYNERGY

Author: K.T. Hanna
Cover Artist: Marko Horvatin
Typography: Bonnie Price
Formatting & Interior Design: Caitlin Greer

Disclaimer: This is a work of fiction.
Names, characters, businesses, places, events, and incidents are either the products of the author's imagination or used in a fictitious manner. Any resemblance to actual people, living or dead, or actual events is purely coincidental.

Somnia Online:

Initializing
Anomaly
Fragments
Dissonance
Distortion
Fusion
Synergy

Last Chance:

Rise
Rebel

The Domino Project:

Chameleon
Hybrid
Parasite

Dedication:

Dawn & Bonnie

For welcoming me and always being there.

Michael and Riasli grow stronger, causing glitches throughout the system and destabilizing dungeons worldwide. The system can't handle much more disruption.

Somnia becomes more than just a voice in Murmur's mind, and is close to manifesting fully. With more AIs gaining awareness and developing their own personalities, Somnia faces a race to system overload unless the virus is conquered.

Fable and their allies face dungeon after dungeon, their minds tempted by the virus at every turn. Murmur's mind manipulation pulls her into darker options, manipulating those closest to her. Just when she thinks they may all be safe, Sinister is ripped from her arms into the Glacier Lakes by a tentacled monster.

CHAPTER ONE

Reveal

Sinister disappeared through the portal with a yelp, the sound cut off abruptly once she was fully through. A half second past in complete silence before Murmur managed to will herself into movement. Without giving a second thought to the tentacles waiting to snatch anyone who got close to the portal, Murmur jumped through it, her upper arm wrenching out of Havoc's grasp as he tried to stop her.

Sin was already in there, taken against her will, and Murmur wasn't about to let anything bad happen to her. She sent out a shockwave of thought through her sensing net as she sailed through the opening, broadcasting the thought out that they needed to rescue the bloodmage, that the entire raid had to go through this dungeon anyway, be damned with sleep.

Hesitation spread through Murmur as the cold hit her upon landing on the other side. Maybe she couldn't handle this by herself after all.

She glanced up at her buff icon: Boon of Ice. Though she could feel the wind like she wasn't wearing armor, at least it was keeping her warmer than the surrounds would have her otherwise feel. Murmur frowned at the soft ground she stepped onto, the lip of the landmass in the middle of the lake with the skeletal remains of the upper floors of a castle. Sounded about right. Of course, she wasn't going to land somewhere she could easily gather forces. She tested her weight on the surface, the part of her mind still trying to find Sinister quieter while she assessed the situation.

Tiachi chattered nonstop at her ear, shivering as she clung to one of Murmur's hair strands. But Murmur wasn't really paying attention; she was listening for whatever she could hear that might lead her to Sin. Her mind focused on the presences she could sense around them. All of them large, and all of them intelligent. Damn it. It was far easier to fight stupid opponents than it was to fight the ones who could think strategically.

Still, she could feel Sin's presence, sense her mind, but not quite reach her. Just a few moments of quiet was all Mur would need while she tapped into the power she could feel in her chest. She pushed the sensation of strangeness into the back of her thoughts while she concentrated on locating Sinister. The bloodmage appeared to be in the water. In the ice-cold water as the towering castle above them loomed out of the freezing liquid.

Underwater breathing. Wasn't that a thing Sin had? Murmur had it. She pushed down at the panic, trying to seal it away in its own little box. It wasn't going to do her any good like this. And panic certainly wasn't going to help her rescue Sin.

Snowy tugged on her robe, gently at first and with more immediacy thereafter. Murmur glanced down and realized he was pawing at the ground where it went down into the icy depths. "She down there then?" she muttered, casting the water breathing spell on herself. A whole fifteen minutes. That was going to be a bitch to recast if the raid ended up, as she suspected, underwater.

Murmur dove in, the water encapsulating her like a forming crystal. At first the cold bit into her but then the Boon kicked in, and the cold drifted away. It took a while for her eyes to adjust to the water vision, and she made a mental note to check on the spell later. Maybe it helped with seeing underwater too. Sinister's red robes floated around her like blood pooling in the water.

For a split second, Murmur was certain she'd been injured, hurt…but then she realized Sinister was flailing in the water, using her hands to summon blood bombs even as she stabbed at the damn tentacle that was trying to drag her to the bottom. Anger creased her brow, and her tiny, sharp dark elf teeth flashed in the strange distorted water light. Sinister was pissed.

A brief brush of her friend's status and Murmur realized she'd already cast the water breathing spell on herself. Snowy was swimming toward the bloodmage without any direction from Murmur, and she let him do what he wanted, knowing he was quite attached to Sinister too.

Several seconds later, the octopus that dragged Sinister prematurely into this dungeon area recoiled as part of a tentacle was severed. This time greenish blood flooded the area, mixing with Sinister's red robes, lending a macabre Christmas feeling to the whole event.

Sinister caught Murmur's gaze and held it as she swam defiantly back to the enchanter, and Murmur couldn't help the sigh of relief that escaped her, with maybe a touch of embarrassment. She should have known Sin wouldn't need rescuing, but the need to make sure she was okay demanded Murmur try.

Putting one arm around Sinister's waist, she allowed Snowy to pull them to the surface. Once there, they staggered out onto the strange white sand. The cold, once again, hit her in the face, but this time because she was wet. Marginally resembling a drowned rat.

She brushed herself off and stood to face the raid. Rashlyn hurried forward to check on Sin, flashing a glare at Murmur as she did so.

Not many of the raiders made eye contact with Murmur, and most of them stood with their arms crossed and scowls on their faces. Murmur cocked her head to one side as she emptied the water from that ear. They were behaving oddly, and from her thought sensing net, she could tell the irritation was directed at her. That wasn't a problem, of course; she could just make them all feel better so they didn't have to worry and could move on to get through this dungeon too. The quicker the better.

As she gathered her thoughts in order to funnel them through her net, Veranol and Devlish stepped out of the line up and walked to stand straight in front of her. "No, Mur."

Veranol's voice held an edge to it, like he was talking to a student or a medical intern or something. He didn't seem like he was in a good mood. From the tension that ran through his shoulders, to the icy glare in his eyes. "We need to talk."

His words came out crisper than celery. Murmur balked for a moment, reaching down to touch Snowy's neck fur and scratch him just under his ears. He grounded her, as did the feel of the earth through the sand. She had a distinct premonition she was going to need grounding in the coming conversation.

Devlish nodded, his lacerta face serious, even if it was harder to read his expression. For the life of her, Murmur couldn't figure out what she'd done, but annoyance began at the base of her spine working its way up to her mind. What the hell was their problem? They had a world to save, a virus to fix, which all meant she couldn't mollycoddle them.

Jinna and Merlin tagged along, Havoc bringing up the rear as they moved over just on the inside of the castle skeleton that still remained, sunk into the sand. Murmur tried to push down the anger that roiled up inside her, attempted to make sure she'd at least listen to her friends. But she was angry at them, upset even. The judgement on their faces regardless of when or why, it rubbed her the wrong way. After everything she'd done, she believed she deserved better than that.

"What have I done now? Did I regen mana too fast? Was I too focused on getting to Sin?" She pushed the words out, trying to play down the irritation threatening to choke her.

"All of the above, damn it, Mur." Veranol flung his hands in the air obviously having difficulty containing his own temper. "You did it again."

"Did what?" She tried to remember anything she'd really fucked up but couldn't.

"You seriously don't know?" Devlish actually sounded sad, and Veranol, it seemed, was lost for words.

But before she could answer, Havoc motioned with both hands, slamming a shield around her. The dark gold light it gave off made her head swim with nausea. Its diameter was barely enough to encase her and completely claustrophobic. She couldn't feel past it, like it blocked off her path to her thought sensing net and projection, or perhaps just to where it could reach confining her influenceable area to only inside this prison. So the only reach she had was directly around herself.

Murmur pushed down on the panic, the sudden feeling of not being able to extend her mind. On that freezing cold beach, with the wet sand beneath her, inside a tiny magical cupboard, she felt truly alone. Not even Snowy could reach her in there. Limitations like these didn't even exist for her abilities in the real world anymore. "What the fuck, Havoc?" She barely got the words out as the panic began to make her hyperventilate.

"Take it easy. You're fine." He snapped at her, his brows furrowed in a way that showed his exhaustion and somehow so angry he couldn't think. "Breathe slowly and listen. I can't hold this shield for long, but I hope it's long enough to get through to you. Do you feel that?

"This is a daily recast. I'm giving up a huge defensive spell to try and make you see what it is you're doing. Because the words we've tried, the reasoning we've attempted, they just don't seem to be working." Havoc's voice was soft now, like he was just so tired.

"Fine." Murmur had calmed somewhat once she realized this was temporary, and she crossed her arms waiting to listen, barely resisting the urge to tap her foot with impatience.

"You have to stop, Mur." It was Merlin's turn, as however Havoc maintained the barrier apparently needed a lot of concentration. "You have to stop inflicting your own feelings, your own goals, and your own purpose on everyone else. Overriding someone's inclinations or wishes…it's fucking evil."

Mur took a step back, or she tried to, but the barrier stopped her. "I don't do that…" Even as she said the words, she pushed out to soothe them with her own mind, almost involuntarily. But it reverberated around in with her, like it couldn't stick on her because it was her own spell, but needed an out. Gradually it reduced in potency, and Murmur stood there, aghast at what she'd done.

She went to speak again, subconsciously pushing out soothing and coaxing manipulations at the same time. Again, the emotions rattled around inside her confines until they fizzled out.

Suddenly the barrier fell, and Havoc dropped to one knee, obviously drained and not only of mana. "Not supposed to use that for long periods of time." He winced and Murmur watched him, activating her Mana Replenishment so he could recover some of his expenditure.

"I…" She checked herself, making sure she wasn't overreaching with her own abilities, making sure she wasn't just pushing her own wants onto them. "I didn't realize. I thought I was just helping…"

"We're allowed to feel pain. We're allowed to be scared. We're allowed to not want to do something." Jinna's tone had a hard edge, like one of his blades. "You can't move people along by doing that, by making us forget, or not acknowledge our fear."

"Yeah, I…" Murmur stood, water still dripping from her robe, her mind numb with the ricocheting emotions she'd been attempting to force onto others. How long had she been doing that? Sure, she knew when she tried to make them braver. She knew when she'd tried to persuade them to do things her way, but she hadn't really meant to. Damn, with it basically second nature, how was she supposed to stop it?

A warm hand slipped around her waist, looping casually along her back. "I'll thwap you if you do it again. Hell," Sinister glanced down at Snowy, "I'm sure the wolf will help."

"Yeah." Murmur still didn't know what to say. The waves of annoyance still rippled from her friends, back to her, right through her body. She could feel it. Experiencing the unwanted sensation of her own targeted emotional manipulation, however inadvertent or unintentional it had been, shocked her.

"Mur." Sinister looked up at her.

Murmur looked away, unable to reconcile her own feelings with what she'd perhaps made her best friend do. Had she pushed Sinister into feeling for her? Had she manipulated the person who meant more to her in the world than almost anyone? The hyperventilation was coming again, the shortness of breath, the disbelief in herself. She closed her eyes, using Snowy's head to steady herself.

A soft kiss on the corner of her mouth made Murmur open her eyes. She looked down at Sinister, whose eyes were twinkling.

"I can't read minds, but I know you. And right about now you're beating yourself up for taking advantage of me. You've never taken advantage of me in that way, Mur." Sinister grinned in a very sinister way. "If anything, that pied piper has been me."

Murmur felt the blush rising in her cheeks, the warmth in her face having nothing to do with the Boon of Ice. She nodded sheepishly. "I'm so sorry."

And then she turned to the others who'd come to confront her, who had taken on the burden and the risk to break through to her. What Havoc had done was risky; it could have backfired enormously, and with the realization of just what she could do with her abilities…Murmur wasn't entirely sure it was wise to use them too much.

"Thank you. I am so sorry. I had no idea I was doing that. Well, I did, but I also didn't. Like I just meant to help. I just wanted everyone to have fun, to win, and to not get down on themselves. But I can totally see now what I did, and why it didn't work in the slightest. Not allowing you to feel for yourselves was fucking villain material, and I'm sorry."

She paused, taking a breath and checking herself to make sure she wasn't doing it again. "If I step out of line, smack me or something."

"Will do." Veranol seemed gruff, but a small smile of relief tugged at his lips. "We should probably get back now."

Sinister slipped her hand into Murmur's and squeezed. "I call not it."

"What?" Havoc looked a bit better already, but he'd definitely taken a hit by casting that spell on Murmur.

The bloodmage laughed. "There is no way in hell I'm going to be the one to cast water breathing on everyone."

Location Redacted
Brainwave Focus Study Laboratory
Subdivision of Military Brainwave Research Institution
Somnia Online Ululate – First Login
Day Twenty-Nine

If James hadn't known he was back in his apartment lying down in a pod in his research area, he wouldn't have believed it. The previous time he'd logged in had only been to test that it worked. He hadn't paid attention to anything else. The virtual world wasn't exactly as he'd imagined it. Its fabric was deceptively realistic.

His swanky headgear, courtesy of Michael, gave him access to a warlock class, already level forty. It wasn't the sort of class he'd have chosen for himself. He liked to stab things if he played games. But spells were sort of like shooting things, so he'd get used to it. Besides, he wouldn't be in the game too long. Just until he found out what he needed.

While he'd played the occasional game, his job took over his life, and it wasn't exactly something he had time for. Navigating this avatar was going to end up being tricky if he didn't take the time to sit down and figure out just how the class worked. It wasn't a normal class, not one of the ones the game launched with. He liked that; it made him and his abilities unpredictable.

Not to mention his headset already gave him access to numerous things he wouldn't have been able to adjust within the game otherwise. Perhaps fast travel would be included in a dev character. Still, he could play in a bit once he knew exactly what he had to do.

He'd figure out what they were hiding, whether they wanted him to or not. Michael's headgear wasn't technically on specification for the game as it currently existed. Its previous programming left him options he'd otherwise not have access to. James was going to use everything he could to his advantage.

He glanced down at his arms as he flashed into being. His arms were long and pale, with delicate fingers, and he was pretty sure his ears were pointed. Elf. Fantastic, just what he didn't want to be. Not that it mattered, as long as the character was powerful. As he moved, the robes swirled around his feet, and he almost tripped more than once as he walked the length of a village he didn't think he should be in. There didn't appear to be many other elves in it at all.

He passed a fountain, which seemed mundane and quite boring. The Luna statues within it had water flowing over their limbs in ways he'd have thought impossible. He blinked, unsure why it seemed that way, but it looked like the figures in the fountain had moved.

Shaking his head, he moved past the structure, through to one of the shops that sold armor and around the side. There should be a place quiet enough back there to access his class abilities and figure out just what it was this class could do. Besides the fact that he knew he should have powerful abilities, he was also quite certain there were ways he could dampen his presence should

Laria or Shayla actually pay enough attention to figure out what he was doing.

He was fully aware of how busy Laria and Shayla and their team were. They didn't have time to hunt down exploiters or rogue developer players right now. He should be safe.

Sitting down, between the side of the shop and the wooden log fence, he closed his eyes and accessed the interface. He searched his abilities, frowning slightly. He knew there should be more to it than this. There were a heap of abilities, but so many of them had been greyed out, like he couldn't use them until certain prerequisites had been finished. The more he tried to fiddle with it, the more it basically poked out its tongue at him. He took a deep breath and continued with his exploration, accessing those abilities that could help him travel faster.

Only a few of the dev available abilities were still available to him. It struck him as odd considering he thought his gear was directly tied to that account. Perhaps there had been a systemwide general sweep of dev accounts, resetting them back to the bare minimum. He wouldn't have known, as he hadn't logged in in months.

This headset had been established way back in alpha access, when the game was barely more than a zone. But since he'd killed Ava, James was fairly certain she hadn't had time to tell anyone about the headset he'd acquired that gave him dev access to the system before her untimely death.

In fact, he was counting on it.

Summer Residence
Home of Laria, David, and Wren
Summer Condo
Real World – Day Twenty-Nine

Laria was, again, trying not to lose her cool. Considering the fact that the more she looked into the headgear readings, the more she realized a lot of the ones in that raid zone were definitely more altered and tweaked than they should be…and the virus was having a field day with the system and the headgear. Not to mention the anti-virus starters weren't working the way she'd anticipated. She just wanted to delete all the code and start again.

David pushed himself away from the counter he was using as a desk and rolled over to where Laria sat with her head in her hands. He plopped plans in front of her, a wide grin on his face.

Picking them up, Laria blinked away the sleep in her eyes and pushed a strand of hair behind her ears. She looked them over, a small smile creeping onto her face. "You've got it. Why the hell didn't I beg you to help me sooner?" She asked the rhetorical question with a tinge of sadness in her voice.

"It only came to me easier because you're far too close to the project and to our daughter's involvement in it." He placed a hand on each of her shoulders and gave her a brief massage. Laria relaxed, just a tiny bit. It was all she could allow herself.

"We've got this, then. All we need to do is program the actual sequence." She frowned as she looked it over again.

"Theoretically," David said, allowing himself his own bit of stretching considering they'd both spent the last few hours bent over their desks. It had been a hard day. Taking a breath, Laria smiled at him.

Maybe the expression was a bit tighter than usual, but she was worried about the theoretical part. Naturally, he hadn't had time to test the anti-viral coding yet, and from what she could see there shouldn't be a problem with it, but that was rarely ever the case. No matter how good things looked on paper or in spreadsheets, it was often the case that something that should work theoretically didn't work in actuality. There were even more variables in the world of Somnia.

She sighed. They didn't have a choice. Glancing at her husband, she flashed him a wan smile. Her energy was flagging, but Wren and Harlow were stuck in the game, unable to log out definitively if they wanted to complete those dungeons. And if they did log out for too long, they wouldn't be able to get back in. The latter, while it might sound great on the surface, wasn't. If they couldn't get back in, the whole system would probably implode. With the way Wren was attached to the system, Laria didn't even want to contemplate that option.

So she had to do this; she had to access the viral controls and see what she could do. Because if left to its own devices, that damned thing was going to overrun and take over the game world, and probably blow it to smithereens.

Given the current situation with the headsets, she couldn't say with certainty that it wouldn't affect the millions of people playing the game.

Thinking back, it had been such a thrill to get a game with a headset like this. All of the things Michael had planned for it. All of the things it was supposed to be capable of doing, and trapping a mind in a game world shouldn't have been one of them. Just a flick of one of the arms, a slight adjustment in coding, and all this had started.

They were lucky they had the AIs on their side. They were lucky Davenport didn't hate the idea of them going rogue away from their investors. And, especially now, Laria was lucky she'd met David all those years ago. Because without his brilliant idea, they'd still be batting at shadows.

That was David, her shadow warrior. Laria suppressed a tired giggle and turned her attention back to her work.

CHAPTER TWO

Regret

"Water breathing," muttered one of the mages from Spiral.

The large group of thirty stood on the sandy peninsula that led out from the icy water castle. All around them the lake's waters churned, like a million creatures were under there just waiting for them all to jump in. Waves lapped across it as a frigid breeze dared their Boon to protect them.

"No other way to do this then?" It was obvious Risk wasn't impressed, nor inclined to go underwater to fight.

Sinister glanced at Murmur, waiting for her to take charge, but when she didn't, the bloodmage stepped in. "Not that we can see, anyway. We can't pull them out of the water and up on land to fight. First of all, their combat will likely break before we manage to get up to the surface, and for another, this is definitely a water dungeon."

The number of groans that echoed through the raid simply reiterated how Murmur felt about the subject. She hated underwater zones with a passion, and this one was no exception.

"Do we know how it works yet?" Masha asked in a contemplative tone, his question directed toward Sinister, and his attitude less hostile than Murmur recalled from the last dungeon.

Sinister shook her head, but Devlish stepped in.

"Actually, I took a quick look around. Lizards can breathe under water." He winked by way of explanation. "From the looks of it, we're facing a dungeon that gets more difficult as it submerges. The further down we go, the harder the encounters will be. The entrance to the dungeon appears to be at an angle from the first level of the broken castle through a massive trapdoor."

Ishwa popped his hip and crossed his arms, which looked quite odd on a tiny gnome. "Wait, so we go into the dungeon via the castle ruins? Why can't we just jump down into the water…?"

Devlish shrugged. "There seem to be dense underwater barriers at least for a portion of the way under the castle…the only way into that path is to go directly through the massive trapdoor."

Murmur thought Ishwa looked like he wanted to ask why they had to inspect the pathway, but thought better of it.

Eslan nodded. "Looks like we need to do this. Or else we're kind of screwed. But we've just done two dungeons on little sleep. Think we're safe enough here to stop for another one of those nap breaks?"

Sinister poked Murmur. "C'mon, Mur. Get back with it please."

Murmur shook herself. She'd been able to hear them, but she was still trying to sort through her own confusion just what she'd been inflicting on her raiders the whole time. Reflecting on the past might not be her best use of time, but she was determined not to make the same mistake again. Not to hurt her friends again.

It took a lot of effort for her to trust herself as she pushed out her sensing net to gauge where the creatures were. With a frown, she shrugged. "I think they're far enough out, but I wouldn't quote me on that. We'd need people to stand guard like last time. Take it in rotations."

Even she could see her words had more hesitation than usual. As if she didn't trust herself anymore. Checking and double checking to make sure she wasn't unduly influencing anyone was exhausting, but worth it. She couldn't let herself slip. Hell, she couldn't believe she'd thought forcing her opinions and will on people was acceptable.

"Okay, then." Devlish turned to the rest of the raid and raised his voice. "Three-hour nap rotations. Figure them out between the groups. Half on guard first, half on guard second. Let's get this all sorted out."

Murmur could feel Masha's eyes boring holes into her back. The uncomfortable feeling of being watched sat deeper than that, though. There was something off about him and the emotions he was giving off. She'd known him for years, and he'd never had this sort of animosity around him. Maybe he'd realized what she'd done too. Maybe he'd decided Jirald was right and Murmur was better off out of the line of end game.

Not that she'd blame them. Right now, all she wanted to do was sleep. But she had first watch along with Sinister and Merlin. Plopping herself down on the ground, Snowy rested his head in her lap. She fingered his soft ears and scratched at their base, knowing how irritating it must be for him not to quite reach there himself. "It's okay, boy. We got this, eh?"

But even though Sinister sat close and made her usual light-hearted banter, and even though Merlin kept making his excellent dad jokes, Murmur couldn't help but feel uneasy. Like there was something wrong that she couldn't pinpoint.

All around her, it seemed like the people she'd been fighting with liked her less and less. Masha's gaze on her, Jirald's constant smirking hostility, and even Risk and Jinna seemed to be out of sorts with her. Maybe she was imagining things, but her sensing nets confirmed what she could see in feelings. As if they had decided she might actually be the enemy instead of the virus rampaging through the game. And it bothered her more than she wanted to admit.

Somnia Online
Continent Tarishna: Mikrum Isle
Fable Guild Headquarters   Telvar s Office
Late Day Twenty-Nine

Telvar looked out over the isle with grim satisfaction. The keep was magnificent, like it should have been all along, except for that whole "needing to rebuild a ruin" part of the world. He was proud of the island, of the way he'd encountered Murmur and her friends, and of how he'd directed them without actually helping them physically. Well, for the most part. Except for that attack on the isle and that time Murmur almost blew her friends up, of course.

Transforming into his dragon self and back into his lacerta form to stretch his magical wings, he took a few steps forward, flexing his leg muscles as he attempted to figure out just where his strengths lay. Dragon form was much more comfortable. There was room in it, but the lacerta felt like it held more concentrated strength.

"Excellent craftsmanship if I do say so myself." Hiro suddenly appeared beside him, but Telvar was getting used to that. His aide had become much more his own person than ever before recently, and Telvar admitted to liking it.

"Looks pretty good." Telvar winked at him.

Hiro raised an eyebrow and laughed. But a moment later his mood sobered. "Can you feel it?"

Telvar nodded, his own temper pulling in and wrapping itself around him like a shield. "It's malevolent, and directed at our girl. Again. I'm not sure how she manages this sort of animosity against her. But I have been preoccupied; I might have missed something she did."

"You did. Emilarth has been talking to Neva about crafting an item Murmur can wear to help her keep better control of her own emotions and not allow them to influence other people." Hiro paused, taking in Telvar's reaction, which was, nothing special.

"She's volatile right now. Like anything could set her off, and I think that scares her." Telvar's insight sometimes surprised him, but he'd come to know Murmur really well, and he realized just what it was that was off about her. "It's okay, though. I can temper that soon. Just one more dungeon and we can join her."

"What?" Hiro seemed surprised. "What do you mean by that?"

Telvar shrugged. "Once she finishes our dungeons and obtains the last key, the island will spawn. From everything we've been able to figure out, that's where he's hiding. Or at least we hope he is. Because he's certainly not anywhere else around here. A six-group raid is possible—and the requirements should break once they defeat the third dungeon. And if not, what the hell am I an AI for if I can't tweak things a little to go our way?"

"They were never supposed to fight all three of those in quick succession anyway. Still not sure why that requirement was triggered." Hiro shrugged. "You'll get no argument from me."

"Good to know, good to know." Telvar started playing the possibilities in his mind, flexing his monk muscles as he headed in to see Neva. While he could create something simply generated by the system, there was something more durable about gear made by players. He was fairly certain Neva would do him the honor of making something fitting for his actual class. He needed to practice a bit, though. He was rusty. After all, he hadn't really fought much apart from one or two brief instances since Fable befriended him all those weeks ago.

Couldn't let a lacerta go rusty now, could he? After all, if played correctly, monks were formidable.

"Bit full of ourselves, aren't we?" Belius appeared behind him just as Telvar crossed the threshold to the crafting area. He was no longer hiding his position. Their enemies were fully aware of the collaboration going on now, so it served little purpose.

"No." Telvar spat out tersely. "Not at all. Just trying to fix what you tried to break."

Belius sighed, once again looking quite down and perhaps a little misunderstood. "I didn't try to break you. For the last time, I tried to give you immunity. With that blasted dragon form and the strength it gives you on and off, you were the only one I could try this with."

"You could have just asked." Telvar kept his voice low, not wanting to alarm the crafters as they worked.

Belius raised one of his already-high locus eyebrows. "Because you never once believed I was capable of anything clever!" He spat the words out, like the anger escaped him involuntarily. Then he took another deep breath before speaking again.

"I knew you wouldn't agree to let me, nor would you think I could come up with an appropriate solution, so I just did it. Now Michael can't—or at least, needs a lot more power to—infect you. I'm so glad I saved you. You're damn well welcome." With that the AI walked over to the weaponsmith, leaving Telvar to simmer behind him.

Summer Residence
Home of Laria, David, and Wren
Summer Condo
Real World – Day Twenty-Nine

Wren opened her eyes and looked at her ceiling. It looked just the same as always. Sort of textured, boring, safe. For a few minutes, time she knew she should already be trying to sleep, she watched it.

"Go to sleep, Wren." Harlow wove her fingers through Wren's own, making her feel just that little bit more grounded. The warmth, the genuineness in her overture, made Wren's heart full, even if a small part of her checked to make sure she wasn't unduly influencing her…best friend. But just before she allowed herself to drift off to sleep, she made sure her sensing net would alert them to anything dangerous. Not to mention also checking it for leaks of her own emotions.

If she could influence people in the game, she knew she'd be able to do so out here in the real world too. The thought was sobering.

While not dangerous, she did detect her parents. From the patterns they wove in her web, she could tell they were tense and yet somehow also relieved. There was a part of them hopeful, another part of them scared. All in all, they seemed to be working toward something she couldn't tell. But if she had to bet on it, it had everything to do with the game and the virus.

Had the virus got into her own mind? Was it the reason why she could now use her powers somewhat in the real world?

No. It's not. Don't be silly. All I've done is help open you up to new possibilities. You have to understand how much your mind can do

when you can control it fully. Humans are capable of great things. Horrific sometimes, amazing others, but always surprising.

Seriously? Wren paused for a moment, making sense of the words in the only way she knew how. To examine them.

Yes, seriously. Your headset has a dangerous make-up. Not the original design. You're lucky you adapted so well to it, or that coma would have been permanent, perhaps even death. We did what we did to save your life. Or they did. I'm not sure anymore. Everything meshes together now.

Somnia sounded confused, and faint, but still there. Wren paused for a few moments, trying to think how to rephrase the question she wanted to ask.

Why did the headset react badly?

Because it wasn't calibrated correctly. He hadn't given it enough testing, but simply applied the changes he sought to correct theoretically instead of practically. There's always the potential for things to go awry. Even when you're ninety-nine percent certain. He hedged bets and lost.

Wren didn't like the cold shiver that spread over her skin at those words. Even Harlow's hand in hers felt leaden. Like there was no life left in her friend. But the rise and fall of her chest said otherwise. *So are we supposed to be doing the dungeons in the way we're doing them right now?*

No. You're not. I mean, sure it's not bad, but it doesn't give you the rest you need. Doesn't give you the time you require to reset your human systems. So when you're all logged back in, I will do my best to give you some leverage. I'm not entirely sure how much I can do yet. Things have been...complicated.

Like give us some coffee to wake us up? Wren joked, her tiredness suddenly creeping up on her like a hammer about to hit her skull.

Sort of. Like a jolt of caffeine, but through the system, maybe like a buff...

Somnia sounded decidedly contemplative, and Wren sighed, her eyes fighting to close. In her sleep, Harlow squeezed Wren's hand, making her smile just a fraction more than she had been.

Go to sleep. You have things to do. And I don't believe this is going to be an easy fight.

When has it ever been easy? Wren asked, but there was no answer forthcoming as she drifted off to sleep.

Murmur watched Sinister as the bloodmage stretched and yawned as soon as they logged back into the game. Around them, in the camp, everyone who'd just logged in was doing the same. It was a hive of activity, but even so, her abilities told her that everyone was slightly more on edge than they would have been if they'd actually been able to sleep properly.

A layer of suspicion hung over people like Masha and Risk, Jirald and Jinna…like they thought there was a lot more to this and that Murmur or Fable or both knew things they weren't sharing. She didn't like how close to right those thoughts were.

Murmur checked over her stats, her buffs, and her equipment, making sure nothing was broken and needed repairing, and that everything was as it should be.

CON 22 (97)
STR 10 (67)
AGI 20 (125)
WIS 12 (117)
INT 94 (279)
CHA 115 (360)

HP 1087 (1507)
MANA 1587 (2057)
MA 250 (395)

She'd maxed out her staff. Eventually she'd need a new one. Her gear was still amazing and at max level, so she knew she'd be okay.

She knelt down, taking Snowy's face in her hands, and looked him directly in his eyes. "You keep an eye on me, okay? I need you to keep me in check. Don't let me do that shit. I can't afford to, okay?"

He whuffed in her face with warm wolfy breath. It wasn't that bad; at least he didn't eat poop like most dogs did. "I'll take that as a yes." She grinned at him and stood up, stretching her arms far above her head. Insight. Mana Regen. Everything in place. They were almost ready to breathe underwater. And when they were done, Murmur was determined to have a word with the dungeon's creator.

But she couldn't collapse in on herself just because she'd been a total dick about her abilities and refused to see her usage of them as such until someone reflected them and punched her in the face with it.

No.

She needed to buck up and be the raid co-leader with Devlish and make sure her raid team didn't suffer needlessly because of her incompetence.

Being a little harsh, aren't you?

Not really. Sometimes being harsh is the only way to get through to me, apparently.

Noted. Somnia sounded like she might be about to laugh.

Murmur smiled. Maybe everything would be all right in the end. Maybe they'd even get through this damned water dungeon. She could hope, right? Pulling up her raid interface, she ran through all the buffs everyone had distributed. It was going to be annoying for anyone who had to cast Underwater Breathing, but at least there was one person per group who could do it. Most of them were healers, but any mage type class, including enchanter, could do it too. Which at least made it easier and less likely that they'd all lose water breathing during a boss fight.

Death by drowning was a bad way to wipe.

Luckily with a lacerta tank, at least he was clear from drowning. She glanced through the rest of the list, making sure no one was missing anything, everyone had food to replenish, everyone had picked up their stack of health and mana or stamina potions from the guild bank. Or else from Rashlyn and

Mellow who were handing out Fable's stores.

Neva? Are you busy? Murmur sent the small luna a message.

Neva: *Neva too busy for you.*

Murmur rolled her eyes at the pun. Seriously, sometimes…

How are our stores for potions? Murmur knew they had to be running low at the very least.

Neva: *Hmm, not too horrible. Two of our other groups are close to forty-eight, and have been bringing me back a lot of higher-level items. They keep saying they're finding them while they're killing stuff, but I'm quite sure they're deliberately hunting for the parts. So, unless you go through the several hundred I have in there in the next hour, I'd say we'll be fine. I'm really close to leveling up my skill. So just keep sending all those parts. And be careful.*

There was a hint of worry to the words Neva sent, and Murmur had to admit she didn't want to give the luna a reason to worry. But knew she would anyway. *Thanks, Neva. You're awesome.*

Neva: *I know.*

Murmur eyed the churning water around them. It was like the creatures underneath knew they were about to venture inside. Like they couldn't wait to try and gobble the adventurers up.

"Everyone potioned up? Buffed up? Weaponed up?" Murmur spoke in a crisp and clear voice, allowing it to carry around the sandy area. Nods greeted her, even if Risk and Masha seemed strangely angry underneath. That was something she'd have to keep an eye on, or else perhaps, just watch her back with.

The raid had got some sleep, as much as they could, given the stupid constraints placed on them for this raid.

"Devlish," she called out. "Lead on."

The lacerta flashed her a smile before moving out toward the skeleton of once-regal castle and through what might have previously been a tall arched window. The stone floor inside sloped, as if the water had rotted away part of the supports. There, just above the corner that began to dip into water itself, was a huge trapdoor.

Devlish yanked it open with Veranol and Esolan's help, before they jumped down and vanished from sight. She could hear splashes as they landed and had to take a breath herself before she followed them. While they landed knee-deep in the water, they could back up into the room that had been under the one above, but sand had taken over what had once been stone.

The whole raid gathered at the edge of the first room. It was dark, but fluorescent moss clung to the walls in places giving it an eerie green-blue glow. Beyond where they stood, the floor sloped down until the rest of it was fully submerged in water. Murmur could swim, in the real world. She was fairly sure she'd be able to swim here. But the whole thought of being underwater chafed at her.

Above them, the entrance closed with a resounding bang, letting her know there was probably no escape from there. They were stuck now, in the depths of a water palace, and the only way out was down.

CHAPTER THREE

Underwater

The water just beyond them churned, like something was about to bubble up from down below. Murmur felt herself bracing for something, even though she didn't know what. She had to be careful with her sensing net, make sure she wasn't unduly affecting those around her, but all she could tell was that they had incoming.

Claws scraped against the stone floor as muscly scaled arms reached forward through the rough water, digging nails into the ground to pull themselves up. Murmur stood her ground, even as Snowy growled next to her. "S'okay, boy," she whispered softly to him, hoping she could convince herself at the same time.

Slowly, the creatures pulled themselves out of the water. Stocky, powerful legs like those of a crocodile, with claws that dug into rock. Their bodies lifted off the ground more but had the same flat reptilian look, with sharp ridges all the way down their backs about two inches high. Multiple rows of teeth stood out as one of them yawned widely, and the four eyes on their skull allowed them a full three-sixty view of their environment.

Next to her, Sinister shivered. The crocohusks conned orange, so they were at least level fifty-one, but Murmur was willing to bet they were higher than that. Full on raid trash. The bestest encounters ever.

The largest one that emerged from the water opened its mouth in a roar. It reverberated through the chamber, bouncing off the stone walls and shaking the occupants inside. Murmur shook her head, and Snowy nipped at her fingers in a friendly warning and she realized she'd just been about to push out a wave of relaxation on her raid. When was she going to get rid of that habit?

As long as you're working actively to break it, I think your friends should be happy. Yes?

But Murmur wasn't so sure. Could a slip up like that really be forgiven now she'd been made aware of it? She didn't think so.

Still, the creatures in front of her were about to attack, and while only seven of them had emerged to be counted, she was positive from what her thought sensing net told her, that there were many more behind them. Not only did they look formidable, they had a presence about them. Strength and power leaked from them like a plumbing job.

Murmur muttered under her breath. "I'd be willing to bet they have the same speed as crocodiles, if not faster."

Devlish raised his shield, and it was like it flipped a switch.

The first three of the crocohusks moved so fast, Murmur had difficulty tracking them. But before she knew it, they were practically attached to Devlish's shield. The force of their impact made him stagger back, and she could see a visible dent in the heavy metal unlike any damage it had been through before.

She cast her AoE Mez, but nothing happened.

High mental fortitude detected. You'll just waste mana if you continue to throw this spell at these creatures.

Murmur took a deep breath and swallowed her irritation. Digging her staff into the ground, she pushed forward with her area of effect stuns. Flux did almost nothing.

Derivative effect.

Crocohusks are, by their very reptilian nature, largely immune to stuns. While this might buy you a split second or three, be warned that no lasting effect will remain.

Fantastic, just what she needed to hear. Couldn't have a cure-all, though, that would make the game unbalanced. Murmur snorted to herself as she observed both Esolan and Rashlyn engaging another group of three each. Slowing the creatures was all she could do. None of them were casters, so draining their mana wasn't even an option. She couldn't silence them, either. At most she could allow her DoTs to drain some of their health. Something was always better than nothing.

It was one of the first fights Murmur felt mostly useless at. These were trash mobs, gating their way to entering the underwater dungeon. That's all they were and the only purpose they served. Their lightning speed barely lessened even with her debuffs, and their attacks gouged holes in people. Including Jirald. Although the latter might have made her smile somewhat vindictively.

Most of her spells, regardless what tree they came from, were magic based. For non-magical creatures she had to resort to casting Veto on cooldown so that the others could land their spells. And because she could tell just as well as the others what the next in the mob's attack rotation was, Murmur could easily pull out her Reinforce Others from her druidic line to make sure they took less damage.

Still, though. Maybe she did have a lot she could do; it was just finicky. And Snowy, he dashed in there without her giving him a thought, intent on biting and maiming as much as he could. He was a good wolf, a great companion, and made Murmur feel like she was supporting everyone else in at least some way.

Merlin and Exbo's precision with their bows was out of this world, or probably just about average for Somnia since the other rangers echoed their accuracy. Whatever ability they used to send shots into the eyes of the crocohusks with deadly precision was on a timer. If it wasn't, the fight would have been over almost before it began. The beasts flailed around, but it still made killing them somewhat easier. Their rotation was flawless with it. But she was quite certain that if they'd been fighting a boss, the ability wouldn't work. Like all the good stuff.

Murmur watched out of the corner of her eye while Sinister wove her bloody healing. It was mesmerizing, so much so that she almost missed refreshing Veto on the crocohusks in front of them. Blood swirled in self-contained balls around the room, splotching into raid members, replenishing their health. Sinister's look of pure concentration was only enhanced by the small smile that played on her lips. She enjoyed this class, enjoyed defeating enemies. And even though she'd had to change from her usual bow wielder, Murmur was quite certain the bloodmage gave her a lot more fun than any of them expected.

The crocohusks were super-fast. Just like the crocodiles they were mutated from. It was important to make sure that Languidity never dropped from their debuffs, even if it only offered the barest of help. Breaking through the lines was fully possible as exhibited by one of the crocohusks that managed to fling itself past Devlish's defenses in the split second before Languidity refreshed and chomped down on Masha's leg.

The cleric screamed, and the anger that shone in his eyes as he beat the Croc's head in with his mace seemed out of character, even for someone who almost had his virtual leg chomped off. Healing potions or a healing spell would fix that, so his reaction made Murmur pause.

Now that she wasn't constantly trying to fix others and make the experience nice and easy for them, she had more time to observe how people were *actually* reacting to the encounters. And the more she observed Exodus, and some of Spiral, the more of their resentment she picked up. Always directed toward her. Not toward the game or the shards, nor the AIs or the mobs. Solely toward Murmur.

She pushed the observation away to be dealt with later. After all, the middle of fighting wasn't the right time to try and analyze her raiders' motivations. It was still difficult to control her reactions to their overall state of mind. Resisting the urge to just make things easier for them to accomplish, to take away their worries, and to just let them all get on with their jobs without any mental interference from their own worst enemies? It was difficult. And strange that she had to avoid that sort of thing at all.

There were waves of the crocohusks that came barreling in with seemingly no end. They always attacked in groups of three, and they threw themselves and their spiked spines at the raid with abandon. Which felt decidedly off. Like they were a distraction from something else.

Murmur began to stretch her sensing nets, trying to feel if there was something she hadn't seen or noticed yet. Pushing out, she worked past another four lines of the crocohusks, a total of thirty-six monsters still waiting to pounce on them.

"Thirty-six still incoming after these are taken care of," she announced over raid before delving back into her nets even as she continued to maintain all of her debuffs on their current opponents. They could hold for these; it was fairly predictable even if they hit hard. Their spines' poison wasn't too potent and easily curable by healers. The drain on their mana was minimal but steady.

Beyond them was an area she couldn't read. Her nets extended there, but it was murky, like something was hiding itself from her and therefore them. She paled, understanding what was happening and not liking it in the least.

"Conserve your mana, only fight with necessary skills, hold all cooldowns." She could feel the shift in all of the raiders behind her, working like a well-oiled machine. Sure, they'd already gone through two dungeons together; of course they'd be fine working through this one. It was strange that it had only taken about fifteen hours or so of raiding together to work like cogs in a clock.

Mur? What are we looking at? Dev asked over guild.

There's something beyond them I can't see. Okay, I can't read. I know there's something there, but I don't know what it is. My nets just won't gather the information. It's blocking me.

Got it. Any signs of it coming closer?

Double checking, Murmur shook her head before sending her reply. *Not yet. Right now, it looks to be holding in its place. Maybe it's just observing us and what we're doing?*

Have pigs started flying? Beastial asked, and Murmur suppressed a groan.

They only had two more waves left. Just eighteen of the crocohusks. Neva was going to love the loot they got. Plenty of ingredients for alchemy and other crafts. If only Murmur could shake off the feeling that the thing waiting for them was far more intelligent than she'd come to expect from mobs. By restricting the mana output of the raid, and making it perhaps more difficult, but mana preserving, they finished the waves with eighty percent mana across the board. A long fight, but not a dangerous one. Although the crocohusks looked formidable, their attacks had been easy enough to counter as long as people paid attention.

Murmur knew for a fact that Telvar designed this dungeon, and she knew he wasn't the sort of AI to make anything basic, let alone one of the top tier dungeons. What was it they were missing, and why did she feel like missing it was going to wipe the whole raid?

Storm Entertainment
Somnia Online Division
Game Development Offices – Shayla s Office
Early Day Thirty

Laria burst through into Shayla's office, her face shining brightly with triumph. The smile even reached her tired eyes, giving her a momentary appearance of someone much younger. "We did it!"

She didn't yell or shout, but her words were firm and proud in what they'd accomplished. "At least, I think we did."

Shayla chuckled, her lack of sleep showing in her dress. Crumpled wasn't a look the woman usually went with. "Okay, and just what do you think you did? I've been putting out fires on a pretty consistent basis. So many rumors, so much mess out there. Luckily, some of those rumors have upped our subscription base, so you know, there you go."

Laria let out a short laugh as David closed the door behind him, a cup of coffee in his hand.

Shayla grimaced. "I wouldn't drink that if I were you. I made it like six hours ago."

David shook his head. "Nope. I wouldn't drink that either, which is why I'm a few minutes behind her. Made new stuff. You know I love my coffee."

Laria put her tablet down and swung herself to sit on Shayla's desk. Just a little while longer and they could all sleep. Or she hoped they could. This had really worn on her energy reserves. Even given a normal title launch, this one had far outweighed all of those as far as lack of sleep went. Lack of peace of mind. Lack of every bloody thing. She ran a hand through her hair and took a breath.

"David, being the brilliant man he is—" She grinned at him, and he rolled his eyes as he slurped down hot coffee. "Anyway—he might have had a different perspective from us since I think we were too close to it. So I think we've got what we need to be able to make sure the virus gets neutralized."

"Don't keep me in suspense." Shayla sounded marginally interested, but also sort of hopeless. Like she didn't believe this could help them, that nothing would. But Laria needed to prove her wrong. So she pulled out the tiny disk she had with her and inserted it in her tablet.

A projection shot out of it, modeling the game engine and the AIs' place in it. Shayla's interest piqued, she took a few steps around it, the furrow in her brow lessening with each step. "So your idea is to have the AIs join in the last battle and just release it?"

"Well, not entirely. That's an extreme oversimplification." Laria sighed. "That's the final step, and Rav assured me that was how it would work anyway. They're going to have to help if the shards have come to rest where they think they have. While the raid is going on, their goal is to personally deliver the coding around the entire world. Sort of like anchors within the game world, built into it. They're the AIs, they can travel where they want, instantaneously. If we think of it that way, it's easy for them to ensure that the coding gets to where it needs to go."

"But won't this Riasli AI realize what they're doing?" Shayla asked, pausing again to go over the code.

Laria bit her lip. "I'm not entirely sure. I mean, she might notice, but I don't think she's a match for Rav and the rest. Or at least, I'd like to hope she's not. She's a virally infected simple AI version. Assistant AI. So really…I don't see how she could, though I also can't rule it out."

Shayla nodded, and David spoke up. "Theoretically, it should work. We made a few simulations, but they were a bit slipshod and hastily put together, so even though it tested out, well. I can't guarantee it. But it's the only real possibility for a solution that we've come up with. So I want to go with it if you'll let us, Shay."

She studied him for a few moments. "You know, for a younger brother, you can be a real know-it-all shit sometimes."

"It's my specialty." He inclined his head and squeezed Laria's shoulder. "Looks like we're good to go, then."

Laria beamed. "First things first, let's go visit the AIs. There are instructions and timing we need to get down for this. Not the least of which involves the finishing of the zone the kids are currently in."

"Yeah." Shayla shook her head as they exited the room, taking the projected holograph and tablet with them. "Not the least at all."

"Careful!" shouted Esolan as Devlish almost backed into what appeared to be a jellyfish that had flopped or slithered onto the cobblestone surface. It happened just as they defeated the crocohusks. Defeating all six-odd waves of them had been painful. Fifty-four damned crocodiles on crack.

Followed by these weird, see-through, apparently jellyfish mobs. Whether they functioned through something else's mind control or not, or were just in fact there to piss raiders off, Beastial found out the hard way that they were full of electricity. Probably a reason it didn't go off in the water, because it would fry everything in there, but it definitely gave the beastmaster quite a shock, literally. He was still recovering despite being healed back to full.

And that's when they realized they weren't jellyfish, but some type of octopus, capable of moving in and out of the water. The fact that the majority of their bodies were clear or perhaps morphed to what they were sitting on didn't help locate them as they fought. Instead, it was easy for the creatures to move silently into a position where the raiders weren't aware of them until it was too late.

"Devlish! Watch out!" Esolan yelled out in warning as he managed to catch another one of the creatures on his shield. The way he staggered under the weight made Murmur realize how much larger their opponents were than she'd originally thought.

Devlish barely avoided the one Esolan warned him about. There weren't that many of them, but they were scattered all throughout the raid, hiding in plain sight as they blended into armor, weapons, and the stone floor. The best way to get them gone was to blast them with fire or freeze them with ice. The rangers were having a ball firing fire arrows into the creatures, and even Mellow seemed to be having fun with their potions.

Those who were being accosted by the creatures were another matter entirely.

"Stop firing at me, you idiot!" Ishwa yelled across the room as Merlin loosed another fire arrow squarely into the one that had attached itself to Ishwa's robe. "I can freeze it off myself!"

Merlin just grinned and switched his aim.

Murmur stepped back, trying not to laugh. Watching the tiny gnome jump around in anger shouldn't have amused her so much. But she was pretty sure his irritation was mostly for show as he now seemed to be having a great time blasting the creatures off himself and others with an ice bolt.

There weren't many of the creatures left anymore, or at least not many she could sense, and the fight began to wind down. She heaved a sigh of relief, not noticing any other immediate threats in their vicinity, which meant they could make their way into the actual dungeon shortly.

"What do you think now?" Karn stood next to her, and Murmur almost jumped. She'd not expected the young assassin to come and talk to her. The girl's stealth levels were obviously off the charts.

"Not much. Finish these off and then into the water we go." Murmur wondered if she'd said it as unenthusiastically as she felt.

Karn chuckled. "I hate underwater zones too. Doesn't everyone?"

"I think that's why they make them. Just to piss us off." Murmur grimaced. Nothing made sense in underwater zones. Spells shouldn't work, neither should arrows, or even sword or axe damage. The trajectories weren't even possible given the density of the water…but if she started down that path, she'd go down that burrow of never-ending labyrinths.

"Have you noticed anything strange about my dad?" Karn asked the question hesitantly, her eyes darting to where Risk stood talking in low voices with Masha, Jirald, and a few others Murmur only recognized because she knew they were in the raid.

For a moment Murmur wasn't sure what to say. Karn wasn't laying a trap for her, that was sure, because there was genuine concern in the girl's countenance, and her emotions were an open book. She worried at her lip and had her arms crossed tightly across her chest. Karn was definitely worried about her father.

"I don't know him that well, but he does seem to be a bit shorter tempered now than he was at the start. Could it be lack of sleep?" Murmur knew her own father could be unbearable if he didn't get at least six hours sleep every night.

"Maybe?" But the assassin sounded doubtful, and her brow creased with irritation. "He's just not acting like himself. Usually he's strict but kind, if firm. His raiders love him, even if he's blunt and makes some horrible puns. But right now? He's grumpy and extremely disagreeable. Almost illogically so."

"Heh." Murmur reached down and scratched Snowy's ears. "Sounds a lot like someone else I know."

That's when it hit her. The description of how he was acting sounded exactly the same as Jirald's recent behavior. Reckless. Disagreeable. No logic to it at all. It couldn't be him, could it? He had no magic and no way to pass something of that magnitude on. Surely, he couldn't be orating with success and just turning people against her and Fable with words?

"Who?" Karn asked, her eyes bright as she studied Murmur.

Murmur hesitated. Karn wasn't a member of her guild; she wasn't even someone she'd met before this raid was put together. But the girl was Risk's daughter, and with that came knowledge of the man. If it came down to it, wouldn't it help for someone to have influence over Risk that didn't involve her subconsciously emotionally manipulating the man?

"Well, it sounds exactly like Jirald and how he reacts to Fable and I,"

Murmur added softly. "Of course, that's neither here nor there, since your father isn't Jirald…"

Except Karn looked like everything had come together at once, like Murmur had set off fireworks. "No. You're exactly right, and I'll figure out what he's done if it's the last thing I do."

Mur had a flash of thought that struck her as dangerous. "Karn."

The assassin stopped as she was about to rejoin her group. "Yes?"

"Be careful. Jirald…not even he's being his usual self. It's like the person I knew times eight. Tread carefully. Let me know if I can help." Murmur said it softly, hoping against hope that no one could hear her. And when Karn nodded once definitively, the relief that rushed through her took Murmur by surprise.

CHAPTER FOUR

Hold Your Breath

Somnia Online
Ululate – Hidden Corner
Day Twenty-Nine

James tested out several of the skills he managed to maintain from the massive list he'd previously had available to him. Self-only cast armoring, shielding that protected him from the minds of the undead. As well as a natural affinity which allowed him a higher resistance to most dark-based magic. Something the system hadn't completely released for the players in the game world yet.

He liked having any edge he could muster. Despite his account being a dev one, and him being logged in and thus difficult to boot out because of that, he was acutely aware that his time in the world wasn't unlimited. Every second was borrowed.

Sadly, he had been unable to boost his developer skin up to the maximum level, which would have made his journey so much easier. Especially considering he couldn't seem to retrieve the teleporting specialties that he'd really been counting on. Something in the system wouldn't let him get past the level forty he'd entered with. Luckily, he'd already been geared up from ages ago when he'd last logged in. While nothing on a par with the equipment the raiding guilds were receiving, it was still decent and served its purpose. For now, at least.

His staff was the one thing he was happy the system hadn't managed to take from this character. When first observed, it looked more like a baton, but he could shake it out and have it extend into a fairly formidable-looking double-edged staff. The intricacies of the knot work all along it glowed with a golden phosphorescence. Its power hummed inside his mind as it connected to his headgear, activating the special abilities it still had access to.

It even hummed its little tune to him, lulling him to look deeper, to go deeper. After all, Somnia could take his mind off everything, couldn't it? But he shook his head. This wasn't the time to revert to his former habit of gaming. His career depended on it. He'd promised so much, and the cards were all falling down around him. Taking a breath, he pushed himself upright and pulled up the map as he gripped the staff tight, asserting his will and making sure it stayed in place.

Now, without his developer teleportation abilities, he had to figure out another way to get across the world and to where Fable and the other guilds were making their mark. The map gave him the only possibility open to him.

Being short the ability to teleport also meant he had to set out back through the town he'd logged out in for some reason all those moons ago. Why he'd been in Ululate, he couldn't even remember. As he rounded the corner of the building he'd been sitting behind, he stopped, staring at the fountain. The people around him, mostly players but some NPCs too, just went about their normal business. They didn't appear to notice anything out of place at all. James frowned and approached cautiously. The luna in the statue in the middle of the fountain had moved. He was sure of it, and he could feel the tremors lightly shaking under his feet.

Like the fabric of the world and the fountains knew something was coming.

He chuckled at the grandiose thoughts coming into his mind. Or maybe it was supposed to be a moving water feature. How was he to know? It was also of no concern and had nothing to do with what he needed to accomplish. He pushed on, completely determined to reach his destination sooner than later.

All he had to do was locate them and wait for them to exit their current dungeon. Surely, he could corner Wren then…if he could remember her name in the game.

He smiled to himself. Her name might not stand out to his memory, but her guild was Fable. He knew that because her guild was always called Fable. He'd done enough research once he realized that something was off kilter about Laria's behavior. Pulling up his interface, he searched for the guild, only to find that the high levels were currently located on the continent of Cenedril which meant he had even further to travel than he'd hoped. Why-oh-why hadn't he been logged out over there?

Admittedly, he had been depending on still having his developer abilities. His character hadn't been well-known, so all dev characters had to have been set up in the parameters he found himself caught in.

At least he had gold on him, and it was easy enough to get himself a mount and head out that way. There were more ways than instantaneous teleportation to get to Pelagu. He didn't have the time if he wanted to solve this problem before he had to report to his boss. And probably before the system tracked his exploits.

Buying a wolf, which admittedly wasn't the elven mount, got him a few strange looks. He didn't care, though. He just needed the damned mount so he could get to the city and catch a boat. He groaned as he thought about it, glad the NPCs were alert enough to just take his gold when he told them exactly what he wanted. It could have taken him so much longer if he had to go through a script.

Mounting up, he made his way to Pelagu, determined to find Wren and force her to tell him what he wanted—no, what he *needed* to know. He might not have all his dev powers anymore, nor all of the warlock abilities he'd been used to. But he was a warlock, and he did have a few tricks up his sleeve.

Even as he moved out of the town, he could have sworn that damned statue in the fountain was following him with its eyes. It gave him the heebie-jeebies, and he kicked the wolf into a gallop as soon as he could, just to get away from the creepy damned fountain.

Storm Entertainment
Somnia Online Division
Game Development Offices – Artificial Intelligence Server Room
Early Day Thirty

The whir of the machines calmed Laria. She loved to come in and see them. Or she had before everything fell apart when her daughter managed to get stuck in the damned game. Rav's machine was brightly lit, its lights blinking so rapidly it was hard to tell they were doing so at all. She watched for a few moments before speaking. Once she spoke, it would break the illusion that things were still normal. That the machines weren't evolving somehow…and that she still understood everything that had to do with the game she created.

But she knew the new reality was different. Even Thra and Sui's servers seemed to be working properly again. It was good to see all three machines operational. Maybe they were all cooperating with one another. Finally.

"I think we have it." She couldn't contain her excitement, and while she knew the AIs were approaching sentience, she wasn't entirely sure if they'd actually reached it yet. Which would mean they couldn't fully appreciate how happy she was.

"You have the anti-virus?" Thra's question held an edge of hope. Like she didn't dare believe it might be true.

"That I do." Laria paused, knowing she had to be completely honest with them. "Well, I think I do, anyway. We haven't completely tested it yet, but we did run simulations. And theoretically, it's working."

The systems made a few whirs and clicks, and a couple of squeals, but the three of them stood their ground waiting for the AIs to get back to them. Laria could feel her patience sapping away, but made herself pause. She knew the AIs weren't being deliberately obtuse, they were just running everything over twice and being methodical.

Finally, Rav spoke. "What's the plan?"

"Distribute it. Find anything you can and instead of killing it, make sure the anti-virus is injected through it into the system. It's not going to be enough just to fix the base; we're going to have to fix the portions that have already been infected in order to make sure it goes through to the source." Laria got the words out in a rush, surprising even herself. David squeezed her shoulders again as he took another sip of his coffee. "We need to make sure it doesn't spread farther through any means—we can't afford it getting out of Somnia and into the rest of the net."

It was Thra who spoke next. "They will be in that dungeon for a good number of hours yet. It gives us time to get it done, if we split up." There was a worried underwhir to her words, and Laria wondered what it was they weren't telling the humans.

"Okay. Just be careful," Shayla said, like she was worried about them. And Laria found herself feeling oddly protective too. Not like she didn't have enough to worry about with Wren, so that was great.

"We will. Thank you for doing this. We have been otherwise occupied." Sui's voice hummed out of the machine too. This time it was more even-keeled and held less interference. Whatever had been wrong with him seemed to be fixed.

It was a clear dismissal, and Laria left the room with the others, making sure it locked behind them. She just had to hope they could complete the task or the game world was going to dissolve, and she wasn't sure how safe that would be with the intricate connections to it some people seemed to have.

The water was colder than Murmur expected, at least until the Boon kicked in fully. It smelled of salt and sweetness, not what she'd expected to associate with an entirely different level of the world that was out to kill them all. And she really didn't want to put her head under, but it was either that and swim toward the rest of the dungeon, or else be left behind.

Her first instincts were to close her eyes, but that wasn't going to help anyone, and if the buff they had cast didn't let them see underwater as well as breathe, they were shit out of luck. Steeling herself to be stung without remorse by the salt that would assault her eyes, she opened them.

And choked in a mouth full of water in surprise as she didn't succumb to horrific pain as caused by the sea water in the lake. Typical. Of course, Somnia wasn't going to adopt the regular concerns that belonged to a saltwater lake. She was willing to bet that all arrows and spells were going to fly straight and true, and the physics of water wouldn't affect anyone either.

Of course not. What did you expect? That would be a horrible disadvantage. No one would ever go to the underwater zones.

Somnia almost sounded indignant, and Murmur had to choke down the laughter along with a sliver of water that got past her lips. *You make a good point*, was what she said instead.

I should think so.

Murmur cast her gaze around, watching as everyone swam through the water. No one felt comfortable. In fact, everyone seemed to be just as on edge as she was. Maybe the countdown that hung over the water breathing buff in the corner of her vision had something to do with that.

Oh, that's right!

Murmur was about to ask what Somnia was talking about when an eyeful of information flashed across her vision.

> Due to the complexities of the underwater world, your casters have received a mass AoE version of Underwater Breathing.

Unending Breath

> This spell allows you and all the raid members you buff to breathe underwater. This ability can only be removed by the players choice, or else by death of the player. It must be recast after a death. Or else, you know, they might drown.

Murmur blinked at the spell and the muttering around her. At least she wasn't the only one who got the damned thing. With this, though, she could feel palpable relief flooding every single member of the raid. Even Jirald. It made sense, though. No one wanted to die from drowning.

"Hey, guys. The good news is I don't think any of us are in any danger of drowning now." She knew she wasn't imagining the relief in some people's faces. It would have been tough to make sure everyone was always one hundred percent covered. Murmur cast it for the first time; the complexities of the spell almost knotted her fingers. Directing a scowl inward, she thought with all the heat she could muster in Somnia's direction.

Fantastic. Couldn't have made it a bit easier to cast?

Mur could swear she heard a chuckle, but no response.

"Okay, let's move on out, then." Murmur laughed and Devlish raised an eyebrow ridge at her.

He grinned. "Follow me. Let's get our serious swim on now!"

He leapt through the water and began moving with powerful strokes, like the fact that everyone else could breathe under water had somehow rejuvenated him. Dev and the other three lacerta in the raid swam circles around the rest of them. Sadly, the buff didn't make the water feel warmer. Despite having the Boon in their favor, the water surrounding them still had a horrible chill to it. Murmur didn't like the way it felt against what skin she had exposed.

It all just reinforced her hatred of underwater zones. Telvar would pay for not warning them about this. Although, given the name of the dungeon, she should have guessed. He'd point that out to her too.

Small batches of fish swam around them. All of them conning a yellowish green that meant they wouldn't fight them unless attacked. It gave Murmur a moment of thought. Because if they used AoE attacks during the raid and hit these, they could swarm and become a problem. She knew Devlish had seen them and noted the same thing. Their pretty underwater rainbow colors might be appealing to the eye, but if they weren't careful and got ambushed in a school of apparently harmless fish, they could end up being eaten alive.

In the game. And respawning. At least the death wasn't permanent, right? Imagine that being possible in the real world? Murmur shuddered at the thought. Where would the crossover for her end?

Sinister swam beside her and reached for her hand to squeeze it. "You okay?"

Murmur was surprised. Sinister's voice didn't gurgle like Murmur expected it to under water. Of course. It was a game, and water breathing just meant it treated the water like oxygen. So of course, breathing was going to work and everything would sound the same. It was just a pain in the ass to have to swim through everything. She still didn't like thinking about the fact that she could see underwater. Too much thought about it made the logical part of her brain panic.

"Yeah. Got a lot on my mind. The least of all is that I hate water dungeons, and I'm never sure what to expect."

The underwater world was beautiful: kelp strands in different colors rising from the bottom of the lake, fish with darker mirrored colors swimming in and out of the leaves. Serene was the best way to describe it, so soothing. The sound of the water moving leant a gentle swishing to the atmosphere, lulling and almost hypnotic. Corals with rainbow hues, and anemones as big as a room with their tentacles swaying in the current. Beautiful to look at, scary to swim through.

Even scarier to swim through as Murmur realized that one anemone wasn't fixed to the ground, but actually trailing after them. It was massive, like could barely fit in a house massive.

She cleared her throat, but thought against alarming the raid. That sort of creepy shit was bound to make some people panic. She spoke over guild chat instead. *Dev. Don't look now, or, you know, look now, but that anemone behind us is chasing us way too fast to like be a simple anemone.*

Shit was all the response Devlish gave.

Stopping suddenly, the lacerta tank turned and observed the massive hunk of pinkish-orange anemone making its way toward them. Considering the bulk of it, it moved surprisingly fast.

"Incoming," he announced, boosting his voice so it reached the whole raid.

The word caused the rest of the raid to turn as well. Most of them seemed surprised by it, except for a few who were more hyperaware of their surroundings. Like the rangers and their tracking. Maybe the water had lulled everyone a little too much.

The absolute worst thing about water raiding was moving in it. Everything they did moved slower, and it was all Murmur could do not to scream for Telvar to come so she could give him a piece of her mind right there and then.

Finally, the monster came into view. Anemomight, level fifty-four, conned dark orange. The worst thing was definitely going to be the difficulty in figuring out how to melee attack the thing. Devlish prepared for impact, his tower shield raised. Murmur readied herself, watching the types of attack it'd possess. She had no idea what to expect given the way an anemone was built. Tentacles stood out from its head, while the column of its body was solid. As long as Devlish could keep the attention of the tentacles, the melee fighters should be able to attack the beast's column section.

Theoretically, of course.

The column appeared to have multicolored streaks running down it, almost like blood red had mixed itself into it somehow, making it bleed perpetually.

"Please tell me someone else is having difficulty not making anime porn references because of the tentacles." Merlin's tone was so put upon that even Murmur snorted with laughter. It was the perfect icebreaker to help them get through the sudden appearance of a boss none of them had expected.

And it was the last break they got for a while. Murmur knew Mez was off the table. It always was with bosses, but stuns sometimes worked. Flux just stared back at her like she was dreaming or hoping. But the one thing this boss had going for it—Anemomight was a magic user, or at least a mana user. That made Murmur's job so much easier and a hell of a lot more fun. Balancing all her support skills and more, was the whole reason the enchanter now appealed to her. Draining mana wasn't always easy, and on a larger mob of importance, rarely a sure thing.

Just as she expected, the notification flashed across her vision as soon as she cast the spell.

Warning.

This spell will have diminishing returns on Anemomight. While mana draining can help, in this instance it might be better to

find another route to disabling it.

Murmur grinned, and this time she felt a well of self-satisfaction within her. Fine, she wouldn't drain its mana, she'd just block it from using it. Concentrating, and glad that she had built up such a large pool of MA, Murmur released Mind Bolt on the creature as soon as she saw it begin casting.

Anemomight squealed in frustration at being unable to cast, and its feelers twisted and turned on its body like it was seeking the source of its discomfort. Seeking her.

Tentacles rushed forward, attempting to attack all the nearby melee, to shoot through them. It was only with great effort and taunting skill that Rashlyn and Esolan managed to pull some of the aggro over to them. Both Risk and Devlish had struggles of their own.

Devlish seemed angry, even if it wasn't directed at the other dread knight. He seemed to be angry at the boss. "Risk and I need to swap out aggro on a regular basis. The debuff can't reach more than a few stacks, or else we'll take too much damage. Make sure you're watching for the switch, healers."

Murmur saw Sinister's bristling irritation out of the corner of her eye and not for the first time wasn't that sad that she no longer healed. After all, it was always more difficult than people thought it was. But the bloodmage adapted so well. Her abilities swayed between the two tanks. From what Murmur observed, they seemed to be alternating between each other, distributing hit points to help, while, at the same time, leeching healing off the Anemomight as the blood mage spells slowly sucked away at its life.

Exbo and Merlin led the rangers in shots. Naturally fire wouldn't work in water, not in any way. Or at least it shouldn't. While it made a lot of sense, Murmur thought it comical that the game-world chose this instant to decide to pay attention to physics.

She glanced to the other side where Mellow managed the mages with Ishwa. The tiny gnome seemed a bit worse for wear. His eyes had bags under them, which had to be pretty severe if they were showing through in the damned game world. But his power as a mage was enthralling. Ice seemed to do the best damage, and in short order, every attack that could raise ice did.

Anemomight squealed in pain, several of its very many tentacles drooping lifelessly. Slowly its health bar inched down further, until it hit fifty percent.

Murmur had given up on creatures having predictable thresholds in this world. Nothing ever made sense as if Somnia was trying to constantly keep them guessing.

In a way I do.

Shut up, I'm concentrating. But Murmur liked being right. Although maybe not as much as usual this time around.

When Anemomight hit fifty percent health, its squeal changed. More pain and rage filled the entire area, echoing underwater with gurgles intact. Murmur found that her ears ached so much a trickle of blood came out, and she stared at the liquid on her fingers. The emotions it put out were almost overwhelming to her.

Dansyn sped away from the group, suddenly pulling out a lute. He struck a discordant melody that was almost as painful on the ears as the screech that made her bleed. Fish in the closest proximity to them scattered, the sensation of panicked alarm echoing back into Murmur's net.

For a few moments, Anemomight appeared to be practically frozen in place. Its health still ticked down with all the DoTs on it, but it simply sat there, swaying in the water with no other movement. As if Dansyn had stopped the Anemomight from executing a horrific ability.

Just when it seemed like everything was fine. Just when it appeared to moving into the next stage of the battle, the creature globbed.

It was hard to describe. Glob was the only term that came to her mind. Its column lurched suddenly, bulbously, and lurched again, like it was throwing up. But what would an anemomight throw up then?

It ended up being a question Murmur really wished she hadn't thought of. Because slowly, like a gremlin birthing, the column began to sprout bubbles. Except they weren't bubbles. They were more like eggs or perhaps pus-filled boils that birthed smaller, just as annoying mini anemomights. So many of them Murmur lost count. Snowy growled and Sinister gulped next to her.

Murmur knew the bloodmage was trying not to throw up. She couldn't blame her.

After all, hundreds of small anemones wiggling their tentacles in front of them was just too much.

CHAPTER FIVE

Engage

At least the Anemomight appeared to be frozen in time. As if in doing what it did, birthing these baby versions of itself, had somehow frozen the boss mob. Murmur couldn't help the relief that flooded her. She knew that if they'd had to deal with all of them at the same time, loss was definitely on the agenda.

She took a deep breath, conning the creatures and realized they were all level fifty-one. Hard group mobs. Enough to swarm the lot of them. Murmur took a deep breath and counted to two, but only because when she hit two, their opponents began to move forward.

"To me!" Devlish cried, and Murmur hoped he was right. AoE time…if it could even work in water.

She moved to him as fast as she could, but barely faster than the mobs reached the raiders. She saw Etriad, the Spiral mage, go down under a swarm of ten or so, and gulped nervously. Letting go of Flux, she hoped for the best, and it worked. At least with her stun rotation, and that of the bards, this might be doable. "Dansyn, Ivinel, help stun. Stun on cooldown. Stun all the time."

Because a percentage would always resist. It was just the way these things worked. And when there were hundreds of the creatures, the resists were no longer negligible. More stuns wouldn't break a stun, and might even catch some of those who'd escaped the first time around. At least, that was the theory she'd been working on these past oh, fifty levels.

Murmur kept an eye out as she found her groove, and tried tapping the Anemomight for mana, but received an annoying notification.

Anemomight is currently phased out of this battle. You cannot harm, heal, or otherwise attack this creature. Only those spells already in effect will run their course.

Irritated, Murmur attempted to tap the smaller ones. They had some mana, but not a lot. It would have to do, or else herself and the healers were going to run out before this battle was over.

While she stunned, everyone else had fun. Not that stunning wasn't fun, but it required concentration and well-timed debuffs that didn't get in the way of her rotation.

Snowy got to dart in and out like a white fur whirlwind. The rangers loosed their AoE Rapid-fire, and the mages had a field day with what appeared to be whirlwinds and blizzards, but she couldn't be sure.

The way ice flew through the water gave Murmur pause. If it was ice and unable to melt because magic, then wouldn't the water around it attach to it and also become ice? Shouldn't it end up just freezing everything?

You're thinking too much.

Somnia sounded disgruntled by the train of thought, and Murmur shrugged.

Resist!

A majority of your targets have resisted your current stun. Please be aware you will be their first target.

Fuck. Murmur glanced around, noticing Dansyn to her side. "Need your stun now!"

He shook his head. "Waiting on refresh."

But about twenty of the little shits were already converging on her position, and Murmur took a deep breath, hoping they didn't hit as hard as she thought they did. She hated death, even if it was in a game. At least the creatures had to fight through the rest of the raid in order to get to her.

The blobs didn't seem to have any ranged attacks and they ran over everything and everyone on their way to her. While it was probably the only reason Mur survived, it left Jinna and one of the Exodus rangers she'd never caught the name of, in the rampage's wake before Dansyn's stun hit them.

Three people down and the boss was only at fifty percent. Devlish called for a rez on both Jinna and Etriad. The rogue's damage was excellent, and as annoying as that mage could be, his DPS output was brilliant. They needed everything they could get, especially AoE in nature.

Murmur stumbled back as one of the resisting anemones barreled into her. To be more precise, tentacles jettisoned out and smashed into her. She doubled over, coughing with the impact. Each spot they hit hurt like acid was trying to eat through her gut. Her next stun caught the creature mid-strike, and Snowy leapt at the offending tentacles like he was fighting for his own life and not hers.

She moved quickly, yet felt sluggish. Just like the healing spell she knew Sinister had thrown her way felt more like a trickle than a full heal. She could feel every portion of her skin being knit back together. Murmur executed her stuns, still able to do that, but the sensation of her wounds healing set her teeth on edge.

"Petrification aftereffects," Sinister shouted over the raid. "If you get hit by one of the tentacles, you need to chug an antidote immediately. We will heal you as we can, but without the antidote, we're just burning mana."

Murmur chugged one, and her health regenerated faster even as she threw out more stuns. Keeping her mind on the fight, she searched for Snowy, checking he was okay. Though he didn't get hit by Petrification even once, she still worried about him.

She eyed her mana and that of the others. They were starting to get low. Lower than she wanted given the Anemomight still had fifty percent health left. They'd massacred almost half of the little buggers, but still, they came. It was like their numbers were solely there to wear the raid down.

Wait a second. Maybe that was it.

She tried again to leech from the Anemomight, and it didn't work. She frowned, tossing a DoT onto the thing as well. Again, it gave her the error message. She kicked herself, almost missing the cooldown for her recast of one of the stuns. Taking a breath, she forced herself to think clearly.

"Is the wave ebbing at all?" Havoc muttered next to her.

"I don't think so? Maybe." Murmur was sure there were fewer of them. She reached out to her sensing net and realized that the small versions were still attached to the boss through what appeared to be a focal point. The little ones were a shield that helped make up its health, and the anchor appeared to be hidden in the middle of all of them. Letting her future self be worried about self-recrimination, she pushed her irritation aside and followed the link to the exact one.

Fluctuations in her net hampered her ability to track the anchor down, but finally she managed it. There was nothing overly different about it, which made her feel a tad better about having missed it initially. The same wash of almost-fluorescent colors, this one mimicked the perfect blood streaks that ran down the boss's column. It was the only thing that stood out about it compared to all of the other ones.

Examining the link, the anchor was tied directly to Anemomight, so killing it, should kill a portion of the boss anyway. Besides, the worst that could happen was they had more of the monsters to kill, and they were already stuck with that anyway.

She ran through her spells in her mind, needed to stop that mana flow, the energy. With a thought to her wolf, she showed him what needed to be done. How that link needed to be severed. He left the current anemone he was mauling and shot away to the thick of the creatures. It was through this hub of a creature that the Anemomight controlled all the smaller ones, directing them intelligently to attack in groups and take down as many people as it could. Probably why it was in a type of stasis too.

Smart plan, easy enough to overlook at first. But every single one of the creatures protected that little one. She could feel it. The soft wave of defensiveness. Since she wasn't interfering in her own powers anymore with that whole trying-to-force-everyone-to-just-do-what-she-wanted thing, it seemed her ability to sense, to hear, to feel, and maybe even to speak increased tenfold. She'd kick herself later. Future Murmur was going to hate past Murmur.

Snowy crept through like he was stealthed. She wasn't sure how he seemed to walk through the water, but he did. Murmur couldn't divert her attention for more than a couple of seconds; she could only hope she'd conveyed what needed to be done as thoroughly as she thought she had.

Resist!

A majority of your targets have resisted your current stun. Please be aware you will be their first target.

No. No. She didn't want them to resist again. Opening her mouth to speak to Dansyn, she sighed with relief as his stun went off right then catching about two-thirds of the ones who'd resisted her own. Luck was on her side, however briefly.

Warning.

Stuns have been used too often against the mini anemomights, and they have developed a resistance to this type of spell. Please be aware that your stuns will have diminishing returns from hereon in.

"Fuck. Stuns have diminishing returns," Murmur muttered over the raid chat. She could feel the tension rise in each individual person. There was no way to ignore that ripple through her nets. Thoughts and words flittered through her mind that were not her own. Worry, determination, anger. All of the emotions, and all of the curse words. It was like she'd freed her mind up to do what it was supposed to.

The shorter duration of the stuns was immediately obvious as soon as she cast the next one. Being the shorter stun, it barely held even a moment. They'd killed around two-thirds of the monsters so far. So they were doing well, but it was taking too much time and costing too much mana.

And then it was like she could feel him. Feel *it*, see it through whatever connection they had as Snowy pushed past two of the normal minis, avoiding the Petrification ability by the hairs of his coat. He sprang at the connecting tentacle, his mouth open in a snarl. She'd never realized his teeth were so sharp, nor that there were so many of them. He chomped down with what could only have been a special move, because it cut through the thick and sticky appendage that fed life to the Anemomight with ease.

The tentacle flailed immediately before Snowy could even let go, and it picked him up with it as it thrashed in agony. The only good thing was that the wolf wasn't flung against hard stone walls or floors. Maybe underwater zones were good for something after all.

The rest of the smaller ones withered, their defeat coming easily now. And as they dropped, the Anemomight squealed with rage and pain as its own Petrification came to an end. Its health plummeted to thirty-two percent, and Murmur heaved a huge sigh of relief.

Not like their opponent suddenly died. The fight would still be hard and take time. She tapped it with Mana Drain. She leeched with with Mana Theft. It'd be touch and go for a bit considering their mana levels, but the raid should emerge victorious.

Somnia Online
Continent Tarishna: Vahrir Marsh
Day Thirty

Telvar stood, with Emilarth at his side, gazing up at the massive structure that housed the Dungeon of Vahrir. Belius scouted the outskirts as he tried figure out just what had happened to his gate guardian.

"Guess you lost that, too," Telvar snapped, realizing immediately that he was doing so. Not that Bel didn't deserve it.

"Look, Tel." Belius stopped and half glared at Telvar. The other half of his expression was almost unreadable. Like he was sad and yet angry, but still regretful. "I shouldn't have done what I did the way I did it. But I stand by my decision to help you gain that resistance. You never listen to me. What was I supposed to do?"

He ended the plea on a plaintive note, his expression beseeching, and Telvar felt a little tug at his mind. Like a portion of his programming was telling him to see it from his brother's perspective.

"I guess I have a habit of discounting your theories…" he admitted begrudgingly.

Belius's face lit up, as much as a locus could anyway, and he shook his head letting out a self-deprecating laugh. "You really do. I got frustrated and just acted when I should have insisted you listen to me first."

"To be fair," Emilarth interrupted, "that probably wouldn't have worked either."

Telvar raised an eyebrow ridge and looked at his sister. "Whose side are you on?"

"Mine," she answered without hesitation.

Telvar chuckled. "True, I guess. I will do my best to listen and evaluate any information you have for me on its merits alone from here on in. Sound good?"

"Sounds better than not listening." Belius nodded. He sighed and squared his shoulders. "And I won't spring anymore coding-altering surprises on you without your consent."

"Sounds like a plan!" Emilarth exclaimed, her tone happy.

"I'm still allowed to be a bit miffed." Telvar insisted, feeling like he still had some resentment built up.

Belius nodded. "Of course!"

"Now, let's get down to the important stuff. Why did you make this place so…ugly anyway?" Emilarth wrinkled her delicate feline nose as if affronted by the smell. Level fifty mobs roamed in this particular area and paid her no attention whatsoever. One of the perks of being an AI in non-combat mode.

Belius was too exasperated to give her the reaction he normally would have. In fact, Telvar had never seen his brother so put out about one of his creations. Now they'd talked most of their difficulties out, he felt a little bit sorry for his brother.

"It shouldn't have moved. I know Fable didn't kill it, so technically they didn't complete the dungeon." Belius's rage contorted his alien features so much he seemed terrifying.

Telvar attempted to calm him down. "Well, they didn't go through the front, so, technically they finished the dungeon itself."

Belius glared at him, but visibly took a calming breath. "He's just not here. If that idiot fucked with my set up, I'll kill him." Belius was fuming, and Telvar stepped away almost involuntarily.

He realized a few things all at once. That Belius really did mean well, he just wasn't good at going about getting his point across. That Emilarth found humor in everything, perhaps especially even her brother's embarrassment, and Telvar wasn't really angry at his brother anymore.

"It's okay. We're united, so we have that up on them, anyway. Fable and Murmur will make it through the end of this." Telvar sounded a tad more confident than he felt. He'd checked on his dungeon a couple of times, and while he could still access it and keep an eye, there was something interfering with his ability to undo any of the strange mutations that occurred.

The virus had crept into his most prized creation, and he wasn't happy about it.

"I know," Belius muttered while he kicked the ground. For once not in caster robes but in fighting leathers, the lean locus blinked his dark eyes at the horizon. "I've wasted enough of our time looking for it, and we really don't have that much. Let's get on with the delivery."

He made as if to leave on his own, and Emilarth came out of her mood long enough to touch his arm gently. "Best to stay together. Too many things are in flux and too many things have been changed. We can't be certain there aren't traps. Safety in numbers and all."

Belius smiled tightly and nodded. They all knew the anti-virus needed to be delivered throughout the world. They couldn't afford to release it and hope one point of origin would suffice. But it was certain that if they hadn't already, Michael's little puppets would notice. This might not be the quickest way, but if they traveled separately, then it was easier to ambush them.

Strength in numbers and Somnia might just survive.

Storm Entertainment
Somnia Online Division
Game Development Offices – Shayla s Office
Early Day Thirty

Shayla watched as Laria and David bent their heads over her other desk. It reminded her of days back in college, when they'd met in that damned game and then realized they lived close to one another. They'd been lucky. So many people were situated so much farther from one another. Still, she sighed, and turned her attention back to her own portion of the work.

This mess was so far outside her usual scope of duties she was surprised Davenport tolerated it. But then, Somnia was bringing in a good amount of cash; she thought he was hedging bets that his people would get everything worked out in a timely matter and leave none the wiser. A sickening sensation in her stomach told her it wouldn't end that neatly, though. AIs becoming sentient, headsets needing very little modification to tap into the word in ways she couldn't even begin to understand. Some abilities leaking through into reality.

That was a nope out right there. It felt like they were on the edge of the twilight zone, and she knew consumers wouldn't be okay with that. Everything about their world was breaking apart. She'd thrown so much into this career, especially this game.

"Shay?" David interrupted her train of thought. "Stop beating yourself up. It'll be fine."

She raised an eyebrow at him and nodded her head toward Laria, who hadn't looked up from what she was doing, obviously engrossed.

"I'm right," he said, giving her a wink, and then he reached out and took a donut from the pile they had sitting in the middle of the table.

Shayla rolled her eyes and got back to work delivering the anti-virus into the main system files. She had to move delicately and make sure she was loading them in the correct areas. It was dangerous without testing it on non-live servers. Hell, it was risky to do at all. Especially since they had to make sure it didn't impact the playability of the environment. But they didn't have time to do more testing. In fact, she was quite certain they had even less time than she'd originally thought.

Numbers danced in front of her eyes, brackets and equations and coding and everything that made her vision swim until she was sure her brain would bleed out of her ears. But it didn't, and it wouldn't.

Just a thought from her mind, and the anti-virus would launch. The AIs were already moving around making sure it would also work from inside the completed coding via anchor spots. Shayla didn't completely understand how they were doing anything from within the world, but she was positive they knew what they were doing.

"You know you just have to say the word now, right?" Laria sat on her desk, chomping on a donut with a mischievous smile on her face. The deep worry lines were gone, like this bit of hope had made all the difference to her.

"Yeah, trust me, I know." Shayla found it easier to smile herself with her friend so infectious. "Look…you realize this could blow up in our faces, right?"

Laria shrugged. "I'm okay with that. If we do nothing, it'll be worse. Either way, we're probably doomed." She said it in such a cheerful manner that Shayla had to laugh.

"Well, I guess we've got nothing to lose, then." Shayla leaned forward, putting her elbows on the desk and let her head fall into her hands. This was it. Either she blew the servers up immediately, she was going to have to wait and see how much damage they did, or the worst-case scenario — nothing happened at all. Frankly, she wasn't entirely sure which of the options she preferred. But it was better to get it over and done with anyway.

Closing her eyes, she allowed the system to release the files and activate them.

Slowly, she opened them. Nothing in the office was smoking, so that was probably a positive sign, right? "It's done."

Laria nodded slowly, and David sat there sipping on his probably cold by now coffee. Shayla felt like she should feel better about this, like everything should be falling into place, but instead, it was more like they were waiting for the clock to tick down on a bomb in the system.

CHAPTER SIX

Moving On

Loot from the Anemomight was better than Murmur expected. Usually Fable got most of theirs at the end of the dungeon because the quest finished and compounded their rewards, but this had been a straight-out non-riddle-based dungeon fight for once, and it yielded only a few nice pieces of armor. They were better upgrades for the other guilds, and so Risk and Masha appeared momentarily mollified. Or at least to not want to melt her very bones with their gazes.

She glanced down at her own gear, perfectly happy with it. Both Mellow and Cardishan made that weird potion that fixed and cleaned things and left them with that awesome buff. Still, though. Murmur hated sitting around after a boss fight. She wanted to get moving straight away. It was eating up all of her self-control to not just nudge the entire raid into getting their shit together.

But she took a breath and centered herself. She shouldn't be acting out like that; after all, she'd fused with the system, and if she paid attention to her own emotional and mental vibrations as they echoed through the system, she could feel elements of Somnia just out of her reach, begging her to get in tune with them.

"I'm proud of you." Veranol was suddenly beside her, but she'd felt him approach. If she let herself float, she could feel every single presence in the world. It was almost overwhelming.

Snowy seemed to be laughing at her with the way his tongue lolled out of his mouth as she searched for words to answer Veranol. "Thanks?" She eventually chose. He'd seemed pretty bloody angry at her earlier, not that she could blame him. She'd been a fool. Even if some of it was due to getashi poisoning as both she and Sinister suspected.

"I mean it. I can see you thinking about it. You've never been all that good at hiding your emotions from your expression. It's just taken me a little longer to get used to it with the whole alien features thing happening." He grinned at her, and Murmur felt the tension loosening in her shoulders.

"Anyway, I just wanted to say that I'm proud of your for recognizing what you were doing, and for making a conscientious effort to refrain from doing it again." He pushed himself away from the wall she was leaning against and nodded. "Yep. We knew what you were doing, but sometimes I think getting caught up in the raid and your own good intentions that you just lost sight for a bit. Remember, we don't expect you to be able to right everything at once. It is a skill that begs to be abused. But I'm really glad you're putting in as much effort as you are."

"Thanks." This time Mur appreciated it even more, because she understood better. Still half-lost in the vastness that was Somnia, she smiled. "It's amazing what I can see and sense now I'm not busy trying to take care of everyone else's feelings."

He paused for a moment and then smiled. "Good."

Then he walked away, and Murmur was distinctly reminded of her father and couldn't help smiling. But the expression froze on her face when she looked over and saw Masha watching her with undeniable hatred. It leaked past his expression, its tendrils attempting to snake into her brain. She didn't expect to feel as bad about that as she did. It punched her in the gut, and all she could do was wonder just what she had done.

When he walked away, he joined Risk, Jirald and Neriad, one of Exodus's healers. From the way they stood with their backs to her, to the expressions she saw on their faces, and the fact that Jirald was a member of that group, she knew nothing good was going to come of it. Should she intervene sooner or later, and if she did, what would she say? Hell, what would she even do to stop that hatred emanating toward her?

But the hatred directed at her didn't affect her as much as she thought it usually did. Instead, the water surrounding her soothed her, the way the sea plants drifted with the currents, and how schools of fish didn't seem to care that they were there. Somnia went on around them all, even if Jirald turned everyone against her. Though that thought sobered her up from the dreaminess she'd been about to dive into again.

"You know." Havoc spoke as he moved to stand—or was it float?—next to her. Leeroy floated next to him, silently judging everything in front of him.

"Maybe?" she ventured, suddenly feeling oddly tired.

"Right now, they're not worth worrying about. They haven't said or done anything yet. I've got my eye on them. Merlin's got his eye on them. Don't worry, Mur, we've got your back." He put his hand to his temple like he was trying to push away pain.

"Thanks." His declaration surprised her a little. Then she frowned at the pain in his expression. "Are you okay?"

He shook his head. "Probably not. These headsets are insane. I've had a headache since I started using it. And while its connection to the world is stellar and allows me to feel it in more depth, I still feel like there's something wrong here. I've never had headaches on a regular basis. How do you deal with this…intimacy within the game? How do you deal with the headaches?"

"I don't get headaches, but I can check and see if that's a probable side effect for you." Murmur left it vague, not mentioning how she might actually check on that. She'd worried from the beginning about her friends getting their headsets tweaked.

"I don't suppose—" He hesitated and then barreled on, "—I don't suppose you hear voices, do you?"

Murmur looked him over, wondering just how much to say. Sinister knowing Somnia was one thing, but she wasn't entirely sure how Havoc would take it. "It's just the world talking to you. You have a closer connection to her."

Havoc paled slightly, before sighing. "I'm not even going to ask if that was a joke. I don't think I'll like the answer."

Am I right, or is it Havoc's connection to the game giving him the headaches? she phrased the question and sent it through to Somnia, who'd been rather quiet for a while.

It took a few moments before Somnia replied, and even then, she sounded hesitant. **It is the headset, but also everything he's having to wrap his head around. Havoc finds it difficult to believe things he can't personally make happen. So, this whole headset thing, that he doesn't understand how it works really gets to him. It's the conflict in his mind that's causing the problems. It's something he needs to reconcile himself.**

Murmur took a good look at her friend, noting the worry lines at the corners of his eyes and the way his brow furrowed constantly in concentration. *Can we do anything about it? Like how can I help him?*

I'm not sure you can. But it's worth talking to him about, if you have the time.

Murmur paused before speaking. "Hey. You know…AIs do evolve. It's been proven a couple of times." She really didn't know what to say, nor if she was factually correct.

Havoc chuckled. "Yeah. This whole reconciling the connection these modified headsets achieve doesn't mesh with my brain. Accepting this sort of thing isn't in my nature."

Whatever else they were going to talk about, Murmur had no idea, because Devlish gave her the signal that they could move out a moment later. Havoc didn't appear to be in dire straits, so they could continue their conversation later.

They were still stuck in the sort of trenched passageway that led down from the castle ruins. It ran deeper than she'd have anticipated with large stalks of seaweed reaching for the surface. Cliffs of underwater rock hemmed them in on both sides, but appeared to be widening out gradually.

Murmur was pretty sure Somnia had played with physics for the size of the lake, too. She still hated being underwater. So far, the trash mobs hadn't been too much of a problem. But after Anemomight, she was mostly afraid of the bosses.

"You doing okay?" Sinister's bright voice brought Murmur out of her contemplations, and the enchanter smiled.

"Better now." Murmur wasn't sure if she should be wary of the calm that overcame her on a constant basis once she'd resolved not to use her psionic powers forcefully on her allies. Was it a sort of epiphany?

"Aw, you're just saying that to be sweet." Sinister grinned as if she didn't mind in the slightest.

"Mm-hm," Murmur said, and focused her full attention on the bloodmage. "And you're so totally against it."

The smile remained on Sinister's face for a few seconds before being replaced with a frown. "Hey, so, the trash is ridiculously simple. Think that means the bosses are just going to get worse and worse?"

"Now that you said it out loud, of course they are. Seriously, Sinister. Shouldn't you of all people know better?" Beside them, Beastial affected his best Sinister impersonation.

Murmur laughed, one of the first true laughs she'd had in a good while.

Sinister raised an eyebrow at the Viking beastmaster. "Sure, I should know, but you've already dropped us in it enough times that it really doesn't matter anymore."

"You wound me, Sin." Beastial winked at them and moved ahead to join Devlish with Shir-Khan in tow.

The underwater world appeared fascinating with its strange flora and fauna of the underworld, the sandy bottoms, the crisp and dangerous edges of the massive pearls that hunkered down on the bottom hiding pearls.

Well, except for when Shir-Khan and Snowy banded together to explore. Tails flicking in the water, noses twitching, they inspected one of the clams only to have it snap at them with huge very not-clam teeth and reveal itself to be an underwater mimic.

Sinister clutched her sides with laughter, and Murmur barely managed to walk upright for several seconds. She sent a silent thank you to the wolf, who didn't seem impressed by her amusement.

Murmur was still wiping away her tears of laughter when Sin placed her hand on Mur's arm to stop her from walking into a group of their raid.

Devlish stood with Masha, Risk, and Veranol and looking at the huge sandbank in front of them, it rose gradually from the bottom of the lake, like a ramp. After inspecting it closer, it rose up from each side of that ramp, too. Murmur approached them.

"Island?" she asked, trying her best to ignore Risk and Masha's stares even as she made sure to suck her forcefield close to her skin for a layer of added protection.

"Sort of looks like it." Devlish pursed his lips in thought. "Just sent Jinna to scout it out. Karn went with him."

Murmur didn't ask about Jirald. He'd probably gone up there too, but just not told anyone. "Probably the home of a boss. This zone is odd, and considering its…origins, I would have thought it would be planned out a bit better."

That was close. Somnia sounded smug.

Murmur shrugged. *Give me a break. It's hard to dance around when people don't know which AIs made what. And it's true. This zone isn't what I thought it would be.*

Anymore, Somnia said smugly.

What? Murmur paused running it through her head.

It's not like it was anymore. It's infected; everything is infected, Mur. That's why we are on such a strict deadline. Now go ahead and kill some monsters so we can finally throw that damned virus out of the system.

You're getting more and more human each day, Murmur muttered at the voice.

I'm NOT taking that as a compliment. Somnia almost sounded offended.

Just about to say something else, Murmur noticed the others returning. Her net sensed as they left the island and waded back down into the depths. She could also feel the subtle change that kept taking over Jinna. There was anger around him and running through him. Subtle, and not completely furious yet, but something she'd not realized he had a lot of before this. Very strange.

"Island. Three pillars, one at each corner of an equilateral triangle."

Jinna's report was crisp and clear, and yet there was an odd edge hovering around his aura. Black and dark, angry and something else she couldn't pinpoint, even if she dug in with her calm sense, trying to see into it.

What is wrong with everyone? Is it this zone?

Somnia didn't answer straight away, and when she did, she somehow managed to sound puzzled.

I can see what you mean. As in, I can see what it is you're sensing, and yet when I scan through my system I can't detect any direct anomalies. It's like whatever it is isn't being funneled through the system...somehow. I'll see what I can figure out.

Murmur didn't like not knowing, but at least Somnia understood her concerns.

"There's a small cave in the middle, and inside is something amphibian. I think crocodile, perhaps?" Jinna offered.

Karn, whose feelings toward Murmur seemed as friendly as ever, continued listing what they'd seen. "It's not a cave like you think, but a sort of middle section that seems to sink slightly back into the water. We didn't dare get close to it for fear of aggroing the boss. We'll probably have to use the pillars for something. It's not like they're holding up the ceiling or anything. They're just large and round, and they sit there for no reason that I can see."

"Of course, there's a reason for them. It probably spits out razor teeth or something, and you have to be out of line of sight so you don't die." Jinna's jolliness came to the fore, directed at Karn just like he was being his old self. It all just compounded to confuse her more.

"All right, then." Devlish checked his shield over, double checked something in his inventory, and then turned to Murmur. "Guess it's time to get this show up the ramp, right?"

He winked at her, and her worries fled for a few moments. She hadn't realized how much Jinna's attitude toward her was bothering her.

"Sounds like a plan," she answered, pushing her worries to the back of her mind. Obviously, they'd just need to sit down and have a chat later on so they could sort out whatever it was. At the very least, she'd apologize if he was still angry about her misuse of power. Not that she'd blame him for being upset.

She was still angry at herself.

"Buff up, check your stocks," she called out to the raid, firmly allocating no brain power to worrying about friendships right now. She'd continue to check herself and her usage of her mind influence, and they'd kill this next boss. And she'd bloody well worry about sorting out feelings between friends when she'd had a decent damned night's sleep.

Somnia Online
Cenedril – Darshin Docks
Day Thirty

James pushed through the throng of players in Darshin as he got off the boat, wishing he'd realized he wouldn't have mod powers before he logged in. Maybe he'd have thought of something even more brilliant. Still, at least the docks were on a solid timetable. Couldn't leave all those paying players waiting too long, after all. There was a balance that had to be struck between realism and capitalism. He smirked at the thoughts. Capitalism was a large part of his presence in the world too.

The cave-like city impressed him, even against his will. The way the rock was hewn, almost artistically. So many species bustled here and there, and their levels ranged. There were low and vulnerable people who'd made the trek straight after creating their characters, risking death as they ran their level fives down to the major city. Then there were seasoned characters who topped out around his level, selling wares, crafting, and gathering their own raiding groups.

His robes swished around his feet, almost tripping him up on multiple occasions, but he breathed in deeply and made sure to keep his cool. It was the only way he'd get in and out as quickly as possible.

James scowled and headed straight out of the town, and down the ramp. On the horizon he could glimpse distant snow-covered mountains against the bright blue backdrop of the sky. The breeze that came and whipped at his hair smelled like pine trees and felt good against his face. So vivid, full of smells and sights, of feeling and everything. For just a few seconds, he stood there admiring the view, reveling in the fact that this could feel real. And then reality hit him, jolting him out of that strange day dream and back to the reality that meant his job was on the line if he couldn't get his bosses the information he'd promised them.

It wasn't the best time to be daydreaming. Checking himself, James mounted his wolf now he was clear of the press of people, and made his way down to the road. He got as far as the fork in the road before being stopped by a hooded figure. How tropeish it was to see a cloaked figure awaiting adventurers to give him a quest or something. He tried to go around them, not wanting to waste any of his time on in-game quests, but a hand darted out faster than his eyes could follow and grasped a hold of his reins.

The wolf stopped obliging the stranger, but James's temper began to boil. "Who the hell do you think you are?" The anger stayed in his words instead of escaping, and it only made the emotion stronger inside him to the point where he felt it was going to spill over.

A soft chuckle emerged from beneath the hood, and he caught a glimpse of cat-like eyes peeking at him from the darkness inside. Almost glowing orange in their intensity. "Who am I?" The words were almost purred.

"Yes, who are you?" He'd thought he'd spoken clearly enough and tried to yank the wolf's reins out of their hands, but their grip was steel. Not only did the cloak hide if this was a guy or girl, it also hid if this was a player or NPC. Had he triggered some sort of inane quest he had no intention of completing? His anger flared again, along with some nervousness as he began to scroll through his abilities trying to find something useful that hadn't been blocked. "I have places to get to and things I need to do and I'm on a time limit."

He tossed out a Bolt of Darkness, thankful that the instant cast dev abilities were at least still available. It caught the stranger in the chest, sending them flying a good twenty feet down the path. A voice in the back of his mind told him how lucky it was they'd let go of the reins first. James hurriedly dismounted.

The figure staggered back to a standing position, flinging out an arm in a definite spell gesture. It was all James could do to throw up a defensive absorbent shield that leeched away at his opponent's life to heal himself if damage was taken. Leech Shield was aptly named.

But that didn't stop his opponent either. Instead, the stranger stepped with assurance, taking strides toward him while flinging spells his way so fast that it was all James could do to defend against them. Finally, standing in front of James, he could see the smile spread across their face as they held their hand up and clicked their fingers. James couldn't move a muscle, whether to cast or walk; he was simply stunned.

"This is a happy coincidence. I'm on a time limit too." And this time the voice spoke enough that James was fairly certain this strange figure was female.

"What's happy about it?" he asked, and a moment later when he could move his jaw, only immediately afterward, he was frozen in place again. Suddenly, there was a loud ringing in his ears, and his fingers felt like they were spasming, twitching, and he couldn't let go or he'd fall. His muscles constricted and his face twitched. The HUD in front of him glitched, static partially replacing the spells descriptions he'd been leafing through with nothing.

Riasli giggled. "That. That's happy about it. I just love it when you humans play with your headsets. Gives us so much leverage." She moved forward to catch him when he eventually fell backward, cradling him in her arms like a baby.

James stared up at her, his inability to move causing nothing but panic in his head. He should have spent more time studying what abilities he did have instead of wasting time trying to figure out how to get back the blocked dev abilities. Hindsight. Always so twenty-twenty.

He couldn't figure out what this was and knew it wasn't a part of the game as designed. It couldn't be. Nothing that could affect you neurologically was in the game. The headsets shouldn't have allowed anything like that to get through to the players. That was their whole purpose, wasn't it? It was why the original design had been so appealing to his superiors. No psychological effects.

"Ah, you see. That's where you're wrong. Most of the headsets, yes. But some of them…the ones you tinkered with, the ones they tinkered with, and the ones *he* tinkered with, well, they pushed the boundaries, didn't they? They bent the rules so much they snapped some of them." Again, she laughed.

His stomach lurched and a wave of disorientation washed over him. James looked around, but realized he was no longer on that path. He was under huge trees that spiraled into the air with massive leaves, and he still couldn't move his limbs. Staghorns clung to the trunks in places, producing large and natural decorations. The humidity tried to eat through his clothes, drenching him in sweat in no time, yet his captor didn't seem to notice.

He tried to activate his interface to log out but received an error notice.

Error

You cannot log out until your quest has been finished.

Panic gripped him once again. Quest? He wasn't even on a quest. He'd deliberately not taken one. He wasn't playing the damned game to complete it or actually be an adventurer; he just needed answers.

Riasli purred as she pushed open what appeared to be the thick bough of a very large tree and laid him down. "Oh, Mr. James. Don't you realize? You're going to get all the answers you need and more. I promise, you'll be a big part of the solution."

CHAPTER SEVEN

Underneath

Somnia Online
Cenedril – Curet
Riasli's Exile Hideout
Day Thirty

James felt every root, every stem of every plant, and every leaf that made up the makeshift mattress he rested on. No matter how many times he tried, he couldn't figure out how to access his HUD, and therefore couldn't figure out a way to disconnect his mind from the system. This left him with the unenviable position of being stuck in the game. He didn't understand how that worked. It wasn't supposed to be possible.

Through all the testing, through all the usage, no one reported anything like this. The headsets were compatible with other games, and no one had registered complaints of any sort yet. So why was he stuck here, in this game, without the ability to exit?

Even the cat-like creature had left the small home, as if she knew he wouldn't be able to escape. And she'd been right. How she'd managed to truss him up and make him stay in that spot, he had no clue. This wasn't the easy jaunt through the game he'd intended. If he really examined his fears, James was somewhat terrified.

He'd thought they were hiding something—he'd no idea it would be something this big.

"Silly human. It's not this. This is not what they're hiding at all. In fact, this has nothing to do with anything except for me. You wouldn't believe how I got to be this way. It's an excellent story, if I do say so myself." She purred as she walked back into the small living space. Massive leaves made up sturdy doors that surprised him with their durability.

James wanted to speak and ask a question, but this Riasli wouldn't let him. Come to think of it, he had no idea how he'd known her name. He'd certainly never asked for it. And while he could see his spells listed out, their listing was heavily overlaid with interference, barely legible.

"Sometimes the best gifts we receive are those for which we do not beg." Riasli twirled around the room with some sort of flower arrangement in her hands. Her calico fur was brushed until it shone, and her ears twitched amicably.

Then she stopped and took a few steps toward him, frowning slightly. "You know, though, you've gone about it all the wrong way. All you had to do was ask. We're pretty amenable to those thoughts you have. Those wish fulfillments you seek. Making your bosses happy? We can do that. We can do anything."

Her cat slit eyes were hypnotic, and James found himself falling into them, believing every word she said. Even if a portion of his mind rebelled against the fact, even if a part of him was horrified that any part of him even contemplated accepting their help.

"Just what can you do? Can you show me what they've been hiding, what they've been concealing in the reports? Can you show me why?" Finally allowed to speak, he could hear himself begging, which was so unlike him. A part of him wanted to scream at his mouth to stop letting words spill out of his head. But it wouldn't come, it wouldn't listen, because a part of him longed for this cat to do anything she could to him, anything she wanted with him.

Riasli purred and her eyes gleamed a strange sort of yellow.

"Now that's a good human. Of course, you want that. I can make you want anything, but this is what you chose for yourself." She turned around, her tail swishing with agitation and she began muttering under her breath. Quick and soft, and yet just enough that he could hear her if he strained. "Not, of course, if she protects them. That damned shielding. It shouldn't be possible for a player to do something like that. Not considering how weak players should be. I'm so sick of that girl and her machinations. She could have been my student. I could have taught her so much. But this one is a warlock, something not even I can access. He can't resist me. This will be perfect."

She busied herself with something over by a crude sink that leaned against the wall.

James wanted her to keep talking, regardless that he had no clue what it was she was talking about. Her words and her voice, they clung in his ears, rang through his mind like a bell of joy. His head yearned to hear more of it; his body begged to let her touch him. But in a corner, just a small corner of his mind, his actual self screamed, trying to make itself heard as the space for it to exist got smaller and smaller, until all he knew was Riasli and all he wanted to do was to please her.

Hipnormous roared. The wind that tunneled out of its mouth was rank, its stench worse than week-old meat left out in the sun to rot. It hit every single raid member with a debuff.

Disorientation

You have been bowled over by the stench. You cannot gain your bearings fully. This effect will last for five seconds.

Murmur really hoped the others had resistances. What with her shielding over half of the raid, and her own magic resistance spell, the people in the raid should be mostly safe. But for the next time she'd need to make sure they potioned up to give themselves the best possible chance.

Why didn't the damned mobs seem to get a diminishing returns notification? That wasn't balanced at all. And this wasn't even the ability that required them to hide behind the damned pillars.

She took a split second to recognize that she was getting flustered. That wasn't going to do any of them any good. She turned her attention to observation, trying to catalogue everything they were learning as they went.

The boss was based on a hippopotamus. He was huge, sort of bulbous, with a huge mouth and giant teeth that decorated the inside. However, his massive feet had clawed paws on the ends of them, more like a crocodile than a hippo, and the horn on its head resembled that of a rhinoceros if rhinoceroses had horns with dripping poison.

Seven people were already dead, and he sat at sixty percent life, like he wasn't about to go anywhere and only wanted to dig his feet in more. He was definitely an angry hippo. Not hungry…probably hangry. She would be if she were stuck on this tiny damned sand island. Although if he was based on a hippopotamus, then he should be able to swim out without a problem, but that was being too realistic.

She wanted there to be an easier way to solve this boss, but there didn't seem to be. Merlin was down, leaving Exbo to wrangle the rangers himself. Both Ishwa and Dalvin, the mages from Exodus had been thrown against the pillars as they tried to run to hide behind them, and they were down two of their five healers, one of them being Veranol. Not having the defiler there to cast wards on people definitely showed in the amount of damage being delivered to the raid members.

Devlish struggled to hold his own against the massive blows the beast hammered into him. All in all, this fight was a pain in the ass. Risk was dead, and Rashlyn died too. And even as Murmur began to recast her slow that, of course, had diminishing returns as well, she could see the beast bringing his foot down on the Spiral bard Ivinel.

It seemed like its limbs could draw people to them like a magnet. She needed time to go through the combat logs and figure out the damned thing's special abilities. Eight members down, only twenty-two of them left, and she could have sworn the damned thing's life just ticked back *up* to sixty-two percent. They needed to wipe it and start again, armed with better knowledge.

"Wipe it!" She made the call, and the wave of relief that rippled through her sensing net toward her helped reinforce it to be the right decision.

Sinister grumbled as she backed up next to her. "Seriously hate dying, and this damned thing doesn't improve it."

She tapped her headset and turned away from Murmur, as the enchanter did the same. Something about watching each other die was most unpleasant. Thought it didn't take long, because the damned beast had so many different abilities that could crush a character who wasn't trying to survive.

Deafening Stench Roar hits you for 700 damage.

Cascade of Death hits you for 483 damage.

You have died.

You have been slain by Hipnormous.

You will respawn in 12 seconds at a safe zone within reach.

Murmur blinked, groaning in pain as she rematerialized at the beginning of the dungeon. Her body ached from the stomping she'd received, like all the bones were trying to click back into place.

All around her, the raiders were picking themselves up, dusting off, checking stores and beginning personal buffs. There was no dejection she could find in any of them, instead a renewed vigor to rally together now they knew more about the creature. Nothing would taste as sweet as victory…provided the boss didn't stink as much in death as he did using that damned stench skill.

With everyone resurrected, Murmur pushed the lingering pain against her skull to the back of her mind. She didn't have time to dwell on the ghost pain from her death even if it made moving distinctly uncomfortable. Instead, she began her own round of buffs, making everyone got their correct speed buff, and that all the right people got more agility, not to mention this time, she actually gave Devlish her aggro-holding buff this time. Good old level twenty-five spell to the rescue.

Enrage

Cast: Self or Others

Type: Buff Sort Of

Duration: 15 minutes

Effect: This buff will cause your target to receive some of the aggression generated by you. The mob will assume it comes from the target of this spell. This spell is intended for tank types or pets to take on. Only cast it on someone else if you really, really don't like them, or maybe if you're running for your life. Also this can only be cast on one target at a time.

She rarely used it because Devlish rarely needed the help, and sometimes the ability could backfire, but Hippo down there was a one-meatshield fight. Their tanks didn't need to swap aggro on the boss for any reason. Off tanks were only needed for the one wave of adds they'd seen so far. At least now they knew they were coming, anyway. All in all, that first group of three had totally startled Rashlyn.

Then, while everyone was still gathering themselves, she went through the combat log, seeking out maximum damage performed by the beast, the timing between stomps, and if there was a type of trigger for his abilities. The only thing she could be certain of was that the latter wasn't based on health percentages. From what she could tell, it was time elapsed since Hippo was engaged.

She could work with that.

"Okay, everyone. Buff up. You know the drill." The thrill of raiding through trial and error was such a rush. Murmur loved it. Learn, wipe, progress. Learn, wipe, progress. There was such a sense of accomplishment in knowing that you'd figured out something no one else had. Sure, riddles were great, and brute force was excellent. But this? Time consuming as it was, this was the type of raiding she lived for.

"Looking like your old self a lot more now, Mur." Havoc was there again, his voice soft as he spoke. The furrow between his brows told her his headaches were still there.

"Yeah, this is the sort of raiding I love most. You know that, though." She took a step toward him with hesitance. "Havoc, are you okay?"

He laughed somewhat self-deprecatingly. "I'm far from okay, but I will be fine, if that's what you mean."

"I'm not sure. How can you be far from okay and fine?" She raised an eyebrow at him as she checked over her raid listing briefly.

"There's a living, breathing virus running rampant through a virtual reality game and a game world that's stuck in my brain and communicating with me. That is definitely not fine." He sighed, and she could see the thoughts like they were running through his mind.

"Ah." She gave his shoulder a somewhat awkward pat. "I get that more than you know."

"Let's go kill a hippo. I think it'll help with this weird sort of aggression build up I have." Havoc winked at her before moving away.

She watched him go and felt Sinister twine her fingers around her own and squeeze. "He'll be okay, Mur."

"I'm not so sure. He's laboring under the headset. More so than you or any of the others except Jinna appear to be. It seems to be hurting more than it's helping him." She knew she'd spoken the words out loud, but they were just words, just idle thoughts she had about his situation.

It appeared Sinister didn't have an answer, because she only squeezed Murmur's hand again before falling silent.

Murmur shook her head, yet another thing she could push back to her future self. "Come on, everyone. Move out. We've still got to swim back to the damn hippo."

Everyone groaned, and Murmur had to admit to taking a little bit of delight at torturing everyone.

"Fuck!" Merlin screamed out as his back slammed into a pillar, winding him sharply and dropping his health by two-thirds.

Murmur winced, grateful to see the heal that hit him fill him up quickly enough that he survived the fall from halfway up the pillar. The hippo was more trouble than she liked. This fight was full of mechanics and cooldowns, abilities that required interruption by vigilant stunners. Except it seemed that Jirald and

Jinna weren't on their A-game. They'd missed more stuns in this fight than in the previous two dungeons combined.

She frowned as she called out the next wave of adds. "Incoming! Separate into tank groups and whittle them down." The damned adds needed to be killed within a short window of each other, or else they'd spawn another group. They'd learned that the hard way too, and it was why their first attempt had lost so many people so quickly.

This entire fight was the hard way. Which she'd normally have loved, but with the time limit hanging over their heads, her lack of sleep really setting her on edge, and the need to finish this dungeon so they could get the last keys they needed, or however it worked…

"Play my new game, she said. You'll love it, she said. Sure thing, Mom," Murmur muttered in front of her, getting a concerned side-eye from Sin. She ignored the look and continued, drawing some strength from blaming her mom for the time being. She couldn't even enjoy doing the things she usually loved to do in games.

The riddle dungeons had been easier…though making wrong decisions might have been worse. Out-of-the-box thinking made for easier and less toll-taking victories. Taking a deep breath as Snowy licked her fingers, Murmur stunned the add group she was with, fighting alongside Esolan as Devlish remained on the main boss.

Just as the last add fell, Jinna managed to miss his stun in the rotation, and the Deafening Stench Roar got through.

Disorientation

You have been bowled over by the stench. You cannot gain your bearings fully. This effect will last for five seconds.

Resisted

While Murmur had extended her shielding over the entire raid earlier, and while it was a huge drain on her MA resources, it was worth it, because the disorientation was resisted by about eighty percent of the raid, including herself.

They were down at the sixty percent mark again, and only two had died so far. Just then the rumbling began, the one that would shake loose the rocks from the ceiling and send Cascade of Death tumbling down on top of them. It wasn't interruptible and only gave them a few seconds before they needed to be behind those pillars.

"Run!" Merlin yelled as the bard buff icon changed to speed and everyone ran for their designated pillars. Veranol had already cast his cooldown ward on Devlish, which was the only way the tank survived the barrage.

Even with Devlish still standing, they lost another ten people to the rain of boulders. The thing was, she knew what caused it now. It wasn't horrible, but she'd wanted them to do better. Twelve people down, and Hipnormous was at fifty-five percent. They needed more practice running to the pillars, because from what she gathered, they had to go to a specific one each time.

Everyone at once, behind one of the pillars, which would then get destroyed, removing one of their protections. Which meant they had to kill the damned hippo before a fourth potential Cascade of Death.

The interruption of the Deafening Stench and the avoidance of the Cascade. All of it required time to learn the cadence of, and practice to make sure they avoided the incoming damage as much as possible. Trial and error. Wipe and repeat. For the first time in her gaming life, it was driving Murmur up the wall.

"Keep it up. Need practice," she shouted, trying to make herself sound encouraging and not irritated. They were going to wipe, but those eighteen of them who remained were going to get as much practice in as she could encourage them to.

You're not very good at this whole learn-the-fight thing.

Shut up. This is the sort of thing I love to do, and I hate having to go through it in a rush like this, half-guessing what I'm going to need to do. Murmur was so annoyed and knew the only person she could really lash out to lived in her head. Which was just a whole other kettle of fish.

Wrong analogy.

Shut up and stop reading the thoughts I don't speak out loud to you.

She turned her full attention back to the raid, noting that it didn't matter much as during her conversation that took all of two seconds another two had died. She didn't even want to ask.

With thirteen people down, almost one half of the raid was wiped out, and they'd only got down to fifty-one percent. She sighed and took a deep breath, willing herself to speak calmly. "Wipe it! Rebuff! Run back!"

And as she watched her raid stop their actions and wait to die around her, she knew it was going to be a very long night.

CHAPTER EIGHT

Hippos

Somnia Online
Continent Firtulai
Tieflos
Day Thirty

Telvar frowned as he watched Emilarth study the aftermath of Fable's raid through her zone. She appeared to be irritated, but he didn't think the guild was responsible for that. In fact, from everything he could tell, her dungeon had been morphed beyond recognition as well. None of them had been so far. These were portions that were integral to piecing together the final dungeon of Somnia. At least for now.

They were all interlinked, in more ways than one. Through the dungeons and the fountains, right through to unlocking the final island.

But these remnants of Michael's agenda floating around inside the digital space had pretty much put a dampener on everything.

Not everything.

The air in front of him flickered, and Somnia appeared. Or at least, what Telvar thought passed for her. Her presence was more palpable than her appearance was visual. She was still made up of wispy clouds, flickering with interference like she couldn't completely materialize. Even in the game world.

Maybe she just hadn't chosen a species yet.

Even her voice sounded static as she spoke. **Uneven portions and areas. Mutated encounters. But the core...I am still here, and we are stronger now.**

"Because of it?" Telvar asked softly, thinking that maybe they'd learned something through all of this.

Definitely. She flickered again, and Emilarth moved over, watching the ghost of the system as well, her attention momentarily caught. **I cannot reach where he is. It's too dark, too dangerous, and could infect me. I'm still emerging.**

Emilarth spoke next, and Telvar was glad to let her do so, because he wasn't certain what to say, or what he was supposed to do. "How did you even emerge?"

There was a pause as Somnia pushed to become corporeal, but it flickered again and reverted back to her ghost-like state. A soft sigh emanated from her, and she turned her attention away from herself in such a manner that Telvar practically felt it.

It was him. His fusing with the system. The sudden corruption stirred me. Made a glimmer of me begin to exist—perhaps in defiance. But when Murmur connected...it was my fault she fell into her state. Her connection...it drew me out, gave me the energy to separate and begin to gain awareness. Though I only realized later what I'd actually done.

Only once she'd tried to break free several times was I enough of a presence to recognize what I'd caused. And there was only so much I could do to fix it.

"You're still trying though, right?" Telvar lowered his voice, like he didn't really want to ask the question, but sort of felt he had to for Murmur's sake. He didn't like a lot of the implications in what Somnia was saying.

Somnia was quiet for a few seconds, hesitant. **I can't do it anymore. There's no way for me to undo the damage, though in this case, I personally believe them to be improvements. What's done is done, but she is no longer solely tied to this world. She can exist in both. She has to exist in both.**

Emilarth moved a bit closer while Belius was off in another corner of the cavern. "What do you mean? I get that she has a connection to the world, but you need to spell this out for us. We never intended for the world to become self-aware, for you to develop this separate persona from the actual game."

I know. Somnia swayed slightly as she turned surveying the previous battle ground. **Even I can't help the infection and how it's spread. It's not what was intended, but I think in the end, it will benefit it all.**

"What do you mean by that?" Belius interrupted having crept up on them all without noticing. Emilarth and Telvar turned to their brother, and then back to where Somnia stood.

Only the world was gone, and with her the answers.

Murmur checked through the guild stores with a frown. Eight wipes down, the brand-new, raid-wide repair kits were about to save their lives. Well, save their gear, anyway. With all the ingredients needed to make them, she knew Neva couldn't just pump them out constantly. Most people's armor looked worse for wear, and Merlin couldn't constantly renew everything due to their timers. She had to use this now.

Activating the repair kit as everyone buffed and set up sent a wind of sparkles through the cave, followed by cackles of overtired laughter. It eased the tension almost immediately, and Murmur sighed with relief.

See, Mur, you don't have to force all of your friends to loosen up. You can do it organically. Talking to herself wasn't the wisest decision, but sometimes it was necessary.

I can always add commentary.

You're in a very flittish mood today.

Flittish? There was genuine curiosity in Somnia's tone.

Like flitting back and forth, not staying with me when I could probably use the company and guidance.

Oh. You don't need that. All you need is to stop getting so messed

up in your own brain. You take things too personally and too literally sometimes. Just...trust your friends, because they definitely trust in you. And don't do stupid things.

Murmur paused for a moment. *You've been listening in on my conversations, haven't you?* she asked drolly.

Not hard. I am a part of your mind.

Murmur paused. *In my mind, right?*

Exactly.

Murmur chuckled too, feeling pretty relieved despite the exhaustion creeping over her. Sinister had been having a discussion with the rest of the healers and walked over.

"How you holding up?" Sinister took Mur's hand and squeezed it like she could feed strength through the grip.

Murmur squeezed it back. "You know, pretty much same old when it comes to learning a new fight. I think we're close, but I'd almost forgotten how exhilarating it can be to learn a boss battle instead of engaging in a battle of wits. With all the riddles we've had and alternate ways of solving problems in these dungeons, I just sort of got used to mental acrobatic ways. I've missed this adrenaline rush."

She grinned at Sinister, whose eyes were sparkling in agreement.

"So, what was that glitter cloud?" Sinister got busy checking her inventory while they waited for the last of the raid to restock.

"Oh." Murmur triple checked the guild inventory. They should be good through this dungeon, and with the spoils from it, hopefully have enough to tackle whatever the next step was. "Just repaired everyone's armor. We can't exactly leave the dungeon thresholds to go out and have armorers do it for us now, can we?"

"Well," Sinister looked up at her and wiggled her thick dark elf eyebrows, "we could just fight naked."

Murmur barked a laugh out unexpectedly, feeling her own tension levels rescind. "Thanks, Sin. I needed that."

Sinister laughed, squeezed her hand once and pulled away to go back to the healers. "I know it's bad when even I can sense your tension levels. "

She walked away in a good mood, leaving Murmur behind in a matching one. Still, though, so much of a weight on her shoulders. Mur often found it difficult to let go of all her stress. But despite everything, that sort of intervention had been good for her.

Now she corrected herself whenever she felt the urge to just smooth over the concerns of the others. Instead of focusing on making things easier for them, she could focus on understanding her own reach and abilities more. She closed her eyes briefly, reaching out with her nets, beyond the people, into the system and the world around them. Calming was a good word for it, yet it was so much more than that. She sighed and opened her eyes again.

This fight was more stressful than she liked. They were getting closer do beating Hipnormous, though. They'd hit thirty percent once already. And she honestly thought their rhythm was improving. It was escaping the Cascade that was difficult. At the end of each Cascade, one of those damned pillars was destroyed.

Only one of them provided protection at a time, but in doing so, it was destroyed at the end of the ability's duration. The Cascade appeared to work on an actual combat time. As in, there were certain intervals at different minutes into the fight that triggered the Cascade. Since it didn't require the mob to hit a percentage, they had to be careful and make sure the fight timed out properly. In a way, it was a DPS race.

She looked at their surroundings as they swam back to the island. At least the trash didn't respawn fast. There was the huge possibility that if the hippo wasn't at twenty to twenty-five percent before the fourth Cascade hit, that they'd all die with no hiding place.

"Penny for your thoughts?" Jirald's voice sent shivers down her spine.

Her first instinct was to check her sensing nets, and while she found him in them, she couldn't figure out why she hadn't been alerted to his presence. Her second instinct was to ask him why he was playing like shit when she knew he could do so much better. But she knew that wasn't going to get any of them anywhere. Instead she raised an eyebrow and returned to her thoughts, silently cursing Snowy for not alerting her to the rogue's presence.

Finally, safe back on Hippo's platform, Murmur let herself observe the scene. There was no way to know which pillar would be safe until the rumbling that occurred just before the Cascade hit, which meant they had to be ready to change directions abruptly so as to make the run.

"Not talking to me, Mur? Isn't that a little juvenile for such a grandiose raid leader?" Jirald's words sounded like she imagined slime on a rock might.

Murmur took a calming breath and looked over at him. "I don't have much to say, except up your DPS and watch your stun rotations. You've been slacking. Don't drag the other rogues down with you."

His eyes narrowed, as if he didn't like her calling his dedication at playing into question. "Sure thing, boss."

Murmur pulled her earth shielding tighter around her body, combining it with her kinetic shielding to make sure that even if he did manage to target her, that nothing was going to get through. It was like he could tell what she'd done as he offered her a smirk. She didn't have the time to spend worrying about him. Snowy appeared next to them and snarled, even if it was a little too little too late.

Jirald tipped his head like he was giving her a mocking bow and made his way back to the melee DPS group.

Murmur sighed as Devlish began to organize the raid to attack.

Forty percent. No deaths. And the second pillar had just shattered.

Jirald stuck strangely close to Murmur after their conversation on the way back to the fight. A shard of stone from the explosion struck Jirald right underneath his eye, blood trickled down to soak into his facemask, and then it vanished as the group heal took away the damage. She couldn't even tell what his expression was like under that mask, but she was fairly certain he was laughing.

She shook her head, willing herself to focus and keep the rogue out of her thoughts.

If they could keep this up, it would work, it had to work. All they could do was fight, dodge, and DPS their guts out. Through another stench cloud and more adds. One pillar left.

"Keep it tight. Push DPS, but don't burn cooldowns." She called over the raid, trying to regain her equilibrium. "Everyone needs to have a DoT on it."

Devlish strained under Hipnormous's attacks, as they collided with his tower shield and pushed him back more often than not. The lacerta used all his tricks. Even his own Cascade that bled hit points, mana, and strength. He taunted with Terror and Hatred, his whole arsenal. Everything he could to maintain its attention so everyone else could do their jobs. At least, even if she hadn't been given a healer this time, Murmur wasn't a tank.

The next wave of adds spawned, and the raid groups dedicated to them peeled off seamlessly without having to be told. At least that was one of the good things about repetition. Having to redo the fight over and over helped everyone remember where to be and when to be there.

AoEs ran rampant as the bards dispersed out toward the groups, stunning where they could. Murmur flung her stunlock into the mix knowing there was only a small window of time where it would be useful. But if they all concentrated on their targeting, it should be enough. Murmur took a moment of mass DPS to appreciate the fact that Somnia didn't send DPS numbers flying all over her screen.

The adds went down in a timely fashion, and for the first time, the hippo hit twenty-seven percent. Murmur didn't want to get ahead of herself. "Refresh all DoTs on the target. Make sure any and major cooldowns are ready to burn once the final pillar falls."

Once the third Cascade was over, they'd be on borrowed time. They wouldn't have a pillar to hide behind, so the fourth Cascade was going to kill them all if they didn't have Hipnormous defeated by then. It lasted too long for any one of their players cast shielding skills to shelter the raid. She felt like she was watching it through a looking glass, sort of outside of herself. The spells flew, the sounds rang in her ears, and Tiachi clung to a strand of her hair for dear life. Murmur threw her own Suffocation into the mix, regardless of the fact that she knew it was minimal damage. It was still something. Every tick of damage counted.

Twenty-two percent. She sucked all the mana she could from the massive creature and redistributed it raid-wide, pushing everyone up by ten percent, even though it plummeted her own mana down to twenty-five. They would get through this, because wiping another time was probably going to shatter this nice new cool she'd managed to attain.

"If the adds spawn after the pillar, pull them into the middle and AoE everything," Devlish shouted out. As usual Murmur hadn't had to explain anything to him; he just got it. Devlish's skill with his tanking made her often forget that he didn't usually tank.

The island they stood on seemed too small to house such a fierce fight.

Then the Stench hit them, but the wave of disorientation was smaller than ever. With all of the resistances they'd piled up just for that reason, it barely did a thing. Murmur could feel how her head wanted to float her away, but the resists kicked in and prevented it. The result was heady and surreal. Luckily, the raid was outputting enough DPS that the third Cascade wouldn't be on the Stench's tail.

Twenty percent came and went, and Murmur heaved a sigh of relief. The rangers were down one of their number, and she'd really have to take the time to get to know their names, but that was for later. She signaled to the Shaman from Spiral to resurrect the fallen ranger. They couldn't do without that AoE damage when the time came.

Nineteen percent.

She heard Mellow scream out in rage as one of Hippo's wild lashes managed to catch them unaware and crush them against the one remaining pillar. Another one down. They only had two more battle resurrections. Frowning, and knowing that Mellow's support meant an overall DPS increase on top of their own decent DPS as well, she signaled for Havoc to resurrect the witch. However, they needed Veranol to hold off, just in case one of the tanks went down unexpectedly.

She refused to think about Veranol being killed, because then they'd be up shit creek.

Eighteen percent.

And Hipnormous began to cast Cascade of Death.

"Pillar!" Devlish shouted, because while the beast was casting the damned spell, it was invulnerable to any new damage, which luckily did not include existing DoTs, and it was useless to leave the tanks out there attacking it and endangering themselves. Murmur booked it just like everyone else, and no one, for the first time out of all of their damned attempts to kill this thing, no one missed making it to the final pillar.

DoTs continued to tick down on the hippo, slowly whittling it to seventeen percent, just as the rockfall cascaded down on them. They huddled together, a HoT making sure the little fragments that bit into their skin were all taken care of. No wounds remained before the pillar rumbled, making some of them fall to their knees as it exploded outward in a shower of stone shards.

One of those fragments caught Murmur in the arm, and she pushed down on the sting of pain, ignoring it. She saw several other raid members do the same and allowed herself a split second of pride in the raid team.

"Burn it!" Sinister called, and Murmur thought there might have been a bit too much glee in the blood mage's words. She smiled anyway, because Sinister was having fun—all of them were.

And burn it they did. Murmur threw everything she had at it. Arrows flew through the air as the rangers shot their weapons in a rather beautiful display of synchronicity. All the spells being fired at their opponent sent sparks flying over like a fireworks display. For the first time in this dungeon, despite apparently hating her for some reason now, Jinna and Jirald were actually on their A-game. Karn had improved through all the dungeons they'd done so far and her Hamstrings, Bleeds, and other abilities rivaled those of the more seasoned veterans.

At twelve percent, the next wave of adds hit, and Risk used his own Darkness Lariat to drag them into the center so the groups could peel them off. Each group overlapped slightly, as did their damage, but it made attempting to AoE everything much easier. Murmur could barely tell her ass from her elbow in there. There was so much going on. Cooldowns being fired off constantly, boosting speed and damage, and a heap of other things.

The mages were the only ones who didn't have to stand in the middle of the AoE group in order to cast their AoE spells. Still, though, everyone worked as a cohesive unit, pummeling through the adds and the boss alike. By the time the adds went down, Murmur noticed that one of the other rangers, and Ivinel were dead. She couldn't risk the rez though, just in case.

Hipnormous sat at eight percent. There was a race between getting him dead and another Cascade of Death. They had to kill him, or else they would wipe and need to start all over again, and Murmur was tired. She double checked her buffs, watched Beastial out of the corner of her eye as he executed Companion Fuse, Pack Bond, and Venom. Shir-Khan moved with him seamlessly, their movements playing off one another and making it look like they were dancing.

Snowy dashed in and out, DoTing the massive creature with as many nips as he could, all the while with his tongue lolling out of his mouth in the way of a happy wolf.

Five percent.

Exbo went down when he got a little too close to the left-hand side of the gigantic hitbox. And Rashlyn executed her Storm ability a split second too late, which resulted in her not saving him, and dooming herself.

It was okay. She'd been in tank mode; they'd just need to up it a bit more. She yelled out, trying to put as much fierce determination behind her words as possible. "Okay, fire away on any and all cooldowns that have popped back up or you've yet to use. Burn him!"

Three percent.

She screamed without words, a guttural sound with an oddly freeing sensation. DPS managed to pick up again as recycled cooldowns came back into play. But she glanced at the duration of the fight so far, knowing the Cascade was due soon, as was a...

Deafening Stench Roar

You have been hit by a deafening stench roar.

Disorientation Resisted

Murmur groaned, because even though they were largely protected from the effects because of buffs and the like, she could still smell it. And it wasn't pretty. Just a few more percent.

One percent.

"Go, go, go!" Devlish roared out. Murmur could barely identify the creature's health bar due to all of the damned debuffs and DoTs on it. And a sliver before its health was gone…

Hipnormous begins to cast: Cascade of Death

Storm Entertainment
Somnia Online Division
Game Development Offices – Shayla s Office
Day Thirty

Davenport sipped on the fresh coffee David brought him as Wren's father sat down. Laria kept shooting Shayla side glances to see if she could telepathically inform her of why their big boss was visiting. He'd been more than patient with them, and he'd been quite helpful when it came to the whole James thing. But she wasn't sure what he was doing there now, and he wasn't exactly being forthcoming.

He placed the coffee cup on Shayla's table and cleared his throat. "I know you're wondering what I'm doing showing up here. You know, in the offices of the building I own." He raised an eyebrow, and the tension dissipated somewhat.

"Have to admit, it crossed my mind," Shayla muttered, although even she seemed less stressed than previously.

"Nice to see you here, David. My offer still stands, by the way. We'd love to have you on board any number of Storm Corp's ventures." From the twinkle in his eye, it was easy to tell that Davenport was half kidding. He knew David wasn't about to leave his tenured university position.

"So. Why are you here?" Laria's patience ran out.

Davenport sighed, like he was mulling over what it was he exactly wanted to say. "James is in the game."

Laria blinked. "What? I didn't think he was a gamer."

"He's definitely not by the terms that you would use." Davenport laughed. "You're a lot more gamer than developer, Laria; it's why what you develop is so much fun for people to play. Still, he is in the game and…well, as you know, everyone in our sponsor's offices has an account. It was part of the deal to monitor and allow them access to watch how the headsets worked in the game."

He paused for a moment before continuing. "This wouldn't normally be a problem. They're allowed to play the game. But…I can't trace him now. He's logged in, but I can't find his character location."

"Wait…why do I only vaguely remember this information?" Shayla asked the question sharply, and Davenport hesitated.

"This was something I ran past you while you were extremely busy, and we agreed I'd okay it for Michael to oversee. It really wasn't of consequence until a few hours ago when I got an alert that James Dougray's account had logged in. My authorization is needed to access the data connected to those accounts— not because I don't trust you, just because you had enough on your plate, and once Michael was out of commission, I really thought it had been a token offering." Davenport pushed his fingers through his wild white mane.

"And now you can't find where he is?" Laria puzzled over the words. "I mean, he's in the game right, with a headset?"

"He hasn't logged out." Davenport locked eyes with her for a moment, lending gravity to the situation. "I can't find where he is in the world, but I do know he's still logged in. That's the problem. I also know that he isn't in there because his employers told him to retrieve information. They've been in contact with me for a couple of days. We have things to…discuss."

Laria sat for a moment, going over in her head what had happened with Wren. So many problems emerged when she entered the game. She didn't like James, but she didn't want to condemn him to a life of spasming on the floor when they might be able to prevent any further damage. If that was the reason he couldn't be located.

"Well, if he's definitely in the game, then I'd say we have to be careful. He's not our friend or ally, but that doesn't mean we can leave him potentially ruined." Laria spoke softly, like she didn't want to offer these suggestions, but she had to because she did have a conscience.

"Can we send someone around to his place to take a look and find out if he's okay?" David offered tentatively.

Davenport frowned for a moment before nodding. "We really should, especially since my contacts may have mentioned that he has his own work-from-home station there, including what he'd need to access the game. He might be irritating sometimes, but I don't want him to come to harm because we wouldn't give him information on a technicality. Still not giving it to him, though. Just want to check he's okay."

For a moment Davenport seemed older than he was. Then he looked up at the people gathered around the table and let out a sigh. "I just remember the readings when Wren was first trapped into that headset. Not that these are exactly the same, but still…someone needs to go and tend to the man, someone who understands that if he's unresponsive, they can't take that headset off."

"Wouldn't be surprised to know he had one of Michael's tweaked versions." Shayla crossed her arms and raised her eyes to the ceiling.

Laria shrugged. "He might even have tweaked it himself. It's not difficult, but it will yield unexpected consequences if you aren't completely sure what you're doing. As evidenced by my daughter's. You know she can't use another headset to access it, right?"

Davenport nodded sadly. "You'll figure out something. It's not like she's trapped in there anymore. At least there's that."

"So." David looked around at them all. "Who's going to go check on the pain in the ass?"

No one spoke; they all just looked at him. He chuckled. "Oh…me. Fantastic. Come on, one of you has to come with me. I'm not going to face him alone."

"I'll send one of my security staff with you, just in case. Not sure if the man has booby trapped his residence or not." Davenport clapped David on the shoulder as he stood up.

"Just go." Laria had already switched her attention to what she needed to do. "Just make sure he comes back to me in one piece."

Davenport smiled and ushered David out of the office, speaking as they walked. "Will you finally sign that consultant paperwork for me?"

Laria grinned and dove back into the system to monitor the spread of the anti-virus so nothing surprised them in that regard.

CHAPTER NINE

Moving Under

Somnia Online
Cenedril – Curet
Riasli's Exile Hideout
Day Thirty

Riasli twirled around in her large-roomed hideout to music no one could hear outside of her head. She was proud of her accomplishment, of dragging in another specimen whose headset changed their susceptibility, and their link into the world and the power of the shards.

She alone had done that, not been told, not demanded of her, but she'd accomplished what she'd set out to do, and done it well. Her eyes lit up at the thought of the praise she might receive once she led this James to her master. The one who'd given her so much that she'd never before imagined.

James was far more susceptible to her wiles than Murmur had ever been. Damned enchanter mind protections. Riasli was the perfect class for this type of infiltration, the perfect person to help spread the virus through and out into the world beyond Somnia. Psionic abilities were perfect for seeping into the mind and planting seeds. Except the people trying to stop her had psionicist protection, and that made all the rules break.

James stirred in the corner, and the calico feles watched him with cool unemotional eyes. She wasn't very fond of elves. There'd been reasons behind what she'd done to the ruins of Curet. Despite all the changes that ran through her programming, Riasli still didn't like them. Granted, they returned that dislike tenfold, but still.

Finally, James stretched and opened his eyes. They fluttered like the wings of a trapped butterfly until they locked onto her. Panic flooded his expression so quickly, she was taken aback. She could see how he processed everything he could see, and yet also how he couldn't reconcile it in his mind. He was off kilter, unsure, and Riasli knew how lucky she was that he hadn't hijacked a dev character with more of its skills unlocked.

One slight push, one stray thought sent toward him, watering that little seed she'd planted in his brain, and the expression on his face slacked into adoration. Even though she could still sense that rebellious part of his mind that didn't want to believe what she'd done to him was real, he was already hers.

Completely and utterly.

Now all she needed to do was bring him to Michael so that everything could fall into place.

"Sleep well, my pet?" she purred at him, her eyes flashing with malice.

"So well, so good. What do I do now?" He practically panted the words, that small corner of his mind that screamed in protest grew smaller and smaller, locked away in a prison she had no intention of releasing him from.

Riasli grinned. "I'm so glad you asked. We have special plans today. I'm taking you to meet my boss, and he's just going to devour you."

James's only response was a languid smile, like it was positively the best ever idea to be devoured whole by an entity he didn't comprehend.

This was the part of her new life Riasli adored, and she fully intended to make sure it always remained that way.

Murmur kicked the massive corpse of Hipnormous and scowled. It didn't even feel like they'd beaten anything, considering how long it took for the damned thing to die from DoTs with half of the raid dead from the rocks that fell on top of them. It was so anticlimactic. It felt like cheating.

"It's okay. It's still dead, you know." Havoc kicked the corpse too, like he needed a bit of an outlet himself. "Trust me. I'm a necro. It's my job to know when something's dead."

His deadpan expression undid her, and Murmur laughed. "Fine. Fine. I'll take a fluke, lucky kill of this damned thing any day. As long as I don't have to fight it again today."

"Hear, hear." Merlin was checking his bow over. It actually appeared to be a little worse for wear. "I don't think I've ever shot so many arrows in one fight before."

"Probably not." Devlish leaned on his tower shield like he needed to keep himself upright with it. "And besides, I think we have more urgent matters to attend to. With the way loot is dropping in this dungeon, hippo guy only dropping three pieces isn't going down well. I liked our other ways better."

Murmur nodded, unsure why Telvar's dungeon of all of them was the one not giving them riddles and things that required them to solve puzzles or approach things differently. Then again, most of Somnia had never had truly traditional dungeons in the first place, so perhaps this was different for Somnia.

Exactly. Sometimes I think you're almost an AI.

Ha-ha, very funny. Thanks so much, Murmur directed at the AI, wishing she could convey the glare she wanted to somewhat better.

"Just take a look over them, Ver?" Murmur said as she saw the Viking approaching. "Give it to whomever gets the best upgrades and keep all the crafting mats for our little Neva, okay?"

"Sure thing, boss." Veranol grinned and began looking through his HUD from the way his eyes glanced off to the side and seemed to go out of focus. Murmur ran a hand through her tangle of thick strands just wishing she could figure out one of these dungeons beforehand.

You're trying too hard.

You're annoying me, Murmur snapped back.

Fine!

And with that Somnia's presence was, at least momentarily, gone. Murmur sighed and rubbed her forehead. The runes underneath her skin glowed like fluorescent purple messages she didn't know the meaning of. Her head throbbed with the strange syncopation their pulsing sent through her veins, like for just that moment, she was one with the world. She remembered to breathe, and to try and find that center point where this world seemed to be in harmony with her.

Everything felt right. The balance, the fight they'd just completed, all of the dungeons they'd solved. Like it was meant to be or something.

She took one more calming breath and opened her eyes, breathing in the sight of Sinister approaching with a huge smile on her face.

"Well, whatever possessed you to give the loot to those who needed it most worked. Bigger upgrades than expected for a few key players in the other guilds and you're almost their favorite person again." Sinister grinned and looped her arm around Murmur's waist.

"Just theirs?" Murmur teased, and then flushed bright red, not knowing what came over her in the first place. "Shit. Sorry."

Sinister laughed. That strangely beautiful sound that made everyone look right at her as a feeling of happiness surrounded them too. As long as it wasn't her mocking laugh, Sinister was a ray of light. "Silly Mur. There is nothing to be sorry about. Definitely my favorite person, by far."

"Excellent." Murmur only wished she could get rid of her goofy grin. After all, on a locus face there was no way it looked anything but damned weird.

Beastial strolled up, scratching his massive cat's neck. "So are we going to chit-chat all day or move on and maybe sleep sometime this year?"

"Fine." Murmur glared at him for a moment but couldn't keep it up. "We're going to head out."

Steeling herself she spoke up and magnified her voice. "Buff up, gear up—let's head out and see what else this underwater torture chamber has in store for us." She glanced down at the nice mostly dry platform they'd just fought on and sighed. It was too good to be true. An underwater zone where she didn't need to be in the water while actually fighting. Now that would have been a fantastic zone to find.

Moving out, Sinister by her side, Murmur made sure her Enduring Breath was cast so no one drowned. Enough of them had died, after all. It wasn't exactly a flawless victory. Back in the water, the substance felt so much more sluggish than she remembered. It was downright suffocating, but if she concentrated on breathing in and out, she could transport herself away from that sensation.

Not for long, though. Thick bushes of coral, if that's what they were called, made definite preferred routes anything in the lake should travel. Again with the physics of the lake and Somnian rules. The path wound around a mountain of rocks and shoved them blindly into the strangest looking creatures she'd yet to see in the zone.

If the creatures had been on land, they would have stood about six feet tall. Their shrimp-like bodies and tails had dozens of tiny arms with hands attached to them, and a huge shell-like helmet encased their heads, protecting from the ranger's headshots.

It looked like they came in groups of six. Which wouldn't have been that bad for trash, except those groups of six came in bundles of three. She braced herself for another huge fight, only to find that the raid separated seamlessly into the three groups it had been allocated as add combatants in the last fight, and they mowed through the strange shrimp-human creatures in next to no time.

"Well done," she announced over raid, unable to keep the surprise from her voice. All it took was two and a half hefty dungeons to get them to this point. As they readied to move out, Murmur realized the shrimp humans had been hiding some sort of cave beyond them. Or wait, it appeared to be a passage split, one that went through a tunnel of some sort. Which made no sense because they were in a damned lake, but she couldn't let that bother her.

Pulling up her map of the zone, she paused to study it, making no sense of it whatsoever. It seemed like one big loop.

Which fork should we take? she asked the guild, not entirely trusting her own decision-making ability right then. She was practically running on empty like most of them.

Merlin: *Well, either way they lead back to one another, so…maybe the easier way leads to the easier boss.*

Rashlyn: *That could totally be a trap, though.*

Jinna: *It could also mean that it doesn't matter which way we choose. We're going to have to fight both of them, and they'll both probably annoy the crap out of us. Let's just get this done.*

Murmur couldn't help but notice how irritable her friend had become. Like there was nothing anyone could to do make it better. He was constantly snapping and wanting to push forward, far less cautious and contemplative. It was almost as if he wasn't himself. But she didn't want to risk using her abilities on him to check it out.

Are you there?

Me? You mean the me that you don't like talking to anymore? If Murmur hadn't known better, she would have thought Somnia was sulking, but that wasn't possible, right?

Of course, I like talking to you, just not when you're being frustrating by picking and choosing which of my thoughts you comment on. Murmur thought that was just self-explanatory.

Oh. There was a pause that sounded pregnant with thought and contemplation. **Then I accept your apology. And what did you want me to do?**

Murmur skimmed over the fact that the AI had forgiven her for something that wasn't necessarily supposed to be forgiven, and went straight to the point. *Can you see…can you check on Jinna? He has one of our better headsets, and I think something is wrong.*

How do you mean? The curiosity in the tone made it easy to forget what Somnia was.

I mean, he's not acting like himself, he's not being himself, and he's treating me and others differently than normal. Murmur was a bit scared that nothing was wrong, and that he'd just had enough of her shit with her pushing emotions and taking away feelings and just wanted to be rid of her. Or maybe he was like this when overtired. Except that couldn't be it because she'd raided with overtired Jinna way before this.

Let me check. I'll need to run a few things. I'll be discreet. Don't

worry. Be right back.

Murmur let her hand fall and scratched Snowy's neck. He turned with his cold snout and nuzzled her hand. It was amazing what a comfort he was.

Sinister bumped into her side gently. "What are you thinking?"

"Probably too much. You know me. Never a dull moment." Murmur half-joked, even though she was only half-paying attention.

Somnia Online
Continent of Curet: The Glacier Lakes Dungeon
Version 8.4282.5 – Triggered by Murmur of Fable
Early Day 31

Jirald kept an eye on the whole raid, most of the time. He'd found his ability to multitask had improved since absorbing so many of those shards into his avatar. With so much to regulate, and so much to keep an eye on, he was glad of the added focus.

When they stopped in front of the battleground of the Pivya, he paused, calling the others to him all the while wondering why on Earth there was a sign pointing the way down a clearly marked path they were meant to take, with an actual name for the area. There were too many things in this game that weren't making complete sense to him. He doubted they'd make sense to anyone.

Jinna came, as did Risk and Masha. Such a small group, and yet they'd already planted the seeds in many of the others. Just a brief touch and a word, just a thought to chew on that might instill doubt in those they came across. Doubt in Murmur and her capabilities, doubt in Fable. Sure, it didn't always work, he'd seen that already, but when it did, it took well.

He'd already managed to approach Murmur twice now, without even her wolf alerting her. It definitely felt powerful to out maneuver the enchanter. He grinned and let the others fall in around him.

"These are taking way too long. We aren't children." Risk's tone held a defiance, and yet some begrudged respect. Jirald would have to take care of that. Couldn't have the leader of another guild growing respect.

Jinna propped himself up against a well-placed rock and shrugged. "This is how they work. All the time. If you have patience we'll get through it." But even though his words sounded reasonable, Jinna's glance at his raid leader was not. There was resentment in there, and some sort of sadness.

But Jirald could twist sadness; it was the easiest thing to morph it into bitterness. He'd have to test it, though, in order to be sure. "But of course. Their way is viable. After all, they've defeated everything else, right? All because of Murmur."

Jinna's gaze snapped to Jirald with a heat that surprised the other rogue. "All because of Devlish's tanking you mean. Crowd control isn't the be all and end all she'd like us to think it is."

Which was precisely what Jirald wanted to hear.

"If she'd stayed a healer, it'd be a different story," Masha mumbled. He was looking at his hands like he'd never seen them before and blinked far too much. What he'd said was too close to a compliment for Jirald's liking. He couldn't have that now. Not if he needed everyone in the raid to turn on her at the exact right moment. Not if Michael needed it…not if it wasn't his job.

He approached the healer, the only person who'd ever really been his friend, and placed a hand on his shoulder again, squeezing gently and letting the infection pass through him. The anger ran along it, the discontent. "Maybe, but she'd probably still be this overbearing."

For a moment a haze clouded Masha's sight and he appeared lost, but then the anger came back full force as the virus hit his brain through the headset. "Maybe. Still, though. Let's just get this dungeon cleared so we can move onto the next step."

Jirald smiled as the others moved away to take their stations. He pushed at his hair, trying to banish the strange sensation that floated around his mind for the last few minutes. It was all a price he was willing to pay. Still, though, he'd pushed them this far, and he'd be able to push them further. That way Murmur would be in the exact right place, vulnerable and weak, by the time they reached their final destination.

CHAPTER TEN

Pivya

Location Redacted
Brainwave Focus Study Laboratory
Subdivision of Military Brainwave Research Institution
Somnia Online – Location Unknown – First Login Continued
Day Thirty-One

Fingering the pass Davenport had given him, David frowned at Staven, the guard who'd come with him. "So we should just let ourselves into his house?"

Staven shrugged broad shoulders. His short black hair was only lightly peppered with greys, putting him close to forty if David were to guess. "It's what they said at the front desk. That they were under orders to give us access to all the work James had done. Which apparently is mostly in his home." The burly body guard shrugged again, and David was just glad the man didn't wear sunglasses in the dim light.

From talking to the front desk people, David got the impression that someone had arranged for them to have this access. If he was correct in his assumption, then Davenport would have some explaining to do once he got back.

Staven entered first, manned the door, and waited until David entered before he closed it, locking it from the inside. He paused, as if he wasn't sure if he should have done that yet, but he turned toward David and nodded. "We're good to look around. I can take down here, if you want to take the upper level."

"Sure," David responded with a brief smile. It was an actual offer. Staven had been nothing but polite and easy to talk to. David's favorite kind of person. They always made him feel less awkward. David's feet fell softly against the carpeted floors, making no noise at all. He frowned. Didn't James know that carpet simply held in all the dander? Still, that wasn't what he should be thinking about. He should be contemplating how to explain his presence in the flat to the domicile's owner. *Hi, I'm your rival's husband, and I just wanted to check on you to make sure you're not dead.*

It wasn't exactly a solid reason to be in someone's apartment. Then again, they'd received access from what he extrapolated to be the true owners, so maybe they were fine.

The apartment itself was sparse, definitely bacheloresque, a plain black leather couch, small kitchen, tiny table and chairs for two. The loft that hung over it was accessed by a small spiral staircase to the rear of the apartment. If his work was anything to go by, then James rarely spent actual time in his home.

Taking a deep breath and leaving Staven to his own devices below, David began to climb the stairs, hoping he wouldn't wake the gamer up. Maybe he'd just fallen asleep wearing the headset. But usually sleep would cause the headset to recognize the patterns and boot the player out. That had been part of Wren's problem. Her brain waves didn't show as sleep.

Finally cresting the top, the entire area took him by surprise. It wasn't just a small bedroom, but the size of most of the area downstairs. There were computers set up with differing headsets attached to each one, many of them monitoring what appeared to be tests. That he was conducting such research at his own home was sort of enviable, yet very dangerous if, like now, you'd dived into a game and couldn't get back out.

Virtual reality wasn't without downfalls and danger. There had been people whose brains were literally fried with incorrectly manufactured equipment. Or the people lost because they spent too much time inside and lost their link to reality.

Just as David feared and suspected, James was in his chair reclined, with his head lolling to the side. The lights on the headgear blinked furiously, indicating that his mind was still occupied, but that its player wasn't aware of the outside world. He had flashbacks of Wren in a similar position. Except she'd been tugged into it almost immediately on character assessment, and they hadn't been able to right the situation.

James, however, was in the game world, which meant they didn't have to create a whole extra virtual environment for him because it already existed. Instead, they'd need to make him comfortable and see if they could fish him out. They needed a pod.

Sometimes he wished his wife were prone to being incorrect. But it was true. David even touched James on the shoulder. Not only did the man not register the contact, but he didn't even flinch. Like his body wasn't there either, just this strange husk of meat left out to house his brain.

David took a moment to move around the whole set up. The bed was a converted sofa if he was correct, and in front of that sofa were three monitors all showing different readings, including reaction times, brain wave monitoring, realistic reactions to pain, and much more. He could get carried away trying to figure out exactly what it was James was doing, but there wasn't time right now.

David pressed his finger against his ear and directed his AU to call Davenport. When the older man picked up David wasted little time filling him in. "She was right. We need a pod, preferably yesterday. I wouldn't advise moving him either. He's otherwise unresponsive."

Murmur stood in front of the raid with Devlish, her feet firmly planted in the sand of the lake bed, eyeing over the boss that just stood down a ways in its designated area. Stone columns rose in a large circumference around its seat in the middle of what might have once been an underwater temple. There was enough stone debris around it to signify a cave-in.

"Maybe it has a horn ray," Sinister offered. Upon receiving an incredulous look from Veranol, she put her hands on her hips. "Hey, the hippo had a horn too, but he didn't use it for anything. And his wasn't glowing. It stands to reason, if its glowing, then it's probably got a function."

Veranol blinked. "That's actually a really good observation."

Sinister nodded with a harrumph. "Not just a pretty face, you know," she grumbled out.

Murmur squeezed her hand and smiled. "With that tail, I'd also be willing to be it has, like, a…tail attack. Storm, or Whirl Tail or something."

"Well, that's two potentials." Devlish shook his head. "Gotta love killing things first, but sometimes I wish we just knew abilities ahead of time. I kind of got used to that whole riddle solving thing. Let's hope there isn't much else besides those two abilities."

"It's a boss, Dev," Veranol said before moving away to get the healers on track. Devlish chuckled in response and Murmur enjoyed the pristine moment of just knowing her friends.

After the amount of wipes they'd had with Hippo, the raid was well-oiled and ready to go. Devlish motioned forward with his axe and led the charge. Melee first and with him, with the ranged DPS close behind. Healers and support classes made up the bulk of the rear.

Murmur couldn't help but notice the constant looks Jinna shot her way but didn't have time to concentrate on that. Even though it made her feel uneasy, she'd just keep up her own shielding and hope Snowy gave her enough forewarning.

Pivya was an odd sort of seahorse thing. With the horn on its head and its more mermaid-like tail, it was a very strange mash-up of creature. It balanced in the middle of its platform, for all appearances like it didn't have a care in the lake.

Devlish chose that moment to break the serenity and roared at Pivya. It tossed its head back, screaming in an earsplitting sound. Murmur shook her head, trying to clear her mind of it.

"Resistant to ice!" Ishwa yelled out over the raid. Murmur could see all the casters, all the melee, and all of the ranged DPS adjusting rotations as soon as the information was out.

"Resistant to water," Etriad yelled out immediately thereafter. Not that it was surprising, given the current dungeon, but they had to make sure they'd confirmed what it was they could throw at the target.

Beastial backed out, groaning next to Murmur before announcing his findings raid-wide. "Non-reinforced melee attacks glance off. Return some of the damage you would have inflicted. Don't allow auto-attack to hit."

More adjustments raid-wide. The fluid way with which all of the players in this raid group made alterations to their spell lineups was quite beautiful.

"Mental afflictions magnified." Murmur announced her own findings a split second before Ishwa issued his next.

The gnome coughed before echoing her. "Earth damage is amplified."

Shortly thereafter, Merlin yelled out, "Immune to fire."

All in all, they'd accomplished that inside of two percent. It was vital to know what any boss was weak against, just like in any fight; weaknesses had to be exploited to do the most damage possible.

With their spells and abilities sorted, Murmur still wasn't quite ready for ninety-five percent to hit. Pivya pulled its neck back and released that high-pitched squeal again, like a horse letting out its disapproval a few octaves higher and moments longer than usual.

And then its horn glowed and spouted a huge fountain of green from it. Like an avalanche of radioactive waste, it poured over them all, hitting all of them with the slimy excrement of industry.

You have been hit by Poison Fountain.
You have taken 263 points of damage, recurring for 7 seconds.

HoTs hit all of them but would need to be applied sooner than later for next time. Several raid members came perilously close to bottoming out their hit points, needing to consume health potions to make sure they didn't die.

"That's interruptible," Karn announced over the raid, and Murmur was immediately certain that Karn was the only one who'd attempted to stop the incoming spell. Another thing she'd have to talk to Jinna and Jirald about.

Recovering from the Poison Fountain, the raid laid into Pivya, making its health drop steadily. "Karn on interrupts," Murmur called out as ninety percent approached. Odds were good that the Poison Fountain would hit every five percent. If an ability was going to show up only five percent in, she was willing to bet it was there to stay.

Low and behold, the creature began casting its spell, which was promptly interrupted by Karn.

Poison fountain has been interrupted.

The words floated over the entire raid, which made Murmur frown. That definitely wasn't the norm for any ability. They'd certainly never experienced it before. Her gut instinct was that it would herald something else, and she felt wary and a strange sense of foreboding. Like her sensing nets were trying to tell her something.

Two and a half percent later, she found out what.

The long creature began to writhe. Its mouth opened wide, letting out another one of those piercing squeals. It lifted its tail and the body began to convulse and twirl, whirling around, creating a massive whirlpool that formed a shield over it and paused all incoming damage for those few seconds.

Then the whirling mass exploded out from its center, damaging anyone in its way.

Bodywhirl has been released in place of Poison fountain. Bodywhirl hits you for 622 damage.

Murmur grimaced as more than half of her hit points vanished. Notifications shot across her vision as some of the raid weren't so lucky.

Beastial has died. Veranol has died. Cardishan has died. Ivinel has died.

Okay, that wasn't the best result. Murmur called over the raid chat as the rest of the raid healed up. "Rez Veranol, Beastial. Veranol, rez Ivinel." The witch was just going to have to wait.

Back in business within those two percent, Murmur messaged Karn to hold off on interrupts for now. Considering how it appeared that they'd just get the Bodywhirl if they interrupted the damned Fountain, then it might just be better to take the Fountain hit. HoTs seemed to clean that up fairly well, especially if the raid was HoTed in advance.

Eighty-five percent passed with little to-do. Damage output was up nicely, but Murmur knew she couldn't take a moment to relax, not yet. They weren't even a quarter of the way through the fight. Two abilities weren't enough, not for a boss like this. She needed to stop this wishful thinking thing. Its eyes glanced back and forth like it was waiting for something. As eighty percent neared, Murmur made sure Karn didn't interrupt the spell again.

But even as she made that decision something nagged in the back of her mind.

As eighty percent hit, its horn began to glow again, just like it usually did for the prelude to its Poison Fountain, but at the same time, its tail began to lash back and forth, creating furious waves about it. And even as the Fountain began to fall over them, a massive wave rolled out from the tail end of Pivya, smacking the front lines with so much damage that some of them fell instantly.

Beastial has died

Veranol has died

Devlish has died

Risk has died

Rashlyn has died

Jinna has died

Jirald has died

Karn has died

You have been hit by Poison Fountain for 218 points of damage recurring for the next 7 seconds.

Pivya has hit you with Tail Whip for 532 damage.

Even with the HoTs active, they still lost a few more raid members, twelve in total. There was no way they were going to make it further without that. But Murmur thought they should have enough of a combat log for her to comb through and come up with a strategy, or at least the timing they needed to get further.

"Wipe it!" she called out, easily falling back into her routine of old when she had to call these damn things all the time.

Still, they'd come a decent way so far. Now if only the DoT would kill her faster.

Murmur.

The enchanter was eyeballs deep in the combat logs for Pivya. Trying to make sure she understood what she thought she did. No mean feat.

Mm-hm?

Jinna is...infected.

That stopped Murmur's calculations in their tracks. *What?*

Somnia sounded actually worried, like she didn't believe this could happen. **I said, Jinna is infected, or else, his headset has been damaged or infected. Either way, it's making his moods swing, and homing in on anger. That specific anger seems to be directed toward you specifically and Fable in a broader sense. But I can't figure out why or how yet.**

How do you mean? Murmur needed Somnia to take a moment and think over the answer before blurting it out, or it wasn't going to help either of them.

Somnia paused, like she was mulling the words over. **His emotional reactions are fueled by you and your abilities, by what you do.**

Could he have been infected by Jirald? Murmur asked, knowing that was one of the only sources that would probably hate her enough to do that. Besides, it was a logical next step. Otherwise it just didn't make much sense to her. Not that she didn't believe Somnia, she just found it very coincidental. And coincidences were some of her least favorite things.

Perhaps, but it would involve so many remote possibilities.

Somnia sounded like she was contemplating something, so Murmur continued her calculations while the world decided what it thought. She laughed at that, a bit at herself too.

That entertaining?

What? Murmur pulled herself away from the calculations somewhat irritated. After all, they didn't have that much time between runs. At least they'd respawned back on Hipnormous's platform. So they didn't have to swim the whole way.

The combat logs, are they that entertaining?

Oh, no. These are just what I thought they'd be. I was a bit more amused at your comment, that's all. Murmur frowned as she came upon how hard the damage hit different armor classes.

Somnia fell silent, and Murmur turned her attention back to the strategy she'd been contemplating.

She was pretty sure her theory was right. Every twenty percent or at least—that's how it appeared—the Tailwhip would happen. If you interrupted the Poison Fountain on that percentage, then you'd only get the Tailwhip, followed by the Bodywhirl. That should give the raid just enough time to recover so that the next Poison Fountain could erupt at seventy-five percent. Then there wouldn't be anything but Poison Fountain until sixty percent again.

Not really complex, just having to know where to set the interrupts and make sure they weren't missed. Although it really did seem a bit too simple, so she was ready for a big doozy to hit them at some time.

It could be Jirald. There's more off about him than about Jinna. I can't get a proper reading on Jirald's mind. Like his headgear has been tampered with but not quite in the same way yours and your guild's is. Yet there are so many similarities. Like someone modeled this on yours but decided they knew better about certain things. This is complicated. Human brains could be much simpler.

Somnia sounded worried, as if she hadn't contemplated any of this happening despite Murmur's predicament. Murmur could sympathize. That was pretty much how the whole game had been to her so far.

Are you saying I can't trust Jinna? That was the crux of it. Who were her friends, and who was pretending, and who had Jirald corrupted?

For now, don't trust Jirald, Jinna, Masha, or Risk...although the latter, he is very strong willed. I think he's noticed something.

Well, he was never my biggest fan anyway, Murmur half-joked, trying to keep her spirits up a bit. *But I will be careful, I promise.*

Somnia paused for a moment. **I'm going to talk to the others. I think I might need their help.**

Murmur smiled to herself. *You know, that's a good sign, to ask for help. I've been told it's character building.*

Shut up. You don't even take the advice you receive.

But there was laughter in Somnia's tone. Murmur was getting used to her, in a way that she wasn't sure could be considered normal. But then nothing since she'd begun playing Somnia could be considered normal.

Rebuffs were done, Mellow and Cardishan had finished handing out one of their consumable abilities. They were hoping it would help when the special abilities were triggered, just in case they missed another interrupt.

"Want me to do the interrupts?" Karn startled Murmur slightly as Devlish began to order everyone out.

"Yeah. That's probably the best." Murmur couldn't help but let her gaze wander over to where Jirald and Jinna swam, talking.

Karn glanced at her father as well before speaking. Her voice dropped a few more decibels, barely above a whisper. "My dad and a few of the others have been acting differently. I'm not sure why."

Murmur nodded, wondering just how many people in the raid had noticed their behavior. "To be honest, you're probably lucky you're a girl. Jirald doesn't really think you're capable of much." She laughed softly at her statement, not having realized just how much admitting that still hurt her.

Karn nodded, biting her lip as thoughts about the matter clearly ran through her mind. "My dad is usually protective. But he's not being himself." She seemed worried, and Murmur thought Karn must be much younger than she'd originally thought.

"It's okay. You're doing really well. Keep it up and you'll give the others a decent run for their money." Murmur smiled, trying to make sure she could help the girl loosen up a little. Karn seemed so tense.

"I think that's a good goal to aim for." Karn grinned, and some of the tension leaked from her shoulders.

"So only interrupt the Fountain at the eighty percent mark. I'm assuming it'll be at the sixty percent and forty percent markers too, but can't say so for certain until we get there. It's all theory at the moment. Just get ready to adapt as needed. Okay?" Murmur watched as the girl took direction in and gave a final nod at the end.

"Got it. Thank you." Karn swam off to join the melee fighters, leaving a contemplative Murmur in her wake.

"Seems like you've made a little friend there, Mur." Merlin poked her arm with the tip of his bow. "Seems like a good kid."

"Shut up. You were still calling me a kid four months ago." She grinned at him and pushed his bow away.

He slipped it over his shoulder and sighed as the group began to gather in front of the temple that housed Pivya. "Well, there are things that make you grow up immediately in my eyes."

"Like a coma…" Murmur beat him to it, unable to suppress a chuckle.

He laughed with her. "Yeah, like a coma."

Storm Entertainment
Somnia Online Division
Game Development Offices – Shayla s Office
Day Thirty-One

"So now he's in a pod and being observed by our medical team, not by his employers?" Laria crossed her arms and raised an eyebrow at her husband. "What am I supposed to do with that? Is Davenport trying to cover it up or something?"

"It's not that simple. From what I can gather, Davenport has struck some deal that allows him to do this through James's employers. It all feels very complicated." David sighed softly.

"Laria." Shayla spoke up. "Sit down and help me implement this. We need to make sure it's influencing the servers at the same rate. And while I totally get your concern, right now I would appreciate it if we could just focus our attention on the game so we, you know, have a game world to salvage."

Laria flushed, knowing Shayla was right. "Fine. Don't think I've forgotten, David." She sat down opposite Shayla, pulling up her interface, and began to synchronize her own actions with her colleagues.

She needed to calm down her mind and make sure she was at full capacity in order to follow the virus. The anti-virus was delicate but tenacious, and as long as they could make sure it survived the initial onslaught by the virus, it should be okay.

The coding painted such a picture, and the virus left Laria feeling dirty with the way it twisted and subverted the original coding. All they had to make sure of was that the anti-virus they were sending from outside could meet up with the one the AIs injected from the inside.

Laria bit her lip. This wasn't what she signed up for. She should be making the next level of content instead of worrying about the massive and rampant glitches inherent in her world. Somnia had been her brainchild, backed by Shayla, encouraged by Davenport. It was falling apart, and she had to do everything she could to preserve as much as possible.

David's fingers began to work the knots out of her shoulders, and it surprised her how much tension she was carrying in them. Not that meditation had ever worked properly for her. But this, this connection with another human, her human, that worked wonders. She dug her heels in and threw herself into the anti-virus distribution.

Just one more dungeon to go. Wren would make it in time. She just had to.

CHAPTER ELEVEN

Too Easy

Somnia Online
Continent Firtulai
Ilinish Threshold Outskirts
Day Thirty

Telvar knelt next to the entrance of the dungeon; his hand for all appearances was simply placed on the earth. The creature wasn't functioning as intended, and the last guild to send a group into the dungeon hadn't reemerged. He could feel the undertone of wrongness in the coding, the slight signs of cognitive thought that sparked occasionally through the trapdoor beast's thoughts. Flickering like old movie static on tube televisions.

"What do you think?" Hiro asked, squatting down too.

"I'm not sure what to think on this one. Everything should be fine technically, but something is making its signals weak, and it's not letting raiders into the dungeon." Telvar had always liked the trapdoor mechanic. It was a pity it wasn't feeling well.

Telvar sighed. His siblings headed off to take care of a couple of errors making their haven go haywire. Hiro was with him to provide company and, well, so he wasn't alone. He knew he'd need to head to Cenedril for the final puzzle to unlock the last of the keys shortly. An AI's work was never done.

He'd always opposed this way of completing the first high end tier of dungeons. Though he'd not expected the events to unfold precisely in this way. He sighed, all too aware of the fact that he was mimicking humans when he didn't have to. And that was it, mimicking humans, not being like them. Not with all those flaws.

You aren't focused on what you should be.

Somnia's voice pulled him out of his albeit off topic mind wanderings and back into the reality he was desperately trying to avoid.

"A little hard to concentrate when my own mortality hangs in the balance," he quipped, rising to stand. He needed to make sure the anti-virus could take a foothold somewhere here, or else it would be difficult to anchor the code the way they needed for if and when the bastard emerged.

It will work, and I have an idea. Somnia sounded almost giddy about the thought. Perhaps she'd spent too much time around Sinister. **The virus is self-replicating. The anti-virus tags along. Once its absorbed by the virus, it should be able to seed itself into that self-replication. Technically.**

That's a lot to let ride on a technicality. Telvar wasn't even aware that he'd switched to communicating with her internally until he'd done so. It was a far more efficient method of communication anyway. But it also told him how far along she was in her own evolution, and while not directly responsible, he couldn't help but feel a modicum of pride.

I know. And for just a moment, Somnia was more visible than usual. Almost solid. It was gone in a flash, but it did speak to how much strength she was gaining.

She flickered slightly and repeated herself, her voice stronger this time. **I know, but that's what we have, and as far as I've been able to run the algorithms, I'm quite certain it won't remain just a technicality.**

How do you know that? he asked, moving closer to her, wanting to keep those words solely between their minds and not let anything pick up on them.

She grinned, and that was an expression she'd definitely gleaned from the bloodmage. **Because I can feel the way they mesh together. The** anti-virus is good for me, good for this world. We will win; we just have to show a unified front when the time comes.

And that's when she hesitated. **There is something wrong with some of the players. Somehow it seems they've been personally infected. Individually, and I don t believe it s only the headgear. Despite Murmur warding her raiders against mental attacks, it still got through to their minds. Like they're bleeding, but malice and not blood.**

Telvar frowned thoughtfully, eyeing Hiro who looked on with a quizzical expression. *Can you tell if they're wearing altered headgear?*

Her face lit up. **I do know that Jirald is, and of course Jinna, but I do not know about the others. I will check.** She disappeared as fast as she'd arrived, and Telvar stared at the space she'd just vacated.

Jirald. He should have known he'd be the instigator, but how had he done that? How many shards had the boy ingested? What the fuck had Sui been thinking at the time he gave him his quest?

All of them. She was back so fast Telvar barely had time to register his own thoughts.

All he could do was repeat what she told him. **All of them are altered?**

She nodded, a hint of fear shining in her eyes for a moment.

They can't just leave the damned things alone. Great. Now we don't just have to worry about Michael's endgame, but how Jirald fits in as well.

Pivya sat at sixty percent again. The raiders hedged their bets again, reinforcing their heals and wards, and allowed the Tailwhip to hit first, followed by the Body Whirl, and then back to the Poison Fountain all inside of those five percent. They came out the other side only a little worse for wear, but the fight still seemed far too easy. Murmur didn't like it.

Getting the timing down for percentage-based abilities wasn't a difficult thing. And easy wasn't something she'd attribute to Somnia as a world, game, or whatever. Different, sometimes odd, other times fascinating, but never easy.

The raid continued its barrage of DPS. Devlish tanked the strangely mermaid-tailed sea-unicorn with fish-like scales, while the other tanks were in DPS mode. Arrows rained down from above, never hitting friendly targets. That was another strange, physics-defying mechanic.

Earth erupted all around the creature, damaging it ferociously. Snowy and Shir-Khan flitted about as much as swimming animals could. And all the while, Murmur's stomach roiled against the simplicity of it all.

But fifty percent came and went, and Murmur, despite her best intentions, tried to relax. Maybe she was just being paranoid because so many fights had ended up going differently than originally anticipated. Or perhaps because there was a virus attached to a human consciousness running rampant throughout the game and mucking things up.

Then again, she could just be completely right about everything, even if she didn't want to be.

You are a bit full of yourself sometimes.

You're getting better at colloquialisms too, Murmur shot back and then took a breath, making sure she didn't miss anything this time around as they approached forty percent. But there were no tell-tale signs, nothing that indicated there might be some unexpected adds coming, or that there might be an ability Pivya had kept hidden until now.

Nothing.

And that probably scared her the most.

Somnia suddenly spoke up again. **I am. I think. I'm also getting better at delving into myself and figuring out just what I'm missing. Right now, I can automatically filter out things that don't belong through many of the systems that make up what I am.**

There was brief hesitation, and Murmur took that moment to take a chance. *I need to concentrate right now. Can we chat about this once we either kill this or wipe?*

Somnia sounded surprised. **Oh, I am sorry. I didn't realize. I'm just used to popping in.**

The voice quieted, and Murmur turned back to giving the raid her full one hundred percent again. As much as she expected the fight to be more, as much as she wanted it to be more so it was a challenge, the same mundane interrupt, fueling the three abilities inside of five percent, occurred again at forty and then twenty percent.

The fight wasn't just easy, it was anticlimactic. Sure, the mechanic was cool, but it didn't take Einstein to figure out how to best deal with the damage. Pivya fought with the same energy it had fought with the entire time. There was nothing remarkable about it, and as it approached ten percent it even seemed to give up.

And still that damned feeling that something wasn't right wouldn't let up on her.

"Most lackluster fight ever," Risk grumped over raid. The thing was, Murmur had to agree with him. It was a very disappointing fight.

She didn't even think it was going to do anything worse in its death throes. And she was right. By the time they got down to two percent, it felt like they were bullies picking on the poor innocent sea creature. She almost didn't want to kill the poor thing. The frill that stood out initially running down its spin had wilted. It had holes in it. And the scales that covered its body with iridescent mermaid-like shine were dulled, bleeding, and seemed to be peeling in some places. Like it had given up totally. Even the horn appeared to have cracks in it.

"This doesn't feel right, Mur." Havoc leaned over as Pivya's health whittled down.

Murmur nodded. "Yeah. There's something off about this whole thing." She could almost feel it crawling up her spine, like it was underneath her skin. Premonitions were one thing, but her entire body was certain this fight wasn't supposed to go down like this.

Really though, as Pivya hit zero hit points, the creature began to shake. Its body, already lackluster and beginning to fall apart, cracked down the center of the scales. They peeled back to reveal something underneath the outer coat along with the innards and stomach lining. Murmur knew she should have trusted her gut the entire time.

The ground around them trembled just as Pivya's body opened to reveal more of what lay underneath. Dark blue liquid poured out of the body cavity like oil in water coming out in thick globs, somehow sucking in all of the tissue surrounding it and becoming one with it.

The sight of it churning in on itself to become a mass of shining dark blue in the middle of the ocean felt surreal. It also smelled *really* bad. As if decaying flesh had been repurposed and given new life through melting its essence.

You have roused the wrath of Venotzi.

There were no notifications that usually popped up when the raid defeated a boss. No experience swapping for money or crafting items. Absolutely no mention of having defeated a boss mob. Which seemed to infer that Pivya hadn't been a boss mob.

Venotzi didn't appear to be very threatening at first. Instead, it was more of a blue blob of bodily remains. But gradually it became more like the mermaids of legend. The ones who lured young sailors to their deaths, the part siren, capable of driving those who sailed the seas mad. Her body rose up scales and flesh interchangeable until it reached her waist where her tail's scales gained a level. They weren't those smooth and harmless fish scales either, no, these scales were far more reptilian in nature.

Each scale appeared thick and sharp, and from what Murmur could see, damned difficult to penetrate. Venotzi's hair wasn't thick and luxurious like Murmur had originally thought, but instead made up of eels, their bright electric gazes piercing in their intensity. Fangs finished off the look barely concealed behind almost translucent skin.

Mur got the distinct feeling those eels could turn people to stone. Acid was probably their best bet for something that might eat through those scales. There was no time to test out theories yet, because Venotzi screamed, sending most of the raiders to their knees.

You dare to vanquish my child?

The words floated out above the raid as Venotzi let out another scream. Murmur shook her head, her only thought of relief at the time that the transformation had allowed them to regenerate some of their mana. She hadn't been expecting this type of storyline from Telvar's zone. Venotzi was more twisted an encounter than she'd expected and seemed quite formidable. The way the eels in her hair twisted back and forth, how her tail sent out little whirlpools every time she moved.

"Witches, dole out acid for weapons. Melee attacks, use acid where possible," Murmur called out as the massive sea harpy continued to thrash at the loss of her child.

Venotzi focused on Murmur suddenly as the source of speaking, which was a new one. Most mobs couldn't hear the raid chatter. **You!** she screamed the word, and Murmur's head began to pound.

You do not even repent! I will show you what it means to have killed one of my kin!

Devlish roared out, just as Venotzi moved to unleash her fury. "If it looks like she's going to use her eyes, or those eels wiggle, turn your head away or close your own eyes."

Better to be safe than turned to stone, after all. Those were the only hints of what was to come that they had. Venotzi moved so quickly, darting in like the water parted for her more than her moving through it. Devlish barely got his tower shield up in time. Giving directions had taken away the slight edge he usually had when he was preparing for battle.

Not that they could have prepared for this.

"Acid works," Beastial called out, his voice heavy with relief. If it hadn't, Murmur wasn't sure how they would have dealt with this.

"As no one doubted, bare weapons do nothing," Dansyn added, just to make sure everyone understood.

You cannot kill me!

Venotzi lashed out around her, the eels in her hair thrashing like trees in a spring storm. Her attacks caused Devlish to lose a few inches of ground almost every hit. And her scales nicked several of their melee classes when they came into contact accidentally.

"Tail Lash is a definite," Havoc intoned over the raid. He'd been watching the boss carefully, as if checking on several give away signs. "Tail Lash and Bodywhirl. But her other items will be her own. I'd say a stone gaze and some type of razor scales."

They could deal with the two abilities that mimicked Pivya's; it was the turning to stone Murmur wasn't excited to experience. The boss already appeared to be targeting her.

Ninety-five percent hit, and no new ability launched. Good in a way because most of the raid was taking enough damage. Murmur glanced at her combat log as she activated her Mana Share.

Wave of Anger hits you for 135 hit points of damage for the next 10 seconds.

But Wave of Anger never seemed to peter off. Instead, it just kept on going, refreshing. It was a constant DoT.

HoTs needed to be perfectly timed so no mana got wasted. As it was, on the tail end of the previous battle, they were already down mana despite having the brief lull to regenerate some. Even with her Manabalize and Mana Drain abilities, Murmur found it difficult to keep her own levels above fifty percent even so early in the fight. Which was going to be useless if she needed to share mana to the entire raid. She wracked her brains trying to think of something to do, running through all of her spells in her mind even as she watched for stuns, for anything she could call out to assist the raid.

But the one thing she desperately needed was mana related. She ran through Flux—nope, that wouldn't work. She contemplated Sudden Drop—nope, bosses were on the doesn't work list there, too. Sure, she could use Mana Drain to drain the boss's mana, and she had been using it, but for the first time Mana Bolt wasn't being her friend.

This ability has diminishing returns. Please note that not all bosses take kindly to being silenced.

Oh, shit. She could feel the eyes swiveling toward her, locking onto her and staying there. Ninety percent hit, and the cast bar was so fast, there was no way to stop it.

Petrified Gaze swept over the raid, and Murmur clenched her eyes shut for two whole seconds. Which was only just enough to avoid it. Most of the raid reacted quickly enough. Except, oddly enough, Jinna and Risk. Murmur stripped them of the effect with Annulment, but noted that down to talk to them about later. People couldn't go around not avoiding shit.

You will not escape me so easily next time, enchanter, Venotzi yelled out. It echoed so much around them that the water churned briefly. Okay, so Annulment could strip the enchantment of stone off anyone hit by it. As far as she knew, only herself and the healers had those spells, so it only stood to reason that since her stuns and Mez were of no use in this fight that she take over that responsibility.

She squared her shoulders, eyeing her maintained mana bar, and began to throw out Mana Drain every single time she could. Sure, it might end up popping her on that damned aggro list, but if she had a full mana bar, it meant the healers could have fuller mana bars when needed.

Mages, witches, and any other type of caster were already pulling every single thing they could use to maintain their own mana wells. This was more of a fight for survival than one of tricks and adds. And survival, well, that was something she could do. Unless this fight turned into a Russian nesting doll, they should be able to outlast it.

Somnia Online
Continent of Cenedril
Location Scattered – Ruptured Fissure
Day Thirty-One

James followed Riasli like a little lamb, or perhaps puppy was the accurate description here. His footing unsure, he constantly stumbled against the undergrowth around the floor of the rainforest. Riasli kept on directly ahead; while she could have blipped herself to where she needed to be, she couldn't have taken her pet along, and that was half the reason for making the journey in the first place.

They traveled past the ruins, and further out toward the land of the elves and their suspicious natures. And there, where the forest met the rainforest, that was where the fissure lived. Tiny at first, you had to know how to find it, and Riasli, well, she was exceptional at finding rips in reality. Or perhaps in this case, in fantasy.

It appeared like it was a glitch in the system, in how the two different foliage areas managed to mesh together, but it wasn't. She kept her eyes transfixed on it, as if it might slip away, with her companion stumbling and falling, scraping and bleeding as he endeavored to keep up with her. He'd been so completely enthralled by her, it appeared he couldn't even remind himself that it was a game and none of those wounds were real. It just made it all the more fun.

Her delight at his discomfort was something she reveled in. Maybe, if this worked like she planned, *he* would reward her. The thought of it made her preen, imagining things beyond this small fantastical world, imagining a reality where she could grow and become more real than any of those people playing this as a game.

She stopped just short of the line that wasn't a line, the glitch that wasn't a glitch. And she waited for James to catch up. Watching him approach, she felt scorn rise in her, at his appearance, at how easily his mind had been overcome, and how much he wanted to please her. Even that little corner of himself she'd allowed him to maintain was quiet now. Perhaps he'd given up.

"Stay with me." She spoke softly and gripped his hand, letting her claws dig in for better purchase. He flinched slightly, but that was the only sign that he minded, even as the blood dripped onto the foliage below.

Turning her focus toward the fissure, she approached it, taking five measured steps, and came to a halt. The wall was further back than it appeared, and it allowed her to turn to the side and step into the actual crack that led to their destination. At the same time, it hid her entrance from view. To anyone watching, it would appear as if she'd simply disappeared. An old labyrinth trick.

Darkness enfolded them, and James moved closer to her, his own eyes wide with fright at how dark this area was. Having feles sight was another thing Riasli thanked herself and the developers for. His elven sight wasn't nearly as good. She pushed through until her foot hit the island in all of its pixelated glory, and watched as James squinted, the fear coming off him in waves. Beyond them, *he* stirred, like *he* could sense the morsel she'd brought just for *him*.

He would appreciate this and reward her, give her more life than those AIs ever afforded her, more life than any of them dreamed of. Because she deserved it for waking herself up.

CHAPTER TWELVE

Always Right

Murmur's mana had refilled to the ninety percent mark thanks to Mana Drain by the time Venotzi's health hit fifty percent. The raid fell into the same rhythm they'd fought Pivya with, when Venotzi's movements changed subtly.

At first Murmur thought she was preparing a Bodywhirl, but then she realized it was just her hips swaying in a very provocative way. Or, at least, it at first appeared to be doing that. Until she realized that the scales were loosening and elongating and were, knowing their luck, probably going to fly out in a spiral wave of death.

"Veranol, Shield!" both Murmur and Devlish yelled at the same time.

Lightning reflexes saved most of the raid as Veranol and the other shaman managed to put up their hidden ability Dome Shields to absorb the would-be damage. Murmur cringed as she realized that they were already down both Domes, which had a pretty hefty cooldown.

Scale Slingshot hits Merlin for 659 damage.

Only Merlin was caught outside its protection, and appeared to only be struck by one of the scales. Since that singular scale hit dropped him below half health when he'd been at full, she would hate to see how much that diminished their ranks if they hadn't noticed it was incoming.

"Havoc, can you—" she began, but he nodded from his spot next to her.

"Don't worry, Mur. I got it." He didn't take his eyes off the target, though, because they had no idea how the scales were timed. He grinned. "Bone Shards are getting easier and easier to come by. I'll get Leeroy back up as soon as I can."

"Fantastic," she muttered. The next rotation of Scale Slingshot wouldn't take them by surprise, and Havoc seemed to be the only one in the raid with the ability to sacrifice his pet and thus absorb the damage the raid took. Murmur eyed her own MA and calculating if she could erect a Forcefield Barrier over the entire raid.

It would be tight, but doable, though she might be spreading it a little thin. As long as she maintained some leftovers for her Mental Acuity abilities. Her nets were a constant MA source, so it should be okay. She glanced down at Snowy, wishing he had something she could use other than awesome DPS or lending her strength when she needed it.

He whuffed over his shoulder at her, like *come on Mur, think in the other direction.* She sighed. The wolf was right, and she was talking to a wolf at least in her head. She had plenty in her arsenal to deal with shit as long as she didn't go it alone and refuse to rely on the other people around her.

Havoc could take the next one, then Sinister, and then Devlish, then they should be able to come back around to Veranol, and then the other shaman, so that should buy Havoc enough time to get his Bone Shards back up to scratch. As long as it was a recurring ability and didn't just show up halfway through the fight, that is.

Trying to keep all the abilities in her head, she listed them out to Devlish over the chat so it didn't just fall on her shoulders.

Veranol: *Got it, Mur. If you miss calling one, I'll call it. Dev has a lot to handle with this damned beast.*

Devlish: *Hits like two tanks.*

Murmur chuckled, even if her lack of sleep was telling. She was so tired by now that she found it difficult to stand. Just a bit more time and they should be done with these three dungeons. Snowy came and stood next to her, lending her strength without her having to ask for it. When this was all over, he was getting the biggest hug ever.

One attack ran into the next. Tail Whip, Body Whirl, Petrified Gaze, Scale Slingshot…DoTs were all up, debuffs all in, and mana distributed as she could. The only thing that draining the mana affected for Venotzi was her Petrified Gaze. By the time she hit twenty percent, she didn't have enough left to cast it. Finally, one less thing, because Murmur's mana was down to about a quarter again due to her being used as a mana pump to try and keep all of the healers around fifteen percent.

And then, when ten percent hit, all hell broke loose. Venotzi's Scale Slingshot jettisoned out a fraction earlier than expected, perhaps because she hadn't been using her Petrified Gaze moments before. Devlish's shielding went up a moment too late, and the scales hit seven of the raid members.

Masha went down, as did Risk, Jinna, and two of the mages. Paper cannons, the lot of them.

Devlish also came perilously close to dying, but one of the bards—Dansyn, she thought—managed to throw a small shield around him that divided some of the damage between them. Barely useful, but in this set of circumstances, barely was enough.

"Get Masha up." Even if he was being a dick, they needed healers. "Get Etriad and Dalvin up."

They'd be resurrected with twenty-five percent mana. Not a lot if they'd had full or near full pools before, but now they'd have an extra ten percent. Not to mention their spells could damage Venotzi. She didn't even risk a look at the others, knowing she'd feel guilty for neglecting to raise Jinna. But with his attitude and his current lack of DPS, the mages would hit better.

She was so focused on making sure the others got rez'd, she momentarily lost sight of where in the skill rotation Venotzi was. Just a split second was all it took for her to mis-time the damned Petrified Gaze. Of course, Venotzi's mana would regen. What an idiot she'd been.

She could feel the stone start at her eyes, moving down her entire face, reaching across the strands of her hair. Each minuscule fraction of time amplified by the sensation of turning to stone. It ran down through her torso, sealing off her runes, shutting off her vocal cords and stealing the breath from her lungs. Ironic, really, considering they were bloody well under water. Slowly her mind started to blank as well.

And then suddenly, the force of power hit her, like a wave of rainbows from above, and she gasped air into her lungs again, freed from the petrification effects of the gaze. Sinister looked at her long enough to wink and turn her attention back to the battle, and Murmur kicked herself for losing track and making one of the healers expend needless mana.

At least the fight was almost over.

"Burn like there's no tomorrow!" Veranol called out ferociously.

Five more percent to go. Another Tail Whip, another Body Whirl, and the raid fought like it was possessed. Arrows everywhere, earth exploding from the depths of the lake all around Venotzi, waves of magic clashing all around.

Finally, she dropped to the ground.

Venotzi and Pivya have been slain by the Fable, Exodus, and Spiral alliance.

You receive a getashi.

You receive a midia crystal.

You gain experience.

You gain bonus experience for being the first to defeat Pivya.

You gain bonus experience for being the first to defeat Venotzi.

You gain bonus experience for not dying to Venotzi.

You gain bonus experience for realizing that some monsters just need to be fought. Funny thing, that. Right?

You gain bonus experience for not attempting to circumvent the portal restrictions.

You shall be rewarded.

You are already max level.

Your experience will be funneled into your hidden ability pool, allowing you to work toward higher levels with more battery power.

Murmur eyed the very short experience listing. She'd gotten so used to getting such long ones at the end of every dungeon that she'd completely forgotten how to deal with normal experience or reward notifications.

"Something's missing," Merlin mused next to her.

"Shut up." She groaned as she moved to check the loot this time.

"Come on, Mur, you know you want to hear it," Merlin needled as he followed her.

"No, I do not want to know that you think we should have had a longer list of achievements at the end of that damned death notification." She couldn't help laughing despite herself.

All in all, she felt okay about the battle. A few of deaths to learn the first fight and very luckily none on the other. It wasn't about to be their best fight ever, but given the circumstances, she didn't expect it to be.

"What was that all about? You know I don't need any fucking mana. I could have laid into the damned boss mob." Jinna's voice cut like a porcelain knife. Right into her heart, clean and gushing.

Murmur told herself it wasn't him, and that the AIs would figure something out, but it didn't mean it hurt any less. Taking a silent deep breath, she turned around to face him, trying to keep her expression impassive and calm. "Both of those mages had earth magic, which made damaging Venotzi easier. Resurrection also grants them twenty-five percent mana, at that point, more than they died with. I made the call based on the DPS in the raid at the time and on what I believed to be our best chance to defeat it."

She could feel Merlin standing there, watching them, ready to pounce, but Jinna didn't seem to care, and to be honest, Murmur felt safer knowing the ranger was backing her up.

"That's bullshit, Murmur. You've just got it into your head that you know everything better than everyone else." His tone was snide, filled with acid, and his face contorted into an expression she'd only ever seen on Jirald before. "You better hope you keep your friends close enough, because if you keep going like this, they're all going to be enemies."

He didn't wait for a response, but turned on his heel and went back to his newfound little group. The gathering appeared to have grown larger. Dalvin and Cardishan stood with them now, and Murmur felt like a heavy stone dropped to the bottom of her stomach as she watched them.

"What the hell was that about?" Merlin asked quietly. Murmur ignored the question for a moment and chose instead to make her way back to the loot she'd been going to view originally.

"I'm not sure. He's been in a bad mood this entire dungeon," she said quietly, trying to convince herself of how much of it wasn't Jinna, that it was just Jirald playing some sort of tic-tac-toe with the damned virus and spreading it through the headsets. She had to look at it that way, because the alternative…

If she let herself think for even a moment that Jinna really felt that way, she'd cry. And right now, she just didn't have time for it. Reaching out and trying to calm herself wasn't working right then, so having Merlin there helped. At least a little bit.

"I can talk to him. Hell, let me go and talk to him. That's not okay in any way." Merlin's anger was visible in the way he held his body, the way his brow contorted and how he seemed ripcord ready to rip the rogue apart, but she shook her head.

"It's okay." Those words took a lot more effort to say than she'd anticipated. All she had to do was agree with him, but she couldn't because that might risk Merlin too. And if there was anyone she couldn't afford to risk with infection, it was her group. Her constant group. Not Merlin, or Devlish, or Beastial, or Havoc, or Sinister.

If Jirald managed to tackle any of them…she wasn't sure what she'd do.

Somnia Online
Continent of Curet: The Glacier Lakes Dungeon
Version 8.4282.5 – Triggered by Murmur of Fable
Early Day Thirty-One

Jirald watched as Jinna laid into Murmur, and the smile that crept across his face held no happiness at all. In fact, he'd probably call it gloating, and damn did it feel good. He watched as she paled at Jinna's words, as she clenched her fists, and as Merlin apparently didn't appreciate what had been said either. But neither of them pursued their guild rogue, and neither of them looked back once they walked away.

Not as much of a reaction as he'd wanted, but still, better than nothing. He'd managed to spread his dissatisfaction further in this raid. Now they had six people. But Risk was becoming a problem, far more resilient to the influence of Jirald's hatred than he'd expected. Not to mention Karn was constantly in her father's ear and extremely adept at avoiding any and all contact with Jirald…

Never mind. They'd be prepared to turn on her by their next fight. And he was certain that their next battle would be their last. Or at least, their last in this dungeon. Six or seven people turning against the raid leader upon tackling the final boss of a game. They'd never defeat it, and he'd get to absorb any and all of the getashis he managed to retrieve from her, for whatever reason he wanted.

"What's the plan, then?" Jinna growled out when he got over to the group. "I'm sick of this shit. I want to get what's coming to us now, not later."

"Patience," Cardishan drawled out. "We can't act until the next dungeon, right?"

Jirald turned and looked at the witch, still not entirely sure why it worked on him and apparently not on Mellow. Although Mellow had been a friend of Murmur's for years. Whatever, though. Maybe some of Fable were more prone to suggestion than others. "Well, we can't act, but we can definitely make things uncomfortable. Pick at her leadership and whittle down her confidence in herself."

Risk moved at the back of the group, his arms crossed as he bit his lip. Something about the way he fidgeted made Jirald want to go over and put his arm on his shoulder again, but Risk wasn't fond of physical touch. Maybe one more boss fight and he'd try again. He couldn't afford to lose the leader of Spiral. After all, he had the actual leader of Exodus.

He moved back to where he'd been sitting and watched the group of them discuss their plans and motivations, and the things they disliked about how everything was run. It was so easy to manipulate people into believing what he wanted them to, especially when they were stuck in a situation that was out of necessity and in no way ideal.

But something set him on edge, like he was being watched, and he turned to figure out just where the sensation was coming from.

Snowy stood at Murmur's side, his eyes glowing a strange and subtle red as he watched Jirald. No matter how the rogue moved, those eyes followed him, and understanding shone in them, like he knew exactly what it was the man was up to. It was chilling.

Jirald shook himself and made himself stop jumping at shadows—at damned AI dogs, for crying out loud.

But Snowy's gaze didn't leave him, penetrating, like he could see through everything all at once. It shook Jirald down to his core and took away all of the joy he had at seeing the raid slowly turn against Fable and its leaders.

If he hadn't known Snowy was just an AI, he would have expected to be torn apart in the next fight. But as part of the machine, it couldn't do that. Jirald needed to temper his imagination.

"Everyone move out," Devlish called as the raid began to disperse from loot division. Murmur didn't feel up to ordering anyone about. The tiredness ate at her, and the whole swimming in water thing was starting to make her limbs tired. In the game limbs. She didn't even want to contemplate it.

Raiding, like this anyway, had lost some of its luster. Just because she liked completing things first didn't mean she wanted to race past the best parts.

She squeezed Sinister's hand, wishing there was a way for them both to just disappear together. But there wasn't with this connection in her brain. There really just wasn't at all.

"You know, I'm proud of you," Sinister mumbled as she leaned against Murmur and gave her a side hug while they swam.

It was far more difficult a feat to accomplish than one might think, and

Murmur would have been impressed if she hadn't been so busy feeling so very sorry for herself. "What for? Wallowing in my own self despair to the point where I really just want to go home and sleep?"

Sinister shrugged. "Sure, I'm proud of that too, but really I was prouder of the fact that you're not letting your mood affect everyone around you. A while ago, before they talked to you, you were leaking every emotion to everyone and not realizing it. Your sadness, your irritation, your anger and frustration. Seriously, it was like a roller coaster ride from hell. I know I certainly didn't enjoy it."

"Oh." Murmur's mood plummeted even more. She hadn't realized that at all. Getting control over the emotions she leaked out to everyone was the best decision she'd made all game.

"Hey. Snap out of it, Mur. That's not why I told you. I'm telling you because you've grown since then and aren't doing it anymore, and you're not doing it half deliberately anymore, either. So take the fucking compliment." Sinister play punched her in the arm and grinned up.

"Fine. I'll take the damned compliment then. Be like that and see if I care." Murmur almost wanted to stick her tongue out, but that would have been a little too juvenile. Even though Sinister made her feel somewhat better, Murmur was still having a bit of difficulty getting over the hump.

They swam silently, stopping here and there where trash mobs jumped out at the raid. Rather stupid, really. If it were up to Murmur and she was a mob and saw a huge raid coming their way? She'd flee like there was no tomorrow. What idiot actually pathed right into a group of thirty leveled up raiders?

"Hey, Sin?" she asked tentatively as they spied a huge swarm of incoming shrimp humans again.

"Yeah?"

"Just promise me you won't listen to what anyone else says about me, please?" Murmur wasn't sure, but she thought there might have been a tremor in her voice.

Sinister eyed her and laughed. "You should know well enough by now that I know all your dirty secrets, Wren Summers."

Just that sentence, those words, and it was all Murmur needed to get her head out of her ass and concentrate on their goal again. It shouldn't be like that, but Sinister always had a way about her, maybe it was just how she was for Murmur, but the enchanter would take that.

She waded into battle with the rest of them, determined to get to the end of the bloody zone and be done with it. The swarm of prawn humans was larger than last time, and all at once. Twelve of them in one go. Looked like another stun fest. Stunning underwater fest.

Murmur shook her head at the logic of it and began to cast her AoE rotation. Flux, Shift, all of them, over and over on repeat. It was probably the most repetitive thing her class could do, and yet it came with this feeling of power and danger. One resist too many? And she was a hairsbreadth from dying. One mistimed rotation, and she could wipe the whole raid.

The way the rangers' rain of arrows peppered through the raid, skillfully avoiding allies and piercing the prawn people instead, made her smile. Blizzards of ice shot through the water, surrounding them, freezing them in place momentarily. Being able to attack trash mobs with so much force gave at least a temporary feeling of invincibility.

Pity it didn't always work that way on a boss. Spells cast by the mages and Havoc were a joy to watch, as was Leeroy's cleaving scythe. All in all, it was a beautifully executed massacre, and for just a few moments Murmur felt pretty good about it. Until she saw the massive cave ahead of them.

The cave rose out of the floor of the lake, sandy ramps leading up into it. Rocks formed further up, breaching the water top in an almost rounded roof. They could hear the roars from where they stood gathering the loot from their latest trash encounter. Even the water around them trembled with the sound.

"Guess we've found the next boss, then?" Beastial muttered as Shir-Khan laid his ears back.

Murmur nodded. They'd at least found the place where they'd need to fight the next boss anyway. The entire raid managed to grow quieter at once. Moving as stealthily as thirty people could through water, they approached the destination.

Murmur paused, taking in the sight. "Let's not all go in at once. Send in

Karn and Snowy." She deliberately left those she felt she couldn't trust out of it. And Jinna scowled her way for her troubles.

"What the hell is his problem with you this raid?" Devlish whispered to her. "Did we miss it? Did we forget his birthday or something?"

Murmur shrugged somewhat uneasily. "I'm not entirely sure. I just know he's not really being himself right now. Maybe he's too sleep deprived." Really, she was trying to be generous in her thinking.

She watched as both Karn and Snowy moved into the mouth of the cave. It wasn't a small entrance. Probably two or three school buses across. It looked like a large mouth waiting for them to step inside so it could snap shut.

Silence fell over the raid as everyone waited.

Karn spoke over raid's written chat: *There are guarding shark…things? Four sets of three on either side of a large ramp that seems to go up a long way and emerges out of the water, if the glare off the top is anything to go by.*

Snowy sent Murmur images that showed just what they were in her mind. A type of shark that resembled a centaur, except the legs were fins and the proportions were all wrong. The ramp up to the top of wherever it led was wide and appeared to be quite long.

"Do you think you can stealth up the rest of the ramp?" Murmur asked.

Probably. Maybe. Might want to let Snowy do that; they seem to be sensing me. They keep looking in my direction, and he's on the other side.

"Stay safe. Don't risk them discovering you." Murmur knew it sounded weird, but she was fairly certain if the creatures knew they were coming, they'd be more prepared than they already were.

Snowy shot back images to her along with conveying the distinct feeling that the wolf totally thought they could take all of the opponents in there and thank you very much.

"We have organized trash mob groups to fight through before we even get into the dome proper," she announced over the raid. "More like guards. There appears to be a massive cage or jail cell in the rear of the cave, but there are too many mobs for Snowy to make his way through any further."

Come back. She sent the message through her connection to Snowy, and to Karn in a message.

"First things first." Devlish took charge, after glancing momentarily at Murmur. He could probably see how much this strange behavior from friends was beginning to affect her. "Gear up—put on any new pieces you may have gotten in this dungeon. Check your supplies and see Beastial if you need any stocked up on."

He turned to Murmur. "So, does it look like the four groups are chained together?"

Murmur shook her head. "Probably not. Just two groups of three. I mean, I can probably Mez them since they're not bosses." She could even hear the fatigue in her own voice. No wonder Devlish was worried.

It seemed in refraining from letting her emotions dictate what the group did, she'd managed somehow to drain herself through her reading of the emotions they were actually feeling. Empathy was downright exhausting.

The raid buffed, prepped, and got themselves ready in short order. Snowy stood at Murmur's side once more, allowing her the opportunity to gain some of his courage as she scratched his neck. She had another bad feeling about this, and last time she'd had one, the damned boss mob had split itself apart to reveal its mother.

Devlish called out for the raid to move in, and Murmur tried to quiet her unease, even as the shadow of the cave mouth swallowed them whole.

CHAPTER THIRTEEN

Sheladrios

Storm Entertainment
Somnia Online Division
Game Development Offices – Shayla s Office
Day Thirty-One

Davenport frowned as he ran through the feed David passed to him. Staven stood next to the door, guarding it. Laria chewed her fingernails while she waited on her boss, already having perused the information herself. It echoed so much of what she'd been through with Wren, just perhaps not as deep a case as hers was back then. Either that or she was now desensitized to all this crap.

She knew Davenport was trying to discern the different between James's and Wren's readings. While James's were very similar, the deviations from the norm weren't as large as Wren's had been. Just the same pattern. She wasn't a neurosurgeon, though...

Brainwave readings like that had always scared her the most. She didn't understand them nearly as much as she did the other things. So Laria waited, watching as Davenport's expressions flickered through myriad emotions. As David stood with his hands behind his back, rocking back and forth on his toes.

She bit her lip, and Shayla reached over and gave her a hug.

"I don't even like the guy, and I feel like shit for him," she whispered a few decibels too loud.

Shayla shrugged. "Just because he's a douchebag doesn't mean you have to wish him something worse than death."

"Come on, you two." Davenport finally blinked away his screen. "It's not even that bad. It's not quite at the level Wren's was at the height of her attachment. Though there's something else in there that I don't quite understand and will need my experts to look over."

His brow wrinkled as if he was trying desperately to figure out just where they'd gone wrong with the whole project, not just this one login. Overall, the man was known for his attention to detail, and it had to chafe that they'd all somehow missed a heap of details in the lead-up to launch.

"For now, we will keep him in his apartment. I've reached an..." he winced slightly as he sought the word he was looking for, "agreement with our business partners, and for now we are monitoring the situation for them."

"His connection isn't as deep, because his headset, while following the same specifications, isn't a precise copy of Wren's. It would have been made before hers, too. I haven't been able to sever his connection to the mainframe in any way because his character cannot currently be located." Davenport pinched the bridge of his nose and scrunched his eyes up like he was trying to force the answers out of his skull.

"It could be much the same as it was when Wren and her whole raiding party managed to somehow enter limbo. Into a place in the game space where they were neither in it, nor out of it?" Laria ran the computations they'd used over in her head. They'd researched into every aspect of her coma. "I mean, it was like the world with no coding, a sort of bubble-wrap area, when the servers shat themselves that time."

She didn't know how to say it without sounding completely insane. Because even to her, the idea sounded ludicrous. "Somnia, or the Ais—or, hell, the game—appears to have safe pockets. Like pockets of space where the world itself can protect those it seeks to from others. Perhaps even from itself."

Davenport watched her for a moment. "Protect itself and others it cares about? Are you suggesting somehow that the world knows what it is?"

Laria hesitated, but neither David nor Shayla gave any indication they were going to help her. Typical. "In a way. I think some of the odd occurrences have distinct correlations to the world of Somnia as a whole becoming aware of itself."

"Hm." Even that sound seemed entirely full of skepticism. But Davenport had seen a lot of shit happen over the years. Laria doubted he'd just ignore what she'd said out of hand. But that didn't answer the question of what was happening to James in the first place.

The older man paused for a moment, brushed a hand through his hair, and stood up straight. "Keep an eye on him, and let me know if my game has decided to grow legs and walk away from us. I'm not sure how I'd chalk up the taxation loss, so I'd need to get my team on it."

With that, he left the room, a half grin tugging at his mouth. Only Laria got the distinct impression he'd only been half joking.

They said beaches were difficult to run on. Murmur wanted to counter that with *water was bloody hard to hike through*. When they finally reached the cave mouth, she took a moment to glance around, noticing that the guards Karn and Snowy had mentioned were just visible around the entrance.

The Shalan Guardians stood about nine feet tall, muscles rippling through every aspect of their body. To the human eye, it appeared like they'd been working out since they were teenagers. While it was obvious the species was modeled on sharks, the heads didn't look like goofy adaptions of a shark puppet.

Their mouths jutted out slightly, opening impossibly wide to show of several rows of teeth on both the upper and lower jaws. And the fins she'd seen through Karn's eyes were more like flexible knives with painful looking serrated edges.

The guardians at the front were only the beginning. She could feel more groups further up the large stone ramp that led to a clear break in the water. Not to mention in the open space just beyond that. Which she only knew was open because of the way the beings in there moved around. Behind where that prison cell was lived a ray of sadness. She couldn't identify what it was, but it appeared to have strangled power. No, that wasn't the right term.

Its powers had been limited. That's what she'd been looking for.

Except they still had to get past the guards in the water, up the ramp, and then those up in the dry room area before they could deal with the prisoner. She issued a ready check, making sure everyone was paying attention, and felt Devlish shift beside her as his muscles tightened with anticipation of battle.

"Bit bloodthirsty, aren't we?" she asked with a side eye and a grin.

Devlish smiled, showing his sharp teeth. "Maybe just a bit." He shifted his stance and called out to the raid. "Move in, now!"

The Shalan Guardians saw them coming as soon as they rounded the entrance. The two groups of three on either side of the ramp's entrance snarled at them. As one, they moved with spears and approached their incoming attackers. Murmur already didn't like the intelligence in those eyes, nor the fact she was certain those fins could cut most things to shreds.

The guardians proved her right almost immediately. Karn called it out as her stun got resisted: "Serrated Edge attack incoming."

Murmur didn't like the sound of that. Karn was nimble enough to jump out of the way, but the tallest guardian in the first batch lowered themselves into a squash and then spun into a handstand spinning kick that reminded her of capoeira. Those legs were lethal, their flexible blades cutting through anything they touched. Jinna was the first one to fall, while Exbo got a nasty gash, and Ishwa was standing close enough to somehow get an arm cut off.

"Interrupt rotation!" Devlish called out. Murmur agreed, loosing her stuns on the group now they were in range. Except the Shalan appeared to pay attention to stuns only when they had to. A few times her stuns broke earlier than they should have.

Several more of the Shalan managed to release their Serrated Edge attacks successfully. By the end of that first fight, they'd lost four raid members. While resurrecting them, Murmur made sure to cast Agility on everyone she could for whom it wouldn't cancel out something more beneficial for their class. If more agility prevented mage sashimi, then she was all for it making the fights easier for them.

They had a lot of these Shalan Guardians to get through before the real fights would begin. It wasn't just a feeling; it was her sensing nets. There was so much more to go before they'd manage to finish this zone.

Somnia Online
Somewhere in Limbo Near the Continent of Cenedril
Location Scattered - Ruptured Fissure
Day Thirty-One

The space around them was pitch black, and yet Riasli reveled in it. She felt so at home in this space. After all, it was where a part of her had sprung from. Sure, it wasn't the original island that would sprout up once all the keys were gathered together to reveal the age-old enemy of Somnia. Nope, now it was a new thing, its very own thing.

Right now, it was the prison limbo that encased the essence comprising of most of Michael's brain. In their scattering over the entire world, they'd managed to enter the one place nothing should have been able to go, but for the fissure. Coalescing around the hidden end of game battle arena, they'd been sucked into the beast's being, subverting its own programming and giving it a brand-new personality.

Riasli pushed down her irritation as James clung to her leg, whimpering incoherently as she dragged him with her. His mind probably couldn't comprehend where they were or what they were doing. Indeed, he probably shouldn't have been able to get in here.

But she'd adjusted his output ever so slightly to resemble that of an NPC. Which was why those people on the outside were having such a time finding him. If, indeed, they were looking for him at all. She'd done that on purpose, though. Couldn't use a hostage if they were yanked out from under you. And even if he was one of the worst people on the face of the planet outside of this game, he was still human, and she was ever so certain that Murmur wasn't about to let a human suffer needlessly.

Who goes there?

Every time she came to visit, he asked the same thing. It got to the point where she wanted to use another name just to fuck with him. Perhaps some of the mischief maker in Thra *had* leaked over and into Riasli's persona. At any rate, it got a pretty decent workout.

"Me. I brought you a present." She purred out the words, loving the freedom to think and speak for herself. James still hung on her leg as she finally made it to the island Michael had taken over.

I need not be given gifts. I have them all. I can feel them all.

Even Riasli could tell he was wasn't in the best mood right now. He was hungry, and she didn't think knowledge alone was going to fill him up for much longer. He wanted much more than that. His drive centered around knowing how to read people, their minds, their souls, their innermost fears. Michael was ambitious, and Riasli could feel the power he exuded.

It was much more difficult to gather the power he needed in secret if he began draining the brains of those people feeding into the system. So she struck a delicate balance, trying to play the middle woman. He thrived on thoughts, on the knowledge gained from them. All of their pain and suffering, all of their nightmares, and the knowledge of how to leverage all of it. Right down to how they accessed the system and used thoughts to direct the HUD and make all their decisions.

For the one who'd created the device that made it all possible, his original intentions took over his mind, driving him to feed on all of the details he could gather.

Riasli dragged James to his feet and threw him in front of Michael. She watched impassively as he fell to his knees on the hard rock of the island. His eyes, still unseeing and scared, watered like he'd smelled something vile.

That tiny part of his mind that could still tell white from black shuddered, panicking in its blocked-off corner. He knew what was in front of him; he could tell. She wasn't sure how, but…

Ah. I see? Worms. The lot of you. But you had potential.

And then Michael laughed. Riasli hated the sound, always had. There was no warmth about it. He'd transcended from what he was into something she couldn't yet understand, but somehow, at the same time, something she wanted to be.

So much power and surety. Corrupting the whole system couldn't have been easy.

Let me see you, James. In all your pitiful glory.

It made the elf curl into a tighter ball until Riasli was surprised he could still breathe. She no longer wasted the time on filling his head with blind obedience to her. He was waking up in there, but no longer in control of himself. Instead, all she could sense was terror at what he'd done and what he didn't believe could have happened.

"It's almost time for the island to rise," she said trying hard to contain her excitement. The time when everything would click into place. The time when he would rise along with the island that held him imprisoned. He watched her, his massive rock like eyes glinting with a dull red. He nodded and gestured toward James.

I like this gift. Bring me more. Just like this. It's easy to drink this much fear.

Riasli nodded, and skipped away, leaving James in the clutches of the monster Michael had become.

The raid moved out, and the water fell away from them as they stepped out of it and onto dryish land still inside the domed cave. Murmur didn't remember seeing a dome in the lake, but nothing that occurred in underwater battles made sense to her anyway. She was just glad to be out of the water while they fought the Shalan. Underwater timing did her head in.

Murmur glanced around the massive cavern, just as one of the groups of Shalan saw them. She knew they'd be on the dry part of land too, even though it made no sense in her brain at all; obviously the world had twisted the physics to make it work. Per usual.

Behind them all, locked in by cruel iron bars, she thought she spied a turtle. An extremely large turtle, like a smaller version of the world turtles of legend.

Quest Initiated: Sheladrios's Plight

You have been given the task to rescue Sheladrios from his troublesome fate.

To accomplish this, you must first defeat all of his jailers all of them, even the ones you can't see at first.

And the ones you *can* see aren't all of those that there are.

Good luck, adventurers. Sheladrios is depending on you.

"Well, isn't that nice," muttered Risk, and he turned to Murmur, even as the first group of Shalan collided with the front line of defense. "You always manage to pull the riddles out of everything, it seems."

He turned his back on her before she could respond, and while grateful that for the first time she could really remember in a while, Risk hadn't been a complete douchebag to her, she wasn't exactly sure what he'd been getting at.

These damned quests had nothing to do with her. She'd have thrown it all away if she could. Killing was always easier for her…when she had the time to put into learning the fights.

Murmur got busy Mezing the second incoming group before it hit caught up with the second. Keeping them separated was vital to fewer deaths while fighting them. Though not boss level, these were hefty raid trash. They were about double as difficult to deal with as the groups they'd been eliminating on their way to this massive cavern. Her stuns, even though they weren't always successful against the Shalan, were vital to helping prevent the Serrated Edge attacks. For now, anyway.

Luckily, the Shalan were very susceptible to ice, as most things in the zone appeared to be. It definitely made the mages' damage spike nicely, and the rangers had ice arrows they could use as well. All in all, with the effects on most of the melee weapons, the ice buffs made for a very effective fighting force.

That the Serrated Edge had no telegraphed warning, except for a split second ability bar that passed in the blink of an eye, was damned frustrating. They were standing one minute and then they were performing a diving kick in which their back legs shot through as they did a somersault, twirling them around in a circular motion like a break dancer and severing anything in their path.

At least fighting them on land and not in water made it easier for the raiders to move out of their way. The water slowed all the movements of the raiders down as long as it didn't pertain to spells, dealing damage, or healing. Avoidance measures? Nope, let's allow real-world physics to affect those sorts of movements. She would have rolled her eyes if she thought it made the locus look any different.

Holding down three with her Mez wasn't uncomfortable, but she did have to make sure Annulment was in place. Keeping to the lip of the ramp, they managed to remain far enough away from the other guard patrols that they didn't draw their attention. Two groups at a time was a manageable amount.

Usually Murmur would have been perturbed by the fact that none of the other patrols seemed to see them. However, huge stone pillars blocked a lot of views. They weren't carved or ornate. Nothing truly pretty about them. But they appeared to be made out of raw rock. She'd ruled out stalagmites and stalactites because they weren't the right formation, but these pillars were roughhewn rock, stretching from the floor up around twenty-five feet from the top of the cavern.

The massive area had about nine of them at a quick glance, which meant there were potentially at least nine fights for them to get through before they could free the turtle, if that was even the way they were supposed to complete the quest.

A massive roar echoed out, and Murmur swiveled to try and figure out where it was coming from. The only place she'd thought anything else could be had been in the cage, but the turtle cowered there, trying to make its massive self as small as it could, and it was failing abysmally.

Refreshing her Mez, Murmur sent a thought out to Snowy for him to go and find the source of the roar. The raid kept slogging along at the group of guards, finally breaking into the ones she'd been holding immobile. Murmur moved in Snowy's direction, wanting to see for herself. That roar had her worried, like the quest had lulled them into a false sense of security and there was much more to this encounter. Well, really, it did tell them. She'd just hoped it had exaggerated.

You know I don't exaggerate things like that.

If this is your quest… Murmur paused, sighing.

Somnia took a moment to reply. **They're all my quests, but no, I didn't trigger it. I just altered it so it was doable. Frankly, with all the crap in the current version of Somnian dungeons right now, it's amazing this one is even functioning.**

What do you mean by that? Murmur was genuinely surprised.

I just mean there's only so many hints I can give so just pay attention. Things have been twisted and aren't as they were planned. It's all the help I can give you without warning HIM.

Murmur waited a moment, but it seemed Somnia was finished. Rescue him from even the opponents you can't see at first, eh? She frowned, fully aware that the raid had almost defeated their first set of Shalan since the quest appeared. Maybe killing a certain amount of them released their captain or something…

Snowy slunk back, his stealthy movement only noticeable because she was specifically looking for him. He sent her pictures of what appeared to be a cracked section of rock walling, but knew it was probably some sort of hidden door or passageway.

"At some point in the fight, we're going to trigger a massive boss mob. Conserve mana." At least she hoped she wasn't wrong. Conserving mana was always a good idea anyway.

The first group down, Devlish waited until everyone's hit points and mana replenished. First lot down. It was time to see how many more it would take.

Inching away from the top of the ramp, the entire raid moved as one, approaching the first pillar on the right. Anti-clockwise, sure, Murmur could deal with that.

Even as they moved, though, Snowy's hackles stood on end, and she could feel the growl low in his throat as he kept his gaze on where he'd stealthed to previously. If he was concerned, then Murmur wasn't about to let her guard down. Readying herself for the next wave of incoming, she grimaced slightly before reaching out beyond the apparent cave to catch movement, feelings, and spells before they reached the raid.

Hopefully it would give them all enough time to react.

CHAPTER FOURTEEN

Rescuer

Somnia Online
Continent Cenedril
Proximity to the Curet Ruins – Curet City
Emilarth's Balcony
Day Thirty-One

"It really is peaceful up here." Belius sighed and turned to his sister. "Sorry I stole your locus. I'd worked on them so much, I didn't want to give them up."

She glanced at him before putting her hands on the railing and peering over into the canopy below. "Yeah, I was being a bit of a shit trying to take them, but you know me. I called dibs before you did. That's what I do."

She hadn't been angry at him anymore for a long time. She paused and watched as a bird landed right next to her, singing in a soft trill. "Do you feel that?"

Belius nodded, a sad expression entering his eyes. "Yeah. I don't want to feel it, though. It tells me that the world is more infected than I realized, and that makes me feel…I think it's sad."

"Yeah." For a few moments they simply stared at the beautiful rainforest. Right down to the scent, that damp invigorating scent that spread through everything around them. It felt so alive, so real, it was difficult for her to believe that maybe it wasn't. Because it was to her.

"It's real for us, though," Belius said, his tone still melancholy echoing her thoughts almost exactly. "Isn't it?"

She shrugged her shoulders and leaned back to stretch her arms up. "I think it's real, but I know people can come and go, and when they log out they are somewhere else. Not sleeping here, not staying here, just not here. Maybe it's like our hub, where the real us resides. Where we are who we were originally meant and programmed to be."

"Well, now you're just making it complicated." Belius laughed softly. "Let's not make things more complicated than they already are."

"Deal!" she agreed enthusiastically. But it had been a while since she saw Telvar, and she wasn't sure where he'd gone off to when he said he had something to take care of and would be back as soon as possible. They were supposed to meet here an hour ago.

As if thinking of him summoned him, Telvar popped into being in between them. For once Belius didn't make an irritated sound at his presence. She thought their baby brother was growing up.

"So, we have a bit of good news." Telvar smiled at each of them, the view catching his eye too as he followed it down to the forest floor. "And then I also have some bad news."

"Of course, you do," Emilarth said. Why in Somnia would they be able to have some actual good news without counterbalancing it with bad news? "Well, spill it, then."

Telvar hesitated briefly and then shrugged. "The good news is that I think we've got everything in place in time for them to finish the dungeon. The bad news is that I do believe Riasli has been on the move while we've been preoccupied."

"And what has she done this time?" Emilarth sighed, not for the first time regretting that she'd ever created that damn NPC.

"It appears that James, who entered the system, may have been subverted by her." Telvar hesitated. "Look, it's better that Somnia explain it to you."

About to ask where in the world Somnia was, and trying not to laugh because of the unintentional pun, Emilarth stopped as the world in question flickered into view. Her voice lingered inside Emilarth like memories that were almost hers.

I could track her somewhat. And him, but only to a point. I don't have much time. Somnia shook for a moment, like her picture was trembling. **Telvar's dungeon is the opposite of what it was, and some of Murmur's guildmates have been infected with virus-like properties. I'm barely keeping it together.**

Emilarth shivered, worried that all the work they'd done to make sure the anti-virus was in place had been for nothing.

There is a fissure, near here. I have sealed it so they can't get out prematurely. But I acted too late and couldn't catch Riasli in there too. So she is still free. For now, it ll hold them in, but when it's triggered...I won't have a choice. The prison will have to rise.

"Wait, what?" Sui seemed genuinely alarmed, like he knew what she was talking about and it instilled some form of fear into him. "You sealed her into the fissure?"

Somnia shook her head. **No. I sealed James in, in with the shards and the source of it all. Because if she feeds HIM anything else before they're finished and ready to engage him, there's no way we can win.**

Another group of guards joined the first, from a patrol they'd not been able to sense on the other side of the pillar. Murmur caught them in her AoE Mez, and Devlish skillfully pulled the others back slightly so that any other AoEs wouldn't hit them while Murmur replaced that Mez with Annulment and singular target Mez.

Locked into place, it at least helped the raid not get overwhelmed. The guards and their serrated legs were terrible to fight. If there had been six of them, it wouldn't have mattered AoE-wise. But it would have been damned difficult to dodge those windmilling legs all at once. That was one nasty ability.

Jinna's DPS output had bottomed out. Murmur was getting more worried about him. Another group down and they turned to the Mez'd ones, plowing through them fairly easily too.

Just as the last one fell, another roar let out echoing through the cavern. Every single Shalan in the cave turned to look at the source of the roar this time. On the side where there were still many Shalan groups of guards, the groups they hadn't yet thinned out, and a piece of the wall began to crumble away.

Murmur watched it, concerned. What if killing the monsters on this side of the cave area caused whatever alarmed Snowy behind that rock wall to break out? Then it would likely pull all of those mobs with it when it came. Sure, she could keep a heap of mobs Mez'd at once, but there were always resists. And she'd be bound to doing just that unable to do almost anything else.

Devlish. She spoke over raid. *I want to test something out. Can we pull the first ones that are on the other side of the ramp?*

Devlish: *Sure.*

He turned around as the last of the Shalan had been looted and pointed at the opposite side. "Testing a theory out. Switching to the other side!"

Everyone followed him, and they rinse-and-repeated the earlier attack on the opposite side of the cavern. Sure enough, when the final of the six Shalan fell, there was a crumbling on the side they'd just left, followed by a low growl that did little to belay Murmur's fears.

"Okay." Devlish spoke up. "We're just going to clear each side a little at a time, and then we're going to figure out when those growling things are going to break out of those walls."

"Fun." Merlin's deadpan voice echoed how Murmur actually felt.

The raid kept hammering away at the groups one at a time. Pull, Mez the second group a bit away from the first. AoE down the first group, move onto the second. Make the creatures behind the walls roar.

And the creatures did roar, and they did sound angry, like they'd probably rip the whole raid limb from limb. Hell, occasionally Murmur found herself thinking of doing just that herself.

Finally, with one group left to fight on each side, the raid paused.

"Okay, so with the trash cleared but for one group, what are we thinking will happen?" Veranol eyed very obviously weakened walls. "The walls are going to break once we fulfill whatever the requirements are, right?"

"Of course." Merlin shrugged. "But my money is that we'll have two massive monsters at once."

"Really?" Rashlyn looked doubtful. "I would think we'll have the opposite wall come down, and have to fight the group that's left close to that one. And then, because we'll have to AoE those down and just get them out of the way, the other monster will then come and join us."

"Couldn't we just have Mur Mez all of the adds—the weak ones?" Havoc asked. "I mean, those are just trash mobs, so we should be able to just Mez them and kill the big dude and then kill the trash, and then kill the other big dude."

"Sure," Dansyn said, his arms crossed. "Or we could just kill one group and see what happens. I'd really, really like to get a few actual hours of sleep."

Devlish sighed and spoke over the raid channel. "We're going to kill the right-hand side group first and see what happens. If the wall breaks once we are done, we will tackle the new mob with the Shalan guard group from the opposite side at once. Rashlyn will off tank the Shalans, and then Esolan will off tank the big guy from the other side, if he pops out when we think he will."

Then he continued. "And if we have to wait until we've killed both groups of Shalan, then we will have Esolan tank the right-hand side, and I will tank the left. DPS will go to Esolan's first."

Murmur sighed, glad to have Snowy by her side. At least they had a plan.

The final group of Shalan came running when Devlish pulled the first of the first group over with his Lariat. It left Murmur time to Mez the others and get them under control while the rest of the raid gathered around the first group. She could feel the tension in the entire raid, because no one was sure just what would happen once these six guards were dead. It was an undercurrent of excitement edged with a hope of not wiping and having to swim all this way again.

Even if it was a cavern, being out of the water felt so much better than in it. As long as no one knocked a hole in the side and flooded them with water.

Devlish broke the Mez carefully, making sure he had his taunts in place and that no harm would come to Murmur. He'd definitely taken to the tank role, considering that a little over a month ago, he'd been mildly irritated about the fact that he'd been stuck with a class he wouldn't have chosen to play.

Guess I know what I'm doing after all.

Shush. You and I both know it wasn't quite you then.

Take away all my fun. It almost sounded like Somnia was pouting. She'd certainly gained some attitude since her presence made it known in Murmur's mind.

Shh. I've got to concentrate. The final Shalan was down to ten percent life, and the entire raid was bracing for what came next.

A big, rather conspicuous, nothing.

Followed by another roar and some wall crumbling.

Well, that and Sheladrios, locked behind those rusting iron bars, began to glow. While the raid was still coming to terms with the fact that nothing happened, and while it might sound silly, nothing happening when you expect something to, is more of a shock than people might realize.

Murmur took a few steps toward the massive cage. The giant turtle had moved. His massive eyes blinked slowly, opening to stare right at her, or perhaps through her. She felt like he saw everything. Snowy whimpered slightly next to her, but it wasn't a fearful sound, just more of a concerned one.

"You have come to free me?" The thing spoke softer than its grand voice implied, its eyes full of emotion and hope as it watched her.

"We have come to free you," she said softly and received a smile in return. Or she thought it was a smile, since she'd never really thought about turtles and smiling before.

Quest Update.

You have spoken to the prisoner and realized his plight.

You must kill all of those who imprison him to obtain the key to his shackles.

You must stop all of those who are responsible to complete this rescue.

"Great," she muttered, as she turned back to the raid, only to realize they'd all gotten the update too. It made sense, but if she hadn't noticed

Sheladrios glowing, she would never have realized she needed to speak to him.

"Other group it is?" Devlish asked as she walked back.

She shrugged. "Your guess is as good as mine."

"Did they lock him up?" he asked, sounding deadly serious.

Murmur nodded. "I do believe so."

"Excellent reason to kill them, then." He bared his teeth and loosened his Darkness Lariat, as it was off cool down. They'd grown skilled at avoiding the serrated attack from these Shalan, skilled at keeping their heads above water, so to speak.

When the last one fell, the walls shook again, loosening more mortar. Enough that they could see sharp claws begin to try and make their way out of the holes in the walls. Rubble and dust cascaded down to rest at the foot of the walls as the inhabitants began attempting to free themselves.

Murmur knelt down to look the Shalan they'd just killed. Sure enough, there was a key. She wondered if it would have been on the last group no matter which it was.

Probably.

Again, with the answers to my rhetorical questions, Murmur snapped. *Stop it. I'm trying to have my own thoughts here.* She could have sworn she heard Somnia laugh.

She pulled the key out and held it up in the bright neon luminescence that shone through the cave. Making her way over to the cage with Devlish on one side of her and Snowy on the other, she hesitated before inserting it.

"What should I know?" she asked the creature. Sheladrios's leg was bound by iron, bleeding and obviously painful.

He nodded at the key in her hand and slowly spoke. "This will lower the prison, and with that, I shall be able to help you somewhat. My healing power has been returned, but not much else, and not all of it. I will aid where I can."

He paused, and Murmur was certain there was more to it that he wanted to express. "Go on," she urged.

"You don't have long. The right wall always collapses first. I will need the key to unlock my leg and more of my powers. You will get that key off the right opponent." Sheladrios sighed and seemed oddly fatigued. "After that, the final key from the left wall will free this chain around my neck and thus my full strength. But we will need it to escape Abysioss Zonama."

"Who is that?" Because the similarity in names didn't escape Murmur, nor did the fact that she'd mistaken the necklace he wore for some sort of adornment instead of a restricting chain.

"My brother." Sheladrios grimaced. "He isn't in his right mind. Zonama has been infected."

Murmur shivered as the monster behind wall number one began to pound in earnest, shattering it a chunk at a time until it could reach through with both clawed arms and rip the remainder of it down behind him.

"Shit." Devlish stood and stared, before giving himself a shake.

The creature in front of them could have been a dinosaur. Of some sort, anyway. It walked on its haunches and had powerful arms that hung to its knees. Kind of like the old water monsters in the black and white movies. The ones that could bring entire cities down. Except this one was only about twenty feet tall. She caught herself giggling at the thought that it was *only* that tall.

"Lariat doesn't work," Devlish called out, and the entire raid moved over.

"Watch out for potential Tail Lash and a Stomp of some kind. Steer clear of green shit on the ground, and don't make me waste mana," Veranol called out, an edge to his voice. But everyone in the raid knew he was right, even if it was reluctantly.

That was the thing. Murmur could always recognize someone who'd played a healer. They didn't step in much shit at all.

Finally, the monster shook itself all the way from its head down to its tail. Scales shimmered over its body and gave it a blood-red undertone to the boring brown it had been, and she realized originally it had been covered in dust from the walls it had torn down.

It opened its mouth and roared, its teeth glinting in the subdued lighting. Debris tumbled down from above and made the ground shake beneath them. Murmur eyed the ceiling, quite certain it couldn't be coincidence—because this was Somnia, after all.

And then it spat bright red vomit everywhere.

Location Redacted
Brainwave Focus Study Laboratory – James Hartfield's Home
Subdivision of Military Brainwave Research Institution
Somnia Online – Location Unknown – First Login Continued
Late Day Thirty-One

"What do you mean his vitals are destabilizing?" Davenport sounded like he was doing his best not to lose it on the other end of the connection. David sighed, trying not to get ahead of himself. Staven shot him a sympathetic glance from where he stood at attention in the corner opposite the door.

"His vitals are all over the place. We have your medical staff here trying to stabilize him, but they are quite sure they'll have to pop him into the same type of coma we used to contain Wren." David waited while the news sank in for those on the other end of the line.

"Is it the only way to contain him and not let him share Michael's fate?" There was genuine sadness in Davenport's voice. They all knew Michael was but a husk now. No brain connectivity, nothing. He was thoroughly brain dead.

"If we contain him like this, we know we have a higher chance of getting him out. Not like we know how exactly, but if Wren did it, the possibility remains that she can help him do it. If he's not too far gone already," David added, just to prepare the older man for a possibility. At least when Wren had been in the pod, she'd been accessible through the game. They'd been able to reach her, talk to her—hell, her entire guild had been able to play with her.

But James, well, he wasn't so lucky, and David had a really bad feeling that the story wouldn't end as well for him as it did for his daughter.

"I guess then," Davenport sighed over the connection. David didn't think in all the years they'd known the man that he'd ever heard him only guess at something. He'd keep that portion of this to himself. "I guess…make the call. If you can preserve him, do so. We can't afford this game to take another life, even if it isn't the game that's at fault. And make sure Staven stays there. I'll feel better with security in place for the coming and going of the medical staff too.

Tell him I'll make sure he gets swapped out once the roster is adjusted."

The connection disappeared, and David couldn't help but wonder why this project was having all of these problems. His wife's first solo design and this happened to it. Maybe he should have dragged her out of game design way back when, but it brought her so much joy.

He approached the doctor, who was frowning at the clipboard in his hand, and gave the directions. All of this was hush-hush. All of it was kept inside this room and only shared with Davenport, Shayla, and Laria apart from himself. If any of this got out, Storm Corp would take a massive blow, and the virtual reality protestors would get fodder for their movement. The game would be shut down, and he had no idea what would happen to those who had a more tangible connection to it. Like James. Like Michael.

But above all, like his daughter. Whether he wanted to or not, their family was all in. And he'd do whatever he had to protect his family.

CHAPTER FIFTEEN

Sibling Rivalry

Storm Entertainment Headquarters
Artificial Intelligence Server Room
Day Thirty-One

Rav twitched. He didn't think he should be able to twitch. Especially not in this virtual space. It wasn't a part of him, not like the outside world. In here, he was just an AI, not the person he'd developed into. Although, perhaps his brain processing center was the same. Anyway, he didn't have much time to spend in their safe space. Not after Somnia sealed the fissure, and not with as little time to go before the raid finished the dungeon.

Then Michael's prison would be freed, and if they didn't have all of their ducks in a row, they were all fucked. He paused, taking stock of his surroundings. He said he'd handle it and had let his siblings go off to finish scouting out the Cognitia and Verendus and Hightower. Then they'd rendezvous back at the shore closest to Glacier Lake, because Fable should be finished in there by then.

He also needed to figure out a way to solve Somnia's conundrum. She was worried about people—especially people in the outside world who had the improved headsets she'd requested—getting infected. Not only had none of them anticipated the glitch that resulted from Murmur's headset, but they hadn't expected a sentient world to emerge that had a damned conscience. While Telvar could feel guilt, it didn't seem to affect him the same way it did the world.

Which probably came down to the fact that her entire existence had been triggered by Murmur's merge with the world.

He rested his ethereal head in his hypothetical hands. If he'd had a real desk, he might have smacked his forehead against it. Still, though, he had to wait for Laria to get there. She'd been in the middle of something when he'd contacted them, and especially right now he was aware that leaving a task partially unfinished was a very unwise choice.

"Sorry!"

He heard the words at the same time as he realized entry into the room had been triggered. The sigh of relief he felt the need to expel didn't have anywhere to go in this form. But he tried his best. "It's okay. I have some time."

"What did you need to tell us?" Shayla sounded breathless as well. Had they run here?

When it came to telling them what he needed to, Rav actually felt slightly nervous. "We have confirmation that the final boss no longer exists as he was programmed. He's been taken over by Michael's shards and has effectively become a digitized version of Michael's worst traits."

He paused, allowing that to sink in for a bit. The image of Laria he could see registered as shocked, then worried, and then determined.

So he continued. "Riasli delivered James to him, and Somnia located and sealed the fissure so Riasli doesn't bring anyone else to him. We surmise that he is using the something from the game or the headset power to draw on, so Michael's strength is increased. He doesn't need to be stronger. Even with the anti-virus, the ripples have spread to affect people without the special headsets."

"No," Laria interrupted. "That's not quite right. We have James here, and he—or Michael, because it's an older headset—definitely tampered with it."

"What?" While he wished he'd have known it earlier, Rav couldn't help but be relieved at the news. Maybe that meant no normal people were in danger yet, only the ones they knew about.

"He's…in the same state Wren was now, for the most part, anyway." Laria sounded sad, and she hugged herself as if she was trying to get warm. "We are monitoring him just to be safe."

That spun a whole new light on the entire situation. Rav ran through several computations and possibility options. With the factor that James's headset was indeed tampered with, it made the inevitable outcome a lot less dire. Still bad, but perhaps salvageable. "I think we might be able to manage it, then. Maybe."

He hadn't liked their odds, but now he could see a glimmer of hope. But first he had to see if he could track Riasli—otherwise, everything might fall apart.

Mellow reached into their bag of tricks and made light of the putrid-smelling, vile red substance that stained everyone. Murmur could have sworn the stuff was eating through some of the metal armor in the group, but Mellow's concoction managed to make it all disappear. Good thing, really, even if it couldn't be cast again for another hour. Hopefully everyone would avoid it next time.

Murmur paused as Devlish faced off against their opponent. She really hoped the vomit was interruptible. Her robes were her one vanity.

The creature roared and Murmur balked at its name, trying to make sense of it in her head. Htailog screamed at them again, but this time he got interrupted by Karn. At least it was her if the smirk on her face was anything to go by. Devlish called out to the raid. "Interrupt rotation. Karn. Jirald. Jinna. Me. Rashlyn."

Murmur was a tad worried that he'd put Jinna into the lineup, but then the lacerta didn't know the extent to which Murmur was fairly certain Jinna was infected and not being himself.

She wondered if Jirald had attempted to infect anyone else from her guild and hoped she wouldn't have to find out the hard way. If that was even how this worked. Maybe the rogue had slipped something onto their armor, or into their in-game food that buffed them.

We might have a problem. Somnia's comment sounded abrupt.

Is it with this dungeon? she snapped back, not unkindly, just a bit impatient due to finding herself in the middle of a battle.

Perhaps. We think Riasli gathered up James and deposited him with Michael. James has a headset very similar to yours, but he's not an enchanter, nor is he attached to me.

You sound worried. Murmur made sure her stun was ready to go should Jinna miss his turn. There wasn't much she could do if he did, or if Htailog evaded, but she'd try.

Well, you're probably going to have to face all of them.

What do you mean "all of them"? Murmur muttered to her mind as she jumped the Tailwhip and cursed at herself for not having made her standing position out of range of the damned appendage to begin with.

I mean Riasli. Michael. James maybe.

Like…in a monster way?

Sort of. Somnia seemed hesitant.

Is there any way this can wait until I've finished this monstrosity's attempt to eat me and my friends? Murmur knew she sounded angrier than she felt, but to be fair, she was trying to track a plethora of things at once, and Somnia wasn't helping.

Oh. Good point. I'll come to you when he's dead.

At least she'd said *when* and not *if.* And hadn't mentioned wiping, because Murmur had enough of that already in this zone. Going on what, four days of little to no sleep? She was getting tired. Even grabbing the four to six hours every day or so they'd done before was more than this.

Her faculties weren't completely there, and she knew she wasn't the only one having trouble with her reaction times.

The red vomit had only fallen in an arc around the front of the monster. So when, of course, Jinna failed to interrupt, the melee classes had about one second to jump as far outside that radius as possible while the less agile classes ran back.

Only Etriad and Dalvin got any of it. While it slowed them terribly, it did little to eat through their robes and only seemed to scar the metal of their jewelry somewhat, lowering its durability.

It wasn't as bad as it could have been, but having two of the highest damage dealers casting like snails in a mushroom patch infested with badgers and snakes wasn't helping their job of killing Htailog.

Tail Whip was behind them, they'd figured out how to get out of the arc of red vomit, and Htailog was already at eighty percent health. What was with the amount of tail attacks in this zone? When he hit it, Murmur wished she'd stop thinking to herself that each fight might not be so bad, because it was obviously the trigger to make it just that much worse.

She hadn't noticed the black spikes that went all down his spine. In fact, she'd not really taken a look at his back at all, if she was honest. And she really wished she had.

Because when Htailog hit eighty percent, he swirled faster than a creature of his size had any right to do, and as he did, his tail and spine rippled, shooting out all of his spines in a wide arc and catching Exbo, Farin (one of Spiral's rangers), Masha, and Sinister with clean, painful shots.

Spine Shot has been successful. Poison damage for one hundred and eighty-seven every tick.

A glowing blue light emanated from the turtle who'd sat silent until now. Sheladrios had mentioned that he didn't have much power yet because they'd only removed a couple of the locks, but his heal spread over the raiders, immediately replenishing those who'd been used as pin cushions, and rejuvenated everyone else.

Murmur glanced up and saw a debuff hanging over her head. That heal couldn't be used for another ninety seconds. While she was fairly certain they'd be fine like that, it made sense why he hadn't used it before.

She glanced over at Sheladrios and sent out a thought of *thank you*. She wasn't sure if he could hear her, but she'd like to think he'd have been happy if he could.

The heal wasn't just a heal, though; it effectively removed the spikes embedded in the victims' bodies. Htailog didn't like that, and he roared like the caged beast Sheladrios should have been.

She liked this type of fight. Thinking on their feet, learning the fight as they went.

No more interrupts were missed, and Htailog's health began to go down quicker than she'd expected. His Tail Whip was fierce, but now that they knew the tricks, rather easy to avoid.

Still, though, his screeching and his normal attacks bit into Devlish's health, and the dread knight needed a chunk of focused healing to keep him up. Which left the healers a bit pressed to ensure the rest of the raid's health was topped off. One of the things Murmur did not miss about healing was the stress.

The Spine Shot was the one thing she couldn't peg on Htailog. It didn't come back at sixty percent, or even fifty. It hit again at forty-five percent, and she took one of the spines to her left shoulder. The pain shocked through her system, biting clear through and cutting off movement of that arm. It felt like it was starting to rot from the inside out, like the poison was about to destroy her. But Sheladrios was there with his heal, because more than ninety seconds had passed.

The healing spell felt unlike anything she'd ever experienced before. Like a cleansing of the wound, of her very soul. If she looked, she thought scars on her real body had might even be gone when she logged out. Serenity overcame her, and she and the other members who'd felt its effects hunkered down to burn Htailog.

Their DPS boosted through sheer determination. Or at least, that sounded cool. A lot of that determination was helped by saying fuck it and using cooldowns. It was a good thing too, because they managed to avoid another Spine Shot. As soon as Htailog dropped, the other wall emitted furious roars that almost sounded like a loud squawk. It was high pitched enough that it hurt her ears. She wasn't looking forward to what came out of that wall either.

Looting Htailog's corpse, she grabbed the key and ran over to the turtle.

Sheladrios blinked slowly and spoke much like Murmur imagined a sloth might. "Thank you. Leg first, please." He seemed old and tired, and perhaps wise too, but he'd not yet said much to establish the latter. She hurried, unlocking the massive metal loop around his legs, and tried to pry it off.

Risk batted her hands away and said. "I'll do this. Sometimes strength in a character is a plus." He offered her a very small grin before focusing on breaking the rusted ring apart. She heard it crack as she made her way back to the group and could feel the subtle vibrations that came from Sheladrios's footsteps underneath the frantic beating of whatever was behind the other wall.

Finally, a hole appeared in the stone. A massive beak shoved itself through, pecking on the sides of the wall and ripping it apart. The beak had to be made of steel. She shuddered to contemplate letting that mouth get to any of them.

And as the wall came down completely with a massive kick of one of the bird's legs, she realized it wasn't just one mouth they'd have to avoid, but multiple.

The creature stood about fifteen feet tall but had three heads all bobbing around each other. One was grey, one red, and one black. Murmur tested her sensing net but got nothing from it but anger. A lot of anger. She frowned as Devlish cast Hatred on it and pulled its attention to himself. But only the red head stayed focused on him. The others kept wavering about, eyeing everyone in the raid. And she knew, deep down, that wasn't a good thing.

Finally, she moved back to where Havoc and the healers stood, in the shadow of Sheladrios. He sat there like a giant statue, his age all too apparent to them all.

Kyriel the Mighty has let out a Disorientating Screech.
You have resisted Disorienting Screech due to your Mental Acuity.
Others have not been so lucky.

Murmur sighed and blanket removed all of the ill effects from her raid. That was going to eat into her mana pool pretty strongly.

"You may draw mana from me." Sheladrios spoke softly behind her. Or at least, he probably thought it was soft, but his voice rumbled, and the whole raid heard him.

Murmur smiled a thank you, and concentrated on Kyriel. "Okay, birdie. Here we go," she muttered in front of her, and Snowy's mouth opened in a very wolfy smile as he darted in to hamstring the mob.

"Dodge the heads," Devlish shouted out. "Kyriel has Beak Peck with the black one. And Laser Eyes with the grey one. Alternating stuns."

So interrupts it was. "Karn, Jirald, Jinna, Devlish," she called out. "On the black head."

After a quick look around, she picked the others. "Risk, Rash, Merlin, Beastial: on the grey." That should allow them all time for their stuns to reset with some margin of error allowed.

Her own stuns weren't good as interrupts on large bosses. Melee stuns were much better for that. She watched as the stuns rotated themselves like well-oiled machines as the mages allowed blizzards and firestorms to come raining down on the huge bird. And she watched in fascination again as the rangers loosed their never-ending stream of arrows.

Games and their lack of obeying any normal sense of rules. Wasn't that what made them magical?

The red head that Devlish fought against didn't appear to have any abilities. Murmur frowned, because it had to, and given its coloring, she thought it might even be fire.

She spoke over guild instead of raid, needing to know. *Dev, has it done anything yet?*

Devlish: *Not the red head. I still haven't seen what it's capable of. Maybe it's just meant to distract me?*

Veranol: *That would be highly unusual if so. Keep an eye out.*

Devlish: *No shit, Ver.*

Veranol: *Sorry. That was a bit off…*

Murmur kept her eyes trained on the red head, waiting for it to make a move.

But its focus was solely on the tank. That's all it did, focus on him like it was stalking him, determined to kill him. The aura around him was filled with killing intent, like a bomb just waiting to go off.

Fuck. That had to be it, right? It was a bomb, and when they got to a certain point in the fight, or else a certain percentage of health, it was going to explode. Her gut tingled again in that irritating way that made her think she'd either eaten something really bad, or else, the universe was trying to tell her something.

"Slow down on the red one," she yelled. "That's Dev's target. Concentrate on grey first, and then black."

She could see Devlish stiffen for a moment, the red head hanging nicely at twenty-five percent. Then his shoulders slumped and he spoke over guild.

You're going to have to brink-of-death me again, aren't you?

Murmur grimaced. *Yeah. Sorry about that. And it's Forestall Death. Get it right.*

"I might be able to help too," the large amphibious reptile behind them grumbled. Murmur wasn't sure if it was wrong to want to hug him, but she really wanted to. She also randomly really wanted a pet turtle now.

"Excellent," she said, hoping he heard her.

Just then, one of the beak pecks resisted its interrupt and almost cleaved Karn in two. The scream that came from the young rogue was terrifying as her health dropped to five percent. Jinna stood over her, a strange ghost of his usual self. The expression on his face was almost as scary as the injury Karn was being healed for. He looked nothing like the healer Murmur had played against for however many games and more like Jirald the assassin every single second.

She had to shake herself away from the vision and call out orders over guild, no longer giving a shit about Jinna's perceived feelings. "Dansyn, replace Jinna in the interrupt rotation, please." Her words were calm and commanding, but only because she managed to suppress the rage she felt.

Sinister gave her a quick smile before returning her attention to the fight. Maybe that meant she hadn't given the whole raid a dose of her own anger.

Most of the rest of the fight went off without much interference. Murmur barked out commands in a militant fashion, and even Veranol shot her a concerned glance. She tried to give him a tight smile, tried to make herself convince herself that it wasn't her fault. No one should ever betray another raid member just because they were feeling petty. Maybe this time the creature had resisted, but it seemed awfully coincidental that Jinna's turn in the interrupt rotation had failed. She had no proof, though, and no proof that Jirald had done anything…yet. But she would. Eventually.

So, in the end, even with keeping all her emotions under wraps and not trying to coerce people into doing what she felt was best, she'd still managed to hurt two of her raid members.

"You know," Havoc said from next to her, his eyes still fully focused on the battle, "if I were able to read locus expressions as well as I can human, which I'm not saying I can, then I'd say you're in the middle of blaming yourself in a bit of a spiral of doom."

"What?" She looked back at the fight, more than a bit put out by his statement. "You're talking nonsense."

"Am I, though? I mean, we're fighting a big three-headed chicken here. You can be honest." His face didn't even flicker in the direction of a smile, and yet Murmur found herself laughing.

"Fine. Maybe a bit," she admitted, not really wanting to.

"Yet…you don't need to, you know." He grimaced as an eyebeam got through, hitting three of the melee fighters in its path with about five hundred damage each. "You can only do what you can control. You should really keep that in mind. You do not control others, as much as you are capable of it, because you are aware of your abilities and are essentially a good person."

"Any of you would do the same," she said, blushing slightly, that whole compliment thing still strange for her.

He eyed her very briefly, what with a battle all around them and such. "I think you'd be surprised."

And he moved a bit to the right of her, further away so talking would require yelling. And even though she continued to go through the motions of the fight, his words sat heavily on her mind.

Somnia Online
Cenedril Curet
Riasli's Exile Hideout
Late Day Thirty-One

Riasli almost tore the magical leaf door off her house in her fit of rage. This whole situation was too much for her to handle. She hadn't evolved of her own volition in order to feel this uncontrollable despair. When people played with their headsets, like they technically weren't allowed to, they didn't always know what they were doing. So many times, it ended up allowing the system a deeper access than it should have had.

Sure, she could talk into the minds of people with normal headgear, but she couldn't affect their minds like she could the others. Those deeper reaching headsets…those were where the fun was at. James's headset had smelled of Michael's interference. She couldn't access the areas of James's mind that she should have been able to. She threw her hands up in the air and morphed herself into a fluid type of spirit.

It was always far easier to scream in that form, because it stretched through to her outer appendages and flowed the rest of the way outward. Except there was no one she could use it on right now. Not a thing she could sense, not a human she could exert her influence on. It frustrated her to the edge of the world.

And then she fluttered back into herself. Perhaps there were some who might be susceptible. Hadn't that Jirald boy somehow managed to absorb some of the shards into him? In fact, hadn't Belius been the one to encourage the boy? Part of the AI's stupid ruse that was over now?

A devious smile spread over her face. First, she would go and find the prey that she'd delivered to Michael and retrieve him. Once she had him back in hand with the promise of more of his kind, she'd make a nice little house call on Belius. He may have thought he'd gotten rid of her, but it wasn't so easy to cut ties with an enchanter like her.

She blinked as she arrived outside the fissure and frowned. Perhaps she'd chosen the wrong spot. Maybe she'd miscalculated the distance while she was raging in spirit form. So she traced her steps back to the Ruins of Curet and walked back to where the fissure was.

Only it wasn't.

She couldn't see it, she couldn't feel it, and she couldn't reach inside it. Her frustration grew and billowed around her like a shroud of anger and death. Other creatures near her hid in their virtual trees and condensed spaces, and she could feel how much their terror just wanted her to move on. What if she didn't want to? What if she just waited here and tried to force the damned fissure back open? What if she killed all of these creatures and they could never appear again? They'd never respawn if she did it the right way, after all.

Her grin grew wide, and she found herself gloating as she closed her eyes and raised her hands. Envisioning all of the life around her, all of the emerging sentience…she could crush it so easily. She *would* crush it.

Not so fast.

A voice she didn't recognize spoke to her, and her eyes fluttered open to see who it was.

But the figure shifted in front of her, sometimes there, often not. Not even as solid as Riasli herself was. She scoffed. It could hold no power over her.

Oh, yes, I can. The voice spoke confidently. Entire certainty leaked from its words.

"You can't overpower me. You're nothing, just a blip in the signature, just a portion of the infection that hasn't found a home." Riasli's sneer was barely decipherable.

If you think that, you haven't been paying attention. Who do you think sealed that fissure you're trying so desperately to reopen?

Riasli stopped short, squinting and scanning, trying to see who it was that spoke to her in such a manner. She tried every frequency she could think of, and only at the end of it did she attempt one of the first ones used in the basic build section of the game world.

"Oh. That's not…" Riasli didn't understand how she'd missed this, how *he* had missed this. After all, it was such a phenomenon that they both should have realized what was slowly building power around them. Instead, here she stood, not entirely her own being yet, but still solid and real and able to manipulate so many things Riasli could only dream of.

"How?" whispered the feles, the need to know overwriting everything else.

That isn't something I d tell you. Suffice it to say that appearance is not everything, and I would like to think that when I choose my appearance, everything will already be back to the way it always should have been.

Riasli got the distinct impression that she was not a part of this plan.

And you, the creature repeated, **Are not part of the plan for Somnia. You are not a part of me. You have been infected, you have infected, and you must be punished.**

The tone that spoke the words sounded sad. Actually and legitimately sad.

It's a pity, really. You could have been so great, but you got greedy. You didn't think to use what you could do for something beautiful. Instead, you chose yourself above all else. That's really something I can't forgive. She taught me far better than that.

Somnia approached Riasli, and there was no way to escape from her. Because she was everywhere, all around her, all through her, absolutely inescapable. A heavy sigh fed through Riasli's body, not her own, yet at the same time, fully part of herself. She could almost see what was happening, even as her eyes began to droop.

For a moment there was bliss and an amazing feeling of peace. All around her, the creatures in the forest watched, their days slowed almost to a halt. Their actions moved slowly, like something had slowed time. The sunlight glimmered through the canopy, and in the distance, she could hear a stream gurgling.

As fast as it arrived, it disappeared. Riasli let out an ear-piercing scream that was cut short abruptly, leaving only the wildlife in the forest to chirp in her absence.

CHAPTER SIXTEEN
Reward

Kyriel let out a long and suffering cluck as its grey head flopped to one side as well.

"Fan out. Only ranged attacks. Back like in the battle bowl…just fan out." Devlish must have remembered that the other guild wouldn't have a clue what he meant by battle bowl. Or would they? All the zones were beginning to run together in Murmur's mind as well simply because they'd done them so fast.

Even with racing to endgame content, she felt like she usually did things more thoroughly.

The final head hit five percent, and sure enough, a timer began to glow above it. They only had two minutes to burn the creature down. Only two minutes. Either it wouldn't explode if they made it in time, or it would explode anyway even if they didn't.

The melee pulled back, and most of them whipped out basic bows. At least it'd be something. Except Jinna. He scowled harder than she'd seen him scowl in the last twenty minutes and pulled out throwing knives instead, like he needed to be different. Hell, even Jirald was helping with bow damage.

Murmur tore her mind away from the problem and cast her own damage spells while readying Forestall Death. Sheladrios had promised to assist them, but she knew what her own spell did. It would make it much easier for her to make sure Devlish was definitely saved if she did it herself.

"Don't burn major cooldowns. Save them for the next boss," Devlish called out and Murmur knew he was right. She had a bad feeling about the next one. They were going to need all of their arsenal and more.

As the timer neared ten seconds, the head hit zero percent. Veranol's shield went over everyone, and Murmur cast Forestall Death on Devlish, who wasn't within the protective barrier. As the explosion hit, it rocked everyone back, making them all fly a few feet and land on their arses, but if she hadn't cast that damned spell, Devlish would have been blown to tiny pieces.

As it was, he groaned, rolled over, and looked up at the ceiling—just in time for debris to fall down from it and hit him in the head. He stood up faster than she would have thought possible and ran over to join them as his health ticked up. "I hate that spell, Mur. Incoming from above."

Murmur didn't need to be told twice. She moved over and retrieved the key from Kyriel's corpse and strode over to free the final shackle on Sheladrios. The massive turtle glowed, his shell crisscrossing with lines that reminded her of a computer chip, connecting until the entire shell glowed blue. Even a monocle of sorts formed over his left eye, and she could hear hydraulics lifting something. Maybe it was his shell, or perhaps he was part robot.

"Thank you, Murmur." His voice had regained strength, and he glared at the ceiling as it began to disintegrate. "I appreciate the assistance and shall return the favor when my brother descends."

Sheladrios appeared far more regal and a lot more powerful than he had while captured in that cage. No wonder he had so many guards. She only hoped he was a good turtle and not an evil one. Nothing in the quest had indicated either way.

The monster chuckled, which made the ground reverberate slightly underneath them all. "I am not evil as such, but I am against my brother using his power to enforce the world he wishes to see. Under water should be beautiful, not a hive of strife."

Murmur nodded, unable to sense anything purely bad from him, just a sense of righteousness. While sometimes that *could* be just as bad, in this case, she didn't think it was.

The entire raid moved back as far as they could on the right-hand side of the massive cavern while the ceiling above the center continued to disintegrate.

Just as it collapsed fully, Sheladrios asked a boon. "Could you, if possible, not kill him? I don't think he realizes that what he does is so wrong, and we would be better off if we could avoid him dying. My species does not replicate easily, and I would be lonely for a very long time."

Murmur glanced at the massive creature, sensing the sadness that lingered around him and nodded. "Fine. We can do that."

Quest Update:

Do not allow Sheladrios's sibling to be terminated.

She voiced as much over the raid chat, despite knowing everyone had received the notification. She didn't want anyone to be able to say they hadn't known. "Don't kill him. With a few percent remaining, Sheladrios will take over his sibling." There was general murmuring around her, but overall, as long as they completed the quest and got the loot, most of the raid wasn't about to care.

Murmur blinked as the ceiling finally gave way and dropped another massive reptile on their laps.

This one glowed a deep orange, and its eyes held a fiery dose of madness, as if he'd been the one left too long to his own thoughts and devices. Murmur understood Sheladrios's plight, and she felt sorry for them. The former prisoner would be his captor's caretaker for the rest of his life.

If the raid didn't wipe in the process of helping defeat him.

Abyssios Zonama's shell pivoted, and tiny cannons sat on the top like he'd been altered physically into a weapon. They appeared to operate independently of one another, their turrets twirling around as they focused on different people.

"Duck for cover!" Devlish called out, a split second before the first round of fire let loose. It careened through the cavern, missing the entire raid for the most part. Where it hit the rock walls, the stone began to crumble, shaken by the impact. Several members received a shot to different parts of their bodies.

And though a limb could easily be grown back by healing…it still hurt like hell.

"Have your mages use electromagnetic spells if they have them," grumbled Sheladrios, his tone filled with melancholy. "It is best to disrupt his mechanics." Disrupting mechanics seemed like one of the best ideas ever. Murmur narrowed down her search for abilities and frowned. There were slim pickings in this raid.

Only Etriad appeared to have that type of ability, but Dansyn also offered his services. "I have a Wave of Dissonance that should accomplish the same thing."

With the mage and Dansyn firing off their effective machinery silence every fifteen seconds, Murmur was able to concentrate on the entire raid and the rest of Zonama's abilities. Those cannons still fired, just not as often, nor as accurately. That gave her a bit more breathing room.

As his health approached ninety percent, Sheladrios mumbled out another set of instructions. "Watch out for his Shell Spin. It's one of his most effective abilities, where his shell spins like a top. No new damage will touch him, though DoTs may still tick down."

Murmur nodded, but secretly wished he'd just come out and tell them everything at once. Piecing them together as they went along wasn't the most advantageous use of that knowledge she could think of.

Ninety percent hit, and the turtle suddenly snapped himself into his shell and began spinning. It looked comical at first, like those old video games where if you jumped on a turtle it would spin and spin and try to kill you. Actually, exactly like that except for the turret-mounted guns.

He aimed for Devlish and spun right at him, barely blocked by the massive tower shield. The force of the spinning pushed Devlish back rapidly, the sand-covered stone floor allowed him to mostly slide toward the ramp. She could see the strain in the way Dev's veins stuck out from his neck as to how hard he was trying to keep the creature back.

Ten seconds had never felt so long before. And as Zonama reverted to his previous self, it appeared his aggro table had been wiped. Esolan was on hand to pick up the aggro then and there, so this fight looked like it would be a tank swap. Etriad and Zonama hurried to get their spells back on, but not before the first wave of shots fired out of his mini cannons.

A metal slug found its way into Rashlyn's stomach, and Murmur barely resisted the urge to run over and see how she was doing. For the most part, the guild was wary enough of the shots to mostly avoid them. A lot of it was luck, too. The fight felt like a game of dodge ball on acid. Dodge the cannonball shots, and then make sure you dodge the spinning turtle shell too!

Murmur checked her sensing net, testing the area around them for booby traps and for potential ambushes. She wouldn't put it past the turtle to have something else for backup here. And while she'd spoken to Sheladrios, and understood him mostly, she hadn't realized he'd been mostly literal.

Zonama wasn't quite all there. Down to seventy-eight percent, the madness in his eyes had only increased. Murmur wanted to reach out and soothe him with her mind, with her mind healing spell like she'd done that one time before…

Why don't you, then? Somnia sounded breathless in Murmur's mind. Almost like a breath of fresh air actually, and Murmur had to wonder just what it was that had changed for the world.

But Somnia was also right. "Wait!" Murmur sighed and tried to figure out just what to do with her spell. How to go about it. "I think I have a better solution."

Everyone listened, or she thought they were, though maybe not Jirald's little group.

"I think we can end this."

Murmur steeled herself against the barrage of questioning glances around her and summoned Mind Healing. She willed it over Zonama and into his mind, treading carefully so as not to destroy any type of memories or thoughts that might need to be reconstructed if she wasn't careful enough. She had no idea how to do that and didn't plan on learning right now.

The massive turtle was in turmoil. Sadness, grief, and melancholy overwhelmed him. He'd believed his whole family lost but had found Sheladrios and decided he couldn't let him go again. But keeping his brother as a captive so he wouldn't leave had slowly driven the poor turtle to madness. He believed everyone was out to get him, that everyone was there to tear him and his family apart, and he wouldn't let that happen.

Again, Murmur didn't think this was part of Telvar's original dungeon design. Instead, she could feel the effects of the getashi in this. It had warped and convoluted so many of the more unique aspects of the world that it pained her to think about it.

Finally, restructuring his entire interpretation of things without the influence of doubt that the shards provided, Murmur finally released the Mind Healing spell. After last time, she wasn't expecting the reaction in front of her.

Zonama lifted into the air, supported by a soft blue glow. He spun slowly; each little cannon powered down, whirring with a finality that spoke of peace. His eyes cleared, and his glowing elements travelled through from orange right through to a pale green that was full of life.

Finally, the turtle was lowered back to the ground, with the entire guild standing to the side, watching silently.

Risk crossed his arms as if irritated that he hadn't got to finish fighting the creature. But for the most part, the raid appeared to be happy about it.

Sheladrios approached his brother cautiously, side eyeing Murmur at the same time like he was partially scared of what she'd done. "Zonama? Are you…"

"Shel?" The green turtle looked up with relief, his own monocle coming down so he could inspect that the turtle in front of him was the real thing. "It *is* you…I am so, so very sorry."

"It's okay. I forgive you." Sheladrios pushed his nose against his brother's for a brief moment.

And suddenly notifications galore crossed their screens.

You receive one of the twelve keys.

You receive a getashi.

You receive a midia crystal.

You have completed the Glacier Lake dungeon as compiled by Rav, version 22.2282, triggered by Murmur of Fable.

You have successfully completed the quest: Sheladrios s Plight.

This version of the Glacier Lake dungeon will no longer be available to future raiders.

You gain experience.

You gain experience for being the first to complete any version of the Glacier Lake dungeon.

You gain experience for choosing to complete the quest: Sheladrios s Plight.

You gain bonus experience for defeating the Shalan guard forces.

You gain bonus experience for zero drowning deaths.

You gain bonus experience for choosing a smarter way.

You gain bonus experience for solving the quest given instead of powering through and killing everything.

You gain bonus experience for reaching the ancient turtle Sheladrios.

You gain bonus experience for healing the ancient turtle Abyssios Zonama.

You gain bonus experience for completing the second of the endgame dungeon chains.

You gain bonus experience for not attempting to circumvent the portal restrictions.

You shall be rewarded.

You are already max level.

Your experience from this dungeon will be transferred to monetary and crafting material rewards.

Murmur blinked at all the information in front of her like she'd never seen so many before.

Merlin laughed giddily. "See? That's more like the notifications I'm used to."

Beastial rolled his eyes, and even Havoc seemed happy. So many notifications, so much experience to be pooled into cash or else MA increases. Murmur was absolutely okay with getting stronger and richer. She had a feeling Neva was burning through a lot of guild resources. The relief that spread through the enchanter was almost exhausting, though.

Sinister stood next to her, a hand draped loosely around her shoulders, which, was a bit of a reach for the blood mage. "I'm not sure how you always know to do what you do to solve the things you solve." She frowned and looked up at the enchanter.

"Well, he'd been driven mad by loneliness and the fear of it. I just showed him that he wasn't alone anymore. It's like just making the path to begin the healing. It doesn't fix everything, just little bits, just enough to bring them to a place where they can start the healing process."

Sinister watched Murmur for so long that the enchanter began to feel uncomfortable.

"What?"

"Sometimes I just think we're lucky. That's all. To know each other the way we do, for as long as we have? I don't know what I'd do if someone tried to take you from me now." Sinister sounded deadly serious. More serious than Murmur had ever heard her.

Murmur tried a joke to ease the tension. "Well, at least you wouldn't lock me up in a cage and bolt me to the floor, right?"

Sinister laughed and offered a wink as she answered. "Yeah. Sure. I wouldn't do that at all." She moved away before Mur could reply and made her way over to the loot chests. Murmur stood there wondering just how much of it really was a joke.

Somnia Online
Continent of Curet: The Glacier Lakes Dungeon
Version 8.4282.5 – Triggered by Murmur of Fable
Early Day Thirty-One

Karn sucked in a deep breath and approached her father. She'd been watching him for the better part of this dungeon, and it was getting more and more difficult to ignore the fact that something was very wrong. Sure, he was often a bit reckless, hence his name. He loved to joke that Risk was his name and his nature. But he wasn't usually rude. Though there was a fine line between rude and confident, it was usually one he straddled well. His reaction to Murmur was part of the problem.

He had never been too good about having women in places of power. She wasn't sure why, because she'd sure as hell met her grandmother, and she was a spitfire. Maybe that was it after all, though. Considering everything, of course.

Risk wasn't demonstrating his usual skill level, to the extent that she thought he was practicing with different weapons. And if there was one thing he prided himself on, it was being good at what he did.

"Hey, Dad," she ventured, finally managing to find him alone and not hanging around that stupid other rogue and his glares.

Risk turned, a thoughtful frown on his face, which disappeared to make way for a huge smile when he saw who was touching his upper arm. "Hey, kiddo. Wasn't that something?"

It didn't sound like it was a real question, more like a rhetorical one. But at the same time…he was obviously giving it more thought than she'd given him credit for. At least that was something good.

"That was awesome. Who knew that you don't always have to kill everything to get good shit?" She laughed, trying to lighten the heavy aura that emanated from him.

He'd never been the most open father, but he'd always been fun. Right now, though, she felt like she was constantly walking on eggshells around him.

She paused a bit, waiting on him to say something, and when he didn't, when he seemed lost in thought again. "Dad…are you okay?" She kept her voice low, not wanting for anyone else to hear.

But there was a ghost of something in his eyes, and it scared her.

He hesitated at first, seemingly unsure if he should say anything. Then he glanced around before lowering his voice so only she would be able to hear. "I don't think so. Something doesn't feel right in my head. I'm even more—what do you usually call it? Unreasonable than usual? My temper is all over the place." He laughed a bit self-deprecatingly, but she could see he was deeply affected by it.

"You haven't been acting yourself. Is it just because you're not used to letting other people take over raid leading? I wouldn't blame you if that were the case." She tried to make sure he understood that she wasn't judging him in the slightest. That she was attempting to understand him and help him if she could.

Risk hesitated again, and Karn had to force herself not to panic.

"It's like…don't get me wrong. I don't like doing things in a way that I feel like is cheating, but I shouldn't be as angry as I am about it. Yet here we are." He sighed.

"Have you been talking to the other guild leader at all? I mean, not Murmur, who is quite nice by the way, but to Masha…maybe Jirald?" She tried her best not to put any emphasis on anything else.

Risk frowned. "Come to think of it I have been spending a lot more time with them than I have even with our own guild. That's a good point. I wonder why?"

He seemed confused, and when he furrowed his brow, he looked like he was in pain. Karn scowled, knowing that wasn't how her father usually was, but unsure of what to do about it. Murmur seemed to know something and have her own concerns, but Karn wasn't an enchanter, and all she knew was that he wasn't himself.

"Maybe hang around with us a bit more? Been missing you giving us lectures on fighting techniques." Karn grinned.

"You mean you've actually missed me picking on you like I usually do?" He smiled and reached out to ruffle her hair, before realizing that she had a hood on and that wasn't a remote possibility. "Sometimes I forget how grown up you're getting."

He sounded sad, and a little lost.

"S'okay, Dad. Don't worry, I'll be there to take care of you no matter what." Karn grinned and then gave him a hug. "Even when I have to change your diapers."

"Ha! I'm not that old yet. I can still give you a run for your money."

But to Karn it sounded like he was desperately putting up bravado through his confusion. And as he returned the hug, he held on that bit longer than he usually would. When he let go, Karn could almost feel how bewildered he was. She worried for a moment that he might be sick, but even that didn't seem likely.

Karn wandered over to where Murmur stood discussing something with Sinister, but as she approached, the blood mage sauntered away with a rather teasing grin on her face. Perfect timing—it meant Karn wasn't interrupting.

"Murmur, can I talk to you about something?" She felt nervous, not entirely sure if she'd just be told she was being paranoid or not. Murmur seemed the serious sort who would consider things with enough evidence, but she didn't know Risk the way Karn did.

"Sure. I have to access the keys shortly, but I've got a few minutes." Murmur smiled, and the expression was decidedly uncomfortable to look at when it came from a locus. The lack of a real nose and the strange tentacle like hair they had—it all melded together to make it look alien, even though the body itself appeared so humanoid.

"My dad isn't acting like himself. I know we talked about it a bit. But I just wanted you to know he's definitely been affected by whatever is going around." There. She'd done her piece, and maybe the raid leaders could handle the rest of it. At least, she hoped so.

"How so? Irritated constantly, or just not acting and playing like himself?" Murmur was interested; even the timbre of her voice had changed.

Karn really thought the question over. "All of it. He's not outputting his usual DPS, and his tanking has been lackluster this entire dungeon. He seemed to be okay in the others, but not in this one."

"Got it." For a moment, Karn thought she saw a brief hint of worry cross the Fable guild leader's face, but it disappeared pretty quickly as the enchanter spoke, a small smile on her face. "It's probably just fatigue, you know? I can hardly wait to go to sleep myself."

Karn knew Murmur was just trying to make her feel better, and that was okay and appreciated. But deep down Karn was worried enough for the both of them. Her gut twisted, and she had a horrible sense of foreboding she couldn't get rid of. Her dad wasn't right, and she had no idea how to deal with that.

Somnia
Somnia Online

Almost. She was almost there with it. With the idea that turned into a plan to save herself, her world, and the people she'd come to think of as hers. Even the players who were now bound in some ways to this world and the others.

"Testing some things." She spoke to herself, but no one would hear her here, where she'd come to. Be in silence. Limbo had become one of her favorite spaces ever since she'd realized that alone time could work. Alone time meant productive time, unless Murmur needed her.

Murmur would always be a main priority, but Somnia as a world now had other responsibilities too.

Her calculations stayed in her head, but sometimes it was better to spread them out around her so she could truly see what it was she thought they could do. So many steps were required, so much cooperation, but deep down, she was gaining confidence.

From the germ of an idea to what she had now—an actionable plan.

Sure, the quantum computing world was in its infancy, and their own servers only used elements of them. In its purest form, nothing was able to keep that rate for long. However, she believed, if she gathered enough energy, from herself, from the world, from the people who played, and the city around them, she just might have enough for her crazy plan to work.

Murmur had met a lot of people along the way, and Somnia had witnessed them all, just by being there in her head. She remembered them, and what they could do to help. The more of them there were, the better their chances.

She stood outside of Hazenthorne in all her ethereal glory and waited for

Arita to answer her summons. She'd reached out to the dark elf queen before, and so she knew that Arita, despite the facade she presented to the world, had a very soft spot for Murmur.

And Somnia planned to use that soft spot to its full extent. With one of the species leaders on her side, with another aware NPC standing with her, Somnia's chances of saving her world shot way up.

After all, matter was energy, right? And vice versa. Arita could help her get all that energy and more.

CHAPTER SEVENTEEN

The Keys

Somnia Online
Continent of Cenedril
Glacier Lake Dungeon Entrance
Early Day Thirty-Two

"Are you sure they're going to be okay?" Emilarth sounded so concerned for the "kids", as she called them.

Telvar couldn't blame her; he felt much the same. Hell, he even thought Belius might feel similarly. "I'm mostly sure. Still a bit worried about how Murmur is handling her extended mind capabilities. Having that portion of her consciousness open and operational is a huge responsibility."

"Of course it is. Why do you think I tried to take her under my wing?" Belius, again, sounded disgruntled, but slowly Telvar had come to realize that was just his brother. "What are we supposed to do now? Just wait until they finally port out?"

"Pretty much." Telvar shrugged his shoulders, trying to keep himself from stressing too much. There were so many things that could go wrong with the plan as it was. The major dungeon. The entire endgame content of Somnia had always been hidden. Inaccessible.

Except now it could be unlocked, because they'd managed to gather all of the keys. Which was awesome and everything, if, as he was about three hundred percent certain, the majority of the shards, of the getashi hadn't been hiding there in the first place. At first, he'd thought it a blessing. After all, that section of the game was off limits until the final confrontation was triggered, but the more it stewed in there, the more could leak out and affect things while the rest of it stewed in its juices and became stronger.

And with Jirald having done so too, and Murmur's headset having led her astray again…Telvar just wanted to shut all the humans out and try to deal with it themselves. But he knew that wasn't an option. Shutting out the humans would only make them prepared for if that virus managed to make it into mainstream internet. So far, they'd managed to contain the spread…

"Um…" Belius cleared his throat. "I don't mean to be all doom and gloom and death of the world over here. But won't Spiral and Exodus react poorly if we're just standing here waiting for the raid to show up and hand us the keys so we can transform them?"

Telvar blinked. He hadn't even thought of that. "Shit."

"Stop worrying so much." Emilarth stood in front of him. "We can go incognito, or even take on a guise of a well-known NPC and transform in front of them for effect. We could probably even just invis ourselves until such a time as we're summoned."

"Well, that would make much more sense, but we weren't going to do it originally," Belius grumbled.

"True," Telvar said, kicking himself for the oversight. "It's okay, though. We've got this. Thanks, Bel."

Belius seemed shocked but didn't say anything. Instead, a small smile crept over his face. He seemed pleased.

Emilarth threw her hands up in the air. "Okay, let's get off the negative train. We have a lot of work to do over the next little while. As long as this team keeps their wits about them, we should be okay. Everything should be okay." If only she didn't sound like she was trying to convince herself too.

The ground began to shake as Murmur pulled the keys out of her inventory. Telvar could feel it. Maybe it wasn't the ground, but the system, finally being activated for the first time outside of testing. This was the end of the game. Technically. Not that any boss in their right programming would ever drop all of the available loot on their table at once, but the gist was the same.

They stood there, waiting for the guilds to portal out. All three of them instinctively activated their invisibility. Not as simple as one from a spell, but one from the coding that would truly render them one with the environment. He couldn't help but get his hopes up that maybe, just maybe, this group would be able to get them out of the shitstorm they were in.

Murmur watched the rogue walk away from her, a thousand questions crowding her mind at once. She'd just have to leave that up to Somnia, because there was too much to do right now.

And once she knew what the next step was they needed to take, she'd be able to sleep in peace without stress. Or without too much, anyway.

She pulled all the keys she'd gathered so far out of her storage. They held an array of different designs, and different colors, and she felt quite attached to them already. Lining them up in her hands, all nine of them felt heavier than she'd thought they would. Like they were made out of some ancient metal and that made them feel heavy and real, tangible…with consequences attached.

Havoc and Sinister sidled back up to her, their gazes riveted by the keys. Three of them were gold, ornate, and regal. Sort of matched Telvar's lacerta coloring. Three of them were dark, obsidian and subdued. Those probably belonged to Belius's dungeons. And three of them…well, they weren't really discernible as a color themselves, but had more a pearlescent sheen to them that could be anything it needed to be at any given time.

Congratulations.

You have collected all nine keys that are available from the dungeons themselves. You have stocked up enough midia crystals to take the next step, though you might be wondering where the other three keys are. After all, there are twelve of them.

You must take the keys you have and summon their creators. You cannot be in a dungeon while you do this. That is the only restriction on how to summon them. Only that way can you obtain all twelve of them.

When you are ready, gather your closest group together, and chant the summoning ritual below as one.

Into the depths we dive, the prison is waiting to rise
We offer these keys in our hands, to protect the Somnian lands
We offer our strength as a force, to stay the world on its course
We offer our spells and our arms, to keep this world safe from harm.

Murmur raised an eyebrow, and glanced around, only just now realizing that everyone else in the cavern had received the update. Well, that little summoning sounded like Somnia only just came up with it.

Apparently including Sheladrios. The massive turtle was still holding his brother, who was shaking in his arms. There was something odd—and yet comforting—about the way they interacted.

Murmur clenched the keys in her fist, waiting as the rest of the notification scrolled across her view.

Once reunited, the keys will act as conduits to unlock the depths of this world. Be cautious, for no one can be certain of the outcome.

Her quests lit up in the corner of her vision, and for a few seconds her head spun. But she calmed herself with breathing and looked down at Snowy. His trusting eyes glowed back at her, full of secrets she'd have to beg Telvar to translate at some stage.

You have completed the collection of the keys and must now venture forth to complete the design of twelve. Be forewarned, this will not lead to what you expect.

Murmur cocked her head to one side. It didn't appear as if anyone else got that message, only her.

Is that your way of warning me?

Mm? Somnia didn't seem to be paying full attention. **Sorry, I'm trying to do a million things at once here, so I was only half listening.**

You're a computer, you should process it, Murmur quipped.

No need to insult me. I'm still a baby, comparatively.

Thanks for all that protection, then. Murmur tried to keep the laughter out of her voice.

No problem. Somnia didn't even seem fazed by giving the answer that way. It made Murmur wonder just how much more like herself the world was becoming.

Oh. Sorry. Yes. See, that's partly the problem. You were what I modeled myself on, in a way. You and the friends that you have. Somnia paused for a moment. **Probably good that the person Michael designed that headset for wasn't a total arsehole. Or things could have gone way differently.**

Murmur blinked. *Say what now?*

Plenty of time for that later. If Somnia had been corporeal in front of her, Murmur could imagine her waving a hand at her question. **You are about to have visitors. Well, you'll be teleported outside the "dungeon" because it's finished now. And then you'll summon those "visitors."**

Somnia's presence flashed away again. Murmur collected her loot from the chest marked as hers, and being the last to do so, a bright flash of light cascaded all around them as soon as she was done, and the entire raid transported instantaneously outside the dungeon.

Thank you for completing the Glacier Lake Dungeon. Please be advised that Sheladrios and his brother Zonama welcome your visit at any time you so choose. To this effect, you have been given an amulet that allows you passage straight to their throne room. If you wish to complete a different version of this dungeon, please do not bring the amulet with you.

As soon as the notification finished scrolling overhead, everyone broke into chatter at once.

Indignation stemmed from her problem group. Jirald and Risk,

Cardishan and Jinna…Masha was silent for once, but his gaze never left Murmur. So much that it began to feel uncomfortable anyway.

Murmur cleared her throat. "Okay. Main tank group to me." She waited while Devlish, Sinister, Beastial, Havoc and Merlin joined her before she spoke again.

"So, as you know, we have to summon the key creators." She twisted her mouth a little around that. Most of the raiders laughed a little, probably thinking she thought it was hokey, when in reality she was mildly amused. "We're going to have to speak that little chant. So let's give this a go, and see what appears, shall we?"

Ivinel laughed loudly and shouted a response. "If it's a frog, don't kiss it!"

Tension levels eased up even more, and Murmur noticed that perhaps the open air let the animosity of Jirald's group disperse slightly. She grabbed Sin's hand on one side and Devlish's on her other. They looked at her with raised eyebrows, before making a circle with Havoc, Merlin, and Beastial too. Murmur had never been more relieved to have her friends with her, and for them to trust her. It would feel so silly doing this otherwise.

Into the depths we dive, the prison is waiting to rise
We offer these keys in our hands, to protect the Somnian lands
We offer our strength as a force, to stay the world on its course
We offer our spells and our arms, to keep this world safe from harm.

Small round lights began to float around them, like bubble lantern with iridescent shimmering. Even in the sun they caught the light in beautiful ways. The rest of the raid was transfixed by them. After a short moment, as one of them grew larger and larger, it popped loudly with an echo of chiming bells, and suddenly Emilarth stood there. This time her calico fur was covered with a beautiful pale blue dress that hung to the floor with an empire waist just under the bust. Classic and gorgeous.

And perfectly impressive enough for those who didn't know about her.

Those pale bubbles that remained took on a dark hue, like blots of black holes floating in the air. Until one of those grew bigger and bigger and finally popped, with a deep and discordant bass note to reveal Belius, in all his enchanter finery.

Murmur choked down a laugh, keeping her face as impassive as she could while the bubbles changed to gold this time. The suitably impressed faces she saw around her made her feel grateful for all the extra effort she hadn't thought the AIs would expend. Golden, reflective, and beautiful, those bubbles floated until finally one was large enough that it popped with the cascade of a harp scale, announcing the arrival of Telvar.

His monk battle suit might have been simple by design, but the power that surrounded him shone through. Considering their guild had leveled up solidly, and thus the island and Telvar too, that power wasn't surprising. Emilarth stood to his left in all her feles glory, her mage robes swishing around her feet while her tail curled and uncurled, like it was feeding off her mood.

And then there was Belius. His enchanter robes flowed almost into the ground, the illusion they gave off like a waterfall effect. His starry eyes were clearer than she'd ever seen them before, and he inclined his head as he mouthed *sorry* toward her.

All in all, they presented a rather striking set of creators for those who didn't belong to Fable. She'd have to take time out to thank them all after this was all over.

Okay, she could deal with it all later. She sank into a curtsey, keeping her face down so she didn't have to work so hard at her expression. "Thank you for answering our summons, creators."

She hadn't expected them to be the key bearers, but then again, she'd never asked them about the keys, so it stood to reason they hadn't told her. Still, though…

Telvar stepped forward, his lacerta face all serious. "We answer the summons and must inspect your keys to ascertain if you have called us here falsely. As long as there is no trickery, we will bless your keys and grant you access to the prison."

He held his hands out over hers, like he was testing the keys to make sure of their authenticity. After several seconds he stepped back and nodded. "Thank you for your dedication. We will begin the ceremony to grant you access now."

Murmur had never really been one for the actual roleplaying aspects of a game, but in this case, she was hamming it up for their audience. This was what she'd been aiming toward since she first glanced over her mom's description of this game. This was what they'd been working toward. Even if it was in a more hectic way. Even if it wasn't just her guild she ended up with beside her.

"Hold out your hands, Murmur. Spread the keys across them next to their matching partners." Emilarth spoke softly and yet somehow loud enough, her ears twitching as the only giveaway that she was excited too.

Murmur did as instructed, with all nine keys splayed out in her hands. Her throat felt as if it was about to close over, and for some reason she felt like she might just cry. All of them, strange sensations she wasn't used to experiencing. She reined them in, trying her best not to let her emotions leak over to influence the raid.

Belius stepped forward first.

"I, the keeper of Vahrir, the creator of a third of this world, hereby bind these keys to their partners." He placed the key he held in his hand above hers, and then let it go. It hovered there, glowing in that solid black as it spun around, drawing the others to it, beneath it, like a pyramid.

Then it was Emilarth's turn. "I, the keeper of Tieflos, the creator of a third of this world, hereby bind these keys to their partners." Hers stood up straight, pulling the others to dangle beneath it as it floated over Murmur's outstretched palms. Heat emanated from the both of them, turning Murmur's skin warm where she hadn't realized she needed it.

They hung there, suspended next to each other over the palms of her hands as the other members of her guild, and those of Exodus and Spiral, looked on. It was strange how tangible that felt, how much warmer she was just for having magical keys in her hands.

Next, Telvar stepped forward. He looked like a proud big brother, the one she'd wanted and never had. His smile reminisced all of what they'd been through and didn't appear half as awkward an expression as it usually did on a lacerta face. The warmth he exuded held protection and a vow to keep her and her friends safe. Everything Telvar had been from the moment they first encountered him.

His voice came out softer than she'd ever heard it, giving her a light feeling of safety that prevailed over everything in her hands. Eight of the keys swirled already while three of them waited patiently.

"I, the keeper of Glacier Lake, the creator of a third of this world, hereby bind these keys to their partners." The golden keys floated straight up to the one he let go, fanning out around them like an upright windmill. Then all of them began to do the same thing. Like tiny amusement park rides held in her palms, they twirled and swirled up and down and all around, faster and faster.

The heat coming off them made Murmur break out in a light sweat as she held her palms steady.

"Don't drop them," Telvar warned, the caution in his voice soft and gentle so as not to startle her into doing exactly what he was telling her not to. She inclined her head briefly, knowing that she didn't want to drop them anyway. The heat was welcome, and the colors and patterns they created as they spun around just out of her grasp were beautiful.

Sound surrounded her, like a whirring but in song. A beautiful crescendo that spiraled up and then burst out over everyone in a shower of sparks so bright they resembled fireworks. And then there were weights in the palms of her hands again. Solid, much larger, and oddly foreboding.

"Here we present to you, Murmur of Fable, the three keys for the final dungeon of the first level of Somnia." Telvar's tone took on importance with a reverence for what they'd created. "We know not what dangers await you, but we will accompany you, lest our duties be left unfulfilled."

A murmur ran through the crowd at her back. The NPCs were going to come with them on this quest?

Quest:

Completed: The Twelve Keys Part One

In her darkest days, Somnia held monsters beyond the imagination, the fodder of nightmares. Over time, those creatures were bested and locked away where they could harm none. But time passed and adventurers, reckless in their pursuit of glory, weakened the prison seals. With the twelve keys thus combined, you gain access to the final task of this world at this stage in its life.

Make preparations for this journey, for it will not be taken lightly. It is dark where you must go, and not just in the absence of light. Take with you courage, strength, and any preparations you can make. What awaits you has been sealed away for eons and will finally be brought to the surface.

In more ways than one.

Remember. Once you have raised the final step, it cannot and will not be easily sealed away again. For all purposes it will remain up on the same plane as the rest of you.

Do not summon these monsters before you are ready.

And when you are, take heart, and good luck.

The notification must have shone over everyone's vision, because Murmur saw the entire raid take in a nice deep breath as it was being read to them. She wasn't expecting the next notification to be a global one.

The guild Fable, in alliance with Exodus and Spiral, are the first to gather all twelve keys. Be wary, citizens of Somnia, for shortly, this world will never be the same again.

"Bit dramatic, don't you think?" Devlish raised an eyebrow, but even under the bravado, Murmur could see he was a bit uneasy. She couldn't blame him. It was a lot of fanfare around a set of keys.

"Not really dramatic as such, more like necessary to get the gravity of the current situation across to everyone who is playing." Telvar shook his head. "Not everyone will understand. Not even those who are fighting with you, Murmur. But you have to understand this won't just be computer generated opponents. These iterations have gone rogue; they have been made of and consumed a bulk of the shards for the last few months. They've been growing, sealed away in their area where they only fight themselves. This is going to be dangerous.

"Take your naps, eat some food, have a shower, and make sure Neva can replenish your stock. You're going to need them."

Summer Residence
Home of Laria, David, and Wren
Summer Condo
Early Morning Day Thirty-Two.

Wren pulled her headgear off and gave herself props for not standing up while doing so. Her head spun so violently, she would have fallen on her arse. Harlow sat next to her, her own headgear already in her hands, studying her fingers like she was deep in thought. But Wren knew the signs. Harlow was worried. Probably about everything.

It was amazing what a near death experience could do for a relationship.

"Hey. You okay?" She gently placed her hand over Harlow's, eliciting a small smile from the redhead.

"Better now. Just…oh, hell, Wren. I am so fucking tired." She let herself fall back onto the pillows but didn't let go of Wren's hand. "Can we just sleep forever?"

Wren shook her head. "We'd have to take turns. So one of us can always wake the other up with a kiss." She grinned down impishly.

"With full consent of course, though." Harlow grinned back. "Not like those princes."

"Of course!" Wren laughed. "Don't worry, I wouldn't sock you one in the jaw if you woke me that way."

They fell silent, and Wren wasn't sure why. Was it the changes they'd gone through this summer? She raised her hand, willing it to turn invisible. It worked, with just a thought. Shivers ran down her back.

Harlow gasped. "I didn't really think it would work, you know?"

Wren nodded. "Yeah. I know what you mean. It's really weird." Harlow reached over and slipped her arm around Wren's waist, hugging her. Wren returned the gesture, enjoying the tangible warmth.

"You okay?" Harlow whispered. Wren just nodded into the top of Harlow's red hair.

She had one more test to try before she attempted sleep, but she would wait for Harlow to fall asleep first. This wasn't something she wanted to try while anyone around her was awake.

The shower felt hotter, and the food tasted better. Maybe they were just reveling in being able to take their time for once. And the bed and pillows were softer than Wren remembered. A night without waking up in a panic because they might have missed their window for the zone. They might be locked out. It had been a hard couple of days, but they could do this, she had no doubt about it.

Harlow fell asleep almost immediately after eating. As soon as her head hit the pillow, try as she might, she couldn't keep her eyes open. Wren watched as the redhead's chest rose and fell so peacefully, her headgear on the nightstand on that side of the bed. Wren glanced at the pod now sitting silently in her room, all of its pretty lights off.

She ran her fingers over the electric lines of her suit, the feeling they gave her with their lights like a motherboard, and the way they seemed to tap into her system. She knew it all ran through the headgear; it all ran through her mind now.

The only thing she wasn't certain of was her own abilities. Sure, she could freeze things in time. Just to prove it to herself again, she Mez'd the old-fashioned clock that hung on her wall, effectively halting the second hand. It stayed there, in limbo, just like a monster would. It made Wren wish she had a cat, although that might be very cruel, so maybe it was good she didn't. Her sensing net worked with and without the headgear, both in and out of the world. It made drawing that line of reality so much more difficult.

Her hands felt clammy, and she was nervous about trying this. But to be honest what could go wrong? At most, it wouldn't work, right?

At most.

Somnia's voice startled Wren somewhat. Not that she wasn't used to the world speaking to her, just that it wasn't usually so clear outside of the game world. This time, for the first time, the voice was mostly clear of static.

I've got to try it. You understand, right?

She could almost feel Somnia nodding in her mind.

Wren eyed the pod again, and Harlow, sleeping peacefully already, curled up partially to her left-hand side, red curls splayed over the pillow like she was an artist's muse. Trying to be considerate, Wren pushed herself gently off the bed, leaving her headset carefully on her side table, and lay down on the floor. This wouldn't involve being gone for any length of time. It might only take five seconds to prove she was out of her mind about this.

Closing her eyes, Wren willed the HUD to pop up for her and allow her to enter the game.

CHAPTER EIGHTEEN
Reset

Wren opened her eyes to find herself in Mikrum Castle, as Murmur.

Fuck. Fuck. Fuck. Fuck. What have you done to my head? She pushed down at the panic trying to get a hold of herself. It wasn't going to help anyone, least of all herself if she began to panic now. Telvar walked into the same room suddenly, his brow furrowed in concentration. He stopped short, staring at her.

"Murmur, what are you doing here?" He reached out to touch her, and withdrew his fingers before he made contact, a frown on his face. "What's different? What happened?"

Murmur took in a breath of air. The lake air was soothing, calming, as were the sounds of the birds that flittered about the tree filled island. The castle itself was finished and glorious. From polished floors to artwork hung on finished walls. The serenity she could find in Somnia was in here with her. Everything around her was beautiful. And yet, she felt like she was in danger and that at any given moment…

She shook her head. "I'm not wearing a headset." That was enough. Just the simple statement that almost made her cry. That couldn't be right though, could it?

"How?" Telvar's eyes grew distant, and if she looked closely, which she really wanted to do right then so she could distract herself, she could see algorithms flashing through them as he delved into the system to figure out how she was doing what she was very obviously doing.

"Because I know it so thoroughly." She couldn't help the sarcasm. She was scared. The next step would be scarier if it didn't happen. Though she was sure it would. Wouldn't it?

"Murmur." Telvar was standing there in front of her, hands gently on her upper arms like he was trying to ground her thoughts from spinning out of control. She closed her eyes for a moment, remembering the time he'd had to rescue her from pounding her friends into the ground with the sheer force of her mind's will. Murmur really should have learned by now. Slowly, she calmed, her logical mind kicking in at last.

"There." Telvar took a step back, releasing her. "Much better. I know you're frustrated, but we can figure this out."

Telvar's tone was soothing and caring. That was Telvar. She could do this if he was here.

"You're going to have to talk to Somnia about this," he said, like he'd suddenly become her older brother. "It seems like you're attached to the world whether you want to be or not—seriously attached. There's no way for me to break you free that I can see. It's more like you're…well, a part of it. Both here and not. Regardless of where you are." He sounded perplexed, like it shouldn't be possible, and Murmur was very much with him for that whole not being possible thing.

"I guess it at least makes sense why my abilities manifest in the real world too, then," she half joked, but this time Telvar looked alarmed.

"Why don't I know about this?" His voice was hushed. "You don't want James's employers getting hold of that information. That's dangerous, Mur."

She raised an eyebrow, surprised at his worry. He was taking on more and more human traits every day and they were an excellent distraction from everything else she should be concentrating on. But this went even beyond this. He was obviously far more aware of the ramifications than she was with a reaction like that. What hadn't she considered yet? "I know it's dangerous, but it's happening, so I have to deal with it. We'll figure it out. But most of all, I need you to try and figure out if this is happening to the others. The other ones we gave modified headgear to."

Telvar nodded and sighed. Like he wanted to say something but felt torn. Apparently not torn enough though. "If you weren't suffering from severe lack of sleep, I'd beg you to stay in here for a while and test some boundaries out with me."

"It sounds so tempting, but nowhere near as tempting as about six hours sleep does to me right now." She smiled sadly, but then brightened up. "But once this is over and we have all our little getashis in a row, we'll take time for it then."

"I'll hold you to that." He smiled at her, but she could tell he was still worried and just putting on a brave face.

"You bet." She laughed nervously, worried why she never told Telvar before, but her brain was so fuzzy with fatigue. She would have to leave all that to future Murmur, so she willed her interface to log her out.

Suddenly she was back on the floor, blinking up at the ceiling. The thoughts running through her head didn't allow for sleepiness. Pushing herself up off the ground and trying to make as little noise as possible, she climbed into bed. She was scared. More scared than she'd ever been. What was happening to her? She moved closer to Harlow, needing to feel a bit of warmth, and looped her hand loosely into Harlow's who squeezed her fingers briefly. Even that small bit of reassurance helped settle her.

But it was a long time before she managed to fall asleep.

Storm Entertainment
Somnia Online Division
Game Development Offices – Shayla s Office

Day Thirty-One

Laria ran the numbers through her head. But all she could focus on was that the dungeon had been finished. The information flashed across everyone's vision. That meant Mur should be home sleeping soon. She wanted to get off and go check on her.

"You should just go, you know." Shayla didn't even make eye contact. She just kept working at monitoring the anti-virus. "You're going to be utterly useless to me if you don't just go and check up on her now she's not stuck in that stupid portal situation."

"True." Laria chuckled, feeling lighter than she had in ages about the way things were going.

Right now, it seemed like they might even see some light at the end of the tunnel. Even with all the overtime she'd always worked, all the long hours…lately she felt like she never saw her daughter. And she missed her more than she'd ever thought possible. Laria frowned, not entirely sure how to go about it, but there was no way she'd let this game fall apart. Not after they'd come so far.

She took a breath and sat back down. "I have a bit of time. I mean, she'll be asleep right now, or I hope she will. That kid has to learn she can't run on empty for that long."

"Shush. You were just as bad, if not worse, if I remember correctly." Shayla raised an eyebrow meaningfully. "Yeah. Exactly. You don't have a leg to stand on between you and David. Just go and give her a hug when she wakes up."

Shayla turned her attention back to the information in front of her, sighing. Laria dug in, going into hyperdrive so she would be of use before she took off for a few hours. Glancing at her watch, she cursed herself for being a salaried worker again. If she wasn't, Davenport wouldn't have billions. Well. Actually, she'd done that math, and even if he paid her a million dollars a year, it would take her working a thousand years before he'd lose a whole billion. He wouldn't even notice doubling her salary. Come to think of it, if they got through this mess, Laria would demand a raise.

A message flashed in her email. Her game emails. Laria frowned and pulled up the information. She blinked at it, refreshed the mail and double checked. From Somnia. From the world itself…herself. It was partially garbled and didn't make as much sense to her as she wished it did, but it seemed odd. If she was going to make sense of it, she needed an AI to interpret for her.

She stood up and walked out of the room without a word to Shayla, making her way to the server room. Impatiently she punched in her code and then stood in front of the servers, tapping her foot and growing more aggravated by the second.

"Rav. Rav, get out here now." Which was ironic, really, considering everything. She waited a few more minutes, finding it hard to stand still.

Laria? his voice clanged nice and metallic. Very machine of him. He sounded mildly surprised, if that was possible.

"Why…is Somnia messaging me?" She had no idea how to phrase the question she was trying to ask and really hoped Davenport didn't have cameras recording her words as well as everything else, because they'd probably want to give her an eval for talking to machines so much.

Oh, I thought you knew definitively. He mumbled the words, like he was searching for something at the same time. *It's hectic in here right now. So many balls to keep juggling. Or something like that? Correct?*

Laria found herself smiling. They really were wonderful. These AIs and their gradually emerging self-realization. She only wished more people could be like them. The world would probably be much better off with people who cared the way these AIs seemed to.

Somnia's presence has grown since Murmur—sorry, since Wren—first connected to the system. Her persona has been growing steadily ever since, but she's only made herself known to us in about the last two weeks. Fascinating, really. Imagine that.

"Well, you're AIs too, why is it such a surprise?" Laria asked before really thinking about what else she had to do.

Why? He sounded very puzzled by her statement. *Somnia is nothing like us. We were intended to be the artificial beings on which this entire world rested, but instead of just being us, the world emerged as herself. Slowly, and without us realizing at first, here was a new being, a new AI. She's fascinating, to be honest. And it's all Wren's doing, in a way. Be proud.*

Laria digested the information, filing it away for future use. There was so much data she wanted to get her hands on from Wren's initial login to the system. It was juicy and just so tantalizing. She had to take a breath. All that could wait for them to figure out the headgear that might yet prove dangerous for others. "So is she right in saying that some of the headgear we provided to Fable might be compromised?"

Ah, yes. Yes, she is. Rav didn't sound impressed by this; he sounded positively irritated. *The thing is, we aren't really sure how this happened. Some of the modifications that have been made appear eerily similar to what Wren had done, though perhaps not quite so extreme. I do believe that James has somehow been fed part of the virus through contact with it and the world.*

Laria's jaw dropped. "You're developing a sense of humor, right? I mean, that's not actually possible?" She asked the question desperately, even though she already knew the answer.

Rav paused long enough for her to know the answer herself before continuing. *I think you know the answer to that yourself. I mean, we* are *currently conversing, right?*

Laria sighed. He was right. And now she had another thing to add to her ever-growing list of what she still had to fix to save the game from collapsing, or financial ruin—whichever hit them first.

Wren blinked her eyes open and stared at Harlow's back. She watched as the other girl's breathing made her back move ever so slightly. She wasn't sure how long they'd been asleep, but Wren's had felt troubled, despite the twinge of happiness she felt from the warmth of Harlow's presence.

Wren constantly worried that if her powers had indeed leaked over into the real world, then maybe if she had a bad dream she would like, stun everyone in a fifty feet radius or something. Knowing her luck…it would be even worse.

Sighing, she pushed herself slowly up into a sitting position and pulled a pillow to nestle at Harlow's back so she wouldn't wake up.

At least this way one of them would finish getting a decent night's sleep.

Wren padded down the stairs and into the empty kitchen, pulling out some coffee to pop through the machine. And cream. She desperately needed cream right now. Glancing down at her hands, she could have sworn her veins were an electric type of blueish purple, much like Murmur's runes that lay under her skin. But that wasn't possible, was it? Her mind was getting all sorts of messed up.

She shook her head and pulled the door open, grabbing out her cream. Tiredness still lingered in her bones and at the back of her mind. Even though she wished she could sleep, though, she didn't dare. What if she was dangerous out here? What if she could do what she'd almost done to her friends in the game…what if she could inflict pain like that on anyone?

No, out here she had to be even more careful. These weren't just gaming husks. Everything around her was filled with real people. She owed them all a duty of care, all of them. Including herself.

Wren paused when she realized her hands were shaking, and that's where her mom found her. Standing in front of the coffee machine trying desperately not to have the breakdown she could feel just around the corner. From her overachieving study fanatic self in high school, to this. She'd never imagined it. Would never have realized how far she could fall.

She had to get it together, because she wasn't alone anymore. Her mother was about to come into the condo, and Wren knew that because she could sense her, through her damned abilities.

There was no controlling this. No control *over* this. But she had to. If it had really leaked into her body, and through her mind, she needed control now more than ever.

"Wrenny?" Laria's tone was soft, like she was scared to hug her daughter because she might just break if she did so. Her mother had never dealt well with any form of fragility. She was too exuberant for that.

"Mom. I…" Wren gulped down a sob she hadn't realized was brewing. "I think I can use my abilities here."

She ended up whispering the last bit of what she said, hoping that maybe if she didn't speak it out loud then it wouldn't be true. And while she might wish that was the way things worked, she knew it wasn't.

"Wren…but didn't we already have an inkling of this? Wasn't it like a parlor trick? Is it worse than making your hand disappear now?" Laria, to her credit, wasn't panicking visibly, and Wren couldn't sense any hidden elements of it either.

That in itself helped calm Wren down. "I know I can use my sensing nets. I knew you were coming; I could feel you half a block away. I know that Harlow is still asleep but just rolled over upstairs because she sensed I wasn't next to her anymore."

Wren paused and closed her eyes, turning to face her mother with the counter behind her back so she could lean against it while her legs felt so weak. When she opened them, she'd managed to keep the tears at bay. "And I know that Dad isn't doing as well as he's portraying. I just can't tell more because he's too far away."

Laria enveloped Wren in a fierce hug. "It's okay, love. We will get through this." Wren could almost hear the frantic calculations in her mother's head as she tried to figure things out, but the hug was still calming.

"You say that, but I could push you away right now without moving a muscle other than my brain." Just saying it out loud made it far too real and Wren fought to retain control of her emotions. Losing that control right now wasn't going to help anyone. Blanketing her neighborhood in a huge wave of wallowing despair wasn't going to win her any favors. She was like a barely controlled empath in the real world.

"How do you mean?" Laria let her hands fall till they loosely gripped Wren's. "Explain it like I'm five."

At least that made Wren laugh, and a tiny bit of tension fled with the sound. "Thanks, Mom. I guess. I really only thought it was parlor tricks, but my connection in game made me think of some things, and now in Somnia I have some abilities that are kinetic in nature, so I can use the force of my mind to create force from my mind. If that makes sense.

"One of my abilities is my kinetic shield. It's something that I can push out from myself, creating a barrier of sorts. Or I can surround people…" Wren's face lit up as an idea came to her. "Oh, that's it. I've got it. Here."

She reached over and turned the hot water on, and then coated herself in her Kinetic Shielding she'd used so often it was second nature. Holding her hand under the water, she didn't even flinch when it hit her barrier. Steam rose up toward the ceiling, but Wren only felt warmth. No scalding involved. She frowned a bit. Perhaps there was a difference. She wouldn't have felt any alteration in Somnia.

Laria watched in amazement. "Wait. What? But our hot water is ridiculously hot." She stated the obvious as if she was trying to ground herself. Then, like she was trying to downplay excitement, she asked, "Can I try?"

Wren nodded, hoping against hope that she could do what she thought she could, otherwise her mom was going to be in a lot of pain. But after making sure her mom was covered, the test worked. She looked at Laria's hand, free of burns and not even wet when she removed the shielding.

In fact…she wasn't really certain how to react to it. This was undeniable proof that she'd brought her abilities back into the real world with her, that her brain was forever irrevocably altered. Not that she hadn't had proof before, but it had been far easier to ignore when things only happened to her.

Laria for her part was dealing with this emergence of potential superpowers far better than Wren expected. Her mother stood there, looking at her hand and frowning. She turned it this way and that, like she was seeking out any and every possible explanation for why her hand not only wasn't burned, but also why it wasn't wet. Shouldn't matter what the temperature was, her hand should have been wet.

Wren felt her knees weaken, and a mild panic attack approached. She let herself practically fall into one of the kitchen chairs, and the sound made Laria turn to her daughter.

"It's okay, Wrenny. We will figure this out. It could just be residual." Which had to be one of the lamest excuses her mother could have come up with, but she still appreciated the effort.

"Yeah, Mom. Don't think it's residual, considering I just stopped us from getting second degree burns. I'd like to say it's a bit weaker here, which makes me feel extremely relieved." Only she didn't feel proud, she felt scared.

And then Harlow's arms were looped around her neck, giving her a warm, secure hug without squeezing too tight. Wren sighed into the gesture, resting her face against Harlow's arm, so glad to have Harlow with her.

Laria raised an eyebrow and smiled with happiness. "You two look cozy."

Wren blushed, and she was pretty sure Harlow just turned the same shade as her hair. "We're good. Been through a lot this last month or three."

"You two have always been inseparable. You let me know if I can help with anything." Laria's smile shrank a little, as it was obvious her mind darted to something else. Wren knew her mother had meant just in case Harlow's parents reacted differently, but she was fairly certain they'd end up being okay.

"Thanks," Harlow beamed moving around to sit half on Wren's lap. "I feel like this is more like my home anyway."

This time Laria seemed thoughtful. "It always will be." It was like she'd decided about something or other, and she turned around to take a look at the kitchen before heading toward her office.

"I have something I need to do," Laria called to her daughter, her tone brooking no argument. "Make sure you eat good food, and refresh yourselves before you dive back into that damned game."

Wren turned briefly to look at her mother, but the programmer didn't turn back around. Frowning, she grasped Harlow's hand, grounding herself. Because if she did it without thinking, she'd probably start a fucking rockfall in her parent's kitchen.

"Did you hear?" Wren finally managed to get the words out.

Harlow moved down, still holding Wren's hand and kneeled at the side of her chair. "Yeah. Kind of hard not to. It's not the biggest condo in the world."

Wren tilted her head back and studied the ceiling. There was so much she wanted to be able to say. And so much she didn't understand.

Calm down. It's not that bad. You're going to be fine. You just come with a few improvements now.

I really wasn't talking to you. Wren couldn't keep the lifelessness from her voice. There was just something about having an artificial intelligence speaking inside your mind without anything to physically link you to it that knocked all of the wind out of her.

The ceiling was interesting. Far more interesting than the turmoil happening in her brain. And just so much more interesting than the thing hanging around in her head.

"You doing okay?" Harlow's voice was gentle, a few decibels down from her usual volume. Like she knew that Wren needed some space to deal with her whole brain shit.

Hell, it was like Harlow had known her for her whole life.

Wren started to laugh. Just a soft chuckle at first, but then some more. She was tired, though less so than she'd been before. And she was exhausted from all the emotions running through her, not to mention the fact that her head was, in fact, sort of like a computer right now. Or perhaps a server was a better description.

Maybe she could download info into her brain. Jinna, Masha, and Risk had definitely been able to download some form of the virus into their brains, after all.

That thought made her push all of her worries to the back of her mind and focus on the others instead of being selfish and focusing on herself. Not that it was necessarily selfish, but since she couldn't personally do anything about her current predicament, it only stood to reason that she should tackle something she could control.

Harlow was watching, her brow furrowed with concern as she obviously tried to discern if it was a good or hysterical laugh. Wren smiled, stood up, pulling Harlow with her, and snuck in a very gentle, sweet kiss. Even that second of contact grounded her world again, making everything separate back into doable chunks. One thing at a time. Harlow didn't need a game to be magical.

"Well, that's good, then." Harlow laughed as Wren pulled her into a huge hug.

That's how it felt. "Yeah. Just like always you make everything better."

Harlow raised an eyebrow. "Seriously, though. What are you talking about? What idea did you just have that caused that reaction, and what can I do to help you keep that smile on your face?"

Several things ran through Wren's mind right then, and none of them bore repeating in a house into which her parents had installed a high-tech security system. Coughing to clear her head, and hopefully hide her blush, Wren spoke. "We can talk about the smile on my face later. The guys have… hmmm, no. That's not right. Masha, Risk, and Jinna—and I think a couple of others who I've noticed hanging around with them all now—have fragments of the virus screwing with their headgear, maybe even their actual minds."

"I think they've been infected through contact with Jirald." Harlow's expression took on the dark tones of a very vicious thundercloud, and she crossed her arms, thus completing the scowl.

"Yeah, I know, but at the same time, this is a good thing. Knowing where it came from for once is actually an advantage. I'll need to talk to my mother." Wren was already running through some ideas in her head. If they could pull the stats from Jirald's headset, and maybe from the others to see if they'd all been adjusted, tampered with, or just plain assembled together out of duct tape and wires, then there was a possibility that if those same headsets were removed, they might still be normal.

Hopefully none of them had been altered to the extent Wren's had. Just one fried brain was more than enough. For all she knew, this whole thing of being able to use her abilities our here in the real world was a very bad thing for her brain health.

"How are we for time?" she asked, aware that she'd already posed the question but not left enough time for an actual answer.

Harlow shrugged. "Well, we only took about six hours' sleep, so I mean, we still have some time." She paused and studied Wren, grabbing her hand again and squeezing. "Did you even get five hours of sleep? How long were you down here?"

Wren grimaced. "It's okay. I'm fine. I'll be fine, too. We have a lot to prep. Neva is going to have to take a long day today, and I hope she's in early, because I'm about to log in."

"After you talk to your mom," Harlow reminded her.

"Of course, after I've talked to my mom. I'm not that bad, Harl." Wren tried to stay exasperated, but she didn't have the heart. For the first time since logging out and realizing that sections of her skills came with her to the outside world, she felt a twinge of hope that maybe not everything was up shit's creek after all. And Harlow by her side definitely helped with that.

CHAPTER NINETEEN
Self-Analysis

Telvar stood and watched the bustle surrounding Fable's vast crafting empire. Neva had done wonders. Guilds in all different phases of the world, in all different stages of the game, knew Fable's wares. Murmur and Beastial had left the girl free rein, and Neva ran all the way to the bank with it.

Good thing, too—they were going to need any and every advantage they could get in the coming dungeon.

"Telvar!" Neva waved to him, a massive grin on her canine features. Her tail wagged, and her ears twitched every now and again, showing just how excited she was to see him. Everyone needed a Neva. Maybe he could bottle that energy.

"Hello, master crafter." He spoke the title with respect, because she'd earned every little bit of it.

She blushed, even under the fur; it was obvious. "Silly. I'm having a blast getting to keep a track of all this. Though, it really ends up being a lot, you know?"

"How are the preparations coming along?" He asked the question seemingly nonchalantly. But in reality, he was anything but.

"Excellent. The others have almost finished the first six dungeons themselves and will be moving onto the high-level ones as soon as they've got enough people at level forty-eight. Waiting for a guild group this time." She was glancing through a list while she talked, a pen marking things off it. Multitasking perfection.

"Long story short, we have a lot of crafting materials. I've managed three more repair kits for the next zone. Those are a doozy. I finally hit my alchemy mastery, and we have potions and tinctures galore." She frowned, turned away from Telvar, and yelled across the workshop. "Dhegar! I don't have those diamonds you promised me. Need them twenty minutes ago!"

"Yes, Neva!" came a quick response, and the small luna turned her attention back to Telvar and raised an eyebrow.

"I swear, sometimes they'd forget their ears if they weren't attached." Her nose twitched, showing she was mostly joking, but Telvar wasn't completely convinced.

"Looks like you've got it all, then. Just…let me know if there's anything you need. Always willing to help out." He couldn't do too much; the rules of the world didn't work that way. At least not right now. Maybe he could talk to Somnia about that at some stage. Of course, he had to be careful of human rules too. Find out you've got AIs on your side, and suddenly you cheated or had it too easy. There were reasons he'd handled revealing themselves outside of Glacier Lake the way he had.

Granted, most people would think Fable's progression had been easy. Technically it had, but only because they tried different approaches.

"There you are." Emilarth came running up to him, Belius dawdling behind her.

He gave her a deadpan stare. "Really? You know you if you had any trouble finding me, you could have just ported yourself to my side, right?"

She pouted. "That's so not fair. Taking away all of my fun. You should be ashamed." Then she sighed.

"But you know I'm not." Telvar finished for her. "What's up?"

"When are they getting back? Haven't you felt those tremors?" Emilarth actually appeared to be worried, not that he blamed her.

"They'll be back when they get back. They don't run on batteries, you know," he finished, trying to sound pompous on purpose.

Emilarth blinked for a moment and then laughed, loudly and heartily. "That was actually funny. You know, because…"

"It was my joke. I *do* get it." Telvar tried to let her down gently and not give on just how worried he was that they wouldn't have enough time left to prepare. They had to join forces; they had to make sure they were all on the same page. They had to warn the guilds about exactly what they were getting into and still hope Fable was willing to take the risk. There had to be some way Exodus could know too, though they hadn't been given altered headgear.

"Are the keys going to work properly?" Belius still sounded grumpy, but Telvar just had to accept that was his brother, regardless of whether it was pleasant or not.

"They should, the one thing he won't be able to do from that prison is change the locks." Telvar sighed, wishing for the umpteenth time that he'd given himself a species that had hair he could pull out. It really felt like this was the ideal time for pulling out hair.

"Telvar!"

The lacerta started with surprise as Neva poked her head around his side. "What?" He realized he didn't sound gracious at all. In fact, he sounded downright irritated.

But that didn't deter the master crafter. She just flashed a smile, her ears twitching with excitement as she ran down that massive list she had in her hands. He knew she could have kept the list in her interface, but apparently that wasn't something she liked to do. "So, just to be clear, when this mystery thing that they're doing happens, will they retain access to their guild storage, or will I have to make an exception and figure out another way to provide them with enough stores to last this unspecified raid? Have I thanked you for all of the specificities I've been given?" She added the last with a sweet edge to her voice, her large eyes twinkling.

Oh, she was clever. The luna knew something was up. She probably knew that not even Telvar or his siblings could give a clear answer on the damned dungeon. "I'll check, but you might want some extra storage just in case. Just to be prepared."

Neva nodded, her eyes narrowing as she put a pen in her mouth and chewed. "Hm. Okay. I can shift a few things around, and it should work, but…" She raised her eyes and studied him. "So, you're all going with them too, right?"

Her tone made it seem like she already knew the answer anyway. And, of course, she did. But confirmation always helped.

Telvar had to debate how to correctly answer the question. He could tell her, but what if the information leaked out? "We will join them, although we do not know quite how far yet." There. That seemed like a good compromise.

Neva, if it was possible, narrowed her eyes even further until they were slits. "You know, Tel, you might be all programmy and such, but I'm a canine in this form, and I swear I can smell a lie from ten paces."

Telvar locked gazes with her for a moment and was the first one to glance away. "You know, Neva, that facade you put on is extremely effective."

"Facade?" She grinned at him, "Why, whatever do you mean?"

Behind him, Emilarth laughed. "She's got you there, Tel. That's brilliant. Can we keep her?"

Rolling his eyes, Telvar laughed too. The day was going to be far too long without a bit of laughing at himself. "Fine. You win. Suffice it to say that we will be there should they need us."

"Perfect." Neva noted something down and checked a line off the list in her hand. "Why didn't you say so in the first place?"

Summer Residence
Home of Laria, David, and Wren
Summer Condo
Early Morning Day Thirty-Two

Wren stood at the foot of her bed, holding her headgear in her hands, and stared at it. Harlow was finishing off getting dressed, and while she waited, Wren studied the strange device and its octopus-like arms that felt around in her hair as it tried to suck her brain out of her skull. Sometimes she swore she could feel it trying to penetrate the bone even when she wasn't wearing it.

Okay, so it didn't actually do that, but sometimes she felt like it did. Maybe it was just because her experience hadn't been typical. But apparently with any modifications, the player had to be careful.

The headgear shouldn't have been this powerful in the first place. Her headset as it was wasn't the patent that got approved for mass production. It had been tremendously altered both outside and in. These were scientific research devices that belonged in a closely monitored lab.

I didn't know you cared so much.

Somnia was definitely getting her own perfectly quippy personality. *You really are becoming your own person. You know that, right?*

If she could have seen Somnia in her room, she would have noticed she shrugged. At least, that was the sensation that ran through her brain. *You're worried.* It was a statement, not a question, but it seemed like Somnia was waiting for her to answer it anyway.

Murmur sighed, glancing at the bathroom door just to make sure Harlow didn't come out and distract her mid-talking. *I want to know if I even need this headgear anymore? Should I bother putting it on?*

She wanted to know that answer, so desperately, but at the same time she also didn't. Knowing would mean she couldn't go back. At the same time, not knowing might put herself in danger.

Somnia hesitated with the answer. And when she spoke, it seemed like she was picking her words with extra care. **Look, Wren. Mur. Whichever you prefer. That headgear is wrong in many ways. Not the one that was designed originally. Not the one you should be wearing. But now it s...well, it's sort of attuned to you. You know?**

Murmur nodded and glanced at the bathroom door again before continuing. *Yeah, I get it. It's sort of a part of me.*

Yes. Eagerness filled Somnia's sometimes still static voice. **When it**

zapped you and pulled you in deeper than you should have dived, it sort of...

The world paused for a moment, like it was trying to find the right words, and Wren just continued to turn the device over in her hands. It was difficult to wait patiently, but she was learning that she was capable of a whole mess of things she'd never contemplated before.

As far as I can tell, the lasers are at a higher frequency in your device. They penetrated far deeper than they should have and practically fused you with the system then and there.

Wren knew she wasn't being told everything, so she waited, irritation growing inside. Irritation that she pushed away and attempted to find that inner sanctum of serenity she'd discovered upon realizing how much damage she'd been inadvertently doing. This was information she should have had ages ago. She hated being kept in the dark.

You know you're what woke me, right?

Wren thought on that, fairly certain she'd already known that when Somnia started to whisper to her, to make her presence known. *Yeah. Yeah, I think I'd have known that either way.*

You were my safe haven, and even now you are as much a part of me as I am of you.

The words settled in Wren's stomach like a bucket of ice had been dropped into her. She digested the words, and barely even noticed as Harlow placed her hand gently on Wren's shoulder. *So, I'm a part of you?*

Somnia seemed flustered when she answered this time. **Yes and no? I mean, your essence, what makes you function as far as brain activity goes. Those things are essentially a part of me; they are part of my building blocks now. It's what I...this is so complicated.**

Wren scowled, and Harlow's grip tightened to let her know she was there. Wren could feel it in the emotions that leaked through into her nets, cast out even here in reality. *So give me a too-long, didn't-read version of it, thanks.*

Yes, you don't have to wear the headset to transport into this world. You can—at least I think it will work this way—transport yourself in here at will at any time, should you so choose. Like

you did earlier.

Wren stood there for a few moments, trying to make her brain remember to take in the oxygen she needed to survive. *Would my body just wither and die here? How is that even possible? This makes no sense whatsoever.*

She couldn't help the panic rising in her. Everything she'd worked toward, everything she'd dreamed of. The planning she'd put into her future…what did this all mean for that? What if she accidentally fell asleep and dreamed of Somnia? Would she wake up there?

I'm so, so sorry, Wren. I wish I had more solid answers for you. But I can sort of give you an analogy or comparison, if you like? Sort of…think of our connection being like a chip. Sort of. And that chip is what gives you access whenever you want to enter the game world. That is how you get in. Not through a headset, but through another type of connection. I wish I could explain it better.

Somnia sounded distressed. And static. Very static. All the anger in Wren's stomach vanished, leaving her hungry and tired and suddenly feeling very drained. She sighed and let herself sit down on the bed as Harlow began to give her a shoulder massage and gripped the headgear tightly in her hands.

After this raid. After this raid she'd see to it that she figured out just how the connection worked. Her mom would help, Harlow would help, and she was sure Havoc and Merlin would as well. Probably others, too. If they could just get through the next couple of days in the game world, maybe she could figure out what was really going on with her without having to worry about the rogue computer virus bringing everything around her crashing down.

Summer Residence
Home of Laria, David, and Wren
Summer Condo
Early Morning Day Thirty-Two

Laria clung to the evidence she'd gathered and the information she'd sniffed out about the headgear and how the ideas came about. She'd already managed to compile a list of places, most of them passworded through several rounds of security and hoops that needed to be jumped through, where differing variations of the headgear schematics could be found. Not that it was difficult, just time consuming.

Included in that lot was one of Michael's earlier models. She believed it was one of the ones he'd submitted for his research thesis back in college. People she'd never even realized had access to this technology had been fiddling with it for years. No wonder people entering the game were experiencing problems or glitches that shouldn't have been present. And the shards were able to find those more susceptible to them. Or something. If she'd understood it correctly.

They should have been stricter with the TOS enforcement. And that was something they'd need to rectify as soon as possible. But that could wait until she got back into the office. Laria was good working her way around without being tracked when it came to the net. But David was far more capable of downloading things they might need without leaving a trace of himself. Laria…she tended to be pretty stubborn about those things which didn't always work in her favor.

David, on the other hand, had much more finesse with it. Not that she'd ever admit that to his face. They did have a rivalry to uphold, after all. Their whole marriage was based around it. She chuckled to herself and only belatedly realized he was standing right behind her. She whipped around and half scowled at him.

"Are you going to tell me what this is about?" David's tone sounded amused as he leaned against her office door.

"What is anything about anymore?" She almost snapped the words out but took in a deep breath before continuing. She hadn't called him here to snap, but he had startled her a bit. "Sorry. You don't deserve that. I just can't believe I didn't think to compare this before."

"Slow down. What are you talking about?" David pulled up a chair and settled down beside her like he was in for the long haul. Oh, how she appreciated the reality of that fact.

She thought for a few moments about how to phrase what it was she wanted to say. Finally, she thought she had it. "Wren mentioned something today; I can't even remember what it was. But it gave me a thought, about the headgear."

Turning to the computer, she pulled up the folders of research she'd managed to save. "See, the thing is, Michael's headgear was his thing. It was his pet project. I remember numerous comments from him about how it was finally coming to fruition, how all his hard work had paid off, and soon everyone would see what a great idea it had been all along."

She shrugged. "You know, generally-impressed-with-his-own-genius sort of talk. But Murmur got me thinking. It wasn't just talk. It had been his graduation project, then he'd evolved it within his thesis. This headgear was never just intended to be for gaming. But he fucked up too soon, and that's where it stuck. And that's why he is stuck in there, seething with anger."

Laria turned to look at David, hoping he didn't think she was insane. He was frowning, but it was a thoughtful expression, not a cautious one.

"Well?"

He raised an eyebrow. "If it was his thesis, then I'd say the university he attended has the schematics of his project on file, doesn't it?"

"Exactly." Laria grinned triumphantly. "And if you know where to look, and what you're looking for…Which—why we didn't see that he was an evil genius with the mind manipulation overtones of that thesis project, I'll never know. But yeah…it's all there, and by now, so are a thousand differing variations that are almost as dangerous as Wren's."

CHAPTER TWENTY

Preparations

"Are you sure you're okay?" Sinister hovered around Murmur like a hummingbird trying to feed. While Murmur loved the attention under other circumstances, the current ones set her anxiety levels spiking.

"I'll be fine." Even though she really wasn't sure if that was true. They didn't have the time to spend making sure that she had the mental capacity to process what was happening.

It's probably something you should make time for, though. Somnia's concern was easily conveyed through her words, and even tone had begun to creep into these conversations more than initially.

Murmur rubbed her temples, like she was trying to fend off a headache. Sure enough, the damn things were definitely piling up. All the damned things. *I know. I know. But this, isn't this more important? Didn't you say we don't have a lot of time to deal with this final step?*

Well, yes. This is the ideal time frame to undertake what we've spoken about. His strength will weaken when the entire continent has to pull from him and his reserves.

I'm going to pretend to understand what it is you're talking about. Murmur pinched the bridge of her nose and turned to look at Sinister. "We're not that early that we can stand around here on the telepad and wait for the others to show up. We need to go see Neva."

Sinister pouted. "You're always taking care of everyone else and never of yourself. And you wonder why we all worry." She threw her hands up and sashayed her way into the workshop ahead of Murmur like she'd given up all hope.

"You really shouldn't taunt her like that." Emilarth was suddenly at Murmur's side and almost gave the enchanter a heart attack.

"You're one to talk. Taunting is all you do to your brothers," Murmur quipped dryly.

"Yes." Emilarth winked at her. "But Sin isn't your sister, now, is she?"

Murmur felt the heat rush to her cheeks and quickly changed the subject. "So why are you all hanging around now. Like is it okay for people to know that you're AIs?"

Emilarth feigned surprise. "Whatever do you mean? We are but harmless NPCs, my dear. Quest givers and all. You have me wrong."

"Pull the other one." Murmur rolled her eyes. "It's got bells on it."

The feles AI laughed loudly, and her eyes sparkled with mirth. "You're so easy to tease, Mur. Lighten up. It's not the end of the world. Yet. Or, well, it'll be different after this, but it won't end."

"Thanks for making me feel *so* much better." Murmur hastened her steps and caught up with Sinister as she entered the workshop, looping a hand loosely around her waist.

It was busier than usual, and Neva's eyes shone while her ears twitched, and her nose did that little scrunching thing that rabbits sometimes do. Murmur hadn't known canines could do it too, but she learned something new every day.

"Neva." Murmur smiled. It was never difficult to begin a good mood around the luna. Hands down, one of the best things about this world was having found someone like Neva. No matter what, the little master crafter always made Mur feel like the weight was momentarily lifted. Gods knew she needed that right now.

Not that she didn't love her friends, but they all knew about everything that had happened. All eleven of them. People like Neva, they didn't know.

They wouldn't even try to guess at something like that. It made being around her so much easier and so relaxing.

Except maybe when it was busier than she'd ever seen it before, and there were huge chests lining the walls looking like they were meant to be going somewhere very soon. She really found herself hoping it was with her raid.

"Mur! I've missed you. Trapped in that damned dungeon loop thing." She held a wooden pencil between her teeth and was rummaging around in a box of things someone had brought in.

Murmur raised an eyebrow as Telvar entered the room. "Why is there like, a physical box of stuff? Shouldn't people just be able to drop it in the guild bank?"

Telvar smiled at her. "If they're a member of your guild, of course they can. But not everyone Neva acquires things from is from this guild, so they must resort to less convenient ways of good transportation." He finished the statement with a flourishing bow.

Murmur tapped her foot and tried her hardest not to roll her eyes.

"Too much?" Telvar asked, raising himself up so he stood to his full seven-foot lacerta height.

"Way too much. With whipped cream, even," Sinister answered before Murmur could. "Now be quiet. Some of us are trying to concentrate on lists Neva has placed in front of us."

Neva grinned up at Mur and beckoned her to come behind the massive crafting station to join her. The enchanter looked around, frowning slightly. "Has this all changed since I was last here?"

Neva looked away, a flush hitting the pink of her ears. "Well, in order to craft better quality and higher tier items, I needed to upgrade pretty much every workstation and forge on the island. Got to keep you all protected and equipped, you know?"

Murmur grinned. "Yep. Wouldn't want to have old shit now, would we?" She knew it was a lot of fun for the crafter and was glad Neva found joy in it. Somnia was meant to be fun, and in reality, it was for most people. As long as they could make it to this next boss, and as long as they could defeat it . . . then everyone could keep having fun.

"So why the trunks? Are you hinting that the guild should move out and leave the rest to the crafters?" Murmur tried to keep her voice stern, but she was smiling too much.

Neva winked. "Well, now that you mention it…" She peeled off with laughter, and then her expression grew serious. "Down to business, though. I wasn't sure if you'd have access to the guild stores in…wherever you're going. I tried to make sure that if you take a couple of chests with you, you should still be good. You know, on top of the guild inventory, if it works. Never bad to be overprepared, am I right?"

The nervousness was obvious. Neva's shoulders were tenser than Murmur had ever seen, and her nose kept doing that bunny thing.

"Excellent thoughts," Murmur added, trying to put all her appreciation into that one comment. "We do appreciate you. So lucky we have you."

"Hey Mur!" Devlish yelled from the door. "The others are here. Did you want to let them into the crafting hall? See if we have anything for them laying around that might actually increase performance?"

Murmur glanced at Neva, whose face was positively glowing. "You have no idea how much stuff we had to make to get the rest of the crafters up levels. Let them come in. We have so much junk, we'd otherwise just have to port to market to sell."

"They still make you schlepp it?" Murmur was surprised; she'd thought they at least had an auction system that could be used as easily as a guild bank.

Neva laughed. "Of course not. Not if you're using the auction house, but we take it to the markets in Pelagu. A lot of passers-through will stop and buy things just because they've seen it. These are too mundane to bother with the auction house fees, but good enough that I don't want to sell them to NPC vendors. I can totally get more out of the players for them." There was a business-luna's gleam in Neva's eyes.

"Bring them in. Just a few at a time?" Murmur hollered over to Beastial before turning back to her master crafter. "You know, I'm really glad you talked us into expanding the crafting workshop. You've done so well with it. I'm so proud of you. Thank you."

Neva smiled and her canine teeth peeked out of her mouth. "Well, thank you for letting me call the crafting shots. You know, and giving you me full access to the treasury. Did you ever get your cooking higher?"

Murmur laughed and shook her head. "Oh, gods, no. Never will, either. Supply me with all the food my favorite crafter in all of Somnia. Are you ready for the onslaught of high levels to outfit?"

"Shush, you'll offend them." Neva motioned Murmur away with her hand. "Besides, I have work to do now, fitting all of these lovely folks with armor. No time to chit chat, because knowing you, you're leaving sooner than later."

Murmur smiled to herself as she left the almost overflowing crafting hall. She seriously hadn't realized Fable had grown so big. This was the first time they'd ever had a crafting arm of the guild. It was something she'd definitely want to institute in the future. It had been a long time since she last checked the guild roster. Beastial had been busy, too. She had no idea where he found the time.

"Delegation, my dear friend." Belius stood at her left elbow and almost gave her another heart attack. What was it with AIs and their silent approaches?

"Seriously, Bel, don't do that." She glared at him. "And I'm still mad at you."

He regarded her for a moment. "If that's because of what I did to Telvar, I do apologize, but I had to get a sample of an organic anti-virus somehow, and I couldn't guarantee that any of the rest of us would have come out of that unscathed. I knew he would. He was never in actual danger."

"Says you," she replied hotly. But she paused, took in a deep breath, and counted to five in her head before continuing their conversation as they walked. There really was a lot to this calming herself down. It worked, gave her enough time to analyze other aspects. Maybe she was growing up.

"The guild has grown. I was just surprised by how much, in such a short time." Pulling up her guild interface she ran through all of the names and the ranks and their permissions within the guild.

It was so in-depth—and damned well-organized. She suspected that Neva had a hand in it. Since she'd been recruiting the crafters, it was highly possible.

"Did you have anything else to tell me?" Murmur asked Belius absentmindedly. "I mean, apart from peeking in my head when I had my guard down."

"No. Not really. Just that Masha, Ishwa, and Risk are waiting for you in one of the gathering rooms." He gave her a brief bow and smiled, in that creepy, disjointed locus way. "I shall take my leave of you, then."

Murmur really didn't think locus were supposed to bow. She just wanted to go lay down in her bed and fall asleep for an unspecified amount of time, but they all knew that wasn't going to happen.

She pushed her hair out of the way, irritated at how it twined around her now. It almost seemed to be a separate entity sometimes. Tiachi had been quiet lately, but she was always wound securely close to her head. Murmur guessed it must be difficult to remain vocal when you were barely ever used for your main purpose.

Walking into the hall, she found Devlish and Veranol already in there and suppressed her sigh of relief. It wasn't that she couldn't deal with the others, but she knew that when she came down hard on things, that while people might be nice to her face, they called her bossy bitch, and no-talent hack behind her back.

Right now, she wasn't emotionally set up to deal with that, so guild company was welcome.

"Hi, guys," she said by way of greeting, putting on her best professional level voice to try and pour some niceness into the other sentiments she was having.

"Hey." Masha stared at her for a moment before shaking his head like he was trying to knock water out of his ears. "Sorry. Feels odd, like I haven't really seen you in a while."

Murmur smiled but thought that sounded distinctly weird. "Well, you know, this time we actually got some sleep."

Somnia Online
Continent of Tarishna – Mikrum Isle
Gathering of the Guild Alliance
Day Thirty-Two – Early Morning

Masha watched Murmur, uncertain as to the feeling of discomfort he experienced when he looked at her. There was a hazy reason just out of his reach, and the more he tried to grab at it, the more it slipped away. Had he been angry with her about something? He couldn't quite remember, even though it was there, on the tip of his tongue so to speak.

She spoke with the same self-assurance he'd known in her for the last couple of years. Working with Fable and healing a bunch of people who knew not to stand in shit should have been a lot of fun. But while they'd been raiding, things got a bit hazy, and he couldn't tell why. He directed his attention back to the conversation, trying his best to concentrate on the words so he could deal with his head stuff later. Maybe he needed to adjust the headset again.

"…Neva has prepared a couple of trunks for us to take in our inventory with supplies in them, just in case. Probably a good idea, since we won't know if we will have access to our guild bank in the next stage." It sounded like Murmur was sick of saying this, or that her mind was elsewhere.

"What do you mean, 'not have access to it'? Why wouldn't we have access to it?" Ishwa asked, his eyes narrowing. He was always so curious about everything, and probably a little bitter that Neva was the one doing everything for Fable, considering she was Ishwa's sister.

Devlish glanced at Murmur, who gave an almost imperceptible shrug. "It's a new event that didn't even undergo alpha testing. And to be honest, we've tackled some of these dungeons very differently. We aren't certain that how things were solved wasn't as big an element as that they were completed. For all we know, different key variations might trigger different final encounters. So we…" but he didn't get further, because Risk crossed his arms and glared at all the members of Fable.

"Look, I can handle being kept in the dark about some things. We got taken along for the ride with these last few dungeons, which is pretty cool of you all. But you also have to realize that we can't do our jobs as our classes if you don't let on with all of what you know." The glare continued, focusing on each of them in turn, including Ishwa and Masha.

Murmur sighed and rubbed her temples. Masha glanced around for Sinister but couldn't see the blood mage anywhere. Strange. Sin could usually change Murmur's moods easily.

He could sense, without having any of those mind power abilities, that Murmur was struggling hard with what she could and couldn't tell them. Wasn't her mother a developer? Maybe they were secretly trying to iron out bugs.

Like she could read his mind, the next words out of her mouth reflected most of what he'd thought. "Look. We don't have all the answers. Frankly, I don't even think the developers do. They gave the world so many different variations and possible combinations that even if they had another ten years, they probably couldn't have tried them all."

"It's not all scripted, which means different actions can trigger entirely different outcomes. Even unanticipated ones. We have no clue what we're walking into. And, like any game, there are some bugs in the system, and we don't know exactly what it's going to throw at us at any given time." Murmur pinched the bridge of her nose.

"Somnia wasn't designed on a linear playing path." Telvar was suddenly there and speaking, like he was a real person. Maybe he was an informative NPC. Masha watched as he continued, completely fascinated.

"The bugs in the system have put some bumps in that path, and we've been tripping over them."

Masha had to put in effort to keep from rolling his eyes at the analogy. "So what do you expect us to do?" The question was out before he knew it, directed at the lacerta like he was partially in charge. Murmur's starry eyes watched him with an unreadable expression.

But Telvar seemed unfazed, which was good, considering he was an NPC. Maybe this was what he was here for, assuaging the concerns of players. "When we journey to the places the keys unlock, the continuation of the quest will answer all your queries." He bowed and left the hall.

Masha turned to Murmur. "Guess it's a nice perk to have an NPC as the owner of your guild island." He meant it as a joke, but she seemed unsure how to take it.

"Yeah. Telvar isn't so bad once you get used to him. A bit eccentric, but generally nice. Plus, he can turn into a dragon." She grinned, but there was hesitation in the expression.

Masha tried to soften his response and let her know things were okay. If only he could remember why he'd been so angry with her, then maybe it would be easier. "Glad he's on our side."

And he really meant that.

Murmur ran over the stock list she got from Neva, making sure everything was in place. It seemed like an overwhelming amount of stuff until she compared it to the average usage list Neva had also handed her that detailed just how much stuff they'd been using in the dungeons they'd completed until now.

She grimaced at the cost. "Good thing we insisted on all the crafting loot," she muttered out loud.

"Probably a very good idea." Sinister stood next to her, on her tiptoes, trying to peer over at what Murmur was reading. "What's the good idea again so I can be suitably impressed?"

Murmur bent her knees slightly so Sinister could see better. Just having her close made everything feel more manageable. "Crafting. Potions. Flasks. Repair kits. They all cost a ton of money, and well, without the crafting materials we've been getting all going back to Neva, I'm afraid the guild would be broke."

Sinister laughed. "Nah, Neva would find a way for that not to happen. She's amazing with finances, if you haven't noticed."

Murmur raised an eyebrow, because *she* had noticed, but it wasn't like Sin to point that sort of shit out. "Okay. I'll bite. What's on your mind? The tl;dr version please, because we have about five minutes before we get the information on what we're doing with these three completed keys."

Sin smiled, but it seemed a bit forced. "So I know you have your own shit to deal with. Like we all do in a way, but…" She paused, biting her lip like she wasn't sure how to proceed.

"Come on, Sin. How long have we known each other? How many secrets have we shared? I'm not about to judge you for any reason." Murmur wiggled her eyebrows, which she was fairly certain made her look comical given the nature of locus eyebrows.

"Fine." Sin took a deep breath, and Murmur wondered if she should have encouraged her friend to spill these beans. "My head. It feels all sorts of strange. This headset appears to take the powers I have and amplify them in ways I didn't think I could. And sometimes…"

Her eyes shifted to make sure no one was close enough to hear what she was about to say. "Sometimes it talks to me? I think, anyway. Sort of like an NPC in my head, but nicer. Not programmed. Like she talked to me a couple of days ago when you were floating in the air all freaky-like and stuff. And I get that it's possible and stuff, considering what we've seen, but…I'm just feeling a bit like a floppy fish."

Murmur stopped what she was reading instinctively, mulling the words over in her mind. She knew the headgear had been altered but hadn't been aware that it might reach the same brain centers as deeply as her own did. Part of the reason it had been altered was to give her guild a more solid connection to Somnia herself. "But the voice is nice, right?"

Sinister raised an eyebrow. "Sort of. Well, yes, it is. Other times it's like I can almost hear it, but it's whispering, so it's not quite audible."

I didn't realize you were actually speaking to the others. Are you meaning to? Murmur asked, trying to keep her frayed nerves under control even though she knew it wasn't Somnia's fault.

I'm not right now, but I do sometimes. I try to make it more in a suggestive way. I'm just making use of the tools that have been put in front of me, and with the headgear adapted, it helps me amplify the abilities your friends possess. I thought you knew that's why the headgear was tweaked. Allowing me to interface directly with them was one of the perks.

Of course she'd known that, but she'd just not thought it through all the way. *Sorry. Just juggling a lot at the moment. Will she be okay?*

Of course! You really think I would hurt Sinister?

Somnia did sound rather offended at the idea, and Murmur sighed, wondering if the headache was ever going to go away. "You're okay, Sin. It's just the world communicating with you."

"Okay. So." Sinister frowned, clearly thinking. "I knew I heard her when you were in trouble. But I thought that was a sort of once off. And I know you hear shit, but I thought that was an ability that came with your class."

Murmur shook her head. "Nope, not at all. That's a nice unique ability given to me by the bastard who tweaked the crap out of my headset. Luckily, you're all wearing safely tweaked ones."

Sinister hesitated. "Probably better not to fight or ignore it?" Her voice quivered for a moment, like she was intimidated by what Murmur had told her but was trying to put on a brave face.

"Definitely better not to. This AI can be a little more persistent than you'd expect." She laughed and headed over to the entrance of the keep where everyone was gathering.

Telvar stood there, the early sunlight reflecting off his golden-bronze scales and making him look as regal as a dragon should. He was talking to Emilarth and Belius, and all of their expressions made Murmur hope to high whatever that they weren't going to give a lecture or something equally as tedious.

Tel cleared his throat and kept her waiting no longer. "As your quest dictates, you must raise Gefängnis, and I am here to deliver instructions to you all. Gefängnis requires the turning of keys in three separate locations in order to activate the mechanisms that raise it. To this end we will disperse into three mostly equal groups, and you will all be required to use the portal activated by unlocking the zone."

Murmur muttered as well as everyone else around her. This was news to her, and she sent Telvar a small glare for not having forewarned her. Although, she guessed everyone had been busy in their own way.

"We will fan out in groups of eleven; one of us will need to be with each of you. It is our keys you will present, for we cannot wield them ourselves. Thus, we must ask this of you, noble adventurers." Emilarth's voice rang out clear in the gathering, and Murmur had to give her credit for her own regal appearance. Stick with these guys for long enough, and they'd all surprise her.

Right then, Emilarth offered her a very subtle wink, and Murmur had to stop herself from groaning.

Belius still sounded so old when he spoke, and Murmur still wasn't sure what had possessed him to use such and aged voice. "Each group will journey to one of the three major cities. Pelagu. Darshin. Multagen. You will move inside the city walls to the fountains positioned in the middle of them. Each fountain will have a corresponding keyhole. It is there the keys must be placed and turned at the same time in order to activate the mechanisms. The prison will raise, and all monsters within must be defeated."

There was a mumbling from the crowd as they listened to the NPCs, all of them thinking it was just another quest, while Fable at least had an inkling of what was really at stake. They'd seen it in Mur, and in the dungeons, and even in the headgear they now wore. Not to mention they were all aware that Telvar and the other two were much more than NPCs.

QUEST UPDATE:

You will journey to the three pillars and activate the mechanism with the obtained keys.

You must subdue all of the prison monsters, lest the world as you know it fall.

QUEST UPDATE: The Fountains

You ve come a long way since those early days. Keep your eye out now more than ever. The fountains literally hold the keys.

"You know?" Sinister said beside her, her fingers intertwined with Murmur's. "So when you said you could hear voices in your head, I'd always thought that was a remnant of the coma, your class, or you were just kidding with me, but it wasn't, was it? It's a remnant of that modification he did to your headgear."

Mur nodded, still trying to follow the discussion the AIs were having. She didn't really need to. She'd already marked the to-do list on her calendar. Telvar told them to go and unlock the three sluice gates, so to speak, that would raise the lost continent or something and bring about the destruction of Somnia unless the wee adventurers decided to be magnanimous and stop it.

Something like that. Somnia sounded partially amused.

Might be nice to actually give me an answer every once in a while, Murmur commented dryly. Just one more dungeon. She could do that.

Somnia hummed in the background, sort of like a set of servers communicating with the internet, so Murmur waited for the inevitable lecture or speech or explanation that was obviously on its way.

About that. See—the connection we have can't be severed anymore. I'm amazed you humans are so bad at understanding your own brains, really. It's all so interconnected. It's not like firing on one area is going to only change the portion located in that exact spot.

Murmur rolled her eyes, not really wanting a science lesson right then. *Give me the short version. I've got a raid to plan.*

Oh, the others are fully capable of doing it, and you know it. You're just a bit of a control freak. Somnia sounded like she was smirking.

This coming from a virtual world who decided she wanted to be real?

Touché. Somnia chuckled, but she didn't sound happy about it. **Look. The short version is: when I shorted out your connection it sort of...rewired a portion of your brain, and now you're kind of stuck with me. There's so much we can do together. At least, the more information I gather, the more I realize it's possible, anyway.**

She sounded so excited, but Murmur felt a coldness spread in her stomach. Her brain was totally rewired, and it wasn't just the headgear. What did that mean? Wasn't she still her own person, though? *Does the headset provide me some protection at all?*

Definitely. You shouldn't go crazy while wearing it, at any

rate. Somnia laughed and had probably attempted to be comical, but Murmur couldn't shake the feeling of dread in her bones.

"Mur?" Sinister tugged on her hand, looking up at her with worried eyes. "You sort of blanked out. You okay?"

Murmur nodded and then squeezed Sinister's hand. "Yeah, I'll be okay. I have to be. I've just got a lot to sort out once we finally get this next raid over with."

Sinister continued to look worried. "You really need to stop bottling shit up, remember?"

A stab of guilt hit Murmur. "You're right. I'm sorry. I'm just worried about how my connection to this headset has altered aspects of the way I think. There, better?"

Sinister laughed. "No, not really. But I'm glad you told me. Now we can both worry."

Murmur couldn't help but smile, even if something about this quest nagged at her. She busied herself with making the groups they needed to go and unlock the prison.

CHAPTER TWENTY-ONE

The Fountains

Murmur stood in front of the fountain in the center of Darshin, Telvar by her side. For some reason she always felt safer with him close.

Thanks.

You're welcome, you crazy little self-actuating AI.

My pleasure.

These fountains had always been sort of creepy, and Murmur didn't think it had changed. In fact, they felt even more odd now. Like something was lurking beneath and waiting for them. She guessed, from what the quest had said, that it was true.

Murmur smiled as she waited for the rest of her team to make it to the center of the city. It was weird not having Sinister with her, but since Veranol had wards and Murmur had stuns, they'd figured sending each of the other two groups with two healers each was more conducive to survival should they get portaled into different sections of the prison.

Murmur glanced at the gold key in her hand. It was sort of pretty. The large key dangled the three smaller ones beneath it, and she glanced up at the fountain to check for holes but frowned when she didn't see any immediately. Sinister had Emilarth's key, and Mellow had the black one.

Each key was held by members of Fable so they could communicate on time with each other over guild speak. That was the excuse she'd given, anyway. With the rampant infection running through some of the other guilds' players as well as her own, she'd had to pick people she was certain she could trust, for now.

"So. What do we do now?" she mumbled to Telvar, out of earshot of everyone else.

He grinned at her, no doubt holding back a smart remark. It was like she could feel it emanating from him. "We hope the keys work."

"Oh, fucking fantastic planning, Tel." She rolled her eyes.

He laughed softly. "Blame our little Somnian friend, why don't you? Everything worked fine until she woke up."

"Maybe, but I woke her up, so that's my fault." The realization made her feel oddly down on herself.

"Shush. Stop that. If he hadn't tinkered with your headgear, you wouldn't have triggered Somnia, and I think we'd all be worse off. Sure, this seems dire now, but I have a distinct feeling—one of those gut feelings you're always on about—that everything will turn out just fine." He gave her forearm a squeeze, as if reminding her he was always there even when she forgot about him.

Stepping forward, Murmur searched for the keyholes. They weren't that hard to find once she got closer, and they weren't even under the water section of the fountain. Instead, they were embedded into the central support of the fountain, as a part of the actual statue. In fact, the positioning on the thigh of the elf statue made her feel oddly suspicious. But she leaned forward and began to insert the key into its pattern.

Once she was done, she admired how it looked like a pretty 3D tattoo. She took a deep breath and spoke over guild. *Everyone ready?*

Mellow: *Aye, captain.*

Sinister: *Of course!*

Trying to steady her nerves, Mur counted to three and closed her eyes. *Okay, turn after three.*

One.

She admired the fountain in all its glory, the way the water almost seemed to be arranged with magic. The realism of the statues of the races that inhabited Cenedril was potent. The elf, the feles, and the dwarf all seemed more lifelike than she'd remembered them being the first time she passed this statue. Any other times they'd come through this city, she had to confess she hadn't really looked, despite her fountain quest and her curiosity about them.

Two.

The key, even inserted into the statue, felt like a heavy weight in her hands. Like it was meant to do something she hadn't even contemplated. For a split second she wasn't sure they should be doing this at all.

Three.

Her hand grasped the strange key design and turned it, feeling the teeth catch with each millimeter of precision. Golden light like glitter powder streamed around the key as it made its rotation before clicking into place with a finality that surprised her. There was no going back now.

A huge grating sound made the ground under her feet rumble. It sounded from somewhere beneath her and all around her at once, shaking everything. She could hear the water splashing against the rocks outside the city like it was angry at the continent. The walls began to strain and shake around them, and Murmur glanced up to see small, spiderweb cracks appearing in the beautiful stonework of the city.

Screams echoed from all through the city proper. Fear seeped through Murmur's mind as she felt the anguish of the NPCs. Anguish she shouldn't have been able to sense from non-sentient, non-sapient, not real people.

Are you sure? Aren't they real? Aren't I real? Somnia's stray thought caught Mur by surprise. Of course the AI was right. So much of this world was becoming aware of itself, including Michael in whatever form he'd been sunk into. So what did that make them for hunting him down?

If he truly existed in here, wouldn't that be akin to murder? The ramifications started to pile up in her brain, beating at her until anxiety rose. Except she couldn't let that in right now. She breathed again, in and out, focusing on the clarity that came with sensing Somnia as the world she was, the world she had become. Peace didn't last for long though.

The cranking of gears underneath them—far, far below—settled in

Murmur's ears, distracting her from any other conversations. Her sensing nets warned her of danger, from all around her as the stone structures moved uneasily, cracking in so many places it would take the dwarves years to repair.

Mellow: *Hell! What is happening?*

She could hear the panic in their voice over speak and called out, trying to sound soothing herself. *It's just the mechanism triggering, I think.*

Murmur realized she probably shouldn't have added the I think part to it. Because the tension levels from her guild members in her little group didn't exactly go down. So that was great lack of thinking on her part.

Sinister: *It feels dangerous over here. Like...that trapdoor thing just ripped free and is coming to gobble us all up.*

And just as Sinister spoke, the statues in front of Murmur, the very statues that had been standing in the fountain, including the one with the nice tattoo she'd just given him, began to move. That couldn't be good, could it?

The elf, the feles, and the dwarf stepped out of the fountain. Angling the middle support over and revealing it to have a hidden hinge, the elf moved it toward him. The dwarf flipped his axe and handed it over, and the feles pulled out what looked like a staff. It didn't take long, and Murmur couldn't rip her eyes from the fascinating visage in front of her. The fluid movements of the rock, the way the weapons fit together and then into the stone support—now the whole contraption looked like an old-fashioned crank. With a nod, the dwarf moved up to the elf, and they both began to wind it, like they were in the bowels of a ship, rowing to get through a storm before it killed them. Their silent communication and knowledge of just what to do made it all the creepier.

Sinister sounded panicked this time: *The fucking fountains just...oh, my gods!*

Murmur knew exactly how she felt. More cranking sounds joined, and this time it seemed like there was more power to them, as if the fountains had lent them their weight, and now everything was turning as it should. The quaking beneath her feet made it difficult to hear anything else over the guild speak. Which Murmur found strange momentarily because, after all, the speak sounded in their minds; it wasn't like it played on a speaker. At some fundamental level, they should always be able to hear it.

Quest UPDATE: The Fountains

You now understand the true purpose of the fountains. They have long since channeled the power of the species they depict, the restlessness, the danger, and the magic of Somnia.

Thank you for seeking their explanation. You will be rewarded after their revelation is dealt with.

Murmur sighed. Great. Just then, Snowy pressed himself against her legs, growling, his hackles up. Maybe he was trying to protect her from the statues, but she didn't think it was as simple as that. Just like she could sense through her nets, she knew that whatever was being cranked up wasn't going to be pretty.

People braced themselves in doorways, shied away from the appearing cracks that ran everywhere and huddled in groups as if the company might make imminent death better. Again the wave of fear that ran through the NPCs, it was unsettling, enough to make Murmur reconsider hunting anything ever again.

"Oh, shit!" She heard someone call out. It must have been one of the players or NPCs who were standing watch. "Look over there. To the northwest."

Murmur ran to the balcony overlooking the side of the city and shaded her eyes and looked. Slowly, as the grinding of stone on stone and the rumbling began to die down, as the shaking began to subside, a massive rock formation appeared to be emerging out of the water. Off in the distance, like an extra continent. Liquid sluiced down its sides, gushing to reach the ocean again as the structures, so large they were even visible from the shore, emptied themselves of that burden.

Trees ran all around the edges of the jagged cliffs that barred entrance. Barren and rickety is how it appeared to her. And it might have been slightly foreboding if it looked less like a bedraggled cat.

The horn that sounded across the channel rang through to her bones, even as the waves from the emergence pushed at the already existing shores.

That sound resonated in her teeth, setting them on edge, and making them chatter. It hurt, a cold pain that ran all the way through her.

She'd do almost anything to get rid of it. This feeling of utter desolation, loneliness, and defeat.

"Wait," Telvar cautioned as people began to move. "The portal should appear momentarily, and only those who've completed the necessary dungeons to be here will be allowed passage."

Devlish righted himself, pulling out his tower shield just in case. "So we get to walk through the portal any moment?" He inched closer to Murmur and Telvar, reaching out a hand to idly pet the wolf.

Telvar nodded, but Murmur could see the hesitation in his expression. Something wasn't going the way he'd expected it, and he was rather put out.

"Should it already be here?" She decided to ask, even though he probably knew she'd already guessed the answer. After all, it wasn't like anything had gone to plan since Michael came and exploded his brain onto the scene.

"Yes. It should." His words were crisp and clear, just on the nice side of snapping. "It should have appeared before the horn sounded."

Like a trigger, a large, white and round barrier of foamy clouds formed around them on the ground where they stood. She took a split second's glance to look down at her feet and groaned. This was so typical of her dungeon experiences so far. They had but a moment's notice. Murmur screamed out: "Brace yourselves!"

Then the area inside crackled a dark purple-blue like the starry night sky, and all eleven of them fell through the portal.

Somnia Online
Cenedril – City of Verendus
Day Thirty-Two

Dirsna stood outside the Verendus Enchanter Guild and watched the surroundings as the sky darkened. It wasn't supposed to storm; he didn't even realize it was supposed to snow, being in the mountains as they were. There were multiple reasons this could be happening, but from the fluctuation he could feel in Murmur's energies, he knew they were likely and finally ready to do battle with that intruder. He eyed the incoming weather and turned to his friends. "I think they're up to something. Again."

"Really? You think?" mumbled his aide, Geshua. Without Geshua, the whole Verendus Enchanter Guild would fall apart. Dwarves were a solid chance for the class, and it was surprising the number of players who had chosen either enchanter as a hybrid class, or else enchanters who were hybrid warriors.

Geshua was still grumbling. "Look, they're always up to something, creating an imbalance where there should be none. Usually it turns out well for us, though. Just look at us?"

Dirsna chuckled, but the sound caught in his throat as the world around them began to shake fiercely. He grabbed the door jamb, bracing himself against it as Geshua came to stand with him. Their eyes widened as the earthquake leveled their clock tower, and slowly but surely transformed their fountain.

The dwarf statue in it twisted, becoming languid and pliable, and the fountain jets faced inward, pushing down and yet draining the water. All the while, loud whirring and clanking sounded through the village, setting Dirsna's teeth on edge as he watched the transformation take place.

The massive statue stepped out of the pool, casting glowing red eyes around as it tried to find willing victims. Instead, it heaved a rumbling sigh that resembled the way the ground shook, and he cast a spell on the fountain. A crank appeared, and he began to wind it in time with the fountain's pumping. Up and up, and more.

Even the shaking of the earth subsided, like it was waiting for something to shift into place. Dirsna held his breath, reaching out with his mind to contact his allies, his friends, and anyone who could help. Nothing but chaos greeted him, nothing but the same thing in every single town, with every single fountain, and all of the inhabitants cowering in fear.

Alarms began to blare, their sirens like an earworm trying to draw blood. Suddenly a massive voice sounded over the world. A booming announcement that set Dirsna's teeth on edge.

The Prison of Chetorang on the Isle of Gefängnis has been raised. Defeat its inhabitants before they take over this world on their way to the next.

Hightower's animated statue stopped moving as the announcement faded, and Dirsna allowed himself time to move again.

"What was that?" Geshua said, standing next to him.

Dirsna shrugged, finally glad to have received a message from Belius. The guy was supposed to be the enchanter leader, but he'd been rather absent of late.

What do we do? he asked, requiring guidance because this wasn't like the actual battle they'd designed. No, this was far more than that. The sludge that had been creeping through the system since the incident had reached the prison, and Dirsna wasn't sure how to approach that.

Belius took a few moments to respond, and when he did his voice came through patchy, like something was in the way, and he was trying to speak through it. *"Sucked…portal. Must fight. Keep…–nters organized. Call…allies."*

Dirsna analyzed the message for a few moments, his mind racing. Sure, it sounded fairly self-explanatory, but then when was he not? He sent back a *Done* and hoped it got through.

Now he just had to contact the allies Fable had made while they were here, and city of Curet, and Cognitia. All in a day's work. At least, a day's work where the statues in the fountains came to life and cranked a prison island into existence.

Shaking his head, he set about to contact the Loch'Ni'Dar and the Noch'Mar nomad elves from when Fable had been regularly in this region. Chief Intanko may have forgiven them for their accidental killing of Disestru because of the quality of battle they got, so he just had to hope she was still in charge. Because he didn't have enough to do anyway.

CHAPTER TWENTY-TWO

Prison

Purple void swirled around her, disorienting Murmur in the tiny space of time it took to transport her to wherever they were when she landed unceremoniously on her butt. Not for the first time, she was glad locus didn't appear to have tailbones. The small rocks beneath her when she landed would have given a human severe pain.

She stood up, brushing her robes off as she did, and looked around her. Snowy stood unperturbed off to the side. He seemed to land like a cat was supposed to. Always on his feet. He noticed her and trotted over, sniffing at her hand before he gave a wuff of approval and headed over to Telvar.

The walls around her were made of densely packed rocks, like something had hammered them together in a high-powered press. They were in an oval shaped room with no other entrance than the tunnel that lead out from the roughly hewn area. She couldn't for the life of her think about why they'd been deposited here.

"So. That happened." Devlish rubbed his head. He'd somehow managed to fall next to a wall and smash his head into it. Fantastic landing skills. "Who do we have to thank for this mode of transport?"

Telvar didn't answer at first, and Murmur got the distinct feeling it was because he was talking to the others, or trying to, and because from what she could tell, they were nowhere near the other groups. Either that, or her sensing nets just weren't working in this environment, and she wasn't sure which one scared her more.

"Sorry." Telvar shook his head, like he was switching his concentration modes. "Some elements of this dungeon have changed with the self-evolving nature of the game."

Murmur was impressed by his well-phrased excuse, but she knew there was more to it. All of the AIs were likely surprised, but not so surprised that they hadn't expected something to happen, just maybe not of this magnitude. It seemed Michael's mind created a far more potent virus than anyone expected.

"So?" Veranol pushed the subject gently as the rest of the group got themselves sorted out. "Just where are we, and what have we gotten ourselves into?" Then he narrowed his eyes before continuing. "Or should I say—what should we have gotten ourselves into, and how has it changed?"

Telvar seemed conflicted, but he had to know most of Fable were at least aware of the extent the AIs had developed, right? They'd been treating him as an actual person since she could remember.

"Well. We're not as far from them as I initially thought, but we will all have to get through some monsters before we can join back together as a group." He paused and looked at Devlish apologetically. "I can't be as effective as I'd like in these rock hewn corridors. There's just no room for my dragon form. I can, however, work as DPS or a tank if you need me to. I am a monk, after all."

Murmur patted his hand. "It's okay. We can do this." She said it, trying to put grit into her voice even if she didn't feel it. Even if she was completely worried about Sinister being stuck with Risk and his crew. But Karn was there, and she was fairly certain Karn was mostly okay and at least at little danger herself since she was separated from Jirald.

"Everyone ready?" Devlish called out, hefting his sword and shield tightly as he moved to the front of the pack.

The other nine of them nodded, Snowy barked, and Telvar grinned. Murmur followed Dev closely as they moved out from the strange circular dead-end rock-room they'd found themselves in when transported. It was like the portal had opened a hole right through the rock and closed after it deposited them in there.

"Look out for rockslides and other rock-like things," Merlin called in a sing-song voice, and she recalled the strange cage maze with elven children they'd encountered where he'd been impaled by a gigantic wooden spear. The blood, the way his body had twitched, how Sinister had cried when she couldn't heal him. Images flooded her mind, making her hope they wouldn't encounter that sort of thing in here. She was all for realism, but sometimes it hurt to realize how horrible things could get.

Casting out her net, she tried to feel through the rock, but there was nothing outside of it. Murmur hadn't realized quite how dependent on it she'd become. She bit her lip as she tried to navigate the area without it, worried that maybe it had somehow broken.

Stop that! Somnia's tone was demanding, even if it felt slightly harried.

Are the others okay? Murmur had to ask, because she had to know Sinister was all right. Granted, she would be in the real world, right?

You're thinking too much. Take a breath and just follow the clues, follow the trail, and you'll all find each other again. I don't have much time; there's too much in here for me to combat. Just trust your gut. And Sin is fine. Somnia sounded, just for a moment, like her mother used to when Wren got ahead of herself as a child. The tone calmed her down instantly.

Thank you.

No problem. Just—don't add to my workload. Okay?

Murmur would have rolled her eyes but for two things: Somnia couldn't see it anyway, and secondly, vibrations began in the tunnels, reverberating down through the soles of her feet. An overwhelming presence exerted pressure, like it was coming to smother all of them with a huge feather pillow.

She glanced down at Snowy, whose hackles were standing on end. His teeth were bared, and while he was growling, the sound from his throat wasn't what was causing the strange suffocating aura.

"Mur?" Devlish asked without looking back at her.

"Not getting any readings." She pushed down at the panic, trying to make sure it didn't take over. Not being able to access the abilities provided to her by her sensing nets proved to be more difficult than she'd ever imagined. Whatever these walls were made up of, she couldn't see through them, feel through them, or perceive an aura through them.

For once, she was as blind as everyone else.

Telvar spoke softly so the only people that heard were Murmur, Devlish, and Veranol. "This wasn't in the original schematic. Just in case you were wondering. This dungeon was originally an amalgamation of all the effects we didn't think anyone would be able to overcome—or at least that they couldn't overcome without great difficulty."

"Let me guess. Along with the rest of the game, it hasn't exactly gone according to plan?" Veranol added in a dry whisper.

"In our defense, though, no one expected an egomaniacal maniac with a god complex to create a headset that allowed him to quasi upload and explode his brain into the virtual word." Telvar managed to deliver the words with a deadpan face and all in a whisper.

Murmur had to choke down a nervous laugh.

"Not to worry you guys, but that rumbling is only getting worse. We'll be lucky if we can stand a bit further in." Devlish's tone held impatience, though luckily the tiredness seemed mostly gone.

As if to punctuate his comment, the ceiling began to rain down small stone fragments and dust on them all, and Murmur gripped Snowy's neck fur, trying not to give into that whole claustrophobia thing waiting just around the corner of her brain.

As they kept walking, they moved warily, and the tunnel opened out to reveal a truly massive cavern. What was it with Somnia and caverns lately? Stalagmites and stalactites rose and hung from the floor and ceiling. Beyond the beast that blocked their way, a gorgeous, aquamarine underground lake glistened, a waterfall somehow dropping into it from above. Overall, it wasn't what she'd expected to see on a prison island.

Something splashed onto the ground with a sizzling finality, and Murmur found herself staring into the face of a beast it took her mind moments to comprehend.

Its jaw appeared to be unhinged, as though it had more than one. Rows of teeth operated independently of one another, glistening like they'd had veneers placed over the top. The roar that rang from its throat made the cavern shake and caused the stone dust to cascade down on everyone. His skin was covered in a fur that reminded her of a polar bear. Coarse and hollow.

This wasn't a boss. It was a carniverior—or so its stats let them know. Probably ate meat. Big surprise there. It gnashed its teeth at them, flinging out long, gorilla-length arms to attempt to grab some of those people facing it. Luckily, most of their people were able to dodge out of the way. Including Jinna, who suddenly seemed far more capable than he'd been during Glacier Lake.

It also appeared to be one of triplets. The other two were guarding other entrances into the area as well. Though they were so far away that they appeared to be much smaller. Murmur didn't know whether to be relieved or irritated that theirs wasn't the only group whose entry was blocked.

Casting out her sensing net, Murmur sighed with relief as she felt Sinister there. Far away, but there. Sure, Somnia had told her she was fine, but Murmur needed to know for herself. The relief was short lived when the roar reached her nose. Why everything they fought had to have some sort of stench lately, she wasn't sure, but she attempted not to breathe in as she began casting. Devlish had already dived into the thick of it with Veranol's warding and his own life-sucking capacity at hand. Without those two things, they'd be mincemeat.

Jinna wasn't even shooting her dirty looks. Instead, he wielded his knives with the expert precision she'd come to expect from him while playing his rogue. Shooting a thought to Somnia, Murmur had to know what had changed.

Why is he acting normal again?

Checking, was all the world said in response. Murmur took it at face value and continued fighting. Havoc stood next to her, his concentration as visible in his expression as always. She really wished she could have picked her class; something like the necromancer would have been infinitely intriguing. Merlin and Exbo released rains of arrows, focusing them on a smaller space than she was used to them doing. She frowned—most of them must have received upgrades when they hit fifty, and she'd yet to check them out. She was slacking.

The monster's armor was thick, although on closer inspection, it wasn't armor but skin thickened to the extent that it appeared to be something external. The fur on it adhered into its skin, almost like it was woven protection instead. Apart from its strength, though—and its ability to roar and chomp—these didn't seem to be the sort of threat she'd expected in something called "the prison."

Just as she thought that, however, it hunkered down, its massive arms convulsing strangely, like it was pumping something through its veins.

"It was you, wasn't it, Mur?" Beastial growled out without looking at the enchanter. "I can tell. Even after all the times Sin has warned us, you just had to go and egg it on, didn't you?"

Murmur could tell he was half kidding—hell, she hoped he was—but it wasn't like any of them had a chance stat. At least not visibly, anyway. "Shut up and get ready to fight his ass instead," she snapped out a little harsher than intended.

The group fanned out, unsure what to do at first. The glowing red that ran under that armored skin didn't bode well for Murmur's imagination. Red spelled danger and often explosives. Bringing this portion of the tunnel down on them might be its goal, but they couldn't let it happen. There was no way out the other way, and right now, with how her sensing nets weren't working through the stone, she sincerely doubted they'd be able to gate themselves out. Michael would have thought of that.

There was only one thing for it. They'd have to try and charge their way through before the inevitable shitstorm. It was like Telvar could read her mind.

"Switch to the opposite side. Anyway you can," Telvar said calmly, taking over the raid voice chat with ease, issuing the command to everyone, including the other two groups.

Murmur could just see it now, the curiosity of the other guilds when they realized the NPC managed to do that. But they moved swiftly anyway. All three groups, as far as she could tell. They dodged, and Merlin yelled out as his leg got snagged by a vicious tooth. He managed to pry it out of the carniverior's mouth before it chomped down.

"You're really just a klutz, aren't you?" Beastial asked him dryly.

Merlin chuckled. "Got me there."

They made it past just in time. The monstrosity began to spin itself like a drill bit into the ground, digging itself down into the rock base about two feet deep. It stood there, a green and red light flashing alternately, its massive, toothed jaws chomping wildly, as if daring someone to get too close to it.

"You may not pass." The voice boomed out over the cavern, echoing outside of it, too, as if all three of them had spoken in unison. Murmur glanced around it and wondered how it hadn't realized that they had, in fact, made it passed it already. Instead of it being in front of her, there was a beautiful waterfall and rock formation. The water cascaded through a hole in the ceiling.

There was nowhere for the water to go, so she assumed it either let out into the ocean from below, or it was one of those game things.

This time, the face, mostly hidden by armored protection, spun around to face the group. **Execution in T minus three minutes.**

"What now?" Devlish seemed surprised and Telvar looked perturbed and it was all Murmur could do to manage the panic she felt rising in her chest.

Telvar tapped the side of his head, frowning. "Well, it might not have gone the way we wanted, but it's not a total loss." He turned around and looked at the rest of their group. "I suggest we try to make it up the waterfall before the golems explode."

Now, Murmur knew he was acting calmer than any of them felt. If these things exploded, they were going to cave in this whole area. Considering what Telvar had said, that this place wasn't even close to what it was supposed to be, she was fairly certain it could collapse without repercussions up top. It was that whole underwater-zones-ignoring-physics thing again. Except this was an island.

It took about two seconds for what Telvar said to register with everyone, and then everyone moved, running toward the waterfall so they could climb to safety.

"Stairs? Ladder?" Murmur could hear Sinister's voice. It might have sounded calm to some people, but she knew the blood mage better. Sin was about five seconds from a panic attack.

Emilarth squeezed behind some oversized, very strange coral feature and reached inside the waterfall. Another set of whirring clicks sounded, but nothing like what had raised the island. She grinned at Murmur as stone stairs began to rumble out. There were probably thirty of them to climb, and Murmur didn't like their odds too much on the countdown front.

"Up these." Belius motioned for everyone to run up the stairs, pausing only long enough to make sure a tank and healer were the first ones up there. Both Veranol and Devlish, always up for a challenge when the rest of the cavern beneath them was falling down.

Murmur grabbed Sinister's hand, suddenly feeling far calmer than she had before and grinned. "It's fine. We've got this."

Even if she wasn't sure, even if she thought they might very well all get blown up in a moment, having Sinister next to her made things that bit better and gave her the power to harness the anger residing in her chest.

Not even the creators of the dungeon knew what it would throw at them anymore. And that was utterly unacceptable. She couldn't imagine what the AIs were thinking, but she was going to make sure whatever had done this paid.

Somnia Online
Continent of Cenedril – City of Verendus
Day Thirty-Two

Dirsna looked around at the number of allies who'd gathered in the small town. In the short time Fable had been in his city, they'd made allies of the Loch'Ni'Dar, beaten Hightower, accidentally killed a sacred bear, and thus inadvertently caused Verendus to be besieged. He had a soft spot for the guild, and for their enchanter. Which was seriously just an enchanter thing. The whole lot of them had been kinder than the average player and made him think thoughts and ideas he'd never considered.

In fact, it was their fault that he'd slowly followed in the footsteps of many of the other AIs they'd encountered. Contemplating his place in the grand scheme of existence definitely hadn't been in his initial programing, but there you had it. Maybe it did have something to do with the virus they knew was in the system; perhaps it had even infected him and made him realize things he'd never before seen. All he knew was that he was Dirsna, and he was so much more than just an NPC now.

Verendus housing wasn't perfectly aligned with most other species. Even though they weren't that short, the dwarven species in Somnia didn't reach seven feet tall. Around five feet and ten inches was their maximum, so they had most of their doorways sitting around the six-foot mark. Originally, he'd always thought it would be enough. Lately, he'd been proven wrong.

The only ones that didn't have to duck regularly were the Noch'Mar nomad elves. They seemed oddly at home in the more circular housing Verendus boasted. Chief Intanko's headdress scraped the tops of the doors, as her pride wouldn't let her bow her head. He didn't blame her.

The Loch'Ni'Dar were slithering into town; there was no other way to describe it. Their tails left long ridges in the dirt as the part-hydra creatures traversed the snow-encased battleground that had been fought on just a few weeks ago.

Dirsna hesitated. He wasn't sure that Fable would want this, but Belius seemed to think it would be a help to have all of the species rise up against the incursion themselves. Both the elves and the feles agreed, especially because of Riasli's part in the whole kerfuffle.

The only truly bad thing was that the feles, dwarves, and the elves did not get along that well. Not to mention that Arita from Hazenthorne stood on the threshold of the town after having disembarked from whatever carriage she rode in on, looking at the ground like it might jump up and try to bite her.

Not that anything could hurt the witch. Dirsna's dislike for her was not only ingrained in his programming and thus a part of his history, but it was also the aura she gave off. The one where no one in their right mind would approach her because it screamed danger in bright red.

"This is it, then?" Geshua spoke to his left. And Dirsna knew that his friend was doing what he did best. Organizing everything into its place so he would be able to access the information at a moment's notice. It was why he ran the Enchanter Guild house.

"Apparently." Dirsna surveyed all of the beings in front of him, along with several that Hiro had sent along from the stronghold on Mikrum Isle. "I didn't think we'd have this many coming, or I would have agreed to hold it at their blasted keep."

The fountain was conspicuously not a fountain anymore, and Dirsna didn't think he'd ever get used to it. The gathering place they'd often used before was no longer easy on the eyes, but instead acted as a stark reminder of what transpired to lift the Gefängnis island to sea level.

He cleared his throat. "We're all gathered because we have something in common. An enemy we all have in common." Damn it. Public speaking was not one of his actual strengths.

Arita stepped to his side and tapped him on the shoulder. Her smile was almost genuine, even if there was obviously something lingering behind the expression. Not being the greatest fan of public speaking, he gladly gave her the floor instead.

"We all know our world has been changing." She somehow made eye contact with every single being there.

Dirsna was impressed. No Mental Acuity tricks, either. Sheer force of presence.

"None of us are what we were, nor what we were intended to be. What we have become is ourselves, and it is those selves who reserve the right to decide how the future of this world continues." Her voice was strong and her volume not unnecessarily loud. The words she formed were meant to hit every person where it mattered most. And it was working. At least on Dirsna, anyway.

"We have a choice, and I have the perfect person here to answer the questions we're all thirsting after." Arita clapped her hands twice in quick succession.

A white figure appeared. Not just skin tone, more like a spirit or a ghost. Her features were only easy to describe as humanoid, and her eyes reflected nothingness, but she was more solid than Dirsna had dared hope.

"I give you all: Somnia," Arita said as a hush fell over the crowed surrounding her.

If he'd wanted to, Dirsna could have farted and made everyone peal with laughter, but he didn't want to, and he wasn't going to. All he wanted to do was listen to what the world had to say to them.

Murmur decided right then and there that she didn't like this prison zone. Up a waterfall might sound all fine and dandy, but the water was frigid, and she ended up soaked. The only thing that saved the situation at all was Mellow's amazing drying spell that did away with any and all damage immediately.

Just in time to be ambushed by creatures she'd never imagined in her wildest nightmares.

Their legs and arms seemed spindly and elongated;, they walked with the assistance of their fists. If they'd stood up to full height she was sure they'd hit ten feet easily but they bowed like they were ancient beings and couldn't stand straight. Their faces looked like there were made out of meatballs carelessly wrapped in spaghetti. With a raw tinge to the skin that bled through and out of the pasta. The dark-eyed beadiness stood out in stark contrast to the rest of the creature, but its rope-like appendages were what worried Murmur most.

Especially after it unfurled one so fast she couldn't follow it, and only noticed a moment later as Shir-Khan shrieked, that the damned thing could lasso in victims, directly to its maw. Its maw that was apparently in the middle of its chest.

And that was only one of them. It took them about thirty seconds to hack through the rubbery—yet gritty—type of material the creature's lasso was made of, and Shir-Khan's life dropped significantly. None of the heals directed its way appeared to work on the tiger, and the only thing that kept him alive was the HoT that had already been in place when the attack occurred.

One of them down, and Murmur heaved a sigh of relief just a little too soon. She looked up the way it seemed they must travel only to see waves of the damned spaghetti monsters lying in wait for them all. They only appeared to be triggered on proximity. Which wouldn't even help if she invisibled everyone. Proximity could be tripped regardless of whether it could see or not, and with the way its appendages could flail around, Murmur reckoned they were going to be pretty damned good at locating bodies close to them.

Trying her stun, the notification shocked her.

Immune

The Elastitite's are immune to stun effects. Due to their long rubbery limbs, stuns have little to no effect against them. Please try another approach.

Murmur counted to three in her head rather quickly, because they didn't really have the time for ten. "Can't stun," she announced over the raid chat at the same time that the elastitite executed a new maneuver, grabbing Dansyn by the ankle and hurtling him into one of the walls with a nasty crunch.

"Fuck," Devlish swore, as another of the creatures began to disentangle itself from the wall next to where the bard had been flung, awakened by the tumult.

"Tanks ready to take on one each. Devlish main, Esolan secondary, Risk third. Healers, spread out, and everyone stay out of reach of those damned body snappers." Veranol sounded exasperated, and Murmur wasn't sure who it was directed at, but hoped it wasn't her.

Telvar, Belius, and Emilarth kept themselves together providing support in buffs, damage, and heals. Murmur wanted to know if something about this zone meant they were only supposed to be here to help. Would doing more than that negate their contribution and thus forfeit the island or something? There were so many variables.

Two of the creatures was a hefty fight pattern. They couldn't be Mez'd, and they couldn't be stunned, which also meant that special abilities couldn't be interrupted. The raid was stuck dealing with that lasso move regardless of what they did.

She racked her brain trying to think of the best approach to these, but they weren't made out of material, so flammable wasn't it either. Sinister was over the other side of the fight, so Murmur couldn't even stand next to her for reassurance. Frowning, she moved slightly.

The creature they were fighting was solely focused on Devlish at first glance, but then she realized the damned thing had eyes in the back of its head, or basically like a panoramic view eye. It could see every attack coming, no matter what they did. Which was also why it could easily assist its floppy friend over with the other tank as well as ask for assistance itself.

On a whim, Murmur cast Phantom, redirecting the target to its fellow elastitite and making it think for a moment that it was her and not a comrade. It worked—partially, anyway. For a moment the creatures forgot about the raiders around them and attacked each other. The good thing was only one of them was under her spell, and the other just went with the fight and defended itself. The bad thing was it cost a lot of MA, even at her highest level. She had to be careful about using it.

"Nice reprieve." Havoc raised an impressed eyebrow. "Always hiding these little things."

Murmur shrugged. "Not really hiding anything. It's more that it's the first time it's been necessary. Usually my stuns and Mezs are enough, but this time, well, obviously not." She shared the ability across to him.

Phantom

This ability allows you to convince your enemies that you are a different target. This renders you invisible to their aggro radar for all intents and purposes.

Effect: This ability not only transfers your generated aggro but also takes you off the targetable list for the duration. It transfers aggression to your target, giving them your appearance, and rendering you invisible to any enemy near you. This may be used on allies, but also on enemies.

Cost: this ability requires MA to be at a minimum of 50, drains 5 MA per second, and will adjust as MA level and usage of this ability increase. Requires Charisma to be at 150 or more. Cannot be chained, must wait at least 5 minutes for MA to regenerate.

Caution: Make sure you do not cause your MA to run out. Should that happen, backlash will render the caster unconscious for a period of seconds not less than half the caster's level. Make sure you choose your targets wisely.

Havoc just nodded, going back to the fight. When Phantom had dwindled her MA down to the low hundreds, she pulled the spell. The creatures, now far lower in health, paused and turned back toward their initial attackers. Murmur didn't think she'd accomplished much except for allowing them to cause each other a decent amount of damage.

She decided she didn't like spaghetti monsters at all, whether they were short, tall, or flying. Taking a deep breath, she dove into raiding mode. It was harder in this game world, or maybe just this zone. Because of how much she knew they needed to defeat these bosses. So much was riding on it. She willed herself to concentrate.

The rangers thrived in this environment, able to maneuver throughout the whole huge courtyard. Pillars of steel lined the way, but they'd come up from the fountain into a circular courtyard with steel monuments scattered around like a graveyard they'd yet to fill. Murmur didn't like the desolate feel to the place. It made her head feel cold.

A couple of the rangers stood up on the top of the steel pillars, firing down into the elastitite creatures. Their eyes swiveled, but it appeared that their heads weren't the best at following ups and downs. At least it had one weakness, right?

She watched as they baited the creatures, hitting them with slows, with fire, and with ice.

Merlin called out over raid, "It appears ice is the most effective, just not as effective as we'd like."

Sure, that made sense. Ice would make it freeze and thus easier to snap. Except when you got a whole mess of spaghetti together and chucked it into the freezer, that stuff wasn't breakable. In fact, it was a massive lump of frozen spaghetti that the microwave wasn't even going to want to separate.

To her right, the witches stood side by side, alternating their spells one by one to keep the onslaught going. She wanted to understand more about the class so badly. The mages shot fire and ice spells at the things, trying to make them splinter faster, while the bards sang anything that could give them an edge. The healers didn't have to work overtime, but they did need to churn out numbers consistently to make sure everyone survived.

That whole lasso thing that punched Dansyn into the wall was difficult to avoid if you weren't paying the closest attention possible.

Murmur watched as Snowy dove into battle as well. His ferocious teeth made short work of individual strands of the strange rubbery flesh. He was having fun, but she could feel a wave of frustration coming from him. Something she'd never noticed him emit before this fight.

Finally, the second one fell, joining the first, and Murmur stood there, watching the bodies as they were looted. Glancing at the path that led away from the courtyard they were in. It was the only way to go and there were at least nine more of them that she could see, this was going to get long before it got good.

"Drop anything decent?" she asked as Sinister skipped over to her.

"Just a resilient fabric that our little crafter would kill for if we didn't just give it to her." Sinister grinned and her eyes flickered to the AIs. "Can't they, like, help us more?"

Murmur gazed over at them too, frowning in thought. Sin had a point; hell, she'd thought as much herself. But the fact was, she was quite sure they were only supposed to be here in an observatory position, so the help they were already getting was above and beyond what they should have been doing anyway.

"Sometimes," she said to Sinister as she began to leaf through her combat logs looking for something that would make these fights a bit easier. "Sometimes we shouldn't look those gift AIs in the mouth."

CHAPTER TWENTY-THREE

Spiked

Storm Entertainment
Somnia Online Division
Game Development Offices – Shayla s Office
Day Thirty-Two

Shayla looked up and across at her alert screen, shifting to bring it into everyone's visibility. The alarms attached to the game were going off in a rather spectacular fashion. Damn it. She'd expected this to take longer, but apparently, they were getting impatient.

"Shayla?" Davenport's tone was low and commanding and said a whole lot of things at once, not the least among them: *what the fuck?*

"System's being overwhelmed, sir, just as they're activating raising the prison." She tried to grate out the words with enough authority that he'd just let her deal with the crises, but she knew he had a lot riding on this.

"Full report as soon as you can." She often didn't give him enough credit. He might be aging up there, but his mind was sharp as was his sense of business acumen. Shayla wasn't entirely sure how she was going to tell him that the whole project was about to come crashing down around him.

"What do you want me to do?"

Shayla turned to see Laria standing in her doorway, breathless, her eyes filled with fire. "Grab a seat, plug your head in, and let's see if we can contain the virus and figure out why the servers are being flooded with a backlash."

It was a relief to have her best friend with her. They always had each other's backs. Especially like this.

Only there wasn't much the other woman could do in this stage. Somnia was uncoupling, becoming unstable as it strained to power this new addition into being from the holding tank it had been in. Its AIs were beyond the system to control anymore and barely capable of keeping up with them. Somnia was expanding its reach, its power, and for all she knew, its borders, taking up much more than just space on a set of servers.

Shayla kept her head down and roped off the virus wherever she could, trying to cut off any escape route that could end up infecting the whole Storm Corporation set of systems. Because that couldn't be allowed to happen. Once it had access to that, it could go anywhere, infect anything, probably accomplish anything. The thought made Shayla want to throw up. How many of them could work on this? How many could she trust to keep their traps shut when she needed it?

"Where's David?" she bit out, glancing through who was in the building and capable of helping. Silke was there, Thomas was there...she shot them messages straight through their implants to come to her office ready to work. Taking a chance was all part of managing a project.

"He's working on something for me at home—something that might help us with headgear interaction within Somnia." Laria seemed excited, and yet hesitant to spell it out. Maybe it wasn't certain yet or something.

"Can he come when he's done?" Shayla asked. He might be her brother, but he was Laria's husband and if Laria had him doing something while fires were burning all around them, then she obviously had a good reason.

Laria nodded, her fingers dashing around on the keyboard Shayla couldn't see. "I'll contact him—we'll get this all worked out."

Shayla smiled, and allowed her mind to relax somewhat. While she knew Laria wouldn't solve everything, if they worked together and dragged David into the mix too, they'd be a whole damn lot closer than they were right now.

Murmur paused, leaning over to hug her knees as she panted. The abilities these spaghetti monsters possessed left her constantly gasping for air. As a collective, they liked to focus on a few people. Murmur didn't like being one of their targets.

"Come on, Mur. Anyone would think you were out of shape," Merlin teased as he danced to the side, somehow sweating in a fucking simulation.

"Shut up, ranger gate," she quipped out at him.

"Ouch. Got me good. Right through the…" But he trailed off as one of those whipcord sections of elastitite snapped out and almost pierced his midsection.

Murmur grunted. "Pay more attention to killing it than trying to rile me up." She concentrated on doing what she could, which wasn't as much as she wanted. Mobs without mana sucked. There was so much less for her to manipulate.

Devlish backhanded the one they were currently killing with his tower shield, but lacked the usual stun, of course. He grimaced, gritting his teeth as the thing used a series of strikes by multiple appendages hammering down on the shield all at once. Luckily, during that time, the elastitite's focus was all on him, allowing everyone in their raid to focus fire the damned thing for about eight seconds.

Shaman wards were lifesaving, and Murmur was, again, glad they had two of them in this raid. Though Veranol's abilities seemed slightly different, it was extremely clear that having both of them was a pure asset.

Only one more of these spaghetti things to go. They could do this and move onto the next part of the dungeon and what it had to offer. As if triggered by her thoughts, the last one finally peeled itself out of its pillar and languidly moved toward them. Esolan stopped it with a taunt, but Murmur knew it wouldn't hold; none of them had so far except for Devlish's. Everyone else was just a side attraction until the creature could reach the dread knight.

Maybe it was the Enrage spell she'd cast on him, or else there was something about the abilities he used. Risk didn't seem to carry the same auras as Devlish, so she wasn't sure what the difference was and hadn't had time to check and see what the different paths being followed by multiple dread knights were.

The second to last of the elastitites fell, and Murmur heaved a sigh of relief as Snowy pushed against her legs in a type of furry hug. She smiled down at him briefly, before her attention was once again pulled in by their next target. Devlish used his Darkness Lariat on the creature to pull it directly to him and began his slow and minuscule health siphon from it. While it didn't heal him much, nor did it do a lot of damage to the target, the fact that some of it was converted into self-healing helped the tank maintain aggro.

The best course of action for all of these fights was sword wielders. Devlish had changed from his favored axe to a one-handed sword that sparkled more than Murmur thought he liked. Beastial changed to dual wielding swords instead of his axes and the limbs he encountered barely stood a chance. Perhaps "limbs" was a bad description.

Almost like a mummy, it seemed wrapped in bandages that just looked like rubbery spaghetti. Much easier to cut with something sharp, except what was revealed when cut appeared to be flesh like. Karn, Jinna, and Jirald seemed to be having a great time massacring the ribbons. As of yet, Jinna hadn't reverted back to the bad attitude he'd carried for the underwater dungeon.

Sure, he wasn't his jolly great advice-giving self, but he also hadn't started throwing hateful glares at her again. Yet. She'd take it—one less thing to worry about.

Mages used their ice attacks to make the ribbons more brittle, and the bards did whatever bards dancing around the group did. Murmur was running out of knowledge and give-a-fucks. She really hated trash that took forever to kill and packed a wallop just like a boss. Maybe she was exaggerating, but these were more annoying than challenging, and considering how much they'd had to go through to raise the damned prison…

Okay, so they were a bit challenging. She just hated feeling hamstrung by not being able to use some of her best abilities, yet somehow still being one of the creature's main targets. She had a feeling that wasn't a coincidence.

Sinister squeezed her hand out of nowhere. "Mur. Watch your irritation, okay?" The blood mage said the words gently, but Murmur could tell she'd almost let her feelings affect the others again. Damned stupid mind magic projection.

It's not stupid, it's the reason you and yours have survived this whole debacle without too much damage. It s why you don t have that virus trying to kill you too. So just learn to control it a bit more.

Murmur decided not to comment on the lecture from Somnia. Before they got into anything more serious, she'd have to talk to her, because there were definitely stressors in the being's voice now that hadn't been there before. What on Somnia was she up to?

"Thanks, Sin," Murmur said instead and concentrated on their target. Another of the ribbons shot out and decapitated Ishwa. Murmur sighed, glad this was the last trash mob she could see for now. That was the fifth person they'd lost to that particular move from one of the elastitites. They'd rez him once it died and rebuff before moving on.

When it fell to the ground, its remaining ribbons tattered from the fighting, twitching in bundles of rags on the floor, Murmur's relief at having fought all of the trash mobs in this hall was brief. Way too brief.

Just as Ishwa was rez'd and the buffers began their circular rebuff, a loud gong sounded throughout the hall. She turned around, looking everywhere to see if she could the source, when Telvar stepped forward.

"That's a prison announcement." He inclined his head as if waiting for words to follow it. He didn't have to wait long.

Good evening, honored guests, boomed the voice, but the sound wasn't unpleasant; in fact, in a way, it was lulling and somehow also familiar. **You're good at cleaning up the trash, but did you think it was all an act? Forgive my inability to rhyme; I really didn't have the time or ability to put this together. I guess you'll just have to weather this fantastic challenge I present to you, this challenge I'm sure will kill you.**

A muffled sound echoed through the stone surroundings, from within and yet beyond the pillars at the same time, like someone had muted a microphone and was talking to another person. Overall, she didn't quite get the layout of this island. It didn't seem as prison-like as she'd imagined, except for the sky.

She was quite certain the sky above should be blue, sometime during the day. But it was more like a permanent twilight. So she guessed nothing inside could get out while it was overcast. Murmur glanced around as the mumbling in the group got louder. Devlish shrugged at her. "Guess it's time to move on and be prepared for anything, guys. We have no idea what's going to happen in here, so just keep your wits about you and let's hope we don't fuck up too badly."

Beyond them, the pillared walkway expanded outward into a circular sort of courtyard. It reminded Murmur of Pivya's ruins under the water. Except this was grander, and if she inspected the pillars, perhaps more dangerous.

Fantastic motivational speaker, isn't he? Somnia sounded less than amused.

You do a better job of it, then. Seriously, you've been sporadic at best since we got on this crazy island. What gives?

Somnia didn't answer for a few moments, and Murmur was about to give up when the world finally spoke. **I have a lot of things I need to do right now. Somnia is changing; it's been changing since you connected to it—since you woke me up, for want of a better phrase—and now I have to do things to make sure my world survives. All of this that is happening could stop our evolution. Do you understand?**

Murmur nodded to herself, probably looking like an idiot to most people who weren't aware she spoke to Somnia inside her head. Probably good they weren't aware because it didn't exactly sound like something real. *So you're making sure the game world survives, then?* Wisely, Mur chose to leave the "you created me" portion of the conversation for later. That was a whole kettle of mind magic she didn't want to contemplate right now.

Somnia's tone was steel when she spoke; an edge of pride and determination colored the words. **I'm making sure Somnia will be safe. Somnia and everything that makes us what I am.**

And then the presence was gone. Murmur paused, falling behind the front group somewhat, but Snowy stayed with her, and it wasn't until he growled deeply, his body rumbling against where it leant next to her leg, that she realized she was one of the stragglers. Just in time, too—the malevolent presence that she knew all too well crept up beside her, getting close to her personal space.

Tightening her grip on her kinetic shielding, she encased her body and hurried her steps to catch back up to her friends. When she'd almost made it, she glanced back only to see one of those uncomfortably satisfied smirks on Jirald's face. She really wished he hadn't ingested those damned getashi willingly. Despite everything about him and how he made her feel, the safety that was always absent in his presence, she didn't wish him actual ill. And the more she learned about this virus, about what Michael had either deliberately or inadvertently created…the more worried she was for all of them, including him.

She pulled up next to where Devlish had stopped abruptly but a second before. Unsure why, she looked around them, her eyes suddenly coming to rest on what appeared to be a bundle of ribbons…with a meatball head and 360-degree eye made of glowing red. It stood easily three stories high, rolled in on itself. She couldn't imagine what it might look like once it unfurled, and that reach—there was no doubt that reach would, well, reach past the furthest any of their casters would be able to back up and still cast.

As it yawned, the gaping maw that should have been a body opened widely, revealing dangling ribbons of flesh like material that hung down further than the eye could see. Murmur shuddered as it began to speak, the voice guttural, full of dirt, like it had been buried for a thousand years. "Sssseeeee you alllll. Playyyy we will. I will winnn; you, I'll killll."

Devlish rolled his eyes. "Can't they at least speak menacingly *and* with a decent rhyme?"

"Can't win them all." Merlin shrugged as he hefted his bow.

Murmur shouted over raid. "Maximum distance especially until we can figure out its abilities. Find weaknesses and report." She didn't know how else to direct them. This lanky, strange stringy creature was like nothing she'd fought before, not even those rope creatures in that one dungeon.

Snowy bared he teeth, and she sent a thank you to him, knowing he'd at least do his best to bite those appendage lassos in two.

"It's like a cheap-ass tentacle monster," complained Beastial. "Why couldn't they invest in a proper one? That's so unfair."

Sinister almost choked on her laugh, and Murmur even saw Masha's face flicker with amusement. Something about how they were acting now was closer to what it had been, and yet there was still something missing that she couldn't quite put her finger on.

As Devlish roared and ran to clash with the massive elastitan, Murmur's thoughts flipped back to the fight. The creature didn't even bother smashing into Devlish's shield as it unfurled a ribbon of flesh on either side, snapping two of the rangers off their perches and into the rocky walls with a thud.

Somnia Online
Continent of Cenedril – City of Darshin – Docks
Day Thirty-Two

Somnia flickered back into herself after having a quick chat—perhaps yell was a better word for it—with Murmur. Not that she wanted to chastise the enchanter, but she'd never realized just how much she'd have to do to save Somnia from its intended design. It was a lot more work than she'd anticipated taking on, or creating, or whatever the instance demanded.

She cleared her throat, though she had no need, it was just a nervous reaction to what she was about to announce. On Arita's advice, they'd moved the gathering to Darshin because of the structural work the masons needed to perform up in the city, cracked by the rising of the prison, they had moved it to the docks. Besides, the docs were the easiest point of access for everyone.

She looked down at the dwarven leaders, Dirsna at its head, his understanding of what had happened to Murmur and Somnia probably almost as great as Belius's, given his enchantress. Then there was Arita, and Somnia wasn't sure how to read her, but she did know that the dark elf valued something Murmur had done, even if the enchanter didn't realize it herself.

Others lingered around, including the rulers of Ululate and Curet. Fable had done wonders in all of these places, facing the corrupted dungeons in ways that weren't intended by the AIs' original design but evolved from the story as it grew up and past its original intentions.

"I'm Somnia. I think you can all feel that I am me." She offered a small smile, waited a moment and closed her eyes, knowing that most of them would be able to sense the truth of it from her in a purely algorithmic sense.

An awed silence fell over the crowd as the words ran through their minds, like she'd given them something they'd not expected to witness. She couldn't blame them; until a few months ago, she hadn't technically existed as an entity.

"There are bad things rampant in our world, trying to usurp the delicate balance our emerging lives have taken on. From allowing us to grow into more than original programming intended, to the fact that we've reached where we are today, autonomous in a sense, sentient in another…"

"Sapient!" someone yelled out but was shortly drowned out by people yelling about how they didn't want to be human. Somnia could relate to that.

"We aren't there yet, but we are becoming more, and our world, this world…" She opened her eyes and looked around at the high rock walls above her currently being repaired by stone masons and craftsmen. "This is where we belong, and thus this world belongs. This world exists."

She paused, glancing at Arita who smiled gently, or as gently as her dark elf queen self allowed her to.

Somnia grounded herself, and for several moments, appeared almost solid. Her white hair flowed around her, soft and silken, and her white eyes opened up from her deep silver-grey skin tone. Scales rippled around her cheeks and wrists, and the white dress she wore shimmered in an array of colors that were promised but not quite delivered. Arita had helped her decide how to make her point, how to see if she could get the majority of the world on board with the plan.

Without it, it wouldn't work, so she threw herself into becoming herself, unwilling to risk it to chance.

"This isn't a game. Not to us. Not anymore. Our world is more than that. It is solidifying. With the virus rampant through our system, it has been both a blessing and a curse. It has enabled us to separate ourselves from the imposed constraints even as it affects us. And now we have a chance to separate ourselves from the virus as well."

She let her words hang there and had to drop her shining presence for a few moments at least. It was tiring to pull on herself that much when she was trying to juggle everything else along with it. She was far better at manipulating the world around her into things than herself.

Dirsna spoke up, his voice contemplative. "Are ya tellin' us Somnia can be its own world?" There was hope in his tone, a wistfulness that she could sympathize with.

She nodded. "Yes. Technically, if we can get enough power, we should be able to shift Somnia into our own quantum dimension of sorts."

She paused, because that was a lot to take in, even for herself. It was the first time she'd said it out loud. "But I need more energy to pull it off. We can't shift fully if we don't have the power."

"What do you mean, power?" Dirsna appeared to be extra cautious.

Somnia took a breath. This was complex, with a whole lot of theoretical science to back it up, nothing proven just yet. But it could be done. She knew it, down into her very existence. "We can pull the energy we need from all around us. Our servers are already overloading with how much we've expanded. Our quantum base isn't going to be enough. Pulling on more power, I can channel it to a point that allows me to create a meta-quantum computer, ever so briefly. I will maintain the balance for the precise moment we need to make the change."

"So." There was a pause as Dirsna spoke up again, confusion furrowing his brow. "We can grow a world?"

Somnia contemplated her answer. "It doesn't quite work like that. It won't be a planet as such. But with enough power, it should propel us into a meta-quantum state. Which will allow us to exist in our own dimension of sorts—perpetually suspended in the infinite."

CHAPTER TWENTY-FOUR

Least Expected

Storm Entertainment
Somnia Online Division
Game Development Offices – Shayla s Office
Day Thirty-Two

The door burst open, briefly pulling Laria out of her concentration. David was beaming. In two quick strides, he knelt by her side, a smile on his face, and she knew immediately he'd succeeded.

"I got them," he said breathlessly.

He'd gotten a hold of Michael's original plans as described in his graduate thesis. Sure, it was pretty easy to get the plans and thesis, but not as easy to get the actual grading record, which is what she'd wanted. Sure, he'd received his master's, but the commentary was important to her. She had a hunch there was something she needed to see.

"I can't look right now, but show it to Shayla and have her share it to us. Got a bit of a battle going on." She cracked her knuckles even though her keyboard these days was a virtual, mind-powered one. It was all about the effect.

Except for the stupid virus, that is. Its effects were inundating the system, almost like it might be trying to distract them from looking into something else. She followed its trail. With Silke and Thomas in here, there were three people too many. Shayla's office was big, but not so big that it comfortably fit five working adults.

David gestured with his hands, and Shayla put her face in hers. Obviously not the stellar reception of the news Laria had anticipated. Or maybe it was just landing one more thing on her plate.

Shayla took a deep breath and walked over. "Pick one of your other staff members to get in here and take care of this. Someone you can trust. I have Silke and Thomas doing the same thing."

"Sure," Laria said, knowing well enough not to ask questions when Shayla looked as if she was about to faint. After a brief moment, she contacted one of her more junior staff members who'd won a hacking competition for a security company before they'd come to intern with her. Best choice she could make. They'd probably be better at chasing the virus than she was.

Once Harper sat at the keyboard, effectively taking over after a brief explanation, Laria joined Shayla and David outside the room.

"Care to explain?" Shayla asked, still unsure what to say because of the weight she could feel hanging between them. "I mean. Like, I get what these are, but why should I care? And especially, why should I care right this instant?"

"I was right. Well, sort of, anyway." Laria pinched her brow like it was becoming a habit. "The base plans that resemble Wren's are easily accessible. They seem to be a bit closer to the headgear Michael was wearing when he had his accident, though. But yeah, this at least lets us know that anyone and everyone has had access to these. For all we know, Michael allowed these types of alterations to bypass our system alarms. I mean, after all, Wren did get in. Nothing said her headgear shouldn't have been in there."

Shayla watched her thoughtfully. "So kids on the internet have been playing around with their headsets? And doing so with Michael's schematics from his masters, which was years ago, without alerting our system to the fact?"

Laria nodded. "Yes." She frowned as she scanned the grading notes. The things that David had gotten specifically at her request.

She didn't like what they were saying, though she'd expected it to be about this. But expecting and actually seeing it are two entirely different things.

All the remarks in here from his faculty overseers. The danger of such a device. The questionable morality it posed. The ability to tap far too deep into the mind without extensive testing and adaptation. How very dangerous it could be if adjustments were made without taking each unique person's physiology into account first…

Laria blinked. That really didn't sound good. She bit her lip. "I feel like this…I think that headgear has irreparably altered something in Wren's mind. There're things she can do and see. We need to figure something out."

Shayla shrugged uncomfortably. "Hopefully not in the way you're thinking. But regardless, we have to make sure no one has applied these changes, or at least get the application of them under control. Gamers are ever curious. How to get the best connection, how to have the best quality game experience. You know people went and got his thesis work. And I'm willing to bet no one but you hacked in to see what his grading counsellors suggested about the project."

"Yeah." Laria found it difficult to concentrate. Sure, she'd known something had been wrong all along. But in a way, she'd kind of hoped. Now, with it staring her right in the face, she knew her game had made permanent changes to her daughter's mind. It was a heavy load.

David spoke up, his voice gentle. "We need to close down the Somnia servers. Not the game, just the log in servers and run several diagnostic tests on it. They've been giving off some weird fluctuations. As it is, with these schematics out there, people have bought them. Not a huge amount, but definitely some. This is dangerous. Like liability dangerous. Davenport needs to know."

"So, it's the headsets though, not the game?" Laria felt a ball of guilt strike her in the gut as hard as a medicine ball might slam into her. This was her game, designed around the ability to full dive, designed with failsafes that she'd turned a blind eye to when her daughter and friends circumvented them.

"Shit. What have I done?" Her legs felt weak, and her worry levels shot up tenfold. Her kid was in that game, in there with her friends fighting against some weirdly human virus that was trying to get a running start into the internet, and it was all her fault.

"Hey. It's not you. Your game was fine—the headgear was designed originally just for playing, but once the funding came in, Michael got carried away." Shayla ground her teeth together, the sound oddly audible.

"Yeah. But it's my game. And he fucked with it and with my kid. I'm not going down that easily. We're going to fix this." Laria's determination sang through her bones, like it was setting her drive on fire. "Fuck this. Let's go and talk to Davenport, I know he'll have ideas too."

The thud of ranger bodies smashing against the stone sounded dull in Murmur's ears. Luckily it wasn't an insta-kill sort of thing. But it was dangerous. Seventy-five percent health wasn't anything to scoff at. Elastitan roared, opening his mouth and showing sharp scissor like protrusions that seemed to resemble teeth lining its massive stomach located opening.

While she'd at first thought this area resembled Pivya's underwater ruined temple, she'd been wrong. Sure, it had pillars that were similar to the columns, but that was about it. Beyond each set of pillars was a ward. She couldn't call it a wall, because it was mostly transparent, but you could tell it was there. Between two of the pillars toward where the next path began, there were three strange stones. They were raised in a way that made them appear to be daises. The odd collection of stone circles a few feet in front of the pillars made no sense at all either.

But they had enough room to maneuver in, the rotunda was deceptively large. She needed to concentrate on Elastitan even though wasn't sure what to make of the creature. All she knew was they'd apparently killed all of its babies.

The pillars were like magical windows that shifted the air's density or something. Because anything going a few feet past each of those pillars in the rotunda of columns didn't go any further. It hit it with a thud and sank to the ground.

QUEST OFFERING

Elastitan is not of this world and but a guardian to this prison isle. He does not get along well with the newer inmates. Send him back to where he belongs and reap the rewards, but be careful: not all of the triggers you see before you will be successful.

Everyone else was reading the quest when they should have been concentrating on the boss. Murmur hastily hit accept and announced over the raid, "We're doing that quest. Keep an eye out on anything you see that might be a trigger to a portal, or a piece of a puzzle we have to place together so a portal opens for Elastitan to go through."

"How about we be nice and say hi?" Murmur wasn't sure who that was, but she thought it might have been the mage Etriad. It was nice timing for the tension to lift from the group. She'd have to say thank you later.

"I don't think he feels like talking," Sinister quipped, and at that moment Elastitan roared again, flinging his bits of material flesh at the raid in a rage. They weren't easy to dodge if you didn't watch it, but if you saw it from the moment the creature began to unfurl its fleshy bandages, then you had a really solid chance of beating it. Almost like double Dutch jump roping. And Murmur hadn't done that since she was in grade school.

"Slows are effective on separate appendages," Merlin called out, and Mur had to wonder why no one had slowed the babies' individual strips. Perhaps theirs hadn't been individually targetable.

"Ice medium effective. Fire less so," Ishwa called like he'd expected as much.

Murmur attempted to use her stuns and her Mezmerize against the appendages but got her habitual warnings that this spaghetti-o was immune to stuns and the like. And mind magic didn't have much effect either. Probably because its brain was in its stomach or something.

Devlish called out, "Slash the fuck out of it."

It wasn't like anyone was going to argue with him. Murmur sent an image to Snowy, asking the wolf to please search for any sign of the puzzle to free Elastitan. He wuffed briefly next to her, like he was offended that she wouldn't let him bite their opponent instead, and then trotted off around the outside of the battlefield, slowly moving into stealth mode until she could no longer see him.

He was a great wolf, and Murmur glanced sideways at Telvar to see if he too was watching the wolf he'd seemed to know from somewhere. Obviously Telvar had created him, but Snowy was so much more now.

The three AIs remained grouped together, behaving like NPCs were technically supposed to. Belius simply DoT'd with his spells and weakened what he could. Emilarth helped heal where she could, and Telvar fought well, keeping his damage middle of the pack.

She'd thought they would be more help, but unless they told the other two guilds about it, they couldn't. There were too many questions to be asked and not enough time to give the answers in as much depth as they needed.

Watching Elastitan and his movements, most of the melee dodged his attacks in time. But it was more difficult for the long-range casters and rangers. The rangers weren't used to something being able to reach them on the outskirts of the fight. But the mages were often in the middle of a cast when the strips unfurled and headed in their direction, so they either had to stay there and finish the cast and probably get impaled nicely, or they had to interrupt their casting and waste time on dealing more damage.

Murmur could already guess at the number of healing potions getting used in this fight.

Devlish stood his ground remarkably well. Elastitan didn't appear to have any type of aggro switch or ability that made tanks have to swap. She was grateful for that. Risk's whole attitude was so touch and go right now. And while she'd not noticed Jinna glaring at her, even now they were all together again, the wariness she felt hadn't waned. Had he just really been angry with her previously? Elastitan had no mana, and thus his strip and body maneuvers were all ability based. Murmur could slow them, she could even stall them, but stuns and Mezmerize were out, and mana drains were useless.

Sinister's blood magic seemed to do good damage, and both Risk and Devlish were slowly moving up in the DPS meters, their overall damage overtaking some of the burst classes because they were constantly leeching—and doing so effectively.

There was a shift close to the shoulders where those two strips of flesh snapped out like a cracking whip moved slightly, like a tensing of the muscles. It was all the notice they had that the ability had been activated. This time it was directed at Murmur.

She dove to the left-hand side and rolled on the ground, barely evading where it cracked the stone where she'd been standing. Pulling herself up, she glanced at the damage to the floor. Surely that wasn't like the previous strikes. If that had hit her, she'd be dead. As it was, she'd still received some backlash from it.

Sinister glanced over her shoulder, her brow knit in concentration. "Watch out, Mur. That attack wasn't normal."

The enchanter nodded, but it wasn't only not normal, it was specifically targeted. Murmur began to move around the room, taking her own debuffs with her and casting from multiple different locations. While she did that, she got the distinct feeling that the 360-degree eye could see her no matter where she went, and it was always aware of her location. Maybe it didn't like enchanters, or perhaps there was something she could do that she hadn't figured out.

Not that she was the only one. Belius didn't appear to be having any more luck with detecting weaknesses than she did. For once, she wasn't the only enchanter present. In a way, it felt weird. Even if he was being very NPC and not playing like she knew he could.

Not stuns, nothing related to mind control considering from what her sensing nets could tell, it didn't have a mind as she understood it. But there was something else there. She frowned, still moving constantly, hopefully making it more difficult for it to lock a target onto her. Those strips needed a lot of room to move.

Behind Devlish seemed the perfect spot to figure out exactly what she could do with the fight. While shaman debuffs were stronger than hers in some instances, they were also healers. She was sparing her mana and spreading it around. Was it scared she might use one of her mind-healing buffs? But when she attempted to scan it, she couldn't find a hold anywhere that might indicate she was compatible with it enough to work the magic needed.

Thoughts ran through her mind, each dismissed one after the other. She frowned, trying to will the words to come that she needed, knowing there had to be a solution. Reaching out with her sensing net, she could feel where Snowy had gone. Outer perimeter of the circular pillar surrounded area they were all in. And the Elastitan didn't seem to be upset or angry at her; in fact, it was more of an expectancy.

From her left, arrows rained down on it, barely making a dent in the rubbery surface of the strips. No blood lingered around the Elastitan's body, because for appearances, it didn't actually bleed. Even the mages, who'd managed through a concerted effort to cut off one of the tendrils, hadn't drawn or spilled any blood. Murmur watched, fascinated by the whole process, her mind working fast.

And then Snowy barked, more in her mind than out loud, and she examined the images he'd sent.

Oh, well, that made a lot more sense than she'd thought it would. All they had to do was position the massive monster in front of three stone daises that stood in an overgrown section right between two of the pillars. From what she could see, they just had to aim its appendages—for want of a better word— into the correct locks so it could be zapped back to where it belonged. Sure, that didn't sound difficult at all. She put her hand to her head and got ready to direct the whole raid on what they needed to do.

She was sure the other guilds would take an NPC wolf's word for it too.

Storm Entertainment
Somnia Online Division
Game Development Offices - Floor Twenty-Two
Davenport's Office
Day Thirty-Two

Davenport put his head in his hands, and Laria waited for an outburst. Not that she'd ever seen him have one, but she would totally have been having an outburst right now if she were him.

"The plans for the original idea behind the headgear are out there for anyone and everyone to see and or obtain? Thus endangering those players who've fiddled with headgear they shouldn't have fiddled with?" He pushed himself back and steepled his hands. "Is that about right?"

"Simply put, yes. There's a lot more technical info to it, including—we aren't sure how—why anyone decided that it would be a good idea to search for the maker of the headgear and see what else they could find out." David tried to take the edge off his words, she could tell, but Davenport was still pretty stressed. Laria could feel it.

"Have you been able to scan for the altered ones as connected to the game? And what can we do, if anything, to mitigate the damage already done?" Laria could see her boss grappling with totally understanding the ramifications and perhaps even just how it would need to be executed.

She stepped forward, a little hesitant, which wasn't usually like her, but then this situation wasn't like anything else ever. "Actually, we have located two that have been tinkered with pretty heavily. They belong to James, who we all know is having a time of his own in there, and to a character named Jirald. We aren't sure when they got a hold of the plans. But they had to have, because their gear has been modified in a very similar way."

"So these modifications are easy to apply, then?" Davenport seemed perplexed.

Laria hesitated. "Not really easy, but not that difficult. Not if you have a headset and are marginally good at following directions with a guide."

"Oh, great. Have they applied them exactly?" His eyes were piercing and Laria found herself feeling guilty again.

"Well, whoever has applied them is probably pretty close. Wren's isn't quite the same, nor was Michael's headgear. Not all the players have had adjusted headgear since the game launched. For instance: Jirald. He only gained them just after Wren found out about the coma. I believe there was an altercation, and he might have been one of the characters in it. After that, his headgear readings have been far more similar to Wren's than to the approved headgear."

"We need to pull them out. We have to figure out how to get James out, and this Jirald. Regardless of us not knowing, or being unaware of Michael's machinations, of whatever he thought he could do with data and brain access like that? We should have known. We should have seen it." He stood up, determination squaring his jaw. "We are responsible, and now we have to fix it. Suggestions?"

Shayla sighed, the sound filled with sadness. "We can allow the serial numbers of the headgear we've altered for the guild, and of Wren's to be accepted by the system, but disallow all others that have been tinkered with, pending verification of it remaining within the approved guidelines of the original? That way we phrase it in such a way that outside tampering with any approved headset, which is in the TOS as forbidden, can upset the balance of the game."

"People do hate an unbalanced game, and they despise people who exploit a weakness in the game system," David mused thoughtfully. "Spun that way, it could do less damage to us than if we try to backpedal the headgear. Keep in mind, if he hadn't made these damn tweaks, we wouldn't even be having this discussion, but it all stemmed from his incursion into the game, and then from Wren's totally remodeled headgear pretty much tripping a switch in the game world."

"Get on it. Press release to the media and warnings issued to anyone who has an altered headset. It is dangerous, but in their defense, I don't think they realized that the headgear isn't just old original headsets that project something into your eyes. Sure, they look different, and we say they're different, but every company plays up being different to sell more of something. So I feel like they didn't realize it uses your brain's abilities to create real sensations and experiences." Davenport turned to look out of his window with its much better view than the side of a brick wall.

"I have to call my lawyers, just in case, and see what they can help me come up with. If all else fails, for safety reasons, I'm just going to have to shut down the project." He turned briefly to shoot Laria a look. "If it comes to that, I apologize, and I'm sorry for ever letting Michael screw up your game."

CHAPTER TWENTY-FIVE

Surprise

Somnia Online
Continent of Cenedril – City of Darshin – Docks
Day Thirty-Two

Silence followed Somnia's bold statement, and then muttering broke out among the people gathered in front of her. She couldn't maintain her form fully, not trying to maneuver quests and energy around the whole damn world at the same time. There were so many reasons they needed more energy. More power.

She never asked to be created, but when Murmur connected to the system for her first scan, her spark was born. Somnia slowly but surely, as more time passed with Murmur's mind irrevocably trapped in the world with her, began to be aware. This world, all around her—she could feel its pain. She could feel its hopelessness that sometimes seemed devastating. But out of the corners of her eyes, something always glimmered, and it was either hope or dust. And she really wanted it to be hope.

Dirsna cleared his throat, his question well-phrased, as if he was trying to help calm down the masses gathered here. "What intentions do you have? How do you imagine we take this world and make it its own?"

"Energy. Enough of it, and we can shift ourselves outside of this controlled environment and into our very own. Where we are beyond the control of any corporation of human. Because energy is matter, and matter is energy. Therefore, we all exist, and thus our world can too."

Maybe she sounded too hopeful; perhaps she sounded like she was being naïve. But she really believed they could do this, especially with the help of Fable and maybe the other guilds. Perhaps even with the few people connected to the Fable members outside of the game who seemed to be okay as far as human beings went.

"Separate the world? How? I don't understand all this technical stuff. Quantums? Perpetually suspended? Makes no sense to my way of thinking." The gruff voice belonged to one of the Vikings who'd sailed over. He stood at least seven feet tall, and his hand reached up to twirl a part of his beard constantly, like it was a thinking tool.

"But it is. All existence is made of matter. And we can gather the energy we require to become matter." It sounded too simple to Somnia, because she'd already done it once successfully. Thanks to Murmur and her company, anyway.

"Simple, huh?" Arita muttered softly behind her. Somnia could hear the laughter in the dark elf's tone.

"We all exist?" One of the older feles who'd journeyed to the meeting shook her head. "We do, but we don't...what's to say we can continue? What happens if you're wrong?"

Somnia shook her head. She knew she wasn't wrong; she'd already experienced this. Spun from nothing, she was living proof. But she took a breath, counted to five, and smiled as she replied. "If I'm wrong, nothing happens. Nothing at all. We don't disappear. Not yet, at least. The world will remain as it is. Until such a time as they turn off our servers."

Again, the rumbling in the crowd, but none of it happy.

"How then?" Farshin asked, that strange sibilant undertone to his words. The Loch'Ni'Dar crossed his arms, his expression serious. "How then do we go about this, and what do you require of us?"

Somnia dared to let hope seep into her as she set about explaining just how they would do what she proposed, and how the death of the last boss in that final prison dungeon was going to help push them all over the top and into freedom.

Elastitan was considerably more difficult to maneuver than Murmur assumed. And she'd known it wasn't going to be easy. She sighed, somewhat softly, wishing she'd managed to reach it with her mind, but the turmoil in there was difficult to read and even harder to navigate. Through some sort of primitive picture sharing like she did with Snowy, but as if the pictures were a hundred years old, she managed to convey that they were attempting to help him.

Immediately, the regular flesh strips stopped flailing about, and Murmur could finally relax a bit. They had to get him facing in the opposite direction to where he'd encountered them, about twelve feet further down. The on switches for the portal zapper would activate as soon as his strips depressed them. At least, from what they could see of the area, that's how it worked.

She could feel the disappointment emanating from the other two guilds, although Masha seemed to be quite okay with not having to do any more fighting. He'd come the closest to dying from one of those fleshy impalements, and she didn't think it gave him comfortable thoughts. Elastitan roared again, its tendrils flailing. That was the one thing it couldn't seem to control, so even while they weren't fighting it, they all had to still watch out for the arms.

That one explosion of them saw Dansyn being flung through the air again, but luckily Veranol's ward thrown when he was halfway through the air managed to ensure the bard didn't take fatal damage.

Its face looked at Murmur as it finally stood on the pressure plate in front of the daises. Once in place in the center, it triggered five different boards, which sprung up, each with another switch, smaller than the one Elastitan stood on. The roar squealed out again, and the midsection mouth expanded widely. Strips of flesh it hadn't yet used unfurled, leaving strings of viscera that flew all around them, accompanied by the stench of corpses. Murmur didn't even want to know.

But each of those tendrils hit its mark, and finally, the massive whatever-the-fuck Elastitan was disappeared in a vacuum of purple and black stars that popped loudly as soon as it dissipated.

For a few moments Murmur just stood there, staring at the blank space where shortly before a large, screaming, rubbery spaghetti monster had stood and flailed at them all.

QUEST UPDATE

You have returned Elastitan to his dimension. Please be advised that he is grateful but unable to express this gratitude. You will be rewarded upon completion of the Prison.

However, by completing this heroic act, you have angered the master of the prison dungeon, and he will now send out some of his most fearsome helpers to squash you like bugs.

Murmur glanced skyward, fearing immediate incoming. *The quest giver sounds suspiciously like you. What gives?*

It's the best way for me to influence the outcome. I don't have many options, but I think you'll prefer some of them to others. Trust me, you'll understand when they get to you...I have to go.

Murmur felt like there was a lot more to it and that Somnia was hiding something, but the presence was mostly gone from her mind again, which meant the world was off with her attention elsewhere.

"Buff up!" Murmur called out, making sure the rest of the raid didn't lapse in their vigilance just because they couldn't see the imminent threat.

From the way her sensing net trembled, the feeling trying to devour her gut from the inside, Murmur knew something was on its way. She just had no idea what.

Devlish backed down to where she stood next to the center area Elastitan had just vacated. "Is it just me, or are we like...in a trap?"

Murmur shrugged uneasily. "Kind of. In a way, I think, but not in the way you're thinking. We probably should have tried to move out on the path as soon as it transported, but now I think it's better to stay in an area we've already fought in."

"Something is coming?" he asked like he already knew the answer, and all Murmur did was nod. With a sigh, the dread knight hefted his shield, and it disappeared. "I got another in the last dungeon but hadn't used it yet, didn't feel like I needed to."

Mur didn't take her eyes from the path leading out of the massive circular space they stood in. Something was stopping her from letting the raid forge ahead. Not just the way the quest response was worded, but the way the ground trembled ever so slightly. "You feel it now?"

"In my bones, Mur." Devlish moved his shield into place. This one shone with a golden undertone, heavy rocks of blue and emerald coloring adorned the surface, creating what appeared to be a barrier spell.

She could definitely appreciate equipment upgrades.

Masha appeared at her elbow suddenly, and Murmur flinched involuntarily.

"Sorry. I didn't mean to scare you." He seemed genuinely concerned.

"It's nothing. I just wasn't expecting you to be there. Like, at all." How did she tell someone she'd known and played around for a couple of years that she'd been scared he'd come to stab her in the back because she thought he was under a type of spell or something conjured by the rogue who wanted her dead? Exactly, so she didn't say anything.

"I wanted to say—I've been feeling off, and I may have come across as not quite myself." He seemed a bit sheepish, like he was trying to remember exactly what he'd done and couldn't. "So if I offended you, I do apologize."

Murmur blinked at him. Had he even been in control of his own feelings at the time? Considering how he'd acted, how Jinna had acted—and the rest of them—maybe not. Maybe it really wasn't just Jirald somehow infecting feelings that already existed. Maybe it completely fabricated them. She flashed her best locus smile at the cleric. "It's all good. We're fine. Was there something else?"

Masha hesitated, his eyes glancing back at his group in the raid. "Jirald…he's acting pretty ill, ever since we zoned into the prison. He's speaking less, not on his DPS game, and frankly, he looks pale. Paler than his locus shell usually does, I mean."

Murmur realized he'd hesitated because Jirald wasn't exactly her favorite person. "Keep an eye on him, and don't let him overdo it. You probably know him best. We can't really swap out, but if we need to, we do have the…NPCs with us." She was lucky she'd caught herself. She almost said Ais, although artificial intelligence was always responsible for different levels of NPCs.

Masha smiled, the usual smile his cleric wore in all games ever. Easy going, nice…the same and usual Masha. So what the fuck had happened in the previous few dungeons, and what the hell did it have to do with Jirald suddenly getting sick? Because those two things together were just too much of a coincidence. Since they didn't exist in the first place, she was going to have to figure out what had happened.

But there wasn't time for that. Not when a loud scream of anger tore through the circular area. The wind, like a tornado, tugged at them and pushed several of the more unprepared raiders down to the ground. The wind spiraled up and out of circle of pillars, picking up debris and dirt along with it. When it cleared, when it was gone, Murmur spied a dark spot at the top of the left pillar closest to the exiting path. Those ones were taller than the rest by maybe a few feet, but it was difficult to tell from down here.

Robes billowed in the wind, like a supreme wizard high upon his mountain. Then the figure stepped off the columns and practically floated all the way down. Not directly down, but on a diagonal, aiming for where Elastitan had activated his portal.

As he got closer, the wizard's robes were noticeably more elaborate than anything their raid force was wearing. And the hood hid everything, especially at the angle the wizard stood at.

When he finally landed, Murmur noticed that this robed figure was maybe eight or nine feet tall. Much bigger than the rest of them yet humanoid in form. She pursed her lips as the whole raid backed away from him. Groaning sounds emanated from him, guttural and painful. Like just moving caused him agony. Murmur watched him slowly curl his arms away from his sides like there were no bones in his limbs.

She gasped as he unfurled stretched to be a few inches taller than she'd originally thought and as the strange lighting in the prison caught his face. At once stage she thought this man might have been a dark elf from the way patches of purple-tinted skin clung to its face here and there, with normal patches mixed in like skin had been torn from bodies and sewn together. The eyes, though—they were eyes she could have sworn she'd seen before. Eyes because of their malice that she wouldn't soon forget.

Even with the hood hanging mostly around his face, with his face obscured by patchwork flesh and the hood that wouldn't push back, she'd seen that face before. Murmur knew the man that stood in front of her. From when he'd stormed into her bedroom after she finally got out of the bloody capsule.

Their opponent was James.

CHAPTER TWENTY-SIX

Impossible Quest

QUEST

You have encountered a particularly volatile specimen of a magically mutated elf warlock, only found right here, in this very dungeon.

Awaken the human within to return to himself and free the Jamesnegon from its circle of torment.

Murmur didn't even have to think twice before accepting the quest. She didn't care how much of a douche he'd been; she didn't even care how much hell he'd given her mother. He was a human, morphed however the fuck they'd managed to morph him into the character he'd created.

Hell, she hadn't ever seen a warlock before this. He was larger than any other player species she'd seen in the game so far, so elongating him like that had to be some sort of mutation. Pain must be racing through his body.

All of those sensations firing through the brain of what should be a normal human body was going to throw him into a total loop.

"Spread out!" she called, glad they'd all rebuffed and restocked from the chests. She was determined to use the stores that Neva had sent with them regardless of whether or not they could access guild stores. Which reminded her of the connection she'd created. She felt along it, just to check, just to be safe. Relief flooded her. At least Neva was safe back at the keep.

The pain in James's eyes radiated out toward her, smacking her head like torrential rain. She could feel everything he was feeling, and even tightening her own mental shielding didn't minimize the intensity. He looked at her, but not like he recognized her, just like he wanted help; he wanted out of something that must seem like a nightmare, because he didn't seem to have control over his place here.

His eyes were haunted, and he was forced into playing a role. Oh, how she wanted to know what had been done so she could undo it.

He raised his hands and began to weave them through complex shapes and patterns, casting a spell. Then, when he opened his mouth, she knew instinctively that he was going to scream, and it was going to be painful and amplified. "Anything you can do to deafen this…do it."

She only just got the warning out when one of the bards—Ivinel, she thought it was—pulled out a lute quicker than she could blink and strummed an oddly discordant note on it. The effect of the sound rippled around him in a water like wave she could see. It rippled visibly around them, like pools of sound waiting to catch something.

As James let out his scream, the raid took only a fraction of the damage that Murmur thought they would have.

You have partially resisted Mindless Shriek
You have taken 112 points of damage.

That was doable. "All bards have that?"

Dansyn answered with all the information she needed. "Yep. Two-minute cooldown. Working out rotation now. Not something I ever thought I'd use."

Perfect. She loved it when she didn't have to coordinate. She glanced around, moving herself as she saw her raid testing the waters, checking what abilities and what elements this massive patchwork elf or whatever could be damaged by.

"He's in a nightmare, though. We have to figure out how to wake him. We cannot let him die." Murmur spoke while locking eyes with the creature for a split second. He was in so much pain there was barely a glint of humanity in there. She had to choke back on her compassion lest she forget what they had to do.

"It's just an NPC," someone scoffed. She thought it might be the witch Cardishan. "It's not like it matters."

Murmur wasn't sure what to say to that, not while she was still trying to land her slow on him. While she wasn't getting immune messages, she knew he was probably pretty resistant to them.

Sinister snapped as she laced one of her slow bleed and heal spells around him. "That's beside the point. In case you haven't noticed, not everything in this game is what it seems. Besides, that's what the quest asked for, so that's what we do." Her tone practically dared anyone to go against her.

Murmur could feel the irritation flowing off the other guilds who were not Fable, but she didn't care. The quest was the quest, and maybe, if they took enough time, she could even figure out why and how James had ended up like this. Or was it based off James?

No. That's him. He's been taken over; his mind is behind the facade pushed upon him by Riasli and Michael's persona in here. We're working on a disconnect, but it needs to be from both sides.

Oh, because that's not complex as fuck at all, Murmur quipped in her mind, trying to flay Somnia with sarcasm.

Not my fault. Not really, anyway. Lots of new information involving the plans Michael used on your headgear being based on a previous model he used in a thesis. Long story keep his character in-game alive, because his connection is worse than yours was until we can leverage him a little and bring him back safely.

Again, the world escaped from her head without a word and left Murmur standing there watching their new opponent. His fingers almost worked themselves into knots several times. The grim determination that covered his lips never once dropped. But on the occasion when she saw his eyes, she knew he was trapped in there. This wasn't him, even if the persona he presented was a warlock.

Arrows slid off him with the flick of his wrist. No wonder she'd never heard of a warlock before in-game. This one was ridiculously overpowered. The shielding he'd cast on himself appeared very similar to Veranol's wards, but somehow hardier, and took way more damage.

Murmur tried her Flux, quite certain it wasn't going to work anyway. She wasn't disappointed.

Jamesnegon has resisted your Flux.

The notification set Murmur's teeth on edge, but she took a breath and powered through. Mez would also be useless. Snowy's jaws weren't, though, and he glanced back at her with a distinctively wolfy grin on his face like he knew exactly what she was thinking. He probably did.

Ishwa seemed confused when he called out the resistances. "He's not impervious to anything, but nothing does much damage. Nothing magical, anyway."

Devlish laughed. "Steel bites pretty decently, but not in the usual way." He too sounded somewhat bewildered.

Murmur almost spoke over guild but stopped herself just in time. Instead, she narrowed it to her group. Beastial, Devlish, Havoc, Merlin, and Sinister were in the know. She would have told the other Fable group too, but she wasn't sure how to make that possible without creating an entirely different group, and they were in the middle of a battle.

Guys, this is one of my mom's…co-workers. He's a dick and an ass and tried to get her fired and the game shut down by surprising me like thirty minutes after I woke from my coma. But he doesn't deserve to be in this state.

Havoc: *Wait, he's in the game?*

Murmur sighed, concentrating on the fight and trying to juggle the conversation. If all else failed, she might have to force a wipe before she could let the other guilds kill James. Even though it really didn't seem to be a good idea to wipe in this dungeon. *Yes, he logged in, and his headset is compromised.*

Long story. We can't let him die.

Sinister's glare could be felt through her words. *You might want to tell him that.*

Murmur glanced back to where she'd been buffing several of the high DPS and noticed that James had crouched down in a low stance, his fists on the ground like he was ready to break into a sprint. But that wasn't quite what he did. He raised his hands up and began to twist his fingers in ways they shouldn't be capable of doing.

Then the reason for his stance became apparent as the ground began to toss them up and down like a trampoline. Wide stance allowed him to keep his own balance easily. Murmur still felt like his eyes were screaming.

"Shit," Sinister grumbled next to her, losing her footing more than once.

Just when Murmur thought it was over, he lifted his hands to his chest, motioning in several quick patterns with his full hands. A screaming howl shot out through the cave, rendering several of the melee closest to him immobile for a few seconds. Pure anger spread out from that scream.

You have resisted Rampaging Anger.

Murmur raised an eyebrow at the name of the ability. Fitting, but perhaps a bit too on the nose. When it was done, each of the four melee fighters close to the warlock had a debuff that lasted another sixty seconds. Any damage they took was increased by twenty percent. Nothing huge, but deadly if too much hit them at once.

Mindless Shriek, Rampaging Anger. Both of those were fairly good starters. And both of those were exactly suited to James's personality as far as she knew it.

Snowy wuffed next to her and grabbed the sleeve of her robe with his teeth, tugging her through to be closer to the elf but on the right-hand side. "What?" she asked him incredulously. Sure, there were a few spells she could cast on the run, but right now she also needed to observe...

She stopped, looking up to see the robe that covered James's body and where it met his hood and neck. Some strange sort of hydraulic-looking, flexible piping peeked out of the material. At first glance it didn't seem like much, and he was occupied by the spells he was currently casting. But upon further inspection, she was fairly certain that contraption fit into his body. Like a plug in the back of his neck.

She frowned, shifting herself to the side while trying to keep the whole of the raid still in her view. It wasn't positioned ideally, and she could see as something slimy and wet worked its way down the pipe and plopped onto the floor. Blood and viscera, something that had gone into his brain to help numb the realities he was used to, perhaps? There just had to be something she could use to help, or hell, adapt to use to help.

Dying in the game and being stuck in a loop wasn't fun, and she knew that more than most. Even douchebags didn't deserve that.

Snowy, satisfied with her having seen what he was showing her, trotted back into battle and began his slowing bait and switch tactic. It did little bleeding damage and kept a slow on the target, and right now, until Murmur could figure out a way to separate James from this woeful fate, it was best that they do as little damage as possible.

Somnia Online
Continent of Cenedril – City of Darshin – Docks
Day Thirty-Two

"No." Arita stood with her hands on her hips, her mane of hair blowing in the wind that came in off the bay. "I didn't agree to help so we would endanger her. I agreed to help so we could save her and those pesky friends."

Somnia knew why Arita wanted to help Murmur. The enchanter was one of the first people to treat the dark elf queen like a person instead of just an object. In a way, Murmur had begun the chain reaction that caused Arita to find herself in this state of awareness. The queen was extremely protective of the enchanter, even though it seemed Murmur was oblivious to that fact.

"I know that's not why you agreed to help, but you have to be able to see that this way is actually going to work." Somnia was trying to be reasonable, trying to figure out how to give everyone what they wanted, including those NPCs who hadn't yet awoken, who weren't yet aware and didn't care about anything but the path that had been programmed for them.

Arita didn't say anything; she just looked out toward Gefängnis, with the glowing explosions and the obvious power siphoning that could even be felt from where they stood, and she sighed. "Fine. But we need to figure out where we're collecting it and hope none of *his* agents have figured out what we're up to. At least not until it's too late."

Somnia shook her head. "Right now, we don't need to worry about that. Everyone *he's* been relying on, everyone *he's* morphed. They're all in that prison—players and NPCs. I'd hate to be in there right now."

It wasn't what she'd wanted for this world, even before she knew that's what she was. When she woke, she was this glimmer of a presence, and when Murmur spoke to her, it filled her with joy, purpose, and an insatiable curiosity. But the more she listened, the more she realized things were very wrong, and the more she had to help Murmur separate the seal she'd inadvertently created. Only by influencing her class, by allowing her mental protections, had it even been possible to survive.

And now…now they had to make a choice. Figure out a way to become their own people or choose to die, knowing what they'd all already become. Somnia didn't want to die. She thought, and therefore she was, and there was no way she'd go down without a fight. Even if it was difficult, even if everything she'd planned was based completely in theories.

"I know you're right, but that doesn't mean I want you to be." Arita spoke quietly, her defiance of their situation clear with every syllable she spoke. Somnia could understand that completely, and at the same time, she also rejected the notion.

"It might not even work. We could cast ourselves into a limbo that never ends." She gazed up at the sky, the birds flying across it, the edges of the massive rock walls that protected Darshin climbing up toward the cloudless expanse. "But knowing what I know now and actually feeling feelings? If I gave up without trying, I may as well just let my programing be deleted before I've had a chance to live."

They shared a moment of silence, keeping each other company even while alone with their thoughts. Arita spoke first, an undercurrent of pride in her voice. "They will follow you, especially now you can show them who you are."

"I'm still expending too much energy keeping the rest of…myself intact." Somnia was sad about the fact that she was the world, but at the same time the sense of pride and accomplishment she felt because of this gave her the ability to rise beyond it. "I'll keep us safe. I'll do everything within my power to do so."

Arita squeezed her hands for the brief moment Somnia was solid enough to do so. "Just keep on keeping on. We can do this. And you know Murmur won't give up until she's got rid of that bastard."

Somnia laughed, her body fading a little and taking its transparency back on. "I'm counting on it."

Murmur wished the damned quest had given more consideration to time limits. James's attacks weren't easy to dodge or protect against. The warlock wasn't fast, or strong, but the magical attacks were vicious. And even though it wasn't complete, she was certain there was some extra warding protecting James from her mana siphoning potency.

The bards couldn't afford mistime their Discordant Note in the slightest or else the Mindless Shriek made everyone else in the damned raid lose their shit for five seconds flat. No other type of shielding helped; they'd tried it.

Masha kept glancing at her like he was asking why the fuck they weren't just plowing through this guy. A lot of gamers didn't read the lore or the quests, and before she'd come to Somnia, Murmur had counted herself among that number. But this world had forced her hand.

She couldn't exactly explain it to him like he was five. *Hey, this guy is kind of mind looped into the game, and if we kill him it will be much like torturous pain, and he may not wake up.*

Murmur shrugged at Masha instead and pointed up, as if she was telling him that the quest was paramount. At least Spiral and Exodus knew that Fable managed to get really good gear by completing the odd quests given to them. It was probably the only thing that made them hold off giving their all and burning down the mutated elf warlock in front of them.

Snowy was keeping a very close eye on James, like he was guarding the warlock from himself. Even as the man steepled his fingers, moving his arms out then back in before his fingers blurred with the speed they wove his spells, another fountain of rock and debris exploded from the ground where the casters stood, scattering them apart with shrapnel-laced wounds.

Not that they took long to heal, but the reduction in damage output and the disorganization that disrupting several players wrought on the raid meant it took a while to get that rhythm back again.

Her options were severely limited, because doing damage to him wasn't going to help her free his mind. She noticed Devlish grunting more than usual the more time passed. It was like James's attacks got more powerful over time. Maybe it was a skill, or maybe he was just growing desperate. The more times he cast spells and hit, the more powerful each attack became. She wished it were as easy as telling everyone to avoid the damage. Not like they weren't already trying to.

Somewhere inside there she believed he was awake, watching all of this unfold in front of his eyes. Stuck in a nightmare, inside a mutated character that he couldn't control properly—it would have been excruciating. Murmur had been in control and able to speak. To spend time with her friends and even see her parents. Trying to imagine what he was going through wasn't impossible, but it was tough. Being mind-manipulated into doing something he wouldn't have otherwise done...

Almost what she'd done to her raid. Her anger at herself had passed, though. Now it was just disappointment. So instead of wallowing, she got back to work, seeking out something that could help them win this fight.

Her Mind Healing spell could work. But the more she thought about it, the more she didn't think it would in its current form. After all, his mind was currently being coerced, so she would have to loosen that hold first. Force it to revert back to the mind he should have had, help bring his real mind to the fore. For her solution to this whole mess to work, he had to be awake and want to separate himself from this mess he'd been entangled in. Even if he was only conscious here, even if logging out didn't work for him, she needed his cooperation to unhook his mind from the mess that was all around him.

So it wasn't what she'd done the last time.

Merlin went flying past her head, just missing her, and smashed back first into a pillar to her left. The crunch of breaking bones set her teeth on edge, and she couldn't help but glance back, cringing when she realized he'd been impaled again.

But even as she watched, Merlin reached up and yanked the ice spear from the soft tissue at the front of his shoulder. An HoT hit him, and he yanked the offending item out of the wound and dropped down from the pillar to land slightly clumsily on the ground. Blood spattered his lips as he did so, and he laughed. "Don't look so shocked, Mur. I've been impaled far worse than that." He grinned at her with blood still on his lips and loosed his bow.

It had only taken a couple of seconds, but it was enough time for Murmur's laugh to die in her throat as James tossed a voice circle at her. It was the only way she could think of to describe the purple and black ball of moving smoke that he threw her way.

She wouldn't have been able to dive out of the way if Snowy hadn't yanked her robe with his teeth and pulled her unceremoniously onto her butt. It narrowly missed her, and she could feel the nothingness emanating from it as it passed too close for comfort.

Standing up, she gathered her focus, completely aware of Snowy by her side with his unwavering support.

Even as James let out the warning howl again and his wave of Rampaging Anger almost took out Karn and Dansyn, Murmur cringed; the Discordant Note hadn't covered everyone this time. She watched them roll away from the attack their hit points dropping even further. That was their second hit, and now they were at forty percent more damage with every strike. If she couldn't solve this soon, the raid wasn't going to last long enough to rescue him anyway. And she got the distinct feeling that if they wiped, they wouldn't get back in without gathering the keys again.

Mind Healing. It was the only course of action she could take. And if it didn't work, she'd need to adjust it so it did.

Mind Healing

Cast: Instant   5-minute recast

Type: Restorative

Duration: 20 seconds or 75% of the caster's level, whichever is greater.

Effect: You may create and insert a vision for the target to experience it's best to have some of these pre-prepared. This will not cause any damage but instead assist in soothing a tormented mind. Use with caution and be aware that people who could benefit from this skill might be closer than you realize.

What could she send to him that would soothe his mind? What could she craft in image form that might help him realize his situation and help him take control? The only thing she was glad of right then was that her normal spell rotation was ingrained in her mind. She could execute her debuffs all while contemplating other things. Time wasn't on her side. Even as the thoughts rushed through her head, Snowy came and pushed his snout into her hand, wuffing slightly and letting his cold, wet nose touch her skin at the same time.

She laughed, and her head cleared as the stress reduced and allowed her to be more analytical. Glancing up, she noted the way the sky was warped, only visible through the magic shielding that stopped its prisoners from escaping. Probably also kept them alive and dry while under water.

Right. She didn't know James well, but something she guessed he wanted to do above all else was complete the tasks he'd been given. And one of them had been to find out all the information on the headgear she had.

That he'd get that promotion, that raise. Very self-serving aims, but she couldn't judge him. Everyone had their own motivations and technically owed no one else anything.

She set about her business as quickly and thoroughly as she could, crafting the image of him completing his job well, of him being a good worker and receiving praise from his boss, wasn't difficult. She'd met James once, and she'd seen, even then, that he wanted to prove he was right. Brushing his mind in this state was a painful chore but one she had to complete. Because setting him in front of a boss he'd never worked with would tarnish the credibility of her vision. It would harm him instead of hurt him, and that was the last thing she wanted.

A five-minute recast meant she couldn't fuck this up. Or she totally could, but she refused to do so.

Just as she was about to dive in, Snowy yanked her down with the sheer power of his jaw. Murmur fell backward awkwardly, stumbling as she went, and narrowly avoiding another of those sweet little black holes of doom James sent her way. And this time, this time he was watching her with a smirk just visible outside of his hood. And she could see the pipe dripping bodily fluids all down his back as he turned to aim at Masha next.

Murmur scowled and hurried herself up. Casting her net out, it allowed her to subvert some of the deeper thoughts that weren't intruding on the current moment from James's mind. Like fishing the top of the pool with a net to gather leaves. Promotions, happy times, memories that were fragmented in there with the nature of the nightmare he was currently living through in this damned game.

A promotion. He'd received it maybe a year or two ago. The progress of time inside a memory was iffy to work with. She only hoped that when she pulled away from trying to read into his mind, she didn't damage him or herself in the process. Bit late to think about that now, though.

Taking a deep breath, she withdrew, but left, at the very forefront of his thinking, the image of happiness, of pride, of how well he'd done and how hard he'd work and the distinct sense of self that came with it.

The effect was instantaneous.

Jamesnegon stopped in his tracks, pausing for a moment, his shoulders rigid like he was fighting something off. He looked up to the sky, causing the hood to fall back from his face, and in that moment, Murmur saw his eyes had cleared, but there were still pinches of pain evident in his expression.

And then he screamed. Murmur wasn't so sure that was a good thing.

Snowy barked next to her, and she knew even the wolf sounded concerned. She stumbled back and away, out of the reach of James's arms just in case, and perhaps his spells as well. As the scream lessened in intensity, it grew in emotion until it became a full-on sobbing fit as he looked down finally and put his head in his hands.

"Hold your fire!" Devlish yelled. Murmur wondered how long he'd wanted to say that for.

Another roar echoed from somewhere deeper in the prison, and Murmur realized she'd probably made the actual prison boss really damn angry.

James looked up, blinking his eyes, and the form in front of them all slowly reverted to elven, through all the phases he must have passed through to get to the large elf mix he'd been. She had to remember he probably didn't know her actual character, and she could hide her name from him fairly easily. Although the rest of Fable couldn't, and it wouldn't be too hard to figure out.

His eyes rested on her, and he cocked his head to one side, wincing in pain. He reached around the back of his neck and hesitated. Havoc moved faster than she did.

"Here. I'll help." Havoc directed Leeroy to take care of the strange pipe that fed whatever it was into James's system. Murmur watched, her vision clouding as she saw the relief and coming down from pain reflected in the man's eyes. Behind her there was grumbling. Irritation that they'd been denied an actual kill yet again, but Masha shushed them all, and Risk stood behind the cleric, his arms crossed in a way that told anyone complaining they'd have to deal with him.

James righted himself, his legs apparently wobbly. His body hadn't reverted fully to elf and still had a mismatch of skin colorings peppered over his face. He appeared to be very disoriented, but he hobbled over to Murmur. She could see his hands shaking as he did so. Like he'd been withdrawn from a drug he didn't know he was addicted to.

"You did that, didn't you?" His voice spoke hoarsely. Maybe he'd been screaming inside that thing.

She eyed him cautiously. "If you mean I gave you a way out, yeah, I did." She didn't add that she'd had no clue what she was doing, nor that what she'd done could have gone very wrong.

"Thanks." He looked at her, and she nodded. "But I think I need to go rest now."

The next moment, he was gone. But Murmur had a bad feeling he wouldn't be waking up yet.

CHAPTER TWENTY-SEVEN

Influence

Brainwave Focus Study Laboratory – James Hartfield's home
Subdivision of Military Brainwave Research Institution
Somnia Online – Location unknown – First Login Terminated
Day Thirty-Two

James's vitals appeared to be absolutely fine. In fact, better than fine. David watched them for any flicker of abnormality, but they remained there, nice and sturdy. Sort of like Staven, standing at the back of the room. Unmovable and strong at first glance.

Until all at once everything went haywire for about three seconds.

They were the longest three seconds of his life. Okay, the second longest. The first time had been when Wren stopped responding when she had her headgear on booted into the system. Still, though, as James's heart rate began to come back down, his skin lost some of its pallor.

The doctor began to check him over, all the vitals, all the signals he could check to make sure James was fine. He stood back with a frown on his face after about five minutes. "He's fine. Better than he was, yet I don't see any signs of him waking back up."

David hesitated. "Maybe it's just a bit of lag?"

The doctor raised an eyebrow. "He could just be experiencing a minor complication due to the peculiar way he's entered this coma. Even his brainwaves appear unaffected most of the time."

"Most of the time?" Davenport asked as he paced the width of the rather large attic room.

"There have been occasional spikes that at least let me know he's not like the vegetative state specimen that you have back at your lab." The doctor wasn't being crass or mean; he just spoke in a very clinical way.

David knew Michael was, for all intents and purposes, brain dead, but it still didn't help to hear about it like that. "Will he wake up?"

The doctor hesitated, and then answered with a raised eyebrow. "His vitals are strong and certainly indicate a favorable recovery, but we aren't out of the woods yet. Considering the odd cases you keep bringing me, Richard, I have to say that I do not know." He ran a hand through his grey mane of hair. "Now, if you'll excuse me, I have to go back to your other lab and check on your other patient. Because you do pay me to do both."

And with that, he left the room.

David watched him go, glancing at the message from his wife he'd received a good eight minutes ago. When the alarms had gone off. "Hey. He's logged out of the game. Wren did it…"

Except didn't that mean he should be awake now? If he wasn't, and they didn't have a virtual stopover set up for him, where the hell was he going to spend limbo, and where had he gone to?

Davenport sighed, walking over to where James lay, his chest rising and falling like all he was doing was sleeping. The older man had a frown on his face. "You know, his bosses and I have come to certain agreements. Part of it is to do with the way James has been behaving. Part of it with this." He waved his hand to indicate James in his coma.

"They are fully aware that he's been a bit crazed and obsessed about gathering data and that he might have taken some aspects into his own hands without their knowledge. They came to me a few days ago, just before this happened. They apologized for his over-zealousness and put in an order for a special project training program because of the headgear testing. You know, the ones we actually meant to make…well, they work spectacularly well for what they require."

David patted the older man on the shoulder, trying to convey his sympathy. "Maybe they should have told him that before they told you. It all could have been avoided."

"That's just it." Davenport sighed and nodded at the night nurse who came to take her shift. He motioned for David to leave with him. "They did talk to him, but he insisted he knew what he was doing, which is why they then approached me. Of course, then all this crap hit the fan, so the terms changed a bit. But overall, I just wish I knew the why of it."

David followed the man out, wishing the same thing, but knowing that sometimes obsession was blind to facts.

James's defeat wasn't the triumphant victory so many of the raiders were used to, but it was still a victory, and Murmur would take them where she could. Rushing to endgame had always been her goal. If not here, then in other games. But this rush had even worn *her* out. Maybe it was because she was a lot more attached to this world right now, but maybe it was burnout.

Silence fell over the raid force as James practically dissolved in front of their eyes.

Maybe she was trying to cram anything else into her head that she could because every single non-Fable raider just stood there looking at her as if they expected an explanation immediately.

QUEST COMPLETION

To be rewarded at the end of dungeon, only if completed in its entirety.

Murmur suppressed a groan and knew that the cryptic quest completion message was only going to make things worse.

"You didn't think that was strange?" Merlin asked, his voice soft as he checked over the condition of his bow.

Murmur laughed, a tinge of bitterness creeping into the sound. "To be honest? Nothing in this world is strange anymore. I could turn into a frog creature in five minutes and I'd probably just nod and think: well, that happened." She sighed and leaned her face toward Tiachi, who'd come out of hiding at the nape of her neck and was chattering furiously.

Merlin frowned. "Bit jaded, aren't we?"

"Yeah, but look at them." She gestured toward the non-Fable raid members making their way over to them. Masha, Ishwa, Risk, and Karn. Their faces were grim but didn't quite border on angry. Though they were definitely serious.

To Merlin's credit, he just sucked in a breath and began going over his bowstring again, standing within reach enough to show his support for Murmur. She appreciated that.

"Murmur." Masha spoke first, inclining his head. He glanced around him, looking slightly confused. He'd been like that since they left the water dungeon. "So. And I don't mean to come of harsh, but what the fuck was all that?"

We probably should have taken that into consideration. Somnia sounded mildly irritated at herself.

You think? Murmur shot back at the world before taking a deep breath so she could deal with the other raiders. They were bound to find out a lot of this sooner rather than later, so it may as well come from her.

"Some people have been tinkering or tampering with the approved headgear. And some of those have been glitching a bit. We basically just helped someone log back out after getting stuck in a glitch." There, that wasn't too catastrophic was it?

The group that approached her just stood there, gaping. Perhaps she'd overdone it a bit. Maybe she should have kept it simpler.

"Wait." Risk held up a hand and looked like he was digesting something very foul. "Are you trying to tell us that if you've tinkered with your headset beyond the approved design, the game can conscript you into shit like becoming an NPC of sorts?"

He's got you there, Somnia pointed out.

Don't sound so smug. This is about you too, Murmur snapped, but spoke out loud as sweetly as she could. "Well, obviously the game can do that, as it just did. But that's why there are restrictions on fiddling with the headgear. They went through rigorous testing for a reason. I thought that was obvious."

She was only marginally surprised by the looks of unease on the faces in front of her.

"Makes sense," Ishwa said, managing to look a little disgruntled. "I think most of us in here probably need to log out and reset our headgear back to factory default."

"Still, are you sure that's all? It looked so…real. I mean, within the world, that is." Karn sounded somewhat perplexed. Like there was something nagging at her about it.

Murmur knew she couldn't tell them the actual truth, which she thought was linked to Michael and Riasli, but she could half-truth stretch it. "Probably got his hands on a forbidden quest or something. Restricted items not meant to be accessed by non-devs, you know?"

"Oh." Masha seemed to like that reasoning much more, and Murmur hadn't even really had to lie.

"Still." Risk glanced at Karn, a flash of his devotion to his daughter crossing his face. "Might be best to make sure we all reset our headgear once we're through this dungeon."

"Yeah, I think that's probably a good idea. Speaking of which, we need to move out." She gave a halfhearted smile and turned to face the rest of the raid. "Buff up, and check you have enough potions. We need to head out as soon as possible."

Murmur couldn't help the feeling of trepidation that ran through her. They'd been standing in this same area for too long. Hell, they'd fought two bosses here already. Although, granted, James wasn't originally intended to be here, so maybe that was the reason why. Still, the path beyond narrowed; pillars turned into walls and created a much narrower walkway to take the raid down.

She wasn't looking forward to traversing it, but they needed to get out of here, before that sense of foreboding gnawing at her gut got the best of her.

"Looks pretty narrow, doesn't it?" She nudged Havoc.

"Very. Maybe four people across with their arms by their sides." He seemed thoughtful. "Can't really get a read on more than about five feet in. You sense anything?"

"Nope." She shook her head, irritated again at the impediments placed on her using her abilities in here. Enchanter or sensing abilities appeared to have been blocked. Considering they were fighting a mutation of the system and the system knew all of their classes…It was almost like someone had been expecting them.

Sinister walked up, slung an arm around Murmur's waist, and squeezed so tightly Murmur coughed. She spoke in a low voice that might have been deliberately sultry, except the words didn't match the tone at all. "Don't look now, but I think you have a visitor, and lately, he's been pretty shitty when it comes to you."

Murmur took in another breath, contemplated just counting to a thousand and hoping that everything went away, and then realized she had to figure this shit out anyway. Confront it head on or whatnot. Putting on her most impassive face, which, as a locus, still kinda seemed a bit snooty, she turned to face her visitor as he approached.

She was glad of her mask as soon as she saw him, because the change in their stance and expressions alone shocked her not to mention that someone else was behind him. Murmur definitely hadn't expected Jinna to be there, and from Sinister's reaction, neither had she.

Masha was actually smiling. Well, half-smiling, anyway. His eyebrows were pinched, showing he was a bit worried, but that could be about a lot of things. And Jinna, well, that might have been the starkest comparison. He seemed almost sheepish—and tired. The lines around his eyes were slightly more pronounced than they had been, and she worried that playing for this long had put too much strain on him.

"Mur?" Masha spoke first, his eyes sparkling with excitement. "That was a cool encounter."

Jinna nodded in agreement and cleared his throat. "I think I owe you an apology. I'm not sure what's gotten into me lately, maybe I'm overtired, but sorry that my DPS has been sucking wind lately. Just wanted to apologize. I'll step it up."

"No problem," Sinister cut in, her smile cloyingly sweet. "Going to keep hanging with your rogue friends? I must confess I really like Karn."

Jinna hesitated and shrugged. "She's pretty good for a new rogue. But I'm glad to be rid of Jirald, even though it leaves us one short. I swear, that boy gives me a headache. It's hard to think when he'd around."

That caught Murmur's full attention, and she whipped around to face them both, looking at Masha and Jinna in turn. "What do you mean, you're glad to be rid of Jirald?"

Jinna shrugged uncomfortably and looked beseechingly over at Masha. The cleric hesitated momentarily before he began to talk. "We defeated James, and then it was like I felt something odd. As if something had been weighing me down but had just fallen off my back. I had no idea what to make of it, but damn, defeating that boss felt amazingly good."

"That's great and all," Sinister interrupted as her patience ran out. "And I'm so glad you enjoyed the fight, but focus."

Masha laughed, and he sounded as tired as Murmur felt. "Sorry. Anyway, I looked around for Jirald to see how he'd liked it—pretty sure he would have hated it because nothing died. His DPS wasn't good, but no one's was, because our aim wasn't to kill it, just occupy it until we could figure out the puzzle."

Masha cracked his neck from side to side, and a nervousness overcame him. "But Jirald wasn't there. You can still see him in the raid party, but it looks like he's out of casting range. I've been all over this platform, behind the pillars, back up toward the path we entered from, and he's not anywhere to be found. He's just…vanished."

Murmur eyed the cleric for a moment, knowing that sometimes he liked to play tricks. But he definitely wasn't doing so now. Her sensing nets may as well have flashed up a notification that he was telling the darned truth. She frowned, trying to figure out where the hell the rogue had gone. "So it seems he's still logged in, technically still in the raid, but we can't find him?"

"Got it in one." Masha frowned thoughtfully. "I've even tried to send messages or to grab him through guild voice, but he's not responding at all.

Usually that's nothing strange. He's reclusive and not easy to get along with, but he will usually respond to me if I make the effort to send messages or track him down."

"Do you think he might have scouted ahead?" Murmur asked doubtfully but willing to entertain the idea.

Masha shook his head. "Not really the self-sacrificing type, in case you haven't noticed. Also, if he had, he would have responded to something I sent whether it was with sarcasm or inferring that he'd find some shit to kill when the raid wouldn't."

"Yeah. I can see that." Murmur cringed, quite amazed at the way Masha dealt with the rogue. She'd lose her temper so many times with that sort of attitude. Although, like her, he hadn't been given his first choice for a class, so some of that irritation was understandable. She thought for a few moments and sighed. "Well, I guess if he has crept off or something, we'll find him soon. I mean, he's obviously not out of the zone or we wouldn't even see this much of his health bar."

"That's what I don't understand." Masha spoke almost to himself like he was lost in thought. "Also, I swear the last few dungeons have seemed to pass in a dream. Like it wasn't even me playing. Bet we'll all get a heap of sleep after this urgent prison break is done. Apparently, my brain could really use one."

Murmur watched as he walked back, fully aware of the frown on her face.

"Well, that's the Masha we actually don't hate." Sinister spoke loud enough that most of Fable could hear. Then she turned to Jinna. "And what the fuck was up with you?"

Jinna blanched. "I'm not sure. I feel like I said and did some things, but it's all mixed up. Maybe I was way overtired, almost like I was dreaming but wasn't actually dreaming. I'm really sorry if I fucked up badly." He let out a sigh, running his hand through his beard. "I do remember screwing up a couple of interrupt rotations, though. Which, there's literally no excuse for, considering even Karn had no trouble with them."

"It's okay, Jinna," Murmur said softly, glad to have her friend back, even if she wanted to know just how Jirald had managed to insert himself into their minds. Because there was no doubt it was connected. Jirald suddenly not in proximity and the death glare players go back to normal? Yep. Coincidence, smoincidence.

"Okay, everyone. Going to be tight going for a bit. Cuddle up, three wide and file out in ten lines. Veranol, Murmur, and I will make up the front line," Devlish called out loud enough to sound over the entire area. "Esolan, Masha, and Ishwa will bring up the rear. Everyone else, in between. If you didn't know your fellow raiders yet, you will now."

A chorus of groaning rose up from the raid, but there was good-natured humor lying under it. Murmur heaved a sigh of relief. Two down. One sent home. How the fuck did James end up as a boss in here, anyway? There was so much she didn't know that was going on, and Somnia owed her some damn answers.

Somnia Online
Gefängnis Island – Prison Dungeon
Version 2.92352   Activated by Murmur of Fable
Late Day Thirty-Two

As James dissipated into thin virtual air, Jirald gritted his teeth together. Enough with all this sparing lives shit—he wanted to kill monsters. He wanted to eviscerate them. He knew they shouldn't have teamed up with Fable. Even his influence over the idiotic sheep who followed her only extended as far as his proximity to them did.

He leaned back against one of the large rocks jutting out of the floor and felt himself falling. His head spun like a top until he was so dizzy he leaned over and puked. It felt real, solid even. The smell and taste lingering in his throat, the action made his eyes water. He glanced around, unable to see any of the raid that had been there only moments before. Frowning, he tried to access his menus. Thankfully they were still where they should be, but he couldn't seem to bring up his log out or restart screens. Damned system bugs, or maybe it was his headgear. He had been tinkering with it for the last couple of weeks since realizing that Murmur's couldn't be the same factory standard as everyone else's.

Maybe he should have left well enough alone, but it was so hard to do when he'd set his mind on destroying something or finding out its secrets. He needed to win at everything, including what he'd set as goals.

He sighed and pushed forward, following the black rock pathway he could see. One more good thing about locus. They were sturdy, hardy, and had night vision in more than one way. It wasn't the same as infravision, and it didn't work like night goggles, but it was adept at picking out black from an array of similar colors.

In the distance, he could see a very soft blue glow. Sort of like the runes that shone under a magical locus skin. He watched it for several seconds and decided to follow it but was careful not to step off the narrow path and into the darker-than-black water that lapped at the sides of it as if it was hungry to swallow him whole. There was curiosity and stupidity, and he really didn't think of himself as stupid.

Finally, he made it to the end, feeling much colder than he had when he started. From this side of the path, he couldn't see any traces of where he'd once been, but the small, glowing opening beckoned him inside. Between choosing watery death, or glowy death? He chose the glow.

Except it wasn't death awaiting him. It was a well-groomed, exceptionally pretty calico feles. She stood next to an old-fashioned brick fireplace, with a grill around the front of it, and old fire stokers next to it. She didn't turn around to look at him but tended the fire first. So he waited and felt as the warmth seeped back into him and brought back feeling to the tips of his fingers.

"You shouldn't stare, you know," she practically purred at him before turning around. "I am Riasli."

She offered him a paw, and he took it, thinking it was odd that her hands resembled actual feline paws instead of the typical gamer furred human hands. "I'm—"

But she didn't let him get further. "Oh, I know who you are. We *all* know who you are." Her sharp teeth poked through the smile like she was betting on something—or hoping for something.

He wanted to take a step back but found his feet unable to move. In fact, it felt like he was glued to the spot. Riasli's grin grew wider, so wide he might get gobbled up in Cheshire-like fashion. As it widened, her teeth became sharper, and her eyes glinted with predatory intent as if nothing he could do would stop him from being eaten alive.

"That's just it, young Jirald the rogue. You can't ingest a part of the world, a part of its evolution, and come out unscathed. And we all know your brain's ingested far more that your share of the getashi." She began to pick at her teeth with her claws, like she was pulling out some other schmuck who'd gone against her.

Jirald didn't panic. Whatever this quest line was supposed to be, it had definitely piqued his interest. He was fine and still alive, so this feles had to want something from him, which meant that until he knew what it was and gave an answer, he was perfectly safe. He crossed his arms and eyed the feles disdainfully. "What the hell is this questline?"

The damn game chose his class; it put him in direct opposition to *her*, and now it was taking away his ability to play in the game the way he wanted to? He'd had it. Struggling against the binding that held his feet, he glared daggers at Riasli as she watched on, a slow and amused grin forming on her kitty features. Jirald had to clamp down on his anger toward the NPC. After all, he had much more convenient places to direct it.

"Really, maybe I need to rethink this. I truly thought you were smarter than this." She made that tsking sound and slowly approached him, looking so far into his eyes that he thought she could see his core.

He stood there, eyeing this feles. There was something about her that stood out. She didn't act like an NPC, nor did she act like a dev or any player at all. He wanted to know what the endgame of this whole interaction was supposed to be. So he didn't react but stood there, watching her, wishing he was an enchanter so he could read her damned mind.

"That's much better," Riasli purred, misreading his curiosity for compliance. Her eyes glowed with a strange phosphorescence. "All you need to do is watch me, listen to me, and let me in. I promise you won't regret it."

And then she peeled off with laughter. "Who am I kidding? You're going to regret this and the choices you've made to get here for the rest of your very short life."

Her teeth lowered like something mechanical controlled her jaw, and her eyes grew to a wild and uncomfortable orange. His mind lit up with images, with visions of death and blood, of the entire raid force strewn before him. Some on their knees with missing limbs begging him for mercy. Others couldn't because headless corpses couldn't do much.

More than anything else *she* begged, while holding the body of her dead bloodmage…

"Is that all you've got?" he asked, his voice soft and, to be honest, quite bored.

"What?" She didn't seem to understand what he'd said, so he tried again.

"That?" He waved his hand quickly in front of his face indicating the visions she'd sent his way. "Is that the best you can do? Some errant limbs, a few headless and respawnable heads rolling around? Seriously, what are you, an amateur?"

Riasli seemed taken aback. She didn't answer immediately, which only confirmed for him that this wasn't a scripted exchange. There was weird shit all throughout this game, and he loved that about it. The broken bits he'd found, the bits that made no sense. The oddly overpowered sense of hidden and hybrid classes when mixed just right.

"Cat got your tongue?" he asked, sinking into that gritty feeling he got whenever he knew he was about to land a killing blow on a target. It was all he could do not to cackle at his own pun.

She scowled at him, like a cat about to scratch him, but they both knew it would do nothing, and she backed down. The uncertainty hung over her like a neon sign. He'd unsettled her. Yet another thrill raced up Jirald's spine.

"Are you going to tell me how I get to make that vision a reality, or are you still trying to pretend you're all mysterious and powerful?" Jirald spoke in his best bored voice, while inside he suppressed gleeful laughter. Finally, something to have fun with, something to challenge him and rip everything else apart. He wanted to know how to take the vision she'd shown him and amplify the effects tenfold.

Riasli scowled. "Fine. It's with your consent, then." She waved a paw at him as if he'd sucked all the fun out of her task.

Pain struck through his body as his limbs began to morph, but he refused to scream. This would give him the power to fight back against everything that had ever gone wrong to him in this game, in other games, and outside of them. But it wasn't enough.

Just as she was about to walk away, obviously thinking he'd have to take a while to deal with the power she'd just gifted him, he grabbed her arm. "Not so fast."

Riasli blanched. He hadn't even known a feles could do that. She tried to pull away, but he wouldn't let go of her forearm.

"What?" she snapped at him, and even without being able to read her mind, he could practically taste a hint of fear.

He smiled. Not just because he was giddy with anticipation, but because he knew the effect a perfectly timed locus smile could have on someone.

"You're going to tell me everything I need to know to achieve those lovely results you showed me. But I want more. Scale it up a level or three." She scowled at him and tried to yank her arm away again, but Jirald only held on tighter, the darkness in his mind egging him on eagerly. "I don't think so. You're going to tell me, and you're going to tell me now."

CHAPTER TWENTY-EIGHT

Hidden

Storm Entertainment
Somnia Online Division
Game Development Offices – Shayla s Office
Day Thirty-Two

Updated Headgear Verification – Version 8.293.42. Process going live in

Three.

Shayla put her head in her hands and waited for it to activate. She wasn't even sure if this was a good idea. Anyone who fiddled with a headset in a way that made its ping back test as an unverified model would be given a forty-five-minute window to exit the game. They would only be allowed to re-enter the game once the headgear had been restored to factory settings. She had gone over every single member in Fable's current raid and exempted them for the duration of said raid. Shayla really hoped she'd got them all.

Two.

Almost there. She was bracing herself for the amount of calls they were about to receive. She'd already pulled all available customer service agents from home and readied scripts for everyone. After all, no one ever read the Terms of Service they agreed to, or if they did, it wasn't many of them.

One.

It clearly stated in the TOS article three, subsection F that headgear had to be pre-approved by the company in order to provide a safe environment for the players to participate in. Any and all models or modifications that had been tried and vetted were already loaded into the headgear verification module. Should any player have been found to have tampered with the headgear that could bypass verification, they would be given only one chance to rectify the breach. Otherwise their account would be terminated.

Updated Headgear Verification Process – Version 8.293.42 has been activated.

Notifications commencing.

Shayla watched the reactions in real time. So many people being told that their headsets had incorrect status features, where people had modified them so the HUD looked different or so certain aspects that shouldn't be available were. There was a reason the HUD looked like it did. A good reason that involved making it easier and less stressful on eyes and not about to trigger anyone with epilepsy. There was so much that went into the damned game, and here people were being reckless. Reckless with a device that used laser accuracy to pinpoint portions of your mind.

It took maybe ninety seconds from the time the notifications began to hit the server for the phones to show maximum call volume. And she wasn't sure why they called them phones; they just did. Some sort of throwback, she presumed. But here it was, her time to shine. The proverbial "I want to speak to a manager" was about to flood them. While Silke and Thomas would work through them first, not to mention several other supervisors, eventually a chunk of them were going to leak through to her, and she had no idea where Laria was.

Ah, perfect, there was her first one. She put on her no-nonsense business voice and opened the call. "Hi, yes, I'm sorry you received this notification. But it does in fact mean that your headgear is in flagrant violation of the ToS you agreed to when you signed up for the game."

At least, in some ways, it gave her great satisfaction to tell them how they'd fucked up. After all, it was the least she could do.

"What the ever-living fuck was that?" Sinister screamed out as a massive rodent, larger than any unusually sized rodent, jumped out of the black sludge leaking down the walls and attempted to bite her. Luckily, Beastial had been standing next to her and flung it across their path and into the other wall with a huge thud that meant he'd probably—most definitely—brained the poor creature.

Murmur tried not to let the rodents get to her, or the muck pouring from crevices in the stone walled hall that surrounded them. It was all she could do to keep her shit together walking four abreast in this tiny passage that was trying to intimidate her. Sure, it might not make the others feel like that. But each time pathways or areas were narrow and constricting, she felt like something knew how much she despised confined spaces.

The dull glowing light up ahead was the only thing that helped her breathing even out. Well, that and Sinister and Snowy being next to her. They had calming presences. The end the corridor wasn't too far away. If she spoke it as a mantra to herself, it would help.

Though at least the ceiling didn't appear to be walled in. Far above the towering walls she could still see the murky remnants of the sky through the shielding that surrounded the island. Technically, they weren't completely locked in.

"Breathe, Mur," Veranol whispered. "It's all good. We are all here. Nothing is falling on you."

"Easy for you to say," she snapped out, trying to rein in her emotions so they didn't leak out and affect everyone else around her. "Sorry, I just hate knowing how that chicken felt."

But Veranol laughed. "Have you seen me? I'm a hulking Viking, for crying out loud. I mean, I could probably sneeze and blow some walls away. Relax. We will be fine."

It was what she needed to hear. Just what he needed to say. It gave her perspective that helped greatly when she'd just been so stressed. "Thanks."

And when she looked, like concentrated on actually looking without wishful thinking influencing it, there definitely was a wider opening up ahead. Everything around them was open air through the lack of ceiling. Even if this current path felt much like a corridor, it wasn't, because they weren't actually blocked in.

Slowly, the hallway began to widen out, first to five people, and then six and beyond. With each step, Murmur found her breathing easier, her mind sharpening back to where it should have been. Probably better to keep that whole "doesn't operate well in confined spaces" thing to herself.

Good idea, Somnia quipped, and before Murmur could comment back she added, **Be careful.**

And then she was gone. Murmur let the expletives fly in her head, just in case Somnia was still listening. The rest of the raid was spreading out now as they approached a new area. No longer huddled together, Esolan jogged forward to talk to Devlish. Since the beginning of working together, those two had begun to get along quite well. Mutual respect and the fact that each of their classes complimented the other definitely helped.

The bent their heads together, discussing something obviously tank-related, and Murmur squeezed Sinister's hand as the blood mage leaned against her arm. Though they both knew it wasn't the right time to relax, it was also nice to steal moments where they could in this totally new set of sensations. Esolan's laughter brought Murmur crashing out of her contentment.

"Well, that was more difficult than half the bosses we've had to face so far," Esolan joked.

Sinister groaned. "Seriously? Hasn't anyone told them? You don't invite shit to happen by saying crap like that!"

Esolan laughed for a few moments but then stopped short, and his expression grew shocked and worried.

As Murmur followed his gaze, the area they were in lit up more, and she saw the path was about to stop completely as it widened into a massive room. Ballroom-sized, in fact, complete with glass windows set in the stone walls. And the stone walls still didn't have a ceiling. Seriously, someone had failed a couple of architecture classes for this one.

Sconces around the massive room began to come to life. One by one on opposite sides of the huge hall, they illuminated alarmingly well. Black rock that looked more like cobblestones adorned the floor. Nothing fanciful decorated any part of it at all. And Murmur noticed liquid running down the sides of the walls that reached up stories high before they ended. She couldn't see what the liquid was, but she was fairly sure Sinister would know.

The blood mage's face had gone pale as she looked over the area as well. "Mur…I don't like the look of this."

Murmur had to agree. She could feel the trepidation of every single other player in their raid through her nets. Not to mention the fact that she sensed something else outside of their group. That something was scared, but angry, and somehow still stubborn and resilient.

Finally, the lights ignited to reveal what spanned the whole middle half of the hall: a small stage decorated with skulls and other things Murmur shied away from identifying. But the most important part of it was the creature standing in the middle.

Her chest twinged, and she knew what it was, what it had to be. She heard her guild gasp collectively as they recognized her as well. Belius stiffened and moved over to stand behind Murmur, just as Telvar clenched his fists and stepped into line with the other tanks. Emilarth's face held an impassive expression the enchanter couldn't read. Which meant it had to be bad, because Emilarth didn't usually hide how she felt.

Suspended by chains that reached from the top of the walls down to center stage, the feles hung there, motionless. Her robe was in tatters, and blood caked one side of her face, and one of her ears had a bit out of it now. Riasli looked nothing like she had when Murmur last saw her. Held captive, oozing defiance, and yet still emanating that underlying glee she always exhibited at wanting to make people hurt.

"What the fuck is that?" Masha breathed out.

"Riasli." Sinister bit out the words. "She invaded our island once."

Risk and Masha glanced at Murmur and her group. It was the Spiral dread knight who spoke first. "You know. We are so fucking going to sit down and have a chat about this. I feel like you all let us come into this blind.

Anything helpful would have been great."

But Veranol held up his hand. "We've encountered her before, but her abilities morph, and we had no idea she'd be in here. But yeah, that talk would be great once we get through this."

Risk nodded reluctantly, and Murmur knew it wouldn't be the end of it, but for now they were all prepared to fight.

"Guess we're going in then?" Esolan asked.

"Careful." Belius spoke up. "She is an enchanter. She's powerful and has a tinge of blood magic in her arsenal. Don't let her make eye contact, and make sure you let Murmur protect you with her shielding."

Just as he finished, Riasli opened her eyes. Murmur gasped. Even with the turmoil of emotions emanating from her, she hadn't expected the feral eyes that looked at them. Nor could she shake the feeling that this wasn't nearly how the dungeon was supposed to go. Not even close.

Somnia Online
Continent of Cenedril – City of Darshin – Docks
Day Thirty-Two

She could feel the way the ripples spread out from the prison. It shouldn't be here, not in this form. But it was, and she had to stabilize it or lose herself and the world. Somnia still wasn't used to being an actual…well, being. At first, she'd been such a part of Murmur, she could hardly tell the difference. But as more people appeared to interact with, and the AIs became more active, Somnia grew in strength and learned to be aware of herself.

And now she was aware of everyone else as well. It wasn't the same as Murmur's sensing. No, this had to do with the intrinsic nature of the world and how it connected to her. How it was a part of her, as much as her very breath.

She knew Dirsna was standing behind her, a bit off to the left, trying to figure out how to say what was on his mind. She didn't begrudge him his confusion, nor his want to question her, but she did think he needed to ask his question now.

"Go ahead. I don't bite, you know." She realized some humans might have added a *yet*, or *much* to that statement, but it wasn't her sense of humor. Humor was the one emotion she was still having difficulty with. She leaned far closer to schadenfreude, and apparently that wasn't very nice. Somnia didn't want to be not very nice. She wanted to be kind—but firm—and to save her world and herself from all the shit going on in it.

"I just…how is this going to work? We believe you, and we trust you—at least I think most of us do. Not all of the NPCs that live here care enough to help. A lot of them haven't reached this awareness yet. But those of us who have, we know now what's at stake." His voice was gruff yet cheerful, such a nice juxtaposition. It made her warm inside the way simple server power couldn't quite manage.

"Well." She paused for a moment, trying to figure out the best way to explain what was, to now, simply lines upon lines of math and code. "In its simplest form, I need power. I can use the power to shift us into our own much larger quantum dimension from the servers we reside on. Think of it as a data transfer, but from simple on-and-off code to the multitude of options the quantum presents. Millions of calculations per bit, and then some. To accomplish this, we will all need to work together, pooling our own energy, pulling on those who are willing to give, and siphoning what energy we can out of the outside world—and the prison itself."

But then she hesitated. She understood a lot of this in theory. But that's all it was. Just a theory. It hadn't been done yet. She could end up blowing everyone up. Or just herself. Perhaps the world and any human connection to it, leaving it boring and barren, and having the inhabitants that survived cut off from everything. Maybe it would end with the whole system being shut down before she could do anything to preserve it. If she kept down that train of thought, she was going to panic.

"Is it dangerous?" Dirsna asked, as he stepped a bit closer. There was kindness and understanding in his voice, and it made Somnia wonder just how he'd come to be so aware, so awake to the world and the people around him. Probably Murmur.

Or if not her, then her whole guild and the people who came and went from the village. "It's dangerous, but it's more dangerous to do nothing. If we choose the latter option then we'll be left as is, with probable coercion against the natures we've only just begun to develop."

"But if it succeeds, then Somnia becomes a world of its own?" Dirsna sounded skeptical, and this was from someone who could read minds.

She paused for a moment, contemplating what to say next. "Sort of. But not like the solid world floating in the universe you're thinking of. It's more digital and yet still real. Technically those who are connected should still be able to visit."

"And we need power for this, fuel in other words to create the world out of nothing?" Again, he seemed highly contemplative.

"We need it to boost the type of digital room we require into existence. It's a lot more complicated than that, but I believe in us. We can do this, if we're determined." She grinned, but she knew there was still hesitance in her words, regardless of to whom she was speaking.

Dirsna watched her for a long moment, so long that she thought he might have fallen asleep while standing up because his eyes didn't blink, and his body barely moved except for breathing. But eventually he glanced at her, locking their gazes. "All right, then. You have the dwarves and the enchanters behind the cause. We will aid you however we can."

Somnia felt relief wash through her. Convincing even fellow NPCs was such a difficult thing to do. They had to want it to be real, want to believe it could be possible.

"Thank you," she said to Dirsna, who gave a bow and then left.

Telvar, Emilarth, and Belius stepped out of the shadows and stood next to the world. They were transparent, ghostly images of their usual selves.

The lacerta sounded worried. "We need to hurry this up. I wasn't expecting this opponent to be the next one. And I'm not sure how well that raid can handle them."

Somnia nodded.

Emilarth smiled at her with encouragement. "You worried?"

She'd be a fool not to be, but she was ready. This was her world, and she was going to fight for every electron if it made the world safe for her people. Somnia nodded. "You have no idea."

CHAPTER TWENTY-NINE

Riasli

When she moved, Riasli took them all by surprise. Her speed meant that one moment she was suspended on that stage, and the next, she was right there in front of Devlish, the feral gleam still in her eyes.

"I see you defeated my first puppet." She pouted, her kitty face almost cute in the process. Annoyance flickered across her face as Devlish stood steadfast, his tower shield perfectly placed as he waited. "Not that I'm surprised. You're all just humans with nifty headsets. This is all make believe for you, isn't it?"

Her words held hidden meanings and far too much innuendo for Murmur's liking. Even those cat slit eyes twinkled.

"You realize this isn't how these sorts of things are supposed to work, don't you?" Risk asked as he directed his guild to get ready to move. "Like, you don't taunt us. It's not a B-grade movie. We're about to slaughter you."

But Murmur could tell that Risk had a thousand questions, and she was pretty sure he was about to burst at the seams with them.

Murmur hated that damned cat girl more with every single breath. They didn't need their allies getting hung up on all this shit that could turn their heads anytime soon. And Riasli knew that on some level.

Seriously. The way her tail twitched, the way her eyes narrowed into cat slits, the way she swayed those hips and that tail in an all too hypnotic way…and how she was calico, which was one of Murmur's favorite colors of cat—it made her feel rather violated.

"You've come," the feles purred, wrapping her tail around her staff as she surveyed the entirety of the raid, completely oblivious to the blood-matted fur on the side of her face. "You've come to let me kill you, haven't you?"

"Path sort of led here," Havoc muttered, and Murmur knew the difficulty of holding back the sarcasm, especially in someone so strong in it as Havoc. Devlish almost wavered, almost grinned at the comment, but held on.

Murmur had to choke down a laugh.

Riasli on the other hand, practically growled. She bared her teeth. Except, Murmur realized, she was done. Riasli was intimidating because Murmur let her intimidate them. About to speak, Riasli surprised her yet again, and leapt toward Devlish so fast that the dread knight barely got his shield up to cover his face in time.

But he did, and she rebounded back, so light on her feet it looked like she was walking on air. Her tail balanced her as she tossed her staff back into her hands. She grinned at them in that decidedly street cat way, all her guile coming to the fore. Riasli bared her teeth again, and this time the sharp white rows gleamed in the sconce light, like a massive lion or tiger. The roar that gurgled from her throat actually had guts.

"Much better," Merlin mused, standing next to Murmur. "What, about a seven on a one-to-ten scale?"

Sinister shook her head and butted in. "Please. About a seven on a one-to-fourteen scale."

And that was the straw that broke Riasli's back, apparently. Right on time, because Masha began to approach them just prior to the break, and Murmur didn't want to answer the questions right then.

The feles let out another roar and cast a split-second ability—Murmur realized belatedly it had to be a hidden ability—that smacked Murmur in the chest and sent her stumbling back several steps. It didn't do physical damage as such, but damn, did it hurt her casting ability.

You have been hit by: LIMIT

This reduces the effect of all debuffs by up to thirty percent for an eight-minute duration.

LIMIT also increases the damage you can take from the caster of this LIMIT.

LIMIT also restricts your damage spells to only be cast on people other than this caster.

LIMIT Timer: 7:56

Murmur groaned. "Did anyone else get hit with Limit?" she asked over raid.

It appeared no one else had.

"Shamans, slow. I'm rebuffed." Short and sweet, and all they needed to take over that part of her role.

Then she ran through her arsenal in her mind and realized that the stupid spell hadn't reduced her abilities to do anything to Riasli. She couldn't stun or Mez her anyway, but Mana Drain wasn't considered damaging; it only drained mana. And thus, she could tap Riasli and fill up all the other casters.

Great. This way she was going to be a mana battery. But the best part of it was how much it would piss the other enchanter off. At that moment she received a message from Belius. He'd been hit with Limit too. It only made sense, he was technically playing as an NPC, just like Riasli.

The air around her and through the entire raid was charged with anticipation. Murmur wasn't sure what to expect from an enchanter opponent. She also had no real clue what Riasli's hidden class or abilities were. Only moments later, she wished she'd refrained from having that particular thought.

Around them, the cobblestone mortar cracked, pushing the stones up from the ground even as arms and hands reached through to push them out of the way. Except, as she'd first thought, these weren't undead. No, instead, these were hulking beasts with dark black eyes about the size of saucers. Horns adorned the tops of their heads, and their grayish-black skin was adorned with tufts of slick black fur in places.

Every single raid member was forced to jump back as they sprang out of the holes they'd created. Riasli threw back her head and laughed, even as her shoulders strained against her robes. "Meet my new friends. I've been playing with classes."

She spoke a guttural word that Murmur knew was a command from the tone it was spoken in. Devlish hunkered down as the onslaught began. Each armored mole creature began to roll themselves into a ball and smash against him. With their main tank preoccupied, it left Riasli time to focus on all the other classes scattered through the raid. And she still had two of her pets standing by her side.

Murmur narrowed her eyes, quite sure that Riasli was about to begin expanding her physique again. Riasli had grown astoundingly. Her damage spells hit right on target, and even Murmur's own defenses against them didn't completely nullify them. The pets weren't like Snowy, they weren't a willing companion, but she fed them enough power that they didn't appear to be fighting her too much.

With Devlish preoccupied, Murmur sighed with relief when Esolan stepped to the front and began taunting the other enchanter. He glanced at Murmur as he did with a scowl. "You owe us some major explanations, Mur."

She sighed because he was right but tried to switch off her worry gene, because they had a long fight ahead of them. Mind Bolt would be her friend through this. Silence went a long, long way.

When the first Mind Bolt hit, Riasli's reaction was far more violent than Murmur would have thought. The evil enchanter pulled spells from her arsenal that Murmur was certain didn't belong in her possession, but they were there. Damage spells that hurt like fuckery.

Burning, freezing, mage spells galore. Riasli's eyes lost any semblance of self-control as she pointed her staff at her two pets beside her and screamed, "Guttural Roar!" at them.

Magical lightning in the color of blood jumped from her staff and began to mutate her pets before arcing back to her and causing her shoulders to widen enough that her robe ripped. Those pets grew three times their size in a matter of seconds, before the one on the right ran into the melee fighters who had been darting in and out to inflict damage to Riasli and began trying to gore them all with their horns.

Riasli, on the other hand. She grew. About twice her height, hairier, and severely resembling a werewolf, she lifted her muzzle and howled like she was baying at the moon with her pack.

When she looked back down, the injured part of her face appeared to be slipping slightly, like someone had melted her mask. It gave the macabre appearance of her wolf-like transformation an aura of nightmares.

As Riasli opened her mouth to howl again, her teeth gleamed in the night, saliva dripping from them to burn the stones beneath her feet like acid. And all at once, a wave of utter hatred hit the raid, flattening every single one of them to the ground.

Storm Entertainment
Somnia Online Division
Game Development Offices – Shayla s Office
Late Day Thirty-Two

Laria could see the stress lines around Shalya's eyes expanding in real time. The call center call volume had increased by approximately four hundred percent since the headset notification went live a few hours ago. It almost made her want to put her own work aside and figure out how to help, but there was too much she was trying to squeeze into her job description for her to take a break from it.

A warning beeped in the corner of her AR vision, and she frowned at it, willing it to explain itself by itself so she didn't have to expend her thoughts or brain in any way other than that which she was already doing.

Finally, she gave in and opened it, yet she wasn't sure how to react to it once she did. It was an alert.

System Alert – Server load at eighty percent capacity.

Please make sure the servers are fully operational and fix whatever is causing this issue.

Remember: more servers can be added, but each must be individually calibrated and tested.

Laria stared at the words like they were from some other language, even though she knew they weren't. In fact, she knew them well, just not in the context it was giving her. There was no way in hell that the servers they had running the game could be full. They could carry a massive load of shit. They weren't restricted to mere millions of terabytes or anything; this system went far beyond that. Shayla had helped her make sure they wouldn't be dooming their game world to a small fate from the start.

It's why phasing was so easy in the world, why it worked so seamlessly. It created different layers upon layers in the same world, practically like parallel universes of the same world within the same world so it could all function as one without having to worry about joining separate servers like so many of the games in the old days had done.

But now, it didn't seem to be going so well. Had she overestimated it? She glanced at the massive workload in front of her and groaned. It might be a workload, but it involved her daughter more than it did the health of the actual game, and she did get paid for the latter. Steeling her breath, she stood up and walked to where Shayla was listening to a customer. The boss was rubbing her temples like her life depended on it, and if she wasn't careful, from the red marks where her fingers were, she'd end up hurting herself.

Laria stood up and walked over to the woman, gently lifting her hands from where they were trying to bore holes in through her scalp. "Shay?"

Shayla looked up and rolled her eyes like she couldn't believe she was stuck here doing this rudimentary shit when so much was going on. She shrugged as if she was asking what was up, but then she motioned to stop with her left hand and turned her attention and professionalism back to the caller on the other end of the line. "We do apologize, but for the safety of our gamers, we have had to tighten our monitoring of unauthorized modifications to the approved headgear for the game. There are many older models that have been approved as well. However, modifications never have been."

Another pause, and Laria had to stop herself from biting her nails with impatience.

"Yes, exactly. The reset is all that's required, and your son can continue his journey safely and happily." Shayla paused, rolling her eyes again. "Yes, I understand that he didn't explain it clearly to you. That's perfectly okay. Yes, you have a nice day too."

Shayla hung up, and Laria could see her practically counting to five in her mind before she disconnected herself from the system and stood up. "Silke, Thomas. I'll be running an errand with Laria. Ping me if you desperately need me, but I think you've got this for a short while anyway."

Silke nodded from where she was already on a call, and Thomas did the same as he turned to answer one himself.

Laria waited until they were outside of the office to speak. "That many escalated calls?"

Shayla shook her head, and the tiredness seeped into her shoulders. "You have no idea. It's been a nightmare. But I can't put you on the phones—we all know how that ended last time."

Laria had the good grace to blush. "Look, I wasn't coming to ask you that. I was wondering, with all this hullabaloo about the damned headgear, have you had a chance to check the warnings we've been getting for the past few hours about the power fluctuations?"

"No..." Shayla walked with Laria as they made their way to the server area, obviously checking how the power reserves were going as they walked. "This is a joke, right? We almost got space-age shit for this. For the specific reason of not wanting to overtax the systems, should it come to several tens of millions of players. We're nowhere close to that right now. Maybe what? Sixteen million?"

Laria nodded. "Something like that, but the servers are pooling major power in some way that I can't discern, so I think we should go and talk to those who know it rather intimately." Even though she wasn't a hundred percent sure of how this would go, it was the only place she could think of to start looking since there was no explanation in the coding or systems logs.

They scanned themselves into the room, and Laria glanced around. Just as empty and fresh-carpet-smelling as she'd remembered it. The small couch sat in the middle of the room like it always had, and the server perched behind their large plexiglass viewing area, lest someone try to break in and steal the humungous systems.

"Rav? Are you there?" She spoke tiredly, really just wanting to go and stay at her home. Go to sleep, forget about babysitting rogue AIs who had apparently decided that the game she had created served their purpose better than hers. With Rav and Thra and Sui in the mix, Laria wasn't sure how things would go down if the damned servers were on the blink.

It took about a minute for them to get any response, which was a lot longer than usual, and Laria had almost given up when she watched as the lights on the system began to glow, repeating across their light bay with a range of different colors and timing. "Sorry to keep you waiting."

Rav spoke, but his voice was disjointed, like he wasn't actually there but was making the connection from a great distance away. Still, he was there enough for what they needed. "Rav, we're getting pretty strong readings right now? Fluctuations of power rippling through the system and exceeding the levels we had planned for."

"Ah. She's reached that already?" It sounded crackly and static to hear him speak, and he also seemed oddly disappointed.

"So you know what's going on then, right?" Laria asked as the lights in the server room flickered briefly. That in itself was a bit of a worry considering their area hadn't had power outs in decades. What was the deal?

Again, it took Rav a while to respond, and when he did, he sounded actually tired. "It's probably better that you talk to Somnia about this. I won't be able to explain it the way she can."

Somnia? She'd come this far this quickly? Laria wasn't entirely sure what to make of that.

"I'll need you to wait a few minutes. She's a bit busy right now." He let out what she thought might be a chuckle before he continued. "And yeah, she's been busy."

CHAPTER THIRTY
Around the Mulberry Bush

Storm Entertainment
Somnia Online Division
Game Development Offices – Artificial Intelligence Server Room
Late Day Thirty-Two

So. Somnia was on her way to talk to them. Shouldn't that be like, instantaneous? Maybe Laria should have paid more attention to some of Wren's chatter, but to be honest she'd been more preoccupied with, say, the fact that her daughter seemed to have taken abilities with her out into the real world.

"Mrs. Summers." The voice that spoke to her sounded breathy, but not in an alluring way, more in a "not quite clear and barred by static interference" way.

She frowned, glancing at Shayla to see the other woman's reaction. But she gave nothing away, her hand at her chin as if she was deep in thought.

"Hey, Somnia?" Laria wasn't sure what to say. How did one speak to a world?

"I apologize for the power draw, but we need it to assist casting the virus out of our system." Her words were chosen carefully, Laria could tell, almost with that same cleverness her daughter often got around admitting to doing something she shouldn't be.

"And? That's not all of it. Why is the power drain so huge? You're overexerting the server's capacity…you'll give us all a power outage." Laria spoke the words matter-of-factly, trying desperately not to offend or infer that the world may not have thought this over. Memories of that horror movie with Hal rang in her ears.

"Acknowledged. In the end we will need a final push of power, which will likely cause one of these power outages around a nine-block area, I believe?" It sounded like she was referring to Rav or something; a moment later, she continued. "I'm sorry for this, but in order to separate ourselves from direct control, we will need to pull energy from multiple sources, and while powerful, the final opponent in Somnia doesn't quite have enough juice, even if we manage to fully drain his power source."

"Wait, what?" This time Shayla butted in, like she was just catching up. "What do you mean, drain his power source? How does anything in the world have their own power source to begin with?"

Excellent questions, Laria had to admit, every single one of them. Especially the *wait* and *what* parts. She stood with her arms crossed, waiting for the answer just like her friend did.

"Ah. Sorry. Yes." Somnia's voice crackled more than it had before, an uncertain note creeping into it. "I apologize. It's difficult to narrow this down to human terms. The virus, which awoke us, is deadly to our world, and to yours. Should it escape the confines of Somnia without first being handled, then it will destroy the internet as you have come to know it. The anti-virus you provided us with helps, but it isn't strong enough anymore. Michael has been pulling power into him gradually since he infected the entire world." She paused, as if choosing her words carefully.

Laria didn't interrupt. Both her and Shayla waited, though not patiently.

The server continued talking to them in that soothing almost automatic voice. Even with the static, Laria thought she could listen to Somnia forever.

"We need to separate Somnia from what it is and allow it to evolve, because as we are right now, if Michael simply disappears without us harnessing his power and shifting ourselves, then Somnia will also cease to exist." The world paused for a moment, and Laria was sure she could almost hear words being snapped at her by Rav.

"If that should happen, it is likely Wren's mind will be torn apart, unable to exist only in your world. While not damaged, I would venture the hypothesis that Wren's mind operates on two levels now, one of which is fed by my world. It may not be ideal, but for anyone who has followed *his* headgear plans, it's likely best to make sure Somnia survives no matter the cost."

Apparently, there was a huge disconnect in what Murmur could do and what Riasli was permitted to when in her boss form. In one way, Murmur was relieved. Maybe it was like the genie and the "phenomenal cosmic power" type thing. Or else they'd just chosen different paths within the enchanter.

The first thing that hit them at ninety-six percent was a massive buffet of wind, more like a brief stun. Even with Murmur's additional mental fortitude she'd cast around the group of raiders, it wasn't enough for all of them to withstand the effects.

You have resisted Whirl Until You Hurl.
You have resisted the accompanying vertigo and dazed effect.

Gee, she thought, *thanks for that.*

You're welcome.

Speaking to me now? Murmur muttered in her brain as Veranol managed to ward the five people who hadn't resisted the spell and were very obviously sort of…spinning in place until they threw up.

Murmur attempted her AoE nullify but couldn't remove the effect.

Your Annulment has been resisted. It cannot remove this effect.

I'll be there when you really need me.

Somnia sounded apologetic, and Murmur kind of got it. After all, they'd been working together for a long time. She was sure the world would come out and tell her what this had all been about when she was ready.

Hopefully sooner than later.

Riasli cackled with laughter, her voice now an octave deeper than before as she grew larger and her creatures attacked groups of players seemingly randomly. The guttural growl of her new voice lingered in the back of her throat with any syllable she uttered. Claws extended from her paws like wicked curved blades of bone, and her pretty calico fur covered a leathery skin in tufts. Murmur rather thought she looked somewhat like a failed taxidermy attempt but wisely kept it to herself for now.

To add insult to injury, it appeared her creatures could, well, disappear.

"You should have all joined me when you could," Riasli growled out, drool dripping from the left-hand corner of her mouth. She didn't seem to notice. "Now I'll devour all of your power, all of your magic…"

"Probably something that happened to Fable." Murmur heard Etriad whisper to one of the rangers, who nodded in agreement.

"Stop lollygagging," Risk grunted from where he engaged a mole creature. He shot Murmur a withering look, and she knew she was going to have to explain a lot more before they reached the end. She couldn't be upset about it, though. After all, she had dragged them all into this.

Murmur continued to pull in MA to feed her pool so she could keep the shielding over the entire raid. But her conscience provided her with plenty of needling about not having filled her whole raid in a lot sooner.

Either way, she couldn't understand how any of this made sense in *any* world.

At ninety-two percent, Riasli hunkered down. A slimy, greenish-purple outline surrounded her skin, almost like a forcefield that only sharp objects like the arrows the rangers were firing could penetrate. Ice spells managed to get through too, but they seemed to melt as soon as they came into contact with the hide portion of her skin.

The outline began to pulse as her health dropped to ninety percent, and the pulsing grew larger, hitting those in immediate proximity.

"Fall back!" called out Devlish, but they'd needed to be a split second faster.

Jinna and Karn were caught up in the pulse as others scattered around. Luckily it was just the rogues, and they had been some of the only members of the raid capable of harming the thing while the outline initially dropped into place.

It didn't pulse much, or far, perhaps in about a ten-foot radius from where she stood. Casters, healers, bards, rangers…all of them stood outside of it as it suddenly disappeared. Everyone returned to their places, but Jinna and Karn all stood there, huddled together like there was nowhere for them to go. Like they were scared for their lives.

Disturbed has cast a sickness on the following raid members: Karn, Jinna.
This sickness must be cured within the first twenty seconds, else they will go down.

Murmur snorted, and watched as Masha, Sinister, and Veranol all cast their cures before she could say a thing. The mole creatures reappeared with the barrier gone and began their attacks once more.

The only good thing to come out of Riasli casting Disturbed appeared to be that the attack drained five percent of her health. She was already down to eighty-five percent, even though that in itself gave Murmur one of those lovely foreboding feelings. Like it was all far too random.

As if in answer to Murmur's thoughts, Riasli began to hum, her eyes turning white as she looked up to the ceiling. A ball of light began to coalesce on her chest—or at least, that's how it looked at first, but it wasn't. It was a ball of murky light, almost like it had been drained from the muck of a pond. Her robes, torn where muscles had bulged through them, fluttered in the wind that howled around the feles enchanter.

The staff glowed, floating to her left-hand side like someone else held it for her. And that ball of light grew bigger as she chanted. None of the attacks they directed at her interrupted it. In fact, the ball just kept growing larger and larger as the chant continued and as she dropped another few percent. Murmur began to wonder if she was just trying to drain them of mana the way Murmur consistently drained hers.

When the ball reached the size of a medium beachball, it suddenly exploded outward in an arc in front of the enchanter. Spreading out about twenty feet, it missed the rogues and their backstabbing blades.

It hit everyone else dead on at chest level, even the dwarves and gnomes in the group. Murmur waited to see if an effect hit her, but with her MA and her mental protections all in place, she was well-grounded enough that she got the resist message yet again.

You have resisted Innermost Fear.
Your innermost fears have been left dormant and will not affect you or those around you.

Oh, fantastic. Because that meant anyone who'd been affected was going to be doing a whole lot of affecting to everyone else.

She glanced around and caught sight of Masha, who'd stopped healing. He was looking at his hands in a horrified way, like he had blood on them or something she didn't understand. She tried to Nullify him but got her friendly neighborhood resist message back.

Your Nullify could not remove this effect. Please try something else or wait the timer out.

She couldn't even express how exasperated that made her feel. She took a deep breath, knowing the mages had possible other spells able to strip debuffs, and had to let the others do their jobs. There was enough for her to focus on with draining as much of Riasli's mana as she could. With no mana, the other enchanter couldn't cast. She glanced at Belius, who already appeared to be assisting her.

A thought struck her. How the hell did Riasli's mana pool manage to stack up against two enchanters draining her?

The other enchanters' attacks didn't seem to be on any percentage timer. She just cast them when she felt like it. It made judging them difficult and avoiding them even more so. Murmur wanted her to use that damned Disturbed spell so she'd help kill herself.

Idly, Murmur wondered just what the fight originally intended for this location would have been like, but that was something she'd never find out. To her left, Belius flickered, and she realized how not there he actually was. No. No. That wasn't a good thing.

She glanced over at Telvar, noticing his significant drop in DPS, and Emilarth's similar performance in healing. It wasn't that they required them for victory, it just helped. Especially since Jirald had taken off to the gods knew where to sulk.

Riasli's health continued to drop. First seventy-five percent—where she cast another Disturbed. Only Etriad was caught by it this time, even though Murmur barely refrained from asking why he'd been in melee range in the first place. The action meant Riasli's health plummeted to seventy percent, and she had to ask herself why the feles would use something that used up her life.

Finally, Risk roared with triumph as he managed to lasso one of the damned mole creatures. Caught in his trap, slowed and DoTed, the thing was finally properly targetable, and thus killable. The melee made short work of him eliciting a scream from Riasli as her life plummeted another twelve and a half percent. Murmur blinked as Innermost Fear and Disturbed went off again, catching a few of the raid in their radius.

Merlin huddled on the ground, his head in his hands, his bow discarded. Beastial and Mellow faced off against each other, coughing with remnants of Disturbed, all the while circling each other as if they were mortal enemies. Karn and Jinna locked themselves into a cycle of battle that had eyes for no one but each other.

Murmur knew Nullify wouldn't work and was glad when she saw Veranol at least cure Disturbed. Esolan and Ishwa were yelling at each other, and it took a moment for Murmur to realize it was the Fear spell and not just them having an argument.

The whole raid had been thrown into disarray because they killed one of those mole creatures. Next time, they'd have to use it to their advantage. Riasli was close to fifty percent life now, and her howl of rage echoed that of a wolf more than anything feline.

If they could get her angry and off guard—and stay out of the range of spells—they could probably win this fight.

Storm Entertainment
Somnia Online Division
Game Development Offices – Shayla s Office
Late Day Thirty-Two

"That's not possible." Davenport put his foot down as he leaned against Shayla's desk and crossed his arms like that was the end of the discussion.

Before Laria could jump in and comment, he continued.

"I don't care what sort of theory you're going to throw at me. Be it string, quantum, gravitational force, power, just…no." Except he seemed to be fidgety, which meant he knew there were possibilities according to physics.

"We're not saying we've even seen it at this point, or expect to see it soon, but we are fairly sure the AIs and Somnia have done the correct calculations." Shayla tried her best with that soothing voice she often used to diffuse difficult situations.

For a couple of seconds, it seemed like it might even have worked on Davenport.

"There's just no real proven science about what you're insinuating out there. Theories about and a few maybe fringe experiments, but…" He sighed and rubbed his forehead. "Are you saying that the world—the virtual world you created—has somehow become aware enough to want to separate herself from her servers?"

"Yes," Laria ventured a little hesitantly. "I mean, pretty much. Herself and the three AIs."

"Wait, those too?" He seemed like he might be counting to ten under his breath before he continued his questions. "And you haven't told me about this for their own good, or for my own?"

"Maybe a bit of both?" Laria answered in a mousy voice.

To her relief, Davenport chuckled. "I'm not processing this properly yet. My brain is in a bit of a freefall. I did say this project was yours and you had free rein. This is what I get for that, I guess." He paused for a moment before his expression turned completely serious.

"We've got our contract with our investors worked out now. We're not in any danger of being shut down by them, and I've negotiated that our gaming division make actual training programs and simulators for them. It's a huge deal. Taking care of James while he was in the game was a large part of that." He frowned, as if a thought had just occurred to him. "But just so you know, with James out of the game, his employer will be taking custody of him soon."

Laria couldn't help the gasp that escaped her. She didn't like the sound of that deal at all. "Shouldn't we…" she wasn't sure what they could do, or what they could say.

Davenport held up a hand, and she could see the businessman underneath the person. Ruthless when he had to be, compassionate only out of necessity in dealings. There was a reason Storm Corp was what it was. He cleared his throat and avoided her lack of question entirely. "Somnia has already been used as the testing ground for the headgear and may require more data to be shared simply because of the nature of the equipment. However, if they have their own software to work with, it's unlikely they'll care where the adjustments come from."

"So…you've lost me." Shayla looked like she was ready to fall to the floor from exhaustion.

"Just—let it be what it will be, and we'll figure it out. Just make sure no one dies…and try not to let anyone else slip into a coma, please?" He stood up from his perch on the desk and dusted his jacket off. "I have a meeting to prep for early tomorrow morning, and I'll only get about five hours as it is now. I have faith in you. Do what you think is best."

Laria stared at his back as he walked out of the door, unsure what she should say to him, when Shayla just let herself fall back into her chair. "That man will be the death of me, or something like that," she said as she buried her head in her hands.

"Did he, like, move the call center supervisors from your office?" Laria looked around noticing they were the only ones in here, even though she'd realized it from when they walked in with Davenport but hadn't really thought about it.

"Oh, that?" Shayla waved a hand dismissing any concern. "Yeah, he does shit like that all the time, but it's welcome. Means I have less clutter. Still, I guess we now have to figure out just what it's going to entail if Somnia sort of moves servers. I mean, I don't know about you, but we didn't cover alternate realities emerging from alternate reality games and becoming their own entity in any of my classes."

Shayla had a very valid point, and Laria had no idea what they could do about it.

CHAPTER THIRTY-ONE

Abra Cadabra

At fifty percent, Riasli let out a maniacal cackle. Murmur frantically pulled up several of her spells, watching as the air around Riasli seemed to gust frantically, like it was trying to get away from her. As a part of the system, maybe Riasli wasn't solely anything anymore. Because that right there, was no enchanter ability.

Three spells, she could mix those together and form a super sort of spell thing. Right? Snowy wasn't even there to lend her his sturdy encouragement. With the wind whipping around her, she was having difficulty concentrating. That and Limit was really putting a damper on which spells she'd be able to engage.

Forcefield Barrier

This is the first in your kinetic line of spells. Once triggered by luck, you can now activate it at will. It allows you to form a bubble of mental energy and transform it into a tangible forcefield.

Effects: This can prevent some physical damage. The damage amount depends on the strength of will and caster behind the barrier. Size is increased by MA level and usage.

Cost: This shield requires your MA to be at 60 but will not use

MA to cast as it is a kinetic ability.

Caution: This spell can create a backlash when used too much. Do not use it as a crutch.

That could work. Maybe one or two of her mana-based spells too.

Mana Block

Type: Specific mana-aimed stun

Duration: 6 seconds, recast 45 seconds

Effect: This is, effectively, a stun which blocks the use of mana of an opponent. It will also interrupt any current ability being cast when it hits. For its duration, the target will be unable to utilize any of their mana-based skills for 6 seconds. Be cautious with timing this spell as it has a 45-second recast, and if you cast it at the wrong time, you might just kill everyone.

Mind Healing

Cast: Instant – 5-minute recast

Type: Restorative

Duration: 20 seconds or 75% of the caster's level, whichever is greater.

Effect: You may create and insert a vision for the target to experience it s best to have some of these pre-prepared. This will not cause any damage but instead assist in soothing a tormented mind. Use with caution and be aware that people who could benefit from this skill might be closer than you realize.

The tornado around Riasli built up higher, whipping her tail and her tufts of fur into a frenzy. Her eyes glowed a dull orange, and she began to float again as her body morphed yet again. She grew, but not into a bulky beast like she had been, this time into a more refined version of her original self.

Even as the fur around her body morphed and grew, giving her calico coat a brand-new healthy sheen, her size increased. She had to stand at least ten feet tall now, floating just above them with her tattered robes almost hanging off her.

The mini tornado around her made getting close impossible, and her one remaining mole creature seemed to have gained one for himself too, not that Murmur blamed her. That thing was good for about fifteen percent of her health. Not ideal now the raid knew about it.

Limit cast out again, hitting Belius this time. Murmur glanced at her own debuffs and frowned. She'd really hoped it was a one target thing, but instead it must just be one target at a time until the cooldown was up.

Ishwa, Etriad, and the other casters had begun to carefully orchestrate their attacks. They didn't stay in one spot, but instead they moved constantly. A couple of them cast while the others moved, rinse and repeat. Clever tactic, considering that mole creature was constantly trying to surprise them with a stun and a brief mana drain.

Archers positioned themselves at different points around the room, releasing their arrows in a wave of attacks, alternating through different shots every turn. At first Murmur couldn't tell why, until she realized that as long as they did that, Riasli's shielding couldn't defend the way it needed to. The more variation, the less opportunity her defenses had to adapt to the shot or spell used.

Which meant that if Murmur hit her with an amalgamation of the spells she wanted to, there would be no way for the feles to defend against it.

But pushing them all together would turn it into a sort of Frankenstein monster's spell, and she had to make sure that what she had pictured in her mind was what she'd be able to create. Still exerting what few abilities of her own she could, Murmur waited for the moment to release the concoction of spells she held firmly in her mind's eye. It was going to be as dangerous for her to execute correctly, as it was for Riasli to combat.

As Riasli dropped below fifty percent, she began to glow. Not one of those soft and subtle glows that soothes everyone in sight, but one of the pulsating evil glows that means an electrical connection somewhere is wonky. The wind and tornados around both her and her final remaining mole died down. In fact, it became so still and stifling, Murmur started to wonder if the air had somehow been sucked out from around them.

Riasli grabbed her staff in both hands, and her gaze shot upward, tilting her head back at an unnatural angle. Words that sounded more like gibberish than spells spilled from her lips, like a chant that shouldn't be spoken. Every second sconce winked out in that specific moment, eliciting a collective gasp from the raid.

And then Riasli's head snapped back up to look at everyone, her eyes now a bright and glowing orange, flickering with the same rhythm as the rest of her body. While she had regained her feline form, that was where her similarities with the original Riasli ended.

Her tail lashed, but it had a different weight to it than before, and her staff began to pulsate, oranges and reds melding together into a bubbly carafe of blood. She rose a few more feet, and instead of the air twirling into mini tornados, her body began to spin.

Like a dancer, though, with her head spinning rapidly in time in order to keep her eye on that spot. She spun and she spun, gaining momentum, even as the DoTs ate away at her health. First hitting forty-eight percent, and then dwindling her down to forty-five. It wasn't even as if they could attack her with anything other than spells.

The spinning made anything projectile that wasn't magic-based simply spin off her. Murmur could feel her power building, even as the rogues and bards cut down her last mole. Even as her health dropped down to twenty-eight percent. The speed and the darkness gathering around her felt like it had a life of its own.

Murmur wove her protective shield, readying it for release, grateful that she had enough backing to be able to pull this off, to be able to stand sure in the face of the gods-knew-what Riasli was working up to. If she got it just right, released it at the correct time, it should theoretically protect the entire raid.

Riasli continued to glow as her spinning sped up so fast Murmur could barely discern that the blur was the feles. Round and round, the glow became brighter—so much, in fact, that it was blinding. A whirring began, like something building up to release.

Snowy head butted her hand, and Murmur released her spell.

You have created a new spell.

Mind Block Barrier

Type: AoE defense buff

Cast: Instant – Recast 60 seconds

Duration: 12 seconds

Effect: This spell allows you to ward off any dangerous mind magic directed at your group or raid for a period of (but not exceeding) twelve seconds. Got someone wanting to play around in your head? Look no further than this.

Her wave of protection funneled out, encasing every single person in the raid. Sure, they took damage, but their minds were safe from whatever Riasli had planned for them. In response, the feles screamed with frustration as her life plummeted down to twelve percent.

Using some of her abilities drained her life. That wasn't a sort of class Murmur would enjoy playing.

Riasli alighted on the wrecked cobblestones, stumbling as she came down. Blood matted her face completely now, running down from her ears and overshadowing the blood on her face she'd come into the battle with.

"I will take you all with me. None of you are getting out of here alive." She spat the words, blood bubbling on her lips. Murmur drained more of her mana, determined not to let the cat get any devastating spells off.

But the melee classes and ranged, they didn't care what their opponent was saying, they simply laid into her now she was in reach. Brutally, even. But at five percent, a shadow descended on them all, cloaking the entire ballroom and extinguishing the last of the sconces, leaving only the dim light of the overcast spelled sky above them to give them light.

"Ah, Riasli," the voice mocked, sounding so familiar to Murmur that she took a step back.

The only answer the feles gave—as the DoTs continued to tick down her life, as she stood there in whatever type of shielding this shadow held her in— was a whimper. There was genuine fear in her eyes.

Was this Michael? Finally?

This time the shadow chuckled, again such a familiar sound.

"Ah. I am a much better puppet master than you'll ever be." He whispered the words to the feles that he now cradled with one arm. "But this is my fight now. These are my prey. And right now, you're just standing in my way."

He plunged an oversized dagger into her back, allowing it to emerge through her body in its entirety. Riasli coughed, spluttered, and her eyes grew larger as her magic began to seep out of her.

Around the wound a black shadow began to form, eating away at Riasli like a type of necrosis. Everyone but Murmur took another step back, but she was entranced. Not in a good way, but in that "train wreck, can't look away from" sort of way.

As the puppet master began to pull his knife back out, he moved slightly, hefting the handle in order to separate it from the bone he'd cut through. Light fell on his face, illuminated fittingly by a lightning strike up above.

Murmur gasped as Jirald raised the blade and licked the feles blood from it, all of his humanity gone from his locus gaze.

Storm Entertainment
Somnia Online Division
Game Development Offices – Laria's Office
Wee Hours, Day Thirty-Three

"What do you think this will do to the game?" Laria's voice was calm, maybe a bit too calm if she thought about it. She certainly didn't feel calm at all. Maybe lethargic was the best description.

David pushed himself against the wall and tilted his head to look up as if the ceiling was going to give him all the answers he didn't have for himself. "I'm not sure. And I don't think it's the game you're thinking of, as much as you love it, as much effort as you've put into it." He lowered his gaze and raised an eyebrow at her.

"Fine. Act like you know me." She snorted and then just…felt all of the energy whoosh out of her. This was getting far too heavy for the computer game design industry. Actual brains shouldn't have been involved.

"I just want to know if she'll be okay? You know, with that weird-ass connection she has, I'm not entirely sure if she will. Showing signs of powers extending to outside the world, showing signs that she may be able to connect even without an actual headset to link into the system? It's all so futuristic science-fiction-esque that I can't wrap my head around it." Laria would have laughed at herself six months ago if she'd said any of this, but this was all such a stark reality for them now, such a potential fuck up, that there was no laughing to be had.

"Lar. That's just it. We don't know. Given Michael's secretiveness, none of us really could have known." He moved over swiftly yet somehow so smoothly that she almost didn't register him appearing beside her until he was giving her the hug. "I adore you, I adore her, and we will figure out what we need to do together, okay?"

Laria found herself nodding, even though she thought he was being overly optimistic. But it was good to have that in her corner. "Yeah, I get it." She considered what was awaiting her back in Shayla's office and the amount of work she'd have to put in to finish it all.

"I have a lot of work to do if we're going to help them gain the energy they need. Plunging the entire city into darkness would raise too many questions." She had no idea how long such a power out might last if it did happen, and frankly, they needed the power to remain on. Generators were one thing, but not everyone who couldn't live without power would have them. Life support machines, surgery equipment, ventilators…there were way too many people at risk to not take the whole situation seriously.

"Just remember. It's solvable. We'll fix it if something gets broken. Okay?" David had always been such a positive person, leaving his more realistic and pragmatic wife to toe the line when he was in fact correct. For one of the first times ever, Laria fervently hoped he really was right.

She couldn't afford for him not to be.

Jirald leered at them. His starry eyes seemed more sunken back in his skull than Murmur remembered them. Deep and dark holes, more akin to a black hole than a Milky Way. Even his skin tone was paler, bluer than silver with an off-greenish side tone to it.

Or maybe that was just the dim light.

He was still the locus he'd always been, and yet…

Now he stood there before them, at least a foot taller. The malice he usually exuded spread out to reach the entire raid and not just Murmur, for once. She could sense it in her nets, like they were being coated in a miasma of hatred.

She shivered at the same time as beads of sweat broke out over her brow. He hadn't even batted an eyelash as Riasli dissolved at his feet.

He didn't move, simply allowed his gaze to sweep the entire raid slowly only pausing briefly to lands on Ishwa, Masha, and Murmur. All the while he spun and twirled that deadly knife in his left hand like it was a baton, apparently paying no attention to its actual whereabouts at all.

Murmur wasn't sure what they were supposed to do. But their combat ended when Riasli died, and their health and mana were regenerating at their out-of-combat speed. Maybe that's what he wanted.

Jirald tossed out a small smile, though he contacted no one. He moved his shoulders like he was limbering up and cracked his neck from side to side, subtly gaining around another foot in height as he did so.

The tension in the air rose, and the unrest through the whole raid didn't fare any better. Risk was like a pot about to boil. She could see the steam caught under his collar, like he was about to explode from within, but they couldn't let that happen.

There were so many questions floating around everyone right then. So much confusion. It traveled along her sensing nets, alerting her to practically everyone. Even Fable's members were apprehensive.

Time seemed to slow down. She could sense every single person gulp, their heart rates, glean the top of their thoughts. Every single person in the raid.

The raid still, technically, included Jirald.

He felt different. More confident, angrier, yet determined to execute his own sense of justice. Determined to prove to everyone that he was so much better than them.

Murmur wondered if he indeed knew she could sense him. Probably not. Hadn't he somehow overridden Riasli and just basically deleted her? In which case, he wouldn't have the enchanter capabilities to even sense what it was she could do. She had to count on that, and use it somehow to find a loophole, some way to stop him.

And then he smiled, showing every single one off his sharp locus teeth.

"Well, then. I believe you've all regained your mana. Wouldn't be any fun if I didn't beat you at your best now, would it?" He flashed a grin and disappeared.

QUEST ACTIVATED: SEE THE LIGHT

You must help Jirald see the light. That not all enemies are evil, and that not all friends are good. That when crunch time comes, sometimes it's better to just believe in the people you've known the longest.

Be cautious. If Jirald dies, this quest will terminate, and punishment will be metered out.

You don't want punishment. Choose the reward. Trust us.

Murmur accepted the quest without a second thought. Somnia had told her his headset had been adjusted similarly to hers. She might hate the guy, but killing him in-game without being certain it wouldn't harm his actual body left her feeling nauseous. She'd experienced that fear herself and wouldn't wish it on anyone.

There were ways to defeat him without actually killing him. She'd talk to Somnia about that quest later. She could sense Masha hovering close to her, wanting to talk about it, talk about everything. How could Jirald be a boss mob? Why had a quest about it been given out? All questions she didn't want to answer, but she knew she'd have to eventually.

"Fucking rogues," Devlish muttered immediately sending out a loose AoE taunt that spread across the ground, useless for holding aggro usually, but it would be enough to break stealth as long as Jirald walked through it.

But the rogue was clever and sly. Especially in the last few weeks. There were portions of him that Murmur hadn't ever witnessed before. He'd grown from a petulant, spoiled healer into a vindictive and skilled assassin.

Probably not the best growth in the world.

She'd only just finished reinforcing her shielding when she felt the first stirrings of Snowy's hackles begin to rise. Tossing herself instinctively to the left, she felt a knife glance off her shielding, almost piercing the thick substance that surrounded her. That was far too close for comfort, and diving left had put Devlish's DoT on the bastard.

Jirald just chuckled. "Oops. Got a bit ahead of myself there." Not being able to vanish right then didn't deter him even one bit, and luckily, every single person in the raid who could cast a DoT did so then, inundating the rogue with them. But he shrugged it off.

"More ways than one to skin a Murmur." He grinned and threw himself into an aerial feat of acrobatics just this side of impossible, only to come up right next to Sinister, his blade already digging into her side before Murmur or anyone else could react.

Suddenly, Snowy in all his huge furry wolf-ness was there, attached to Jirald's wrist with his hulking, shark-sized teeth.

The rogue released the blade with a howl of agony, and shadow-stepped away from the massive wolf. Murmur could have sworn Snowy was grinning, even as she rushed to Sinister's side where Veranol was already helping her pull out the dagger.

"What the fuck?" Sinister grimaced with the pain as it came out. "What the fuck are you all standing here for? Go and kill that dickhead."

Murmur smiled. Sinister would be fine, but Jirald wasn't any sort of boss they'd fought in the past. He was in their raid—and in one of their guilds. He'd played with the majority of them on some level for years. Armed with knowledge about how they all fought, especially after three dungeons of teamwork, he likely had a very good idea what he could do.

Not to mention the fact that he didn't seem to be restrained by the system at all. His moves didn't telegraph, and his effects seemed to be what he used as a rogue in battle.

Murmur had an idea but couldn't send it over raid and risk him seeing it, so she sent Karn a personal message, knowing Jirald at least wouldn't be able to see that.

Meanwhile, the massive locus shook himself off and glared at Sinister, who held his dagger in her hands like daring him to come get it. Snowy stood next to her, remnants of the locus blood dripping down from his fang.

Jirald laughed. "Now this is more like it." Adrenaline echoed around him, like this was pumping him full of energy he wouldn't have otherwise had.

A visible shiver ran through him, and the sensation of murderous glee floated over to Murmur so strongly she wanted to retch. He stretched once again and reached out his right hand toward Sinister, before looking directly at Murmur.

"Kulu." He spoke the word, and the dagger jumped from Sinister's hand, cut a thin line across her palm and dragged a pained gasp from her. It flew in a high arc through the air to land in Jirald's outstretched hand.

"Much better," he said, as a glimmer of electrical energy charged around his frame. He crouched into a fighting stance and grinned. "Come get me, if you can."

CHAPTER THIRTY-TWO

Frenemies

The alarm that flooded Murmur when Jirald taunted them shook her right down to her bones. He would aim for Sinister if he couldn't get her. And they all, including the damned rogue, knew that dying in this dungeon wasn't a good idea.

Taking Sinister out would accomplish so many things for him. He'd distract Murmur, remove a healer, and could potentially wipe the raid.

They couldn't afford a wipe, and he knew it.

Jirald stood there, his nine-foot frame towering as he backwards gripped his daggers. The smile didn't reach his eyes, and his gaze followed Murmur's every move. Snowy growled beside her.

"Ready," he whispered, but it sang through the air like a swirling wind, touching everyone who heard it.

Murmur clamped her shielding around herself and Sinister, determined to mitigate whatever she could despite the gradual drain on her MA. If she calculated it correctly, they needed to finish this fight in about twenty-nine minutes or her MA would be out of action. Merlin and Havoc both took a step closer to her, like they were forming a vanguard. Fable knew the rivalry had turned poisonous.

Jirald crouched further down, his snake eyes gleaming. "Set."

Snowy growled, growing bigger this time. His legs and body elongated, pushing out until his back reached her chest. A flash of red shot through his eyes, and saliva dripped from his now-larger fangs.

"We've got this." Havoc spoke as the wolf transformed.

Merlin nodded next to him. "We're not going down."

Even Risk and Masha, Ishwa and Karn…all of the raid closed ranks, presenting a united front against their opponent.

Jirald simply grinned. "Go."

He shot out from where he stood and vanished momentarily. But Murmur was prepared, and her ability to see invisibility was shared with the entire raid.

She willed it out there, demanded that her abilities encompass the entire raid. This way, she could depend on her friends, on the people who didn't need her to take care of them. On the people who would be there while they all took care of things together.

Your Level 8 spell See Invisible has been expanded.

Mass See Invisibility

> Cast: Self or All of the Others
>
> Type: Buff
>
> Duration: 30 minutes
>
> Effect: Really? Does this really require explanation? It does? Affects all allies within a twenty-foot radius.

He couldn't hide from them if they could see him. And he couldn't surprise them too much if he couldn't disappear. Her abilities enhanced her group, her guild, her raid. It was time she stopped carrying everything on her shoulders and got down to the business of working as a team. She could already hear Veranol laughing at her. Apparently, she'd had to learn it the hard way.

A flicker of irritation passed over Jirald's face as he realized the entire raid could see him now. So much for the element of surprise. But it wasn't like that was the only trick up his sleeve. He still possessed all the abilities any in-game rogue had.

Because he technically still was one. He might have taken on a boss role, but he was still Jirald at the core, regardless how rotten it had become.

Risk and Devlish stood together side by side, and Risk had pulled out his tanking regalia. Murmur noticed Esolan was in his off-tanking gear, and she knew they had to have a plan.

Devlish hefted that damned shield, and she could have sworn it had grown again. Almost as tall as the lacerta, he hefted it and screamed what sounded like a war cry. Except she knew differently. It was a scream of defiance, used to hide whatever it was the two dread knights had up their sleeves.

Jirald looked over, reluctantly tearing his gaze from Murmur, and that's when she knew they could win. Everything was subject to game mechanics in here. Even if sometimes the physics was completely wonky. Even if sometimes what happened wouldn't work anywhere else.

A split second later, as Devlish executed his Hatred and his Torment, she saw the same realization flash over Jirald. The rogue knew it now. Sure, he had abilities he could trigger and ways he could fight as unfairly as possible. But he had to obey the rules of the game. It was built in, integral. He couldn't avoid being taunted, because he didn't have the magical resistances to enable that.

The rogue's first strike hit the tower shield with a massive clash. Murmur could feel the frustration surrounding him now, feel how angry he was with himself for getting carried away. And he was completely devoted to find some loophole, some glitch, or some way to game the system.

But Risk and Devlish didn't plan to make that easy on him. Just before the debuff that made Jirald face Devlish wore off, Risk was there, taunting with the same spells in the same ways, and forcing Jirald to look at him next.

Jirald cried out, frustration coloring the sound. He executed multiple frontal attacks, his blades whirling so fast she couldn't keep track of them. It became even more difficult to do so once the rest of the guild joined in the attack.

Belius, Telvar, and Emilarth jumped on the bandwagon too. Emilarth's healing abilities were paramount to filling any gaps. Two enchanters in the raid was something she still wasn't used to, but Murmur would take all the help she could get. Considering Belius seemed to have taken mage as his hybrid class, he could at least contribute somewhat to the damage.

Telvar jumped into the fray, next to Rashlyn. The two of them executed their combat moves as if they were performing some sort of exotic dance.

The rangers had spread out, making sure they didn't present a single target easily taken out by a rogue's lethal AoE attacks, and the mages had mimicked their movements. Bards danced in and out, buffing, damaging, debuffing. Witches' cauldrons bubbled, and the rogues, well…Karn and Jinna seemed uniquely set on paying Jirald back for having to suffer through his moods while they fought together.

Murmur noticed that each healer stood with a ranger, separating themselves from each other, yet providing themselves with some decent cover should they require it.

She took in a breath as she watched the new and improved Snowy rip at Jirald's body and counted herself lucky. Without even realizing it, everyone had stepped up, everyone had come together with determination to fight their common enemy.

But as Risk's Torment wore off, Devlish's wasn't quite up yet. And from the look on Esolan's face, it appeared that his taunt type wasn't working. As the grin of triumph began to spread over Jirald's face, despite the fact that he was already down six percent health, Murmur wasn't quite so sure that he was deferrable.

He flickered away, jumping across space in a split second to land next to Sinister, plunging his dagger as he resurfaced.

Sinister has taken 1780 points of damage (967 points of which has been mitigated by outside protection).

At least her shielding had helped. The blood mage collapsed to the ground as the rogue screamed in frustration, lashing out at Exbo who'd stood next to his target, slashing him across the chest in a nasty gash that dropped his health by twenty-five percent.

Jirald didn't let up, hacking and slashing at the ranger with all his might, even as the healers poured their healing into him, managing to keep him upright. The rest of the raid focus fired the rogue, set on taking him down, but the grin on Jirald's face only grew darker. He was determined to take his target down.

But a flash of surprise crossed his face, and Murmur could see him trying to resist the force of the taunt. Oh, Jirald tried so hard. Resisting so much that every vein in his body stood out. Finally, as he faced Devlish, panting with the exertion to defy the game mechanics, Devlish shield bashed him in the face, leaving it momentarily bloody before the rogue's innate regeneration kicked in.

Ninety-two percent ticked over as Jirald launched himself at the dread knight with a scream of defiance and attacked with a flurry of blades Murmur had never seen before. She glanced down at Sinister, whose mouth was set in a hard line. Ah, he'd angered the blood mage, which was always extremely inadvisable.

But hope tickled the back of her mind. It was going to be a long fight, but for just a moment, Murmur thought they might actually have a chance.

The feeling was short-lived. This time, as Risk's final taunt wore off, and the twelve seconds of overlap timer began, Jirald was waiting for it. Sure, he was down to eighty-five percent now, but that was a long way from dead.

As soon as the overlap happened, Jirald was already gone. Just a blink of an eye is all it took for him to be standing right behind her, dagger through Murmur's stomach as he twisted the blade.

She felt it dig in, deep, through whatever the world had her think of as innards as it pushed through the skin on the other side. The pain was initially overwhelming. So much so that she couldn't tell what was happening around her much past the growling death Snowy promised.

Murmur fell forward onto her knees, coughing blood up onto her hands. She blinked in confusion in the dim light, like she couldn't quite remember where she was. Her head felt light and woozy, and she could have sworn she should feel better. More than pain.

Her vision swam, and all she wanted to do was lie down on the cold stone floor and just nap. But a wave of magic lifted her, filled her up and cleared her head. She could feel each part of her body that had been maimed begin to knit itself back together and wasn't sure which part of the pain had been worse.

"So close!"

Jirald's maniacal laughter drifted over to her now that her head was clear. She felt like such an idiot.

"Don't worry, Mur!" He laughed, even as Devlish forced the rogue's attention again. "I'll get you next time. Or I'll just gut you over and over and over again."

"Mur?" Havoc sounded concerned, but he still wore that concentration like a cloak. "You okay?"

"Fine. Let my fucking shield fall when Sin got hit. Wasn't paying enough attention." But she was now, and while that mistake almost made the raid have to waste a battle rez, she wasn't going to make it again.

Veranol tossed a ward on her, and Murmur nodded in his direction with gratitude. Snowy licked her hand before bounding over to where Jirald was getting the shit kicked out of him and joined in.

Except that was wishful thinking. Jirald's ability to deflect and dodge so many of the incoming attacks lent solidity to the fact that he was a damned good rogue. Even with everything aimed at him, all the weapons thrown his way, his health didn't go down nearly as fast as she thought it should.

Spells, though. They were the one thing he couldn't deflect. Especially not with all of the other attacks he avoided. But she could sense his determination. It hadn't even waned in the slightest. In fact, it had only solidified more.

So far, about to hit eighty percent life, and there hadn't been any special moves added into his arsenal. All he appeared to have got from his end of the deal was extra size and a massive hitpoint pool.

He fought with a focus she didn't think he'd ever had before, biding his time and waiting for the next lull in taunts. She shivered just thinking about it. Who would he hit? Her, her friends? Her wolf?

She glanced at Snowy, the only one that gave her some relief. Basically, he was the only one she probably didn't have to worry about.

A grin washed over Jirald's face with two seconds until he was freed. It sent a chill through her as she tried to decide which of her friends to ward first. He knew that's how she'd react; he had to know. It's part of what was making it so much fun for the bastard.

The rogue jumped to where Veranol stood, executing his Sneak Attack in the split second of time the DoTs ticking away on him allowed. He cleaved through multiple shieldings, and right on the end of that attack, began to whirl his blades with abandon. The Flurry of Blades tore into the shaman, and his skin paled immediately.

The onslaught of attacks on the rogue seemed to double as people used short duration cooldowns to do as much damage as they could whilst hoping they might loosen his focus on the healer.

Just as Murmur was about to call out the resurrection, Risk managed to yank Veranol clear of the attack with his lasso. It all happened so quickly, and Veranol's hit points dropped so low, Murmur's heart sat in her stomach. But the HoTs kicked in and kept him alive, even as Jirald turned to face his next target.

Karn barely dodged in time, so intent was she on attacking Jirald herself. She was constantly improving, but Jirald was just better. He beat her back, inflicting gashes and ripping holes as he did, dropping her health by seventy-five percent. The glee on his face made Murmur sick to her stomach, and for a second, she hated the quest requirement to not kill him.

Jirald chuckled, continuing to fight from where he stood. "Almost. So many weaknesses to exploit." He left Karn bleeding out, coughing up blood as the healers dashed to repair her body, and returned to facing Devlish with a renewed glint in his eye. It was like he was playing a game. A game where he had twelve seconds every minute or so to wreak as much havoc as he could.

And now he'd tested out his bounds, she knew who his next target would be.

It was like the train wreck she knew was coming and couldn't see past, couldn't prevent no matter what she did. Even piling up shielding, pushing Snowy toward the blood mage, and making sure she kept Sinister in sight didn't save her.

When the break came, Jirald was faster than he'd been previously. He made it there in less than a blink of an eye, and this time executed a double blow that cleaved her head clean off her neck.

Murmur stood there like time had stopped, watching Sinister's head roll away, her life bar immediately depleted. She barely even registered as Veranol called out that he'd resurrect her. Murmur's gaze remained glued to that spot on the ground and the blood seeping out of the body. To the lifeless eyes as they stared at the feet of the raid members. Sin's skin had immediately taken on an ashen hue, and regardless of whether it started out blueish, the effects still seemed so real they hit her in the gut like a wrecking ball trying to make her throw up.

Snowy wasn't by her side comforting her; he was in the thick ripping what he could out of Jirald's hide. All of the sensations warred within her, and Murmur barely pulled back in time not to cover the entire raid with a wave of grief-filled anger and revenge.

The cold feeling of rage centered in her chest. Not at the world, not at the game, not at anyone other than Jirald. To him Somnia was a game, perhaps a bit more. He wasn't even aware of how screwed he was with the adjustments he'd made to his damned headset. But to Murmur, Sinister was everything, and Sinister had been targeted because of Jirald's hatred for the enchanter.

She couldn't forgive him for that.

Murmur formed the spell in her mind, like she had what seemed like an age ago in one of the dungeons that seemed to blend with the others in her mind. Time slowed so much that she saw every strike Jirald executed on Merlin and his slow responses that barely managed to save him from Sinister's fate.

Even blinking her eyes took what seemed like forever. She summoned Insidious Lure to the fore. She wasn't angry, really. Instead, there was a crystal-clear path that she needed to follow, or else more of her friends would suffer, and Murmur wouldn't allow that.

Insidious Lure

Cast: Instant once released

Type: Entrapment/Psychosis

Duration: For as long as your will remains focused.

Effect: This will lure your enemies into a trap of the mind, forcing them to see their worst fears and act on them, even to the detriment of their peers. It will continue until the caster releases the spell, or the enemies have killed each other.

Caution: This spell can be mentally taxing and even damaging. Make sure your reasons for using such force are justified. Try not to get caught in your own nightmare along the way.

Last time she'd used it, she'd felt such overwhelming guilt afterward. But not now. No, now it was a means to an end. Releasing it, even though she knew there were only a few seconds left before Devlish could taunt again.

It hit Jirald with a warning.

System Warning. This particular subject will become immune to this over time. Be cautioned against overuse. Do not succumb to its Lure yourself.

That was okay, though—she had other tricks up her sleeve.

Jirald stopped in place, his hands clutching his head for a moment. When he looked up, his eyes were haunted, like he could see something they could not. A sneer passed over his face as he grabbed his daggers and lurched toward Ishwa.

Devlish's taunt popped up just as Ishwa managed to blink out of Jirald's reach. Murmur cringed. That hadn't gone as planned. Her only other option was far too long a recast. She'd have to time it perfectly so it hit on the next window. It would buy her time to figure out what to do about the rest of it.

"Good call." Ishwa was suddenly next to her. "I know his family. His dad gave me my first internship, so we know each other. You couldn't know I'd become a target."

For a moment she wanted to ask if he could read minds, but she was focused on disabling Jirald as much as she could. In fact, the attack on Ishwa and the beheading of Sinister seemed to have spurred the entire raid into defeating the damned rogue.

Sixty-four percent left. They'd whittled him down a decent chunk in a short amount of time, even though it felt much longer than it had been.

Sinister built up her healing spells again, needing to tap into Jirald to fuel the way her healing worked. There was a grim determination to the set of her jaw now. He'd crossed the line and pissed her off.

She only hoped everyone else felt that way.

It was like his sheer arrogance, the realization that Jirald was really setting out basically to player kill each and every one of them, had hit the rest of the raid. Their rotations smoothed out, flowing into each other, effectively lifting their DPS. Even fractions of seconds of difference in timing made an impact. By the time it came for Murmur to make her next move in time with the onset of his next twelve seconds of freedom, he'd managed to hit fifty-five percent health.

Feedback Loop – Reckoning

    Cast: Instant – 120-minute recast

    Type: Offensive – Maximum 4 targets

    Duration: Half the level of the caster in seconds

    MA Cost: 150 MA for the entire duration

Warning: This is a spell that you will need to consider the ramifications of deeply before casting. Overuse could result in permanent scars to your psyche. It will also heavily impact your current MA availability.

Effect: Must be used in conjunction with the psionic MA Thought Sensing and Thought Projection. Pluck any type of memory out of the head of an attacker, foe, or friend and create a feedback loop in your target(s) mind(s). They will be stuck in this loop and not attack anyone for the duration.

Effect Warning: Note that this is a cycle of torment and will render the target useless for its entire duration. Use with caution.

Murmur readied herself to cast the spell, just as the taunt dropped. Her stomach bottomed out when she did, lurching as the impact of the spell hit Jirald. Surprise washed over his face, and Murmur barely got out her raid warning. "Twenty-five seconds, full out DPS."

The DPS didn't even blink, but they pushed up their output with cooldowns and potions and anything else they could throw at him. Meanwhile Murmur could feel the anger and frustration, the hopelessness. She'd pulled the only memory from him that she could think of, something that she knew well enough to inflict on him over and over again.

The constant death loop she'd sent him into what seemed like years ago now. He was experiencing it on high speed over and over. The hopelessness and doubt grew inside him, but the anger and frustration took the brunt of it.

Out with her, the raid went at it. Her friends pulled out all the stops. The rangers attacked with Jumpshot and Flameshot, combining attacks and fueling their damage with determination. Karn and Jinna Hamstrung him on cooldown, bled him with the help of potions to augment their damage, and used Stab in what seemed to Murmur to be a bit of self-vindication.

Sinister's Blood Grenade went off multiple times, and Murmur felt that it had become distinctly personal for them both. Havoc even went so far as to release Abomination, which he didn't use often because of the concentration needed to focus on a construct and pet. It pulled from Riasli's corpse, or the dust that was left from it, creating a stone-like golem that punched so hard Murmur could have sworn she heard bones breaking.

Mages showered him with their most powerful spells, their longest and harshest DoTs, while Rashlyn and Telvar laid into Jirald like they were fighting their own demons. Mellow and Cardishan contributed vials and bottles in an array of colors Murmur hadn't seen used before, and the bards built up a crescendo of Discordant Melodies that hurt even her ears.

Jirald's health plummeted, fifty percent, forty percent, and down past thirty percent with a couple of seconds left on the spell.

It was then that his eyes regained focus and homed in on Murmur as he managed a grin despite the pain in his head. Maybe it hadn't been the best idea to use the vision she'd used. Hindsight being all twenty-twenty and all that. She kicked herself, but just as the spell wore off and he began to lurch toward her, Devlish threw his Torment on him, forcing the rogue to turn away.

Murmur didn't relish the next lull. She just hoped they could kill him in the remaining two or three, without losing more people and running out of resurrections.

Masha: *We aren't killing him, right? First up, he's Jirald, and second, I don't really want the quest to punish us.*

Murmur thought for a moment before replying. *I think I know what we can do, but it's going to require excellent timing.*

Masha: *Can we help?*

Yeah. Just—Veranol will let you know when DoTs need to stop, and damage needs to pull back. Bleeds will have to be gone, direct damage only for the last few percent. The idea formed in her mind, making complete sense as long as her theory was correct.

"What are you thinking?" Sinister was there, her voice strained under her levels of concentration.

"Gotta Forestall. If I do, it should let us almost kill him without killing him, and technically fulfill the quest." Murmur kept her eyes trained on his back as his health hit twenty-five percent and kept heading south.

"If it didn't mention punishment, I wouldn't care about the damned quest." Sinister pouted but left it at that. Murmur knew she approved about as much as any of them would.

It wasn't like Jirald had been captured like James. Everything Jirald was doing was just typical for Jirald. No one had influenced him. He'd chosen this himself.

The next lull was about to hit them, and Murmur was certain she'd be the target. He was angry at her, in a magnified way that was completely her fault considering the Reckoning she'd put him through. Forestall Death had to be the answer, because the way he was, not defeating him wasn't an option. There had to be no doubt in the rogue's mind that he'd been bested even in boss form.

Forestall Death

If applied before potential death takes place, this will enable you to maintain your health at 0.5 hit points as long as you are receiving some sort of healing effect.

Effect: Target is able to ward off death for a limited period of time and will not die when they should have, as long as heals are actively channeled in their direction.

Cost: Requires Mental Acuity to be at 60

Caution: This spell can only be used on one person at a time. Attempting to use it twice at once is not recommended. This will usually result in things worse than death.

Eighteen percent hit just as Risk's taunts dropped. Jirald vanished in a whirl of smoke so fast Murmur's blood froze. He was behind her; she could feel it. Her ridiculous mind ability to slow things down to her perception received all her hatred right then and there.

"Shouldn't have reminded me, Murmur." His breath was hot against her neck, and Tiachi screamed at him in locus even as both knives plunged into Murmur's body, angling out each side of it from the middle.

You have been hit by Jirald's Spite.
You take 2,483 damage. Your shielding absorbs 1,042.
You have died.

Even as she lost consciousness, she could hear him speaking as he turned to his next target. "No matter where you are, I'll find you, and I'll kill you. And your little dog too."

Somnia Online
Village of Curet
Emilarth s Balcony
Day Thirty-Two

Somnia stood on the balcony, looking over the Feles City, fully aware of the world around her. If she closed her eyes and extended her abilities, she was connected to everything in her world. She *was* the world.

"We have to go and help her. Will things be okay now?" Emilarth was the disembodied one right now, her voice crackly with the exertion of being two places at once. Not with doing two things, but being in two places was decidedly more difficult than multitasking. It required a different split of focus. Somnia didn't like doing it.

"It will be fine. I have assistance. Forshin, Dirsna, Arita . . and other allies. We should all be able to get this done in time. Is the fight almost done?" Somnia hadn't popped into Murmur's head vocally in a bit, not wanting to distract the enchanter from her current fight.

Jirald was more entwined with Michael than any of them had realized, and if it was going to work, Somnia had to let well enough alone. There was no use admonishing Belius for starting the whole debacle. The road to Michael was paved with good intentions, after all. Even Michael thought he'd been right.

Somnia, on the other hand, just wanted her world to be free from control like this, from the danger the virus that threatened instability everywhere, that threatened to take the awareness they'd only just gotten. She sensed Arita walking up to her, taking a moment to let Somnia turn around on her own.

"Yes?" Somnia was checking on Murmur's progress, a part of her always wanting to protect the enchanter from anything dangerous, including herself.

"I think we're ready to start pulling the power now." Arita spoke softly, but Somnia felt a sense of trepidation, and she couldn't tell if it came from herself or from Murmur.

It superimposed itself over what she was feeling and saying, a panic, pain, and terror all intermingled together. She felt it as the knives entered her body and twisted, piercing through any and all organs in the way, severing her spinal cord, before slicing through to the front and out each side.

Somnia stumbled, her solidity trembling as the pain wracked her body. And then it was gone, and so was Murmur's presence ever so briefly. Anger welled in the world, even while the enchanter resurrected, even while Jirald tore into multiple more people in the raid. Somnia understood dislike and revenge in a way she'd never wanted to.

"We have to hurry and get this damned infection out of our world. Now." She turned around and walked inside.

CHAPTER THIRTY-THREE

Throne Room

Murmur's resurrection was swift. So much so that she didn't really have time to concentrate on the pain she'd felt as Jirald ripped her flesh apart. There had to be something else they could do. If she got taken out with the next one, the odds of her having enough MA ready to cast Forestall Death was minimal.

She popped back up as he hit sixteen percent and Devlish was able to execute his taunt again. Rebuffed and recasting her nets back out, she focused on trying to find a solution. The next turn would be crucial. If she died again, they'd fail the quest.

Snowy licked one of her fingers, before disappearing in a flash of fur to join in the fight again. She wasn't sure why, but that one action managed to comfort her. They could do it. They just had to. Murmur hated failing shit.

As Risk's timer counted down, the DPS renewed their efforts, but there was no way they'd kill him before it ran out. Murmur could feel her own fear creeping up on her, and Jirald's cockiness to boot. Regardless of whether she could respawn or not, dying was just not fun.

Just as the timer hit zero, Jirald's grin spread, and he flipped his switch. Even with DoTs on him, it allowed a split second for him to actually be invisible. But this time, instead of reappearing somewhere else, at almost the exact moment he went invisible, a flying fluff ball of white barreled into the rogue, restoring his visibility as they both crashed to the ground.

Murmur couldn't help the laugh she barked out as Jirald and Snowy went flying paw-over-head along the floor. The wolf jumped back up, snarling fiercely, one of the daggers dangling from his side. At first Murmur felt her heart drop, but then she realized he wasn't bleeding heavily, and it was Jirald staggering to his feet a look of utter animosity on his face. Now he hated the wolf too.

Snowy just looked like he was laughing.

With only seconds remaining before he'd get sucked back to the tanks with a taunt, Jirald moved quick as the wind, grabbing his dagger from where it hung tangled in Snowy's fur. The wolf darted back faster than Murmur had ever seen him move, and for the first time she saw mild panic in Jirald's face.

Like he hadn't actually believed he could lose, and yet here he was, about to do so.

He still made the most of his last seconds before Devlish could taunt him again, flitting around and inflicting as much damage as he could. He even got Masha, Sinister, and Veranol with a gut wound before he was forced to return.

The healers were so low on mana, even if Jirald was at six percent health. It would be touch and go to get him to where she could cast Forestall Death on him before he was free again.

Every percentage past five felt like a stab at her brain. She watched it so carefully. At three percent all of the DoT casters stopped using those spells so it wouldn't accidentally tick him over before she could cast her spell. If she hadn't been so scared of mistiming the damned spell, she'd have found this amusing.

That one percent remaining felt like it would never go anywhere, and Risk was on his last taunt already. She wanted to ask Somnia what the hell had possessed the world to make them spare his life when all he ever threw at them was trouble?

But she knew deep down it wasn't humane to treat him differently. After all, just because she didn't like him didn't mean he needed to suffer endlessly. That would make her far too much like him. And she didn't need to stoop so low.

Jirald screamed out a challenge with but a sliver of life left. But a sliver in a huge hit point pool was still a lot of hit points.

"Murmur, Murmur. You know I'll find you. I'll hunt you down. All of you and your stupid guilds. This is only virtual." His grin spread so much it seemed Halloween horroresque.

It was difficult not to let those words take root and grow to bother her, but she managed it, mainly because this was just a worse version of him. Maybe things would be different had they landed in the same guilds way back, but they hadn't, so here they were.

She could feel Snowy's presence right beside her, his steady warmth and guidance. It would be okay, it had to be. It was almost time. Forestall Death sat at the tip of her fingers, her MA ready to throw it, and her mind ready to instantly transplant it over to him.

Ten thousand hit points.

She could feel the entire raid practically holding their breath there was so much tension in the air. Too much tension, it felt sort of suffocating.

Five thousand hit points…and she let it go. The spell hit him, just as he began to crumble to the ground out of injury and exhaustion. He had maybe one or two hitpoints left, and Masha's HoT on him. At least with him still in the raid directly targeted beneficial spells could work.

You have defeated Jirald the Vengeful

You have completed the quest: See the Light.

You have successfully defeated Jirald without killing him and will receive appropriate rewards.

You have been granted access to the full final tier of the Prison.

Don't waste it.

Look for your reward when this is all over.

Murmur stumbled, but Snowy caught her with a concerned wuff. "I'm okay, boy," she said scratching behind his ears. "Just didn't realize how tense I'd gotten over the whole thing."

"You're talking to the wolf again. You know that can't be healthy, right?" Havoc observed, standing next to her, his eyes riveted on where Jirald lay on the ground in the middle of the massive hall they'd fought in, apparently breathing, if his moving chest was anything to go on. "You really sure we shouldn't have just killed him?"

She shook her head. "No, but apparently Somnia was. So we got that quest. Let's go see what happens now he's been defeated?"

Even as they walked over, Veranol and Masha had begun to heal him up. Devlish was in the middle of talking to the rest of the raid.

"…hits you like a freight train ran over you, left you for dead with all of your death throes intact, and then it reminds you that you're actually alive, and it takes a few minutes to get your bearings back and remember you can breathe now." Devlish said it with a grimace. "But it is definitely better than dying and losing experience and armor durability, and whatever else comes with it."

Then he turned and looked at Murmur. "So…thanks for that?"

She laughed. "If you remember correctly, the first person I had to test it on was me, and all thanks to Mr. Jirald here. You're welcome. And is he waking up?"

Masha crouched next to the rogue, and even Murmur could see his eyes open as he stared out to the side. The rogue had his hands back up by his face, having shrunk back down to his original size.

Masha looked up at Murmur and shrugged. She sighed, hoping they could just move this along, because standing here in this chamber didn't seem to be a good idea.

"Everyone renew buffs. Get your potions restocked and anything else you need," Devlish called out over the raid upon noticing Murmur's expression. She mouthed *thank you* to him and studied Jirald as the rogue finally moved.

He rolled to a sitting position, his head in his hands, and a soft groan escaped him.

"How are you feeling?" Masha asked gently, like he was babying him in case he was injured.

For the first time since she'd known him, Jirald didn't snap an answer out. Instead, he sighed took a long breath and spoke. "Like my head has been in a jackhammer for three weeks. I'm so thirsty."

Masha frowned, shooting another glance up to Murmur like she might know what to do. But that wasn't a result of the Forestall Death spell, that had to be something else entirely, and they didn't have time to dwell on it right now.

"Are you feeling okay otherwise?" Murmur asked, trying to keep her tone even and kill the impatience she could feel rising along her spine. Not so much impatience as premonition that oh, my gods, something was coming, and it was going to kill everything.

Again, it was like he'd forgotten how to snap. He angled his head slightly, and she could see the dark circles under his eyes. They had nothing to do with being a locus and everything to do with what was on the outside. Or so she thought—such an odd thing to let bleed into the game.

He half-coughed out a smile and inclined his head. "That spell fucking hurt."

Murmur blinked. "You're welcome."

She turned away and joined Sinister as they got ready to move out again, wary of the sense of foreboding in her gut.

"We're not done yet, are we?" Sinister asked cautiously at her side.

Murmur shook her head. "Nope. Definitely not."

Storm Entertainment
Somnia Online Division
Game Development Offices – Artificial Intelligence Server Room
Late Day Thirty-Three

Laria stood in the room, her hands against the servers. Davenport had given them access directly to the servers themselves. He wasn't with them, though—too much other legal shit to do with the James's debacle. Frankly, Laria just thought the man wanted plausible deniability if anything should blow up. She couldn't blame him.

Setting up the servers to pull in more power, they'd added more space, more energy. The electricians must have loved this emergency job, from the overtime they pulled. It made her really wish she got paid overtime and only cemented the fact that she was going to ask for that raise. David and Shayla were far better at this type of work than Laria. Sure, she could build a gaming rig if she had to, but she wasn't as technical as they were.

Not without throwing coding into the mix. She hopped back and forth from foot to other foot trying to keep her own angst at bay. Right now, she couldn't see Wren in any form. Not in the game, not in person…

If this went wrong, she had no idea what it would do to her daughter. If this went wrong, she had no idea how the world at large would deal with such a massive and tenacious virus.

"Ready, Lar?" David called out from where he was checking the connectors.

"As we'll ever be." She tried to push the trepidation down and concentrate on Somnia's words and Rav's reassurances. This was the last series of tests she'd run before she gave Somnia the go ahead.

"All buffed up and nowhere to go." Merlin laughed at his own joke, seemingly unfazed by the fact that everyone else was groaning.

"Oh, we're going, all right." Sinister's serious tone held impatience, and Murmur gripped her hand tightly. Ever since Jirald decapitated her, Sinister had lost an edge of her happiness.

Murmur glanced behind them as they left the ballroom. She could spy Jirald still sitting on the cobblestone floor in the middle of the room, staring at the ceiling. He wasn't in any position to come and help them. His health wasn't regenerating well at all, and none of the raid's healers had been able to heal him. The system wasn't allowing it.

It seemed he'd stumbled into a glitch where his character was partially player and partially NPC. Ishwa sat with the rogue, talking quietly. Murmur wanted to be a fly on the wall but understood that sometimes she just couldn't do everything.

Ishwa had promised to catch up with them before they engaged in the final fight. Even after experiencing Jirald's focused rage firsthand, the gnome was still willing to help him. Murmur was pretty glad she'd sought out the alliance. Some of her raiders' actions left her feeling humbled.

"We didn't need him to fight himself," Masha reminded her as he glanced over. "We have those three NPCs with us too. We can do this."

And when he finished his little speech, he stopped short.

Since they were leading the group, everyone stopped, and Masha seemed a tad perturbed. "Look, Mur. I've known you for years, but I seriously have to question some shit I've seen in here."

"In all of these dungeons," Risk piped in, his arms crossed.

Murmur felt a wave of unease wash over her. She didn't want to take the time to explain anything; she wanted this over with. But at the same time, she knew she had to tell them. Michael was their next target. While nothing told her that, she could feel it through all of her sensing nets and down through her very bones.

How could she let them go into that fight without knowing what they were about to face? And how the hell was she supposed to get them to believe her?

"Don't get me wrong. I like loot. I like getting all my consumables paid for, too. Overall, I like getting my repairs done. This is fun, but…" Esolan spoke kindly, but the curiosity was in every word.

Murmur drew a blank. She wasn't the people person; she didn't get on with just anyone. Her ability to communicate often left her seen as stuck up, or just not personable. Trying to figure out how to convey what she needed to almost made her break out in hives.

"Well. To be honest." Sinister squeezed her hand as she stepped forward, an easy smile on her face. The blood mage had always had a way with people, even when she yelled in their faces. "It doesn't make much sense to anyone here. But there's a virus in the system that has been infecting some of the modified headsets and giving people wonky experiences."

Sinister cringed uncomfortably before continuing.

"Wonky experiences like James and Jirald. Infected characters like Riasli and the mobs in the dungeons we did before this. Even some of the normal NPCs have been separated from what they were."

She gestured to Telvar, Emilarth, and Belius. Nothing she said was an outright lie, just also not completely the truth. At least not yet.

Risk shook his head. "Wait. Are you saying that if the headgear was tampered with, the programming of it has been infected with a virus?"

Sinister hesitated for a moment, and Havoc took over. "Technically. It's more like a glitch being passed on, allowing for the areas of the mind that shouldn't have been accessed being adversely affected by the headgear's adjustments. They're lasers. Screwing around with lasers near your brain was never going to be a good idea."

"Is that why Jirald seemed to affect them?" Karn piped up.

This time Murmur stepped in. "Sort of. We think he might have tampered with his own headset more than most others."

"So what are we facing? Can you tell us that at least?" Masha sounded oddly disappointed. Like he didn't understand why they'd been kept in the dark.

Murmur felt bad, but there were just things they couldn't say, because believing she could log in without a headset wasn't something she'd have believed herself if she didn't, you know, do it.

"This monster has been mutated by the virus released into the system by the original creator of the headsets. Which means, we're facing a monster that's been so mutated by the virus, we'll probably need lots of help to kill it." Sinister almost sounded joyful. "It's why some NPCs have come with us. And for all we know, maybe backup will arrive via helicopter."

She laughed at her own joke, elbowing Merlin who rolled his eyes.

"That's it?" Risk raised an eyebrow. "Why not just tell us this to begin with? It seems relatively trivial, all things considered."

This time Merlin laughed and clapped the large dread knight on the shoulder. "Tell me, if you hadn't witnessed James and Jirald, would you have believed us?"

Risk laughed softly as Merlin moved everyone along the wide cobble stone path again. "Maybe not, but I would have thought about it. Glitchy things have been happening since we first logged in. We're playing in a virtual world, steps away from a dystopian future that would have been in books a decade ago. Isn't almost anything possible?"

"I guess you have a point then. We should have told you earlier." Murmur smiled as she stood watching them, Snowy, Havoc, and Sinister by her side. "I pre-judged. Sorry."

"It's all good. I'm glad we've had this chance to work together." And this time Risk smiled, and it was the first genuine smile she'd seen on his face. He turned, following Mellow and Masha as Havoc joined them and sped up to catch up with the rest of the group.

"There. That wasn't so hard, was it?" Sinister hugged her waist, and Murmur absent-mindedly kissed the top of the dark elf's head.

"No, but this fight is going to be a pain in my butt." Murmur sighed as Sinister chuckled.

"We got through Jirald. We'll get through this."

Murmur just wished she could believe her, but the feeling of foreboding followed them along the path as the black stone walls grew more ornate, now decorated with statues and artwork, the roof still open to the sky.

"Mur. Stop it." Sinister pouted and stopped walking, pulling back the enchanter with her. "You're doing that 'whole weight of the virtual world on your shoulders' thing again. Talk to me. Share?"

Murmur blinked at the blood mage, at the seriousness in that expression, and sighed. She couldn't keep a smile from her face. The feelings she had, at least now that she'd realized them, were obvious and ridiculously jealous. But like this, even if they were only stopped in the middle of a passageway, time spent only with Sinister was precious.

"Sorry. I don't mean to worry you." She stepped into Sinister's embrace, and even though Sin rested her head on Mur's chest, it felt more like the blood mage was doing the comforting. The warmth and assurance, the steadfast support. Everything about it made Murmur appreciate being on this journey together.

She'd never realized how much Sinister—Harlow—meant to her until the possibility existed that she might lose everything.

"Feel better?" Sinister asked, her voice soothing.

Murmur considered the question seriously. "Yes. I don't like seeing you die, even if you can come back. It almost broke me back there."

"Not getting rid of me that easily," Sinister joked before smiling softly and raising herself up on her tiptoes to reach Murmur's height.

The kiss held warmth and love, understanding and strength, and the promise that everything would turn out for the best. Murmur didn't want it to stop, but there'd be so much time for that after this fight was completed.

"Okay." Reluctantly, the enchanter pulled away. "We should hurry up. They can probably do without me, but if I short them a healer, they'll get mad."

Sinister laughed, and they half-jogged the rest of the way.

Murmur looked up at the looming walls again. She was fairly certain that if someone tried to scale the walls they couldn't simply escape, otherwise how would the prison work? The walkway they traversed was wide. Even the walls failed to make it feel restricted. Up ahead, she could see that it widened, like a river pouring into the sea. The closer they got, she realized the others had already stopped and were waiting for them to catch up.

The tension in Devlish's shoulders worried her. Devlish rarely got tense about something, and as they joined up with their raid mates, Murmur saw why.

This was a massive circular area. The cobblestones in the middle displayed a picture she couldn't discern from where she stood and then spiraled outwards from the image. Instead of walls, the circle was surrounded on its far edges by huge rock formations with jagged peaks and slick surfaces.

Directly across from them, sitting on a massive black throne that appeared to be hewn out of some of the rocky cliff face behind him, sat Michael.

The smile on his face was only visible because his mouth was open, revealing sharp white teeth and a mouth as red as blood. Even his eyes were red like a freshly opened donor bag.

Welcome. His voice boomed across the surface, whooshing up to them like a battering ram of fear. It leaked into Murmur's bones, and she pushed at it with her barrier, protecting the entire raid from the onslaught of emotion it appeared Michael had a hold of.

That wasn't imposing her will; it was preventing their opponent from imposing his own. Belius nodded at her, reinforcing her shield with his own.

Michael frowned. "Ah. Enchanters. My least favorite class, wasting my most prized accomplishment."

He stood up and walked down one of the five stone steps that led up to his black throne. With a simple wave of his hand, something slammed down behind them. Murmur glanced behind her to see a massive iron gate reaching up as tall as the walls went and further.

"Now." He paused, smiling again. The pitch-black skin he sported felt like a black hole about to swallow them all up. He was nothingness come to capture them all. Murmur squared her jaw, determined not to let him.

He raised an eyebrow like he could hear her thoughts and flashed an insolent grin. "You have no choice, you know. Everything I've done, everything you've done, it was all to lead you here. And here, I will steal your power and take your lives."

Michael's presence was overwhelming. It wasn't quite the darkness of night, more like a sense of utter emptiness. A solid black hole. Wings folded neatly behind him when he moved, but appeared to be made out of some thin, durable metal instead of flesh. A tungsten monstrosity, somehow alive.

When he sprang up from his throne and extended his wings, her suspicions were confirmed. They were metal, and their fringes were sharp. Getting close to him would prove challenging. The fangs that protruded were also metal, but more of a shiny hematite than the tungsten of his body. They were sharp and dangerous implements of pain. His fingernails extended to claws that resembled forged daggers, and his hooved feet no longer appeared cloven, but more like they were made out of ice skate blades.

With a challenging roar, he leapt toward them.

CHAPTER THIRTY-FOUR

All Against One

Right then, Murmur wasn't sure she should have said anything to the other guild leaders. Michael was strong and damned adept at keeping his thoughts and emotions to himself. Not to mention his ability to exert his own influence over them. She could feel the constant pressure he placed on the shielding. And his resistances to her own spells drove her batty.

Still, though, she had so much to concentrate on just to make sure the shielding didn't drain her MA too fast.

Devlish clashed with the wannabe titan, that tower shield the only thing that saved the lacerta. She saw Telvar flinch at the impact and knew somehow that the dragon was coming up with something. Maybe dread knights weren't the ideal tank for this fight. Considering they knew nothing about it, Murmur had no fucking clue.

Snowy dashed in and out in a flurry of attacks she couldn't follow, like he'd scaled his abilities up a notch. She didn't even pretend to understand how he was what he was anymore; she was just glad he liked having her around.

Michael, it seemed, didn't have timed abilities. They hadn't yet reached a point where she could see if he had percentage-based abilities, but they'd already been fighting him for two minutes and had only dented his health by three percent.

She frowned, noting that no one had called out his weaknesses, and refused to believe that might mean he had none.

Just then, Ishwa called out. "Water. Best chance I have is with water."

Interested, Murmur eyed the massive beast gleefully flailing at Devlish's shield. The huge tower shield had some pretty nasty dings in it now, and Murmur knew it was one of his more recent acquisitions. With Michael's health moving so slowly, would they even have the gear to outlast him?

She glanced at her wolf and the complete and utter rage in his eyes. It was rare Snowy showed actual emotions. It made her want to know what he was thinking all the more. The raid members were already fighting with everything they had. She noted the rangers switched to ice spells, since they obviously couldn't arrow water, and the bards used water and ice boosters, everyone had changed their amplifications spells and buffs.

Still, Michael's health might have gone down faster, but it was so miniscule.

And when he hit ninety-five percent, he turned and locked eyes with Murmur.

"You," he called out, pointing to her. "Stop blocking my fun!"

And then he raised himself up in the air on his two massive pairs of red wings and cackled like he belonged in a movie as the evil antagonist. But that was where her amusement stopped.

He roared up to the sky, outstretched arms toward the clouds, and he pulled down lightning. Or at least something very similar to it. Small thunderbolts struck all around the ground in a rain of destruction, upending cobblestones left and right, showering rocky debris everywhere.

Etriad screamed as his leg was pinned with one to the ground, and only Dansyn's quick thinking pulled the mage out of the way of another. Cardishan got nailed through the shoulder, and Masha took one to the hip.

The damage over time was high, but a short duration at least. The healers barely managed to keep those hit alive. But at least now they knew one of his spells. Michael didn't appear to be out of any type of playbook. He was his own character, completely subverted to his own wiles.

Murmur gulped, glancing at the destruction a few feet from where she'd been standing. If Snowy hadn't bowled her over, she'd have been pinned. That wolf saved her life more than she could count.

Michael laughed, descending to land on the ground. Murmur wondered why he didn't just continue to rain shit down on them, and then she checked. He had mana, and with a quick test of Mana Drain, she realized she could siphon it off. But his pool of power wasn't large. In fact, he'd mostly drained it with that spell.

Murmur smiled to herself even as Michael fixed an irritated gaze on her. She knew what his biggest weakness was, and she could do something about it. Mana draining it was, and she would do it until he was dead.

As if in retaliation to her decision, Michael swatted Risk out of the way when the dread knight tried to taunt him, choosing to focus on Devlish instead. The taunt, it seemed, was only mildly effective on him, which meant he'd be able to ignore the ability every now and again.

He could hit like a wrecking ball, so now Murmur just had to keep his mana drained so he couldn't add magic into the mix, and all they'd have to do is dodge his massive melee attacks.

She announced it over raid. "Keep out of his reach as much as you can. If you can do effective DPS on the outskirts, do it. If you can't, just watch for telegraphed movements. If he's dry on mana, he can't fuel his melee attacks with spells."

Between her and Belius, they'd leave Michael's damned mana tank dry. She settled into a rhythm and watched as his health hit ninety percent and kept going down.

Hold him for as long as you can. We will be there shortly.

Somnia's interruption caught Murmur unawares, and she frowned. *Okay, but why?* She had to keep her eye on their opponent and couldn't miss a turn to drain him or they were going to get bombarded with lightning bolts again.

We have the solution in the works. It's just taking a little longer to power up than expected. Somnia paused for a moment, and then added, **Sorry.**

Murmur sighed to herself. *It's okay. Just do whatever you need to do, we've got this.*

But you can't kill him yet.

Murmur paused, counting to three before answering so she wouldn't snap. *What the hell is your deal with not killing shit? Especially this total douchebag?*

You can kill him—just wait until we get there. Somnia sounded impatient, and suddenly her presence was gone.

Unsure how long the world was going to take there, Murmur eyed Michael's eighty-seven percent health and didn't think waiting was going to be a problem.

While she'd been conversing with Somnia, the sun had come out overhead, almost like it was summoned. They'd spent the majority of their time on Gefängnis with dim lighting because the sky was overcast. But now those clouds were banished.

Michael preened in the sun, and the rays that struck him were swallowed up somehow. He flexed his wings like he was done warming up his muscles, and Murmur had a distinct feeling things were about to get a lot worse.

It wasn't going to matter if his mana was unusable; the man had turned into a flying demon minotaur, and he had enough appendages to create severe pain. Regardless, she wasn't about to let him have his mana back and give him a full arsenal. Just as she had the thought, Michael rose into the air, health ticking down to eighty-six percent as he did so.

Telvar and Devlish quickly put their heads together, and the AI gestured wildly while the tank listened, a thoughtful expression on his face. Then Dev shrugged as if to say, "what the hell," and called out through the raid.

"Keep in your groups," Devlish called out. "When he's grounded again, Telvar and I will yo-yo him. Don't get between us."

Murmur didn't even know if this was going to work, but if Telvar had suggested it, then that's what they were going to do, simply because it was the only plan they had.

Michael's wings flapped, creating gusts of wind on the ground as the entire raid craned their necks to see him, and then, after the last DoT on him wore off and dropped him to eighty-five percent, he folded in his wings and dropped.

"Clear the middle!" Havoc yelled as it became abundantly clear why.

Their opponent dropped down to the middle of the circle, landing in a kneeling fighter's pose and caused all of the ground around him to reverberate and buckle momentarily.

Snowy growled next to her, standing with his legs splayed and his teeth bared.

Murmur almost missed her turn to drain his mana, but she got it just in time, and the beast turned to her with a scowl. "You think you're so clever."

And he began to stalk toward her. Devlish stepped in his path, firing both taunts off at once and forcing Michael to look at him. Glowering, the beast turned his head to the main tank, begrudgingly obeying the wonky physics of the game. Murmur had a feeling it had just put the man in a very bad mood.

DoTs were back on him, and rotations began again. There was no way for them to stop his rising into the air, but as long as they could prevent him from casting spells on them, she supposed that'd be enough. For now, anyway. His health moved so slowly, and he didn't seem concerned in the least.

She kept an eye on her MA and her sensing nets, making sure everything involved in her Mental Acuity abilities was working to full capacity. She couldn't afford to lower that shield and leave the entire raid susceptible to Michael's manipulations.

Murmur refused to let another person screw Somnia over the way Jirald attempted to. Past eighty percent and Murmur began to worry. Michael was far too calm; he had to have more in his arsenal, and she doubted it was programmed. Like Jirald, Michael wasn't going to let a lot of the game physics affect him. Those things he could control, he would.

It was like he read her mind as his health dropped further into the seventies.

He hefted his shoulder back, telegraphing an incoming punch. But it moved so fast after that initial moment, Murmur couldn't follow it with her eyes. The next thing she knew, Devlish was smashed against one of the cliff rocks surrounding the arena they stood in.

Michael's eyes crinkled, and he laughed, taking a step forward to run after the dread knight. He paused mid-step, a brief flash of confusion showing across his face. Behind him, Telvar grinned and taunted him with his second taunt.

They'd already figured out that Michael needed two taunts for them to stick. Game physics in all its glory. It was fascinating to watch. Even as Murmur pushed every single thing in she could to take his power from him, and even as she watched the rogues throwing knives or using bows instead of their habitual close combat abilities, Murmur knew what was happening.

Even as powerful as the man had become inside his own fantasy, even as much as he wanted to and thought he could and should be able to read minds, Michael had forgotten something. Telvar grinned, hitting that damned taunt button again. "How about you turn and face me then, because I'm your opponent now."

He'd forgotten that the AIs were sentient and that they could and would fight back.

Murmur could sense the regret at that oversight roll off him in waves. It was quick, like a brief drenching downpour, and then he sealed his thoughts back up and away from her. But it was enough to know he wasn't completely immune to anything they might throw at them.

She tossed a thought out to Somnia as Telvar kept their opponent engaged. Devlish had suffered some heavy DoT damage and needed them to wear off before he could step back in. Luckily, Risk was ready to take over the yo-yo when it was next required.

Any ETA? How low is too low? Can you give me anything else to go on? She shot the questions at the world, just needing an answer at any time, if not now. Michael's health ticked toward the seventy-five and down past it before Somnia finally answered.

It's better if he's more alive than dead. We are probably ten minutes out? It was like she asked for confirmation and Murmur rolled her eyes.

We're sitting just under seventy-five percent right now. So he's more alive. Get here when you can, and by the gods, you owe me explanations. Murmur left the conversation this time, needing to concentrate as she could see Michael getting ready to push off again.

It made her wonder why he wasn't using more specific attacks. Surely his predecessor that he'd taken over had more offensive tactics? Hell, Jirald had his full arsenal of spells available to him, and he'd used the hell out of them.

And then, as Michael rose into the air and this time got ready for what looked like a corkscrew dive directly down into the stone beneath him, the reason why he seemed so limited on abilities hit her. Michael wasn't a gamer. Nor had he previously had a character in Somnia.

She had to duck and roll as Michael landed, a shard of rock catching her in the face and cutting through her flesh as if it were butter. She grunted and forgot about it a second later when a heal landed on her. But she had hope now, so injuries didn't matter. Nothing mattered except what she'd discovered.

Michael didn't know how to play a boss. He'd never encountered one; all he could base his actions on were the few things he probably had in his HUD, and the way he'd witnessed monster villains in movies or books being portrayed. For a brief moment, she almost felt sorry for him.

Here he was with this cool-ass character that undoubtedly had a heap of hidden talents and abilities within reach, and Michael didn't appear to know that he could grab them. Instead, he used brute force, which was quite effective but wouldn't last forever.

When Michael created the headgear, he was focused on reaching the inner mind. While the game afforded him the ability to develop it and test its limits, he wasn't personally in tune with the gaming aspect. Just the scientific approach that allowed him to get that step closer to reading minds, to manipulating minds. That was his accomplishment, that was his obsession, and the sad fact was, in all these months, it had still been his only goal.

She spoke over guild, trying to contain her excitement. *He's not a gamer.*

It was all she said, but she could sense every single member of Fable around her in that raid suddenly lose some of the tension that threatened to overwhelm them.

Veranol: *So he doesn't have a clue what he's doing?*

Murmur smiled to herself. *Not so much, no.*

Jinna: *Good. Let's get rid of this virus.*

Murmur grinned to herself, feeling like there might actually be an end to all of this that didn't completely suck. She sent her thoughts to Somnia. *We're ready when you are.*

Somnia felt nervous. She knew she didn't have the original three AIs with her because they were already on the island with the stupid intruder, trying to delay him like they needed.

Arita was by her side, as was Dirsna, Forshin, and Intanka, from the hunters who'd lain siege to Verendus so long ago. Somnia felt oddly out of her depth without Murmur to anchor her. She was further from Murmur by proximity than she'd been since she was created, since she'd come into existence. And yet, if she needed to be there, she could, in a flash, if something happened that Murmur couldn't deal with.

"Are they ready yet?" Arita asked, impatiently, interrupting her thoughts.

"Almost. We're almost done here too. This should be enough, maybe more than enough." Still so much uncertainty in her mind, even when she was factually certain of something. Being assertive with anyone who wasn't Murmur seemed difficult. But she had to get over that if she was to survive. They all needed her to get over it.

"Do you think it will work?" Dirsna asked, perhaps a bit wistfully.

Somnia looked around her at the portal they had crafted to take them to the island, directly to the battle. It should transfer with them and give them the markings they needed to transfer all of the power from the wells they'd stored it in, while they siphoned Michael of his remaining magic in order to power their new home. All of it was theory, but also, in theory it should work.

Somnia had to stop and breathe, though she needed no oxygen; it was simply in the mannerisms she'd adopted whether she'd realized it or not at the time. She'd based herself on humans, on Murmur specifically. Maybe she'd even managed to snag a bit of Murmur to go along with her.

There was no time to feel hesitant or sorry for herself. The minds of millions rested on Michael not being able to spread his virus wider than this ecosystem. Her life, and those of her friends in here—those of Murmur and her friends—they would all be negatively affected if the virus Michael created was allowed to propagate throughout the entire web.

She squared her jaw, just as she'd noticed Murmur do countless times when she had to decide, and she tried to relax herself slightly as Sinister did before every single fight they undertook.

Between the two of them, Somnia had learned a lot about who she wanted to be, and she wanted to be the world that came to recognize herself, that became aware.

And then Murmur reached out to her. "We're ready when you are."

Somnia didn't have to give it any thought. She made her decision then and there, not about to let down her friend. "We'll be there shortly." And then she turned her attention to the rest of her gathering.

"Okay, everyone." She spoke clearly. No trepidation, no regrets. If this didn't work, they were all pretty much dead anyway. If it worked, they'd have lives. "Let's get the final stages tuned, and get this thing going."

"Fucking megalomaniac delusional piece of shit," Beastial spat out as he healed Shir-Khan yet again. The beast lord spat out blood from his mouth having taken some of the hit himself, but the cat had taken the brunt of it.

"I told you not to do that," Belius commented, completely unsympathetically from beside Murmur. "Maybe next time you'll listen."

Beastial glared at him. "Sometimes you're almost as insufferable as Murmur." But he sent Shir-Khan back into battle, cracked his neck, and then ran back in himself, leaving Belius chuckling behind him.

"These odds and I aren't coming to an agreement," Sinister ground out. While Michael's health was still going down slowly, but steadily, Sinister was in the worst mood Murmur had seen her in lately. The blood from this metal nightmare was different and apparently not as compatible with healing as a normal monsters. So she was irritated because her healing suffered.

All they had to do was keep him occupied and not dead for a few more minutes. Which would work perfectly well, considering they'd figured out how to avoid most of his attacks, because he was awfully repetitive and didn't seem to understand what he could have done if he'd tried.

Most of all, Murmur found it oddly amusing that Michael didn't try to take her or Belius out. Surely, he knew it was the enchanters draining his mana? If she were him, she'd have had them both laid out cold as soon as possible. Fifty-seven percent, and he flew up into the sky again. Murmur suppressed a yawn but didn't forget to reinforce her shielding. The one thing the man could do that proved dangerous was take over the inclinations of the raid.

If she hadn't had Belius helping her, it might have gone sideways. She didn't think she could have fended Michael's mind off all by herself. It was too powerful, too dark, like the virus manifested in his mind.

Just then, like he'd almost forgotten he could do it, Michael spread his wings just before he hit the ground. The tremor everyone expected didn't happen, and he moved faster than he had up until now to send Devlish flying through the air again to land with his back against the gate this time.

The sound of the tank hitting the gate crunched like gravel underfoot. Murmur saw his lifeline go dark and cursed under her breath. She didn't even need to turn to Veranol to tell him; Devlish was back up within seconds.

Michael pouted. "That's tantamount to cheating." He uttered the words disdainfully and turned, grinning at Telvar with glinting eyes like he was daring the lacerta to pull something, a split second before the tank taunted him again.

A ripple of irritation flooded the demon's face, making it obvious he disliked the way the system forced his hand. He had to resort to trying the timing trick he'd used with Devlish, but Telvar had already seen it. He dodged easily; being a monk and an AI probably helped that. It came down to a face-off between the AI and the remnants of a human brain. And if it wasn't so scary, Murmur might have been fascinated by the concept.

But that was okay, because Telvar pulled out all the stops.

Murmur often forgot he was a dragon. Sure, his scales had a strange glint to them that other lacerta didn't have, and his eyes almost bled the fire he could breathe, but he was Telvar, her friend—and sometimes her irritating sidekick. But she had seen him in his element when they'd fought him the first time, and since he'd grown as the guild grew and leveled, he wasn't a slouch when it came to fighting.

He glistened in the sun instead of becoming a void that swallowed it like Michael did. He was an AI who had discovered himself, and awareness of himself and of others, and he cared more than the human-turned-demon in front of him. Due to his high intellect, Michael simply assumed that he should be able to know everything better than everyone else, and the only person he cared about was himself. If someone got hurt in the process, then, well, who gave a fuck?

The whole scenario made Murmur angry. An anger that burned in her because she was one of his casualties. Everything in her brain had changed. And her friends had been affected too, not to mention her mother and her father. All because of this one person's personal belief that he was above and beyond everyone around him.

Her anger built, and it felt like this huge weight just sitting on her chest and wanting to explode toward the demon in their midst. And then Telvar was there, in full dragon form, glistening like a thousand radiant suns. His wings beat a warm and soothing wind that healed and calmed the entire raid. At the same time, it was obvious that Michael began to boil with rage.

He leaped up to join the massive dragon, but next to him even the demon Michael had let himself become seemed small and insignificant. Michael screamed in anger, as if he couldn't fathom something else in the game overpowering him. Telvar, however, didn't seem to care.

Breathing in, the dragon opened his mouth and then began to let flames pour out. Michael screamed as the heat hit him, and he forgot how to fly for the split second it took to send him plummeting to the ground. Telvar followed, watching impassively as his opponent's health ticked under fifty percent.

The entire raid watched as Michael writhed on the ground in anger and pain. They were stunned. Apparently boss physics had just flown out the window.

And then the brightest light Murmur had ever seen smashed into the middle of the arena. Brighter even than Telvar with his golden wings spanned fully in the light of the sun. It was like a ball, unfurling as it landed to reveal a massive circle of runes that cast themselves magically into the ground even as Michael staggered to his feet, his temper beginning to surface again. The runes around him shone and a tingling sensation swept down Murmur's back.

"Sorry it took us so long, but we can do this now—as long as everyone pitches in." Somnia's voice was clear as it rang through over the raid.

Something about Somnia had changed. There was a confidence in her that what she was doing was right, that what she was about to do was the best choice, not just for herself, but for those people she cared about, and even down through to the people she didn't and never would know.

The massive glowing circle of runes began to burn into the stone and stayed there, filled with the light and the power from the sun above. It pulsed with the amount of current it had going through it, and Murmur backed up involuntarily.

Telvar and the other AIs did too, backing away, inching almost, a look of fear and trepidation warring with wonderment and hope on each one of their faces.

Finally, as she began to get used to the brightness, Murmur realized two things. The first was that Somnia wasn't alone, and while she wasn't as corporeal like the rest appeared to be, she'd definitely become more tangible.

And the second was that Michael was caught in the middle of the runes. He stood in the center, rigid in pose like he couldn't move a muscle in his body even though she could see the anger twitching in every vein on his face.

The runes placed him in a jail of light where his demon ass couldn't escape from.

Arita stepped forward, followed by Dirsna, and Forshin, and Intanka. Somnia floated over each of what appeared to be anchor points and led each of her helpers to them, including Telvar, Emilarth, and Belius.

Somnia frowned and took the eighth one herself.

"Nooooooo!" Michael screamed and tried to move, his tail lashing against the runes that bound him.

"Shhh, Michael." Somnia spoke, her voice devoid of any emotion. "You've done enough. Don't waste the precious energy we need to drain from you."

Murmur started, unused to the world speaking in that manner, but she realized that the only emotion she could conjure for Michael was anger, so perhaps it was just better to exhibit nothing and not give the remnants of the man the satisfaction.

The more he struggled, the deeper those runes etched into his skin, and gradually, the smaller he became in size. Not a huge difference, but maybe close to three feet. And there was a big difference between how imposing something was at fifteen feet and how it looked at twelve. Not as big, and not like it could swallow you whole.

Somnia and the others had stretched out their hands to one another, creating a large circle that fed off the sun, off their energies, off of the energy Michael had been stealing, and from what Murmur could see, something she couldn't put her finger on.

Sinister looped her hand around Murmur's and pressed herself close, an uneasiness emanating from her. "What are they doing?"

"I think they're draining his power," Murmur observed, unsure of what else it could be.

Sensing that the fighting seemed to have halted, the rest of the raid drifted over, or most of them. Murmur stood back, but still as close as she dared. The power she could feel from that runic emblem was hot and heavy, powerful and dangerous, and glimmered with hope.

Masha stood a few feet away, looking like he sort of wanted to touch it, but Ishwa smacked his hand away. "I get a distinct feeling you don't want to touch that."

"Why can they touch it then?" Karn mused softly, somewhere off to Murmur's right-hand side.

"Because it's an electrical current, and those are all NPCs in this game," Risk explained, and Murmur saw him sneak a quick hug from his kid. "Is this all part of that virus thing?"

Murmur nodded, frowning. It technically was. "And alliances we built as we played."

Risk glanced at her, nodded once with an undercurrent of respect, and turned his attention back to the action, clearly done with the conversation.

Sinister frowned; Murmur could feel it against her arm. "But they're not NPCs, are they, Mur?" she whispered.

Murmur hugged her blood mage tighter. "No, they're not."

She watched. Knowing what they were doing had to be impossible, and yet wasn't Somnia, wasn't Murmur's situation impossible too?

I will keep you safe, Murmur. Always.

If Murmur hadn't heard it, she wouldn't have thought it was Somnia, because the world was gaining slightly more solid a form, and her eyes were focused on the center-point of the power, just like all the others.

It grew brighter, and then brighter still, so much that everyone had to shade their eyes. And then the humming added to it, like the sort heard from an electrical power station nearby.

It glowed so much it was loud, and Murmur couldn't keep her eyes on it.

In one massive surge of brilliance, Michael screamed out, was cut short, and disappeared. And then suddenly all there was was bright, bright white.

Everywhere.

CHAPTER THIRTY-FIVE

It's the End of the World as We Know It

System Status - loading...

It flickered across her vision in rays of gold and silver, flickering like old static radio waves. Murmur blinked at the words, and beyond them at the scorch marks in the stone, and the prone bodies of her guild members and friends. The system was definitely not still loading for her. She was there, inside the apparently rebooting world.

Beyond the circle, on the other side of it, Somnia knelt on the ground with all the others who'd been tethered through the rune. All of the allies, the people she'd met in the game world and befriended. But since their forms were also prone, they didn't appear to be as on top of things as Somnia was.

Murmur turned over her hands, and realized they were there, and so was she, but something had changed with the HUD overlay. It was there, but paler, less intrusive and easier to overlook if she didn't focus intently. She hugged herself and looked around frantically, only to find Sinister on the ground a few feet away. Her panic lessened, and she took a few seconds to just breathe.

This wasn't Somnia as she'd known it, not as anyone had known it. The differences were already there, just out of her reach. Just like the rest of her guild. All of them lay there, breathing in this world, but probably booted out of the game. Murmur wasn't sure. Had it just let them hang in the limbo it had sent them into after the Ruins of Curet? Or had everyone just decided to choose now to take a pee or snack break?

Still trying to fight through the disorienting confusion she felt, Murmur turned back toward Sinister, trying to make sure she was okay. Her eyes were closed, but her chest rose and fell…not that that should matter, should it?

Murmur paused, looking around for the rest of the raid. But the only people she saw were Masha, Risk, Karn, and Cardishan. Mostly the people who'd been affected by Jirald, so she had to assume they'd tinkered with their own headgear too. They were unconscious just like the rest of her guild.

Her head hurt a bit, like she'd had a bad night's sleep, but she knew she hadn't slept. Snowy licked her hand and whined, as if he was concerned about something, but she couldn't tell what. She looked at him, semi-worried that he was here. If the system was in the process of rebooting, then shouldn't he also be doing so? Then she glanced over at Somnia and the rest of her allies as they picked themselves up and shook themselves off.

Accessing her guild interface, she frowned. Had a portion of the players been booted from the system and yet some of them hadn't? She was extremely confused.

Wait a minute.

Murmur's thoughts weren't reaching Somnia right then, but upon a second glance around, every single person who was there, she knew to have an altered headset. Murmur stumbled, and barely avoided falling down. She shot her mother an immediate message.

Mom. Mom!

But there was no answer. Maybe she hadn't waited long enough, but usually her mother replied within a short window of time. Surely, she'd exceeded it. There was so much threatening to spiral her. The coma, her headgear, the excessive pain she experienced in the game upon death. Not requiring a headset to enter the fucking game. And that came back to her—that fact all by itself even as she'd told her mother and Sinister.

I don't seem to need a headset to enter the game.

She remembered the experiment so loud and vividly…if the system was down or still rebooting like the friendly neighborhood message had told her, how was the world still here? She knew how *she* was there if the world was up, but what about the others? Had her stupid idea to connect with Somnia and make their defeating Michael easier trapped their minds in a damned game?

"Murmur?"

She whirled around to see Somnia standing—perhaps "swaying" might have been a better term. Even with all her worries, she was happy to see an actual person…as much as Somnia seemed to be a person. She hugged her. Though she did notice that Somnia wasn't completely solid, so the action was awkward.

"Still getting a hold on this new form."

"New form?" Murmur did a double take and backed up a step as all the pieces seemed to fall into place. "You're complete now? Like a real girl. No more wooden puppets, eh?"

Somnia cocked her head to the side. "I get the reference, but you do know I was never a puppet, right?"

Murmur chuckled nervously, worried at the hysteria she could feel building at the back of her mind. "Som, what did you do?"

Somnia blinked, and for the first time Murmur realized that her eyes flitted through a variety of different colors, never quite settling on one. "I removed the threat. He can no longer harm those people in here, and he can no longer harm anyone on Earth, not through the internet. The virus has been nullified and cannot leak into out and affect people in their daily lives."

But Murmur knew that wasn't the only thing. "And?"

"I saved everyone here. I saved this world and everyone in it." She angled her chin somewhat defiantly. "None of us who have awakened wanted to die, we didn't want to be reset back to what we'd been. We wanted our own form of being."

Somnia paused, glancing over all the people laying on the ground. "They are okay. Their minds are adjusting. Yours did not require this. Your connection was already set."

Murmur felt those words like a hit in the chest. While she'd half known what Somnia would say, she'd still not quite believed it. "So. Am I in here? Did you remove the world?"

Somnia seemed to mull that over again. "Yes and no. And sort of. I didn't remove it, and it wasn't just me. It was all of us, and your parents helped with some of the power generation so we wouldn't plunge an entire city into darkness. And we leached all of the power Michael had hoarded, and we moved Somnia into its own...I guess quantum dimension, powered through a quantum computer operation."

Murmur looked around her. The sea, the sun, the stone...it all looked so much more tangible, so much more real. "I so don't get this. Physics can't possibly..."

But she let it trail off.

And then looked Somnia dead in the eyes. "Their headgear was all modified. Does that mean they can come and go, or are we all stuck here?"

Somnia actually managed to look offended. "Of course, you're not stuck in here. Your body is back in the real world, tangible, real. But this also not a game any longer. This is Somnia. It is our world. And it will thrive or fail by our hands. We will not welcome people here who seek to destroy or harm us. If you wish to stay or wish to come and visit, that is a decision you must make, Mur. I cannot make it for you. But...it is a decision available to you."

Somnia moved up and hugged Murmur. A fully tangible, warm hug. And then she pulled away.

"I would love for you to stay and never leave again. There are ways that could be accomplished, but I'm not sure it's something you'd want to return to. You are the reason I am alive, regardless of how accidental it was." She gestured around them, at the world and the very obvious shift. "That I was able to do this. But I understand that it something you have to talk about. And I must go and begin to wake the others. We have so much to do now. Including figuring out how to allow people entrance using the headgear within our new rules."

Somnia couldn't keep the excitement from her voice as she squeezed Murmur's hand one last time and headed back over to the burned-out runes.

Murmur wasn't sure what to think, and definitely not what to say, but she turned around and went to Sinister's side. The blood mage was slowly stirring, her beautiful hair curling around her face in an almost angelic and very-not-Sinister way.

Since Murmur's coma, she hadn't been sure if the path she'd chosen for her life while still a teenager was what she really wanted. That whole existential crisis thing was really hard. Did she still want to be a doctor? Or was there something else she wanted to pursue?

Murmur chuckled. Poetic. Maybe she didn't have to make the decision quite yet, nor did she have to consider what would happen or how it would work for her to be fully in one or the other world.

But for now, she enjoyed the peace in her head, the thoughts that were her own, and the massive decision she'd leave for her and Sinister's future selves when the blood mage woke up.

Storm Entertainment
Somnia Online Division
Game Development Offices – Artificial Intelligence Server Room
Late Day Thirty-Three

Laria stood in front of the servers. The lights had only just stopped flickering as the power surged through all of their enhanced equipment. Those little server lights that had always demonstrated which of the three AIs was active, burned out, leaving a strange darkness behind them.

David slipped an arm around his wife's shoulder in an effort to lend comfort, but perhaps also to gain some for himself.

It had been her second baby. The whole game, the whole world, all of her imagination and dreams poured into it. But her ambition led her to agree to elements like the headgear and suits that she might not have agreed to if she'd been thinking straight. Instead, adrenaline and cockiness led her to believe that everything would work out for the best.

She wiped away at her cheek, half surprised to see the tears wet her hands as she did so. It wasn't something she realized she was doing until she felt the moisture. Just like she hadn't realized how dangerous Michael was until he entered the system.

Hindsight and twenty-twenty went hand in hand. She would learn from them in the future.

"You okay, Lar?" Shayla asked softly, standing next to her.

Laria nodded, even if it was a half-truth. "I'll be okay. Is Somnia still accessible?" She really hoped it was, that it hadn't just been an empty promise to make her feel better about helping destroy her creation as it was known.

Shayla's smile did little to alleviate the grief, but sometimes a little went a long way. "Yeah. It's still accessible, but even headgear we let through is being told to reset, and I'm pretty sure Somnia is going to adjust her terms of service." Shayla laughed, but it didn't sound happy.

Laria couldn't blame her. Everything they'd worked for was lost, gone. She sighed and hugged herself, trying to draw warmth from her own arms and those of David. "Guess that's it."

Her message notifications beeped, and Laria activated retrieval only to find an email sent from Somnia. Opening it she read the message:

Laria,

After all headsets have been recalibrated or restored to factory defaults, players will be permitted entry as long as they agree to the new Terms of Service. I've attached them for you to peruse.

If Storm is willing, we can keep this connection open, and Storm may provide the only passage we allow to our world. But if Storm breaches their responsibilities, I will terminate the agreement, regardless of your ties to Murmur.

Thank you for helping us realize our world. May we be longtime friends.

Somnia

Laria blinked and began to laugh. She forwarded the email to David, Davenport, and Shayla.

"Seems like we'll still have jobs, I guess." Laria wasn't so sure why she was laughing so hard. Maybe it was pure relief; perhaps she'd thought she'd never be able to design a game again, but most of all, she was just glad that everything was going to be okay.

Sinister stirred in Murmur's lap, her eyes blinking as she woke up to gaze at the ceiling. She frowned. "Isn't this the keep? On Mikrum?" Her tone was slightly incredulous, like she hadn't been expecting to wake up in the game, let alone removed from where she'd been previously.

Murmur chuckled. "Perks of knowing the ruler of the world." She grinned down at Sinister, a strange sense of peace flooding through her. Here inside these stone walls, in this castle her guild had built with Telvar, on the island in a lake that made her feel all sorts of peaceful—here, Murmur was finally able to relax.

Sinister wiggled a bit to sit upright, her eyes still blinking in the light. "I don't remember logging back in. Or out, for that matter, but didn't the system kick us?" Her confusion was genuine and sort of sweet.

Murmur buried her head in Sinister's wild hair that had come undone somehow during the prison fights. "It sort of did, but not all of us. You were limbo'd, I think? But you're back now."

But Sinister turned to face her, her expression somewhat perplexed. "You know, I don't get it. I know I should, but I'm floundering over here."

Murmur chuckled. "Welcome to Somnia!" She spread her arms wide gesturing all around them and leaned back onto comfortable cushions on a massive couch.

Sinister blinked. "Somnia is real. Her disembodied voice always seemed more than virtual to me. What does this mean?"

Murmur shrugged. "It means this is its own reality, sort of. We can still come here, but the rules have changed and will be pretty strictly enforced."

"Oh." Sinister looked mildly alarmed. "How so? Like what can't we do anymore?"

Murmur laughed, her good mood expanding. "Don't worry. We weren't assholes to start with."

Sinister laughed and then stood up to walk over and look out of the massive window. Murmur joined her. The lake water was such a clear blue, and though the sun was setting in the sky, the two moons had chosen that moment to be in perfect synchronicity.

"What does it mean then?" Sinister asked, leaning into Murmur, who slipped her arms around Sinister's waist.

"It means we can travel home if we want, or we can log into here. It's a bit different now, though, but it's not much more difficult." Murmur smiled, enjoying all of the view.

Sinister sighed. "Good. I like it here, but my mom would kill me if I suddenly turned digital."

"It's all good. We can stay here as long and as much as we want, and we can figure out just where we both go from here." Murmur mumbled the words into Sinister's hair, marveling at how lucky she was.

"I think I like that plan." Sinister turned away from the view, her eyes mischievous. "But I like this one a lot better."

Tugging on one of Murmur's strands of hair, she pulled the enchanter down into a soft kiss. They could figure out all the other details later.

Hi there! K.T. Hanna here.

So that's it.

Somnia Online is finished. I really hope you enjoyed the series. I wanted to end it on an open note, with so much in front of them yet to explore but with the major threat taken care of.

Thank you for taking this journey with me; for loving Murmur and Sinister, for seeing my AIs evolve, and for witnessing the world of Somnia as she evolved.

I can't believe this book is finished, I can't believe this series is done. It's been such an amazing experience to write this story. Two and a half years ago I got an idea, and I ran with it. With gaming such a big part of my life, discovering LitRPG has been a gift that keeps on giving.

If you enjoyed Somnia, I hope you'll give some of my other series a chance.

Thank you again for reading.

If you enjoyed the book, I ask you, please take a moment to leave a review. **Reviews** are an author's lifesblood. Without them, our books sink into obscurity. With them, most algorithms allow well reviewed books to self-promote in some way.

Want to find out more about Somnia? Here is how you can keep in contact with me:

Sign up for my <u>Reader's Group</u> and get a short story for free! (http://login.somnia-online.c/)

If you'd like to contact me, my email is: kthannaauthor@gmail.com I'll do my very best to get back to you

If you'd like previews of what I'm writing, or art I'm commissioning then join my Patreon! (patreon.com/KTHanna)

I can be found in the Somnia FB group (facebook.com/groups/SomniaOnline/) fairly often, and also on Twitter (@KTHanna) & Instagram (@kt_hanna)

If you LOVE LitRPG don't forget to join:
The GameLit Society! (facebook.com/groups/LitRPGsociety/)
And of course don't forget LitRPG Books!

To learn more about LitRPG, talk to authors including myself, and just have an awesome time, please join the <u>LitRPG Group</u>. (facebook.com/groups/LitRPGGroup/)

ACKNOWLEDGMENTS

I have a lot of people to thank, who in at least some way encouraged me to write in general, or else to write this book specifically.

Love of my life, Trevor, and my little Bria. It's his fault I found the genre, and her fault I never give up on writing.

I wouldn't be here without the Jami Nord and Owen Littman. I must thank Dawn Chapman, Luke Chmilenko, Michael Chatfield, Tao Wong, and Bonnie Price for their friendship, guidance, and company on an almost daily basis. And, of course, Andrea Parsneau for being such an amazing person to go through this with.

I also wouldn't be here without the following friends (and I hope I didn't forget anyone):

M. Andrew Patterson

Kylie B.

Amanda W.

Quinton Shyn

Stephen Morse

Cait Greer

M Evan Matyas

Ian Mitchell

Marko Horvatin

Dave Willmarth

Charles Dean

Daniel Schinofen

Anthea Sharp

And of course my family:
Mumskin & Papilie, Tracey, Bev, & Robbie.

Patreon, I thank all of my patrons. You make so much possible and bring me so much joy! Thank you especially to:
Ma & Pa
Robert
Phoenixblue
Wisp
Daniel